A WOLF IN STONE

What Reviewers Say About Jane Fletcher's Work

Silver Ravens

"Fletcher serves up tasty, trope-filled political intrigue with a side of wholesome lesbian love. …Fletcher succeeds in crafting a gentle, fanciful lesbian love story about questioning cultural bias."—*Publishers Weekly*

"*Silver Ravens* flows nicely and Lori's adventures have kept me deeply engaged. Though my first try at Fletcher's works, I am now convinced I have to read more of her novels."—*Hsinju's Lit Log*

Isle of Broken Years

"Fun, fast, and deeply entertaining, *Isle of Broken Years* is one of the better uses of the Atlantis myth I've yet seen in fiction. I enjoyed it a lot, and I feel confident in recommending it."
—*Tor.com*

"*Isle of Broken Years* is an amazingly inventive story that started off being the tale of a noblewoman being captured by pirates and veered off into something way more interesting and fantastic."
—*Kitty Kat's Book Review Blog*

"How fantastic was this story? Taking history, future, sci-fi/fantasy, mystery and magic and just putting it all together to make the most amazing adventure for the reader and the characters. When I first started reading Catalina and Sam's story, I wasn't sure what to expect, and it spent time building up a scene which I soon learned would be vital to explaining the rest of this brilliant story. This took an amazing amount of creativity and imagination, which I thank Jane for. This was unlike any other fantasy I have ever read, the historical element and the hint of romance gave the adventure an edge but the adventure was the complete focus of the story which was quite the change."—*LESBIreviewed*

Exile and the Sorcerer

"Jane Fletcher once again has written an exciting fantasy story for everyone. Though she sets her stories in foreign worlds where the traditional roles of women are reversed, her characters (are) all too familiar in their inner lives and thoughts. Unlike the Celaeno series (which I highly recommend) where there are no men, this series incorporates male characters that help round out the story nicely... Fletcher has a way of balancing the fantasy with the human drama in a precise way. She never gets caught up in the minor details of the environment and forgets to tell the story, which happens too often in fantasy fiction... With Fletcher writing such strong work, readers of fantasy will continue to grow."—*Lambda Book Report*

"*The Exile and the Sorcerer* is a mesmerizing read, a tour-de-force packed with adventure, ordeals, complex twists and turns, and the internal introspection of appealing characters. The author writes effortlessly, handling the size and scope of the book with ease. Not since the fantasy works of Elizabeth Moon and Lynn Flewelling have I been so thoroughly engrossed in a tale. This is knockout fiction, tantalizingly told, and beautifully packaged."—*Midwest Book Review*

"*Tempura Mutantur*" in Women of the Dark Streets

"This is certainly a haunting and love-intensive story. A darkly and overpowering obsession morphs into a reunion that knocked my socks off. Splendiferous!"—*Rainbow Book Reviews*

Wolfsbane Winter—*Lambda Literary Award Finalist*

"Jane Fletcher is known for her fantasy stories that take place in a world that could almost be real, but not quite. Her books seem like an alternative version of history and contain rich atmospheres of magic, legends, sorcerers, and other worldly characters mixed in with ordinary people. The way she writes is so realistic that it is easy to believe that these places and people really exist. *Wolfsbane Winter* fits that mold perfectly. It draws the reader in and leads her through the story. Very enjoyable."—*Just About Write*

The Shewstone

"I was hooked on the plot and the characters are absolutely delightful."—*The Romantic Reader Blog*

The Walls of Westernfort

"Award-winning author Jane Fletcher explores serious themes in the Celaeno series and creates a world that loosely parallels the one we inhabit. In *The Walls of Westernfort*, Fletcher weaves a plausible action-packed plot, set on a credible world, and with appealing multi-dimensional characters. The result is a fantasy by one of the best speculative fiction writers in the business."—*Just About Write*

"...captivating, well-written stories in the fantasy genre that are built around women's struggles against themselves, one another, society, and nature."—*WomanSpace Magazine*

"*The Walls of Westernfort* is not only a highly engaging and fast-paced adventure novel, it provides the reader with an interesting framework for examining the same questions of loyalty, faith, family and love."—*Midwest Book Review*

"*The Walls of Westernfort* is...a true delight. Bold, well-developed characters hold your interest from the beginning and keep you turning the pages. The main plot twists and turns until the very end. The subplot involves likeable women who seem destined not to be together."—*MegaScene*

"In *The Walls of the Westernfort*, Jane Fletcher spins a captivating story about youthful idealism, honor, and courage. The action is fast paced and the characters are compelling in this gripping sci-fi adventure."—*Sapphic Reader*

"Jane Fletcher has a great talent for spinning yarns, especially stories of lesbians with swords. *The Walls of Westernfort* is a well written and suspenseful tale... Fletcher effectively intertwines the intrigues of the assassination plot with a young woman's inward exploration...and yes, there is romance. ...This book is a page-turner; you will have a hard time finding a stopping place."
—*Lesbian Connection Magazine*

Rangers at Roadsend

"In *Rangers at Roadsend* Fletcher not only gives us powerful characters, but she surprises us with an unexpected ending to the murder conspiracy plot, pushing the story in one direction only to have that direction reversed more than once. This is one thrill ride the reader will not want to get off."—*Independent Gay Writer*

"*Rangers at Roadsend*, a murder mystery reminiscent of Agatha Christie, has crossed many genres including speculative fiction, fantasy, romance, and adventure. The story is an incredible whodunit that has something for everyone. Jane Fletcher, winner of the Golden Crown Literary Award 2005 for Walls at Westernfort, has created an intelligent and compelling story where the reader easily gets drawn into the fascinating world of Celaeno, becomes totally absorbed in the well-designed plot, and finds herself completely enamored with the multi-faceted characters." Jane Fletcher, an amazing talent, gifted storyteller, and extraordinary plot developer, is one of the best authors of contemporary fiction today—in all genres. *Rangers at Roadsend* will convince you of that."—*Just About Write*

Dynasty of Rogues

"Jane Fletcher has another triumph with *Dynasty of Rogues*, the continuing story in the Celaeno series. This reviewer found the book clever and compelling and difficult to put down once I started reading and easily could be devoured in one sitting. Some of the characters in *Dynasty of Rogues* have visited us in other Celaeno novels, but this is a non-linear series, so it can be understood without having read the other stories. ...*Dynasty of Rogues* has it all. Mystery, intrigue, crime, and romance, with lots of angst thrown in too, make this fascinating novel thoroughly enjoyable and fun."—*Just About Write*

"When you pick up a novel by Jane Fletcher, you will always get a riveting plot, strong, interesting characters, and a beautifully written story complete with three-dimensional villains, believable conflicts, and the twin spices of adventure and romance. Ethical and moral dilemmas abound. Fletcher writes real characters, the type that William Faulkner once said 'stand up and cast a shadow.' The reader can't help but root for these characters, many of whom are classic underdogs. I give the highest recommendation for *Dynasty of Rogues* and to the entire Celaeno Series."—*Midwest Book Review*

Temple at Landfall—*Lambda Literary Award Finalist*

"*The Temple at Landfall* is absorbing and engrossing tale-telling of the highest order, and the really exciting thing is that although this novel is complete and 'finished,' the door is left open to explore more of this world, which the author has done in subsequent books. I can't wait to read the next Celaeno Series volumes, and this book is a keeper that I will re-read again and again. I highly recommend it."—*Just About Write*

"Jane Fletcher is the consummate storyteller and plot wizard. Getting caught up in the action happens as if by magic and the fantasy elements are long forgotten. The world Fletcher creates, the characters she brings to life, and the rich detail described in eloquent prose, all serve to keep the reader enchanted, satisfied, yet wanting more. A Lammy finalist, *The Temple at Landfall* is surely a winner in this reader's book. Don't miss it."—*Midwest Book Review*

Visit us at www.boldstrokesbooks.com

By the Author

Celaeno Series

The Temple at Landfall

The Walls of Westernfort

Rangers at Roadsend

Dynasty of Rogues

Shadow of the Knife

Lyremouth Chronicles

The Exile and the Sorcerer

The Chalice and the Traitor

The Empress and the Acolyte

The High Priest and the Idol

Wolfsbane Winter

The Shewstone

Isle of Broken Years

Silver Ravens

A Fox in Shadow

A WOLF IN STONE

by

Jane Fletcher

2024

ISBN 13: 978-1-63679-640-6

This Trade Paperback Original Is Published By
Bold Strokes Books, Inc.
P.O. Box 249
Valley Falls, NY 12185

First Edition: July 2024

CREDITS
EDITOR: CINDY CRESAP
PRODUCTION DESIGN: SUSAN RAMUNDO
COVER DESIGN BY JEANINE HENNING

Dedication

For Joanie

INTRODUCTION TO KAVILLIAN NAMES

In the Kavillian empire, family allegiance is a vitally important yet fluid matter. Over the course of their lives, individuals will change elements of their name to indicate their current situation, juggling family, economic, and political concerns.

Personal names

These are normally given to gain favour with grandparents, rich relatives, gods, or anyone else who might be flattered into looking favourably on the baby. Most people will have two but use only the first on a daily basis. However, should changes in circumstances render it advantageous, switching to the second name, or taking on a completely new one, is common. Personal names are normally shortened by close friends and lovers, denoting a degree of familiarity.

Family names

This is where judgment calls and changing circumstances come into play. The final name always denotes the primary family allegiance. Other families added are a matter of personal choice. The basis of the association is given by a prefix. Notable options are:

dom—birth family
con—by marriage
ado—adopted
pars—a parent or grandparent's birth family
dimi—freed slave, owing allegiance to former owner

Common people rarely cite more than one family. Nobles pick whichever secondary family they feel confers the most prestige. A third association is very occasionally added, but while it is possible to extend a name indefinitely, claiming links to more families than this would smack of desperation.

Titles—family

Doyen/Doyenne: The leader of the family. Major families automatically get a seat in the Imperial Senate. The method of choosing a leader varies between families, generally for reasons lost in history. They might be elected by all or some family members, nominated by the previous leader, picked by an oracle after examining goat entrails, or whatever else tradition dictates.

Senator: An elected or nominated member of the Imperial Senate. They might represent a city, a province, or a wealthy faction, such as a confederacy of minor families or a trade council. On occasion, senators are nominated to stand in for their doyen/doyenne due to illness or as a result of internal family power struggles. Major families will often contrive to get two or three of their members into the Senate.

Lord/Lady: Senior member of a major family. Acquisition of this status varies between families in a similar fashion to the role of leader.

Master/Mistress: Member of a minor family, or a junior member of a major one, or someone in a position of authority who doesn't fit into any other category.

Civis: A free citizen lacking noteworthy money, power, or family connections. Since this is the default title covering the overwhelming majority of the population who are not slaves (and hence without any title at all) it is rarely used, except in official documents.

Titles—other

Primus: The elected leader of the Imperial Senate, and the most powerful person in the empire (in theory).

Magistra/Magister/Scribe/Prefect: A civilian official who has renounced family allegiance to play an impartial role in administering the law, e.g. judge, lawyer, policeman. The family part of their name will reflect being "adopted" by the prefecture.

Legate/Tribune/Centurion: Military ranks

Example names

Doyenne Pellonia Valeria dom Konithae ado Passurae: Passurae family leader who joined the family via adoption. That she chooses to still cite her birth family, the Konithae, could be seen as a subtle insult, i.e. she didn't think they were worth staying with.

Lady Cassilania Marciana pars Vessiolae dom Passurae: A senior member of the Passurae family who was born into it. Also related by birth to the Vessiolae family.

Magistra Vessia Gallina ado Prefectae: A judge who has therefore become a member of the prefecture.

Master Branius dimi Passurae: A freed slave who was once owned by a member of the Passurae family. Now important enough that people feel the need to be polite to him.

Legate Jadioleus Camillus con Nerinae dom Passurae: A senior army officer born into the Passurae who is married to a woman from the Nerinae.

Mistress Salina Helvia dom Nerinae con Passurae: Jadioleus's wife. Although born into the Nerinae, her primary allegiance is now to her husband's family.

Civis Marcella dom Rissanilae: A nobody.

ARIAN

A moment, frozen in stone. The wolf stood, one forepaw raised, head turned, staring over its shoulder at whatever lay behind. But what had the sculptor captured? Arian could never make up her mind. The backward look—was it fear of pursuit, relief at escape, doubts over the path taken, or an exile's regret?

Depending on her mood and the way the day was going, Arian might identify with any of these. Both she and the wolf were out of place. They belonged in forests, where you could hear wind through the branches, smell the wet soil and leaves. Yet here they were, trapped inside stone walls, as an ornament for others to look at and comment on.

Which was not to say life in the city was all bad. As long as you had the money, Kavilli offered luxuries she could never have imagined before arriving from her homeland. Goods from all over the empire and beyond made their way to the capital, wine and olives, silk and satin, perfumes and jewels. Not to mention the everyday marvels of sewage systems, smoke-free chimneys, and roofs that did not leak.

On a personal level, there was also a freedom to live her life in ways her people would not allow. With each passing year, the thought of giving this up became harder to face. Not conceding so would be dishonest. Arian bit her lip at the twinge of unease. Dishonesty in others was an unfortunate fact of life. Dishonesty in herself was unforgivable.

She sat on a corner of the plinth and leaned against the statue's rump so she could look into its eyes. There was no dishonesty in wolves. They were never more or less than they appeared. Even as a foe, there was no deception. They were a fitting totem animal for her people, the Lycanthi.

The statue was what had drawn her to the villa, when the Imperial Senate offered her a choice of dwellings in the city. And whenever the longing for home grew too strong, she would sit in the courtyard and try to block out the ceaseless clamour of voices and traffic in the street outside. Even the tranquillity of night was shattered by the march of patrols, drunken revels, and the rumble of horse-drawn carts, bringing tomorrow's produce to the markets and carrying today's refuse away.

Arian closed her eyes, trying to draw on memories of home, the peace of the sacred spring, where the only sounds were the ripple of water and rustling of leaves in the ancient oaks.

"Mama. Mama." Feran's wailing cries. Her six-year-old son rushed into the courtyard.

"What is it?" She scooped him onto her lap.

Unshed tears glinted in his eyes. "Ulfgar's being mean."

"I'm sure he's not." *Not deliberately.* The priest could be firm and exacting, but never petty.

"He said I can't go to the academy next year."

That's a new one. "Do you want to?"

"Kario's going, and Daril, and Luce. Everyone. All my friends. I'll have no one to play with."

"You can make other friends."

"Only stupid ones who aren't good enough to be army officers."

"It's not about being stupid. The academy is for Kavillian boys. You're not Kavillian."

"So? I bet your friend Cassie could sort it out."

While Cassie undoubtedly could, Arian had no intention of asking her. "If you go to the academy you'll be far away from here. You won't see me or Eilwen for months."

"The other boys aren't bothered."

Were their mothers? How did Kavillian noblewomen cope, saying goodbye to their sons so young?

A tear trickled down Feran's cheek. "The empire army is the best in the world. They can beat anyone."

"And that's why we've allied with them." Not as if there had been any choice.

"So why can't I go with my friends?"

"Because you're king of the Lycanthi. That's better than being an army officer."

"S'not." More tears fell. "I don't want to be king."

Ulfgar arrived in the courtyard. At Feran's protest, his normally stern expression deepened into what could only be called a scowl. The Lycanthian bodyguards, Olric and Durwyn, also appeared.

Arian lowered Feran to his feet. "It's time for you to go. We'll talk later."

"Promise?"

"Promise."

Feran scrubbed away the tears and trotted over to Olric and Durwyn. That Feran needed bodyguards for the short walk to school was a symbol of everything wrong with Kavilli. Back home, in the king's capital of Breninbury, any child could go wherever they wished, without thought of kidnap or robbery—or could normally. Unfortunately, these were not normal times. Not all of the Lycanthi were happy to accept empire legions in their land. Feran was safer in Kavilli until either things settled down or he was old enough to defend himself.

Once he and his bodyguards had left, Arian turned to Ulfgar with what was intended as a sympathetic smile. "Don't worry. He'll get over it. I'm not—"

"He cannot stay here." Ulfgar spat out the words with a startling vehemence. "A king's place is with his people."

"This nonsense about the academy won't—" Again, Arian did not get to finish.

"The academy." From Ulfgar's tone it might have been an obscenity. "Of course he can't be allowed to go. Though, in truth, it would be preferable. At least he'd be in the company of warriors, rather than this...this cesspit of depravity."

Arian rose uncertainly to her feet. "Ulfgar? What's wrong?"

"Do you need to ask?"

Yes. Now she thought about it, Ulfgar had been ill at ease for the better part of a month. What had Feran been saying? "He's just a child. He didn't mean about not wanting to be king. In another day or two he'll have forgotten it all."

Ulfgar turned away. In profile, his hawk nose jutted out over the beard covering the lower half of his face. "I've failed in my duty. I'm supposed to instruct Feran in the ways of our people, so when he returns he can be a fitting king for them. But this city can corrupt even the purest soul." He glanced her way. "And some succumb more readily than others."

Meaning me. "Feran will be a good king. He'll be the bridge between the Lycanthi and Kavillians. There's no other way."

"He'll be a bridge with both feet on the same shore. The empire will have a puppet of its making on the throne. I was sent to ensure Feran knows our laws, our gods, our history. Not to sit by while his heart and soul become those of a Kavillian."

"If you want, Feran can spend more time with you, receiving tuition." Which was something else that would lead to argument. Feran clearly preferred going to school with his friends.

"That will not do. Feran must leave at once. Another day in the city is one day too many."

"No." That was not an option. "Feran stays here until it's safe for him to return."

"When will that be?"

"Whenever Earl Kendric says." Arian folded her arms. "There's no point Feran going back before he's old enough to take on the responsibilities of kingship. In the meantime, Kendric's doing an excellent job as regent. Things are calming down. People are seeing the benefit of our alliance with the empire."

"Then it's safe for Feran to return."

"Maybe in another year or two."

"A year or two! You think Earl Kendric and his warriors can't protect one child?"

"I think he has more than enough other things to deal with." Breninbury might be a fort atop a hill, but it was built to protect against enemy raids, not internal threats. The houses did not even have proper doors, let alone locks to put on them. "I won't take a chance with Feran's safety for no reason. Some powerful people would be quick to use him as a pawn."

"You think that isn't happening at the moment." Ulfgar said it as a challenge.

Arian had no illusions about the extent to which Feran was a hostage, ensuring the newly established protectorate stuck to the terms of its treaty with the empire. However, in the Kavillian power games, no side stood to benefit from Feran's death. In himself, he was of little importance, the client king of a small, outlying region, but his safety ensured the flow of valuable ore from Lycanthian mines.

"If you want, I'll write to Earl Kendric and ask when he thinks Feran can return to Breninbury."

"And how long will it take for the message to get there and back? Three months?"

"Probably." If not longer, with winter on the way.

Ulfgar snorted into his moustache. "That's not acceptable."

"I will not send Feran into danger." Arian said each word with emphasis.

"Is it truly Feran's safety that keeps you here?"

"What else?"

Ulfgar turned an icy glare on her. "Do you think I haven't heard what every tongue in Kavilli wags about? You and Lady Cassilania. I've put nothing of it in my reports to my brethren, but there is much I could say. Do not force my hand."

Arian's skin prickled. Of course Ulfgar knew. He would need to be deaf and witless not to. It was not as if she made any effort to hide the truth. In Kavilli there was no need. Unless you were married to the people concerned, love affairs were purely a topic for dinner party gossip, The gender of those involved was irrelevant. Regrettably, although the Lycanthi were more open in some ways, taking a same-sex lover was outlawed. If news got back, the consequences would be serious. But, whatever the outcome, Feran's safety was not up for negotiation.

"I'll write to Earl Kendric. But Feran stays in Kavilli until it's safe for him to return. That's an end to it."

Ulfgar drew himself up to his full height and glared at her. "If that's your last word."

"It is."

"Write to Earl Kendric. Insist preparations for your son's return move ahead with speed. See to it, or the outcome will be on your head." He turned and stalked away.

Only when the beat of his footsteps faded did Arian allow herself a deep breath. She returned to her seat beside the stone wolf. The courtyard was again at peace, yet she was not alone. A shadow crouched in a dark corner of the courtyard, hidden behind a potted fern.

"How long have you been there?" Arian called out.

The shadow huddled down further, making no sound.

"Eilwen. Come out. I know you're there."

Eilwen sidled from her hiding place. "How did you know it was me?"

"Because you're the only one who'd eavesdrop so shamelessly." Regrettably, her daughter was becoming ever more adept at Kavillian games of intrigue.

Eilwen took a seat beside her on the plinth. "You're not really going back to Lycanthia, are you?"

Lycanthia. The name jarred on Arian's ear. As far as the Lycanthi were concerned, their home was simply "the Land" granted to them by the gods. When the Kavillians needed to distinguish it from everywhere else, they made up a name. Arian was forced to use it when talking to them, although never by choice. Yet the name came so naturally to Eilwen—as did speaking Kavillian, instead of their mother tongue. With surprise, Arian realised she had automatically switched to the language when her daughter appeared. Arian had learned Kavillian as a child, and three years in the city had enhanced her fluency.

"Mama." Eilwen nudged her for an answer.

"It's up to Earl Kendric." *And the Kavillian Senate.* Despite Ulfgar's disapproval of their relationship, getting permission to leave the city would require Cassie's family connections.

For a moment Eilwen was silent, except for the sound of her heels bouncing against the stone. "I want to stay here."

"We all go together."

"Ulfgar and Feran can go. You and I can stay in Kavilli." The rhythm of her heels increased. "Breninbury is a dungheap. There's no parties, or nice food, or books to read, or anything."

"It will have changed."

"It's only been three years. They'll still be living like pigs in shit."

"Eilwen! They're our family. Don't you want to see your cousins?"

"Why don't they come here?"

"Feran is king of the Lycanthi. He has to return to his people. And you're his sister, you have to—"

"I know and it's not fair." Eilwen jumped down. "Feran can father his own children if he wants them. He doesn't need me."

"That's not how our people do things."

"Then our people need to change and stop being stupid."

And Ulfgar thought Feran becoming more Kavillian was a problem! Eilwen had embraced the empire's ways completely. As a bright, stubborn, eleven-year-old, she was far harder to coerce than her younger brother.

Ulfgar was definitely guilty of overlooking her. But then, Lycanthian men rarely gave any thought to what women wanted. Feran dreamed of joining the imperial legions, a warrior of sorts, which was suitably in keeping with Lycanthian ideals of manhood.

Eilwen wanted to be what? A businesswoman, a politician, a spymaster? For the Lycanthi, none of these were suitable roles for a woman. Eilwen was the keeper of the royal bloodline. Feran's heirs would be her sons, just as he had succeeded to the throne from his uncle, Arian's unmourned brother. The idea Eilwen might not want to go along with this had probably never drifted through Ulfgar's head.

Eilwen leaned against her. "Please, Mama. Why can't we stay in Kavilli together?"

"Once Feran goes, the Senate will want this house back."

"I bet, if you asked her, Cassie could find you a rich husband. Then you could stay, and I could have a baby sister."

As with Feran's suggestion earlier, there was no doubt Cassie could indeed make it happen, and Arian had just as little intention of asking her. "Aren't you supposed to be at school?"

Eilwen pouted. "It's private study this morning. I've got a book to read."

"Then go and read it."

"Mama!"

"Go."

Alone at last, Arian sighed and returned to leaning against the stone wolf. Feran, Ulfgar, and Eilwen. Three different demands, the most serious one accompanied by a threat. All of them dependent on Cassie's intervention.

Arian put her arm around the wolf's neck. Today, her interpretation of the backward look was definitely leaning towards doubt over the path taken.

❖

"Lady Cassilania is expected home soon. I'll let her know you're here when she arrives." The maidservant gave a polite bow and left the room.

Arian wandered to the window. Heavy cloud hastened the approach of dusk over the scene. The Passurae residence was a sprawling maze of interlinked courtyards, towers, gardens, reception rooms, domestic workshops, and luxury accommodation. In total, the mansion covered an area more than fifty times larger than the villa she lived in, and the rooms forming Cassie's apartment were far more lavishly furnished.

Rain splattered against the window glass. Arian watched water droplets trickle down, distorting her view of the garden outside. Despite the absence of any visible fire, the room was warm, thanks to the underfloor hypocaust.

Window glass and central heating were both unknown luxuries in her homeland. Even the small villa with the wolf statue made the king's capital at Breninbury look like a squalid collection of overcrowded hovels. Which, to be quite honest, was what it was. Lycanthian homes were built with dry-stone walls, using a daub of clay and horse dung to fill gaps. No windows. No sewers. No bathhouses. Choking smoke from open fires seeped out through sod roofs. Hanging blankets over the doorways were the only thing to keep out the cold. Was it any surprise Eilwen had no wish to return?

The door opened. "Sorry. Have you been waiting long?" Cassie swept into the room, trailed by the maidservant.

"No."

Arian turned and rested her back against the wall, watching Cassie strip off her wet cloak and hand it to the maidservant. "This needs to be washed. The hem's muddy."

"Yes, my lady." The maidservant withdrew.

Cassie dropped her jewelled cloak pin on a side table and smiled apologetically. "I meant to be back sooner, but things were…" The smile broadened. "Getting interesting." She planted the briefest of kisses on Arian's lips before going to her desk on the far side of the room. "I need to make a few notes while everything is fresh in my mind, but then I'll be all yours."

The soft emphasis on the last two words still had the ability to send shivers through Arian. She watched Cassie dip a pen in the ink pot and start writing. The notes would be all about overheard whispers. Who said what about whom. Who talked too much. Who kept suspiciously silent. Who was not where they were supposed to be.

It was all part of the game of imperial politics. The leading families of the empire were in a constant state of diplomatic warfare, fought with spies, intrigue, secrets, and blackmail. The war was not something Arian wanted any part of. Yet, just by her association with Cassie, she was drawn in.

Arian idly picked up Cassie's discarded cloak pin. It was larger than needed to secure her clothes, a good five inches in length. The narrow, bladelike pin clipped into the back of an ornate silver brooch, styled as a fox. Its one visible eye was a diamond, its ears, snout, and tail were picked out with gold and onyx. At market, it was undoubtedly worth more than the entire king's treasury from Breninbury.

The cloak pin had been custom made for Cassie, a gift from her mother for a birthday, or some such occasion. A casual display of the family's wealth and prestige. A silver fox was the Passurae family emblem, featuring prominently on banners and crests around the mansion.

To a first glance, the brooch was an ornate work of art. But there was more to it. Cassie had shown her the trick. If you opened it fully, then gave a quarter twist until you felt a click, the pin became a stiletto with the silver fox as a handle. It was quite deadly, Cassie had assured her, if you knew where to stab. The brooch was a perfect analogy for Cassie herself. Exquisite, utterly unique, and far more dangerous than it appeared.

Despite her disquiet, Arian could not help playing with the cloak pin. It was captivating, and even knowledge of its concealed menace only added an edge to the allure. And that was perhaps, in turn, a perfect analogy for her relationship with Cassie. Arian put the cloak pin down and returned to watching rain trickle down the miraculous window glass.

The ink pot lid snapped shut. "Done." Cassie's gown rustled as she left her desk.

Arian did not move, concentrating instead on the sound of Cassie's footsteps, crossing the floor. Then Cassie's arms slid around her waist, and the warmth of Cassie's breath flowed over the nape of her neck. The lightest touch of Cassie's lips tickled her skin. Arian twisted around to return the kiss in full.

Eventually, Cassie broke away. "Are you hungry?"

"I ate earlier."

"Wine then?" Without waiting for an answer, Cassie went to the door and rang a bell.

Arian listened to the tone rather than the words that followed, the maidservant's deference, contrasted with Cassie's serene confidence. Anything she wanted was hers for the asking.

Once they were seated with full glasses, Cassie asked, "What's bothering you?"

"Why do you think anything's bothering me?"

"The pout on your lower lip, and the wrinkle between your eyebrows. You always do that when you've got something on your mind."

Why deny it? Cassie had always been able to read her. "Feran. He wants to go to the military academy with his friends. Ulfgar wants him to return to Breninbury as soon as possible. And Eilwen is determined to stay in Kavilli."

"Someone's going to end up unhappy." Cassie looked thoughtful. "But there's no reason why Feran can't attend the academy for a year or two. It'd be good experience for him, and it's not without precedent for the sons of allied nobility."

"No."

"Why not? Mother will arrange for you and Eilwen to keep the villa. After all, Feran will need somewhere to come home to on leave."

As if the house was her only concern. "I want him with me. He's a young child."

"He'll be the same age as my three sons when they went."

"Didn't it bother you, waving them off like that?"

"Oh, I missed them dreadfully at first. Worried about them." Cassie shrugged. "But, from the day they were born, I accepted they'd leave me when they turned seven."

"Well, I don't accept it. He's staying with me."

"All right. Feran draws a short straw. Who gets the other, Ulfgar or Eilwen?" Cassie's tone was light-hearted. Then her expression sharpened. "Or is there more to it?"

"Ulfgar tried to blackmail me."

"Did he now? I'm intrigued. What naughty secret is he threatening to reveal?"

"You and I are lovers."

Cassie laughed. "Does he know it won't come as a surprise to anyone here?"

"Probably. But things will be different back in Breninbury."

"Ah, yes. There is that angle. Your people do have strange obsessions."

"Ulfgar's threatening to send a report home if I don't agree to return at once."

Cassie's smile changed to a frown. "Why's he suddenly so keen to leave?"

"He's worried Feran is becoming too Kavillian."

"Enough to try his hand at blackmail?"

"Apparently." Arian shrugged. "I fobbed him off with a promise to write to Kendric and ask about the situation."

"That's a temporary fix. Would you like me to have Ulfgar taken care of permanently?"

Was she joking? Even after three years together, Arian could not be sure. The allure of danger, cloaked in a beautiful form. If ever she learned to see through Cassie's facade, to whatever lay beneath, would the attraction fade?

"It'll take over three months for the reply. Ask me again then."

"Do you think the situation will have changed?"

"Who knows?" Thinking about the future came with its own set of issues. "What would you do if you were me?"

"I've already said. Sort out Ulfgar and get permission for Feran to attend the academy for a year or two."

"I've told you Feran stays with me."

"All right. So is it Ulfgar or Eilwen who also loses out?"

"What do you want me to do?"

"Whatever will make you happiest." Cassie at her most irritating. Was she really not bothered either way?

"I asked what you wanted."

"And I told you my answer. I want you to make your own decision."

"You don't care whether I go or stay."

"I didn't say that."

But you might as well have. Arian glared at the wine in her glass, not that there was anything wrong with it. Like everything else in the mansion, it was of the highest quality. Cassie could have whatever she wanted. Why settle for less than the best? But not everything could be bought. What did Cassie want for the two of them? How did she see their future playing out? She always sidestepped the subject.

Arian knocked back the wine forcefully enough to burn her throat, leading to a bout of coughing.

Cassie's amused expression changed to one of concern. "Are you all right?"

"Yes."

"If I didn't know how much you hate lying, I'd be tempted to call you out on that."

"Whereas you lie as easily as breathing."

"No. I have to think about which lies I want to tell. Breathing just happens." All said without a trace of guilt.

"You don't care about the truth."

"The truth is generally easier. Less taxing on the memory. It's just not always wiser."

Not caring about wisdom, Arian poured herself another glass of wine. "Do you care whether I stay in Kavilli or not?"

"You know I like you being here."

"Like?"

"I'm very fond of you."

"That's it? Or do you want to add you're also happy to have me in your bed, when you're not too busy with something else?"

"I'm not quite that shallow." Cassie looked exasperated. "What would you like me to say?"

Say you want me. Say you love me. But Cassie would never make any commitment that might conflict with her duty to her family.

Arian put down her glass, removing the temptation to toss the wine in Cassie's face. "I'm tired of all the games. I'm tired of not knowing where I stand."

"I'm not playing games. I'm…" Cassie closed her eyes and sighed. "Do whatever you want."

"Good. Because what I want right now is to leave." Arian got to her feet.

"Arian." Cassie beat her to the door. "Please."

She slid her hands around Arian's waist and rested her head on Arian's shoulder. And that was all it took. Anger ebbed away, unable to hold back the wave of peace radiating from the touch of Cassie's body, pressed against hers. The tightness squeezing Arian's stomach softened and melted. *Am I really this shallow as well?*

They stood for a while by the door, arms around each other, until Cassie pulled back so their eyes met. "I'm not playing games with you. You are important to me. More than I can say. But I won't make promises to you I can't keep. And you can't make decisions about your life, based on expectations of me. You have to understand my family must come first."

Once upon a time, Arian would have agreed without question. Family was what bound the Lycanthi to each other and the land. "I feel so alone here, and I know I need you more than you need me."

Cassie's lips brushed Arian's throat, then moved on to nuzzle her ear. "Let's see what I can do to make you feel less lonely."

It was not the answer Arian wanted, but still she let herself be towed toward the bedroom.

Cassie

Cassie dragged herself free from a confusing tangle of dreams and opened her eyes. The first ghosting of daylight lay over the room, though dawn was still a ways off. A trill of birdsong came from the garden. No point trying to go back to sleep. Nor did she make any attempt to recall the fading dreams. Nothing about them had been good. A lingering unease assured her of that. She raised herself on one elbow to look down at Arian, still asleep beside her.

Arian's face was almost translucent in the muted light, especially by contrast with Cassie's own copper-coloured skin. A halo of golden hair fanned the pillow, marking Arian as coming from the barbarian fringes of the empire. Blonds were so rare in Kavilli, apart from those found at the slave market. Even less common was the green of her eyes. After all their time together, there was still a startling quality to them.

She reached for Arian's shoulder, but then stopped. Before they spoke, she needed to marshal her thoughts. Rekindling the previous night's quarrel was the last thing she wanted to do. The conflict had been dodged, not resolved. But what resolution was possible? Cassie bit her lip.

I know I need you more than you need me.

Arian's words from last night. So bleak. So hopeless. Were they true? Cassie was far from convinced. Yet surely, the day was fast approaching when she would be forced to find out.

Already, their love affair had lasted far longer than she expected at the outset, but it could not go on. With each month, the fractures became more blatant, the arguments more frequent, more painful. How much longer until the strain tore them apart? Tears stung Cassie's eyes, but she would not let them fall.

Sometimes, as with the night before, she was able to bury their differences under the comforting routine of lovemaking. Sometimes she could not. But it was never a solution. One time, and it could not be too far away, Arian would walk out and not come back.

And tormenting herself with the thought was a waste of time. Cassie shook Arian's shoulder. "Good morning."

She slipped out from the sheets before Arian fully woke, rather than face her immediately. Better to give herself a little more time to compose her expression.

Arian groaned and rubbed her eyes. "Is it?"

Cassie pulled on a robe and drew back the window drapes. The darkness was retreating from the courtyard garden. "It's stopped raining."

"I guess that's something."

Cassie rung the servant's bell. "What would you like for breakfast?"

"Nothing for me. I want to get back before Feran leaves for school. I promised to talk to him." Arian sat on the side of the bed and reached for her discarded clothing.

Cassie watched her, drinking in the sight. The muscles of Arian's back, the curve of her neck, the fullness of her breasts. How many more mornings would she be able to enjoy seeing the perfection of Arian's naked body? Then the maidservant arrived, and by the time Cassie had finished giving instructions, Arian was dressed and ready to leave.

Cassie delayed her departure with a leisurely kiss.

Eventually, Arian broke away. "Will I see you later today?"

"Maybe not. Mother wants me at the lodge. I don't know how long it will take, or what it's about."

"It'll be more fun and games with the Imperial Senate."

"Most likely. I'll send word when I get back, though it might not be till tomorrow."

Arian made no answer, merely nodding as she headed out the door.

The maidservant returned with a tray of food. Sitting alone by the window, Cassie picked at the pastries without enthusiasm.

You don't care whether I go or stay. The pain in Arian's voice had ripped through Cassie. She had been an inch from breaking her unspoken vow. An inch from lying to Arian and pretending she could make the world other than it was—pretending that somehow they could unpick the web of imperial politics and free themselves to do whatever they wanted.

On one level, it would have been so easy. She could have said, "I want you to stay in Kavilli, because it will break my heart if you leave me." It would be the truth, but it ignored other truths. If the family required it, Cassie would pack her own bags tomorrow, leaving behind Kavilli and everyone in it, including Arian. No matter how strong her feelings, she could not turn her back on her family, because without her family's support and protection, her back was merely a target for all the other imperial players.

The problem was that Arian was simply too honest and straightforward for her own good. Arian hated the political manoeuvring and double-dealing. But that was the way the empire worked—the way it had always worked and would always work. Trying to change it was as pointless as raging at the tides, and ignoring it was as dangerous as dancing on quicksand. The world would suck you down and swallow you whole.

Cassie snatched up a bowl of cut fruit, tempted to hurl it across the room. But the stronger the emotion, the more important to keep it hidden. Mother had taught her that. She carefully selected a slice of apple and returned the bowl to the tray.

You lie as easily as breathing. She would not lie to Arian, except for the one big lie of omission. "I love you." Cassie whispered the words she had never dared say to her. It would not be fair to give hope that the bond between them could withstand the weight of the empire.

The food formed a hard lump in Cassie's stomach. After another few bites, she gave up on breakfast, and instead got ready for the drive to the lodge. Time to see what Mother wanted. Time to put the pointless worrying out of her head.

One day—one day soon, Arian was going to walk out the door and not come back, and there was nothing she could do about it.

❖

The carriage negotiated the last bend in the road and the climb levelled out. On either side, the marshalled rows of vineyards gave way to rough pasture. Tufts of long grass fluttered in a chill wind from the north, while sheep roamed between spindly shrubs. Winter was closing in. Crowns of white were growing on the distant mountain peaks. Up ahead, Mother's lodge broke the skyline on a ridge between two wooded hills.

They were expected. Even before the driver called out, the gates to the outer stable yard swung open. Cassie was not the only one summoned. Two other carriages had recently arrived, judging by steam rising from the horses' flanks. Whatever Mother had planned was more than a routine catch-up session.

Marcella, the housekeeper, was waiting in the entrance foyer. She bobbed a curtsy as she took Cassie's cloak. "The Doyenne's waiting for you in the salon, my lady."

"Who else is here?"

"Lord Xeranius and Master Branius."

"Is anyone else expected?"

"No, my lady."

So as Arian thought, it's fun and games with the Senate. Not that it was a hard call.

The foyer took the form of a portico, with the entrance in the middle of a long wall, facing an open row of columns running the length of the other side. The inner courtyard lay beyond. Marcella disappeared into her office at one end of the foyer, to hang up the cloak.

The hunting lodge had been built in the rustic style, fashionable several decades earlier. After acquiring it from the previous owner,

Mother had expanded the buildings into a comfortable villa, adding a second floor to the main block and facilities for year-round habitation, but leaving the deliberately uneven plasterwork and gnarled wooden beams as they were.

The salon was directly across the courtyard from the foyer, on the other side of the small enclosed garden. In keeping with the lodge's origins, statues depicting mythical huntsmen were set amid the flower beds. The roses had been pruned back for winter but, come summer, the garden would be a riot of scent and colour. Mother loved her roses.

On the left of the courtyard, several doors gave access to the guest bedrooms. On the right, an open wooden staircase climbed the wall to a veranda and Mother's private apartment on the upper floor. Near the foot of the stairs, an archway led to the kitchen yard, workrooms, and servant's quarters.

The salon was where Mother entertained visitors to the lodge. The seating could comfortably accommodate a dozen diners, yet still had a cosy, intimate feel, helped by the low ceiling, richly coloured wall paintings, and large stone fireplace. The lodge had been built without central heating, and Mother had not attempted ripping up the floor to add a hypocaust.

The others attending the meeting were already present. Mother stood by a window, looking at the city of Kavilli on the lowlands below, like a hawk, hunting for prey. The thick green glass would warp the view, but the miles and distortion counted for nothing. Few could see the city as clearly as Mother did, and even fewer were as deadly, when the moment came to swoop.

Xeran lounged on a couch. He looked up as Cassie entered and gave a friendly grin that held an undercurrent of ice, if you knew to look for it. He was her first cousin, son of her father's sister. His easy charm belied a casual ruthlessness. More than anyone else in the family, he was responsible for various unfortunate accidents befalling those who had made a nuisance of themselves. At thirty-eight, just two years older than Cassie, he had already notched up a body count she would never get close to.

Bran was at the side of the room, pouring wine. He held the bottle up. "My lady?"

"Please." Cassie smiled at him as she took a seat.

Bran's pale skin and blond hair were a match for Arian's. Unsurprising, since they came from the same tribe, although he had renounced any link with them. Ex-Lycanthi, ex-farmer, ex-slave, and undoubtedly the most valuable employee working for the Passurae family. Bran ran a network of spies and informers that wove through every warp and weft of Kavillian life.

Cassie accepted the wineglass and settled on a couch. No matter how serious the matter at hand, there was no reason not to get comfortable. For his part, Bran picked an upright chair by a table and opened a leather dispatch wallet, although he did not, as yet, remove any documents.

Mother turned away from the window. "There's an issue we need to deal with." She seated herself at the other side of the table from Bran and continued. "The position of principal magistrate is up for election in eight months. Which means we have time to ensure the right person gets elected."

"Does the right person have a name?" Xeran asked.

"The wrong person does. Which is our first concern. Other families will have their own preferred candidates. Most stand no chance and will be knocked out in the first round of voting. The Konithae's nominee is the one we need to worry about."

The fierce rivalry between the two families went back decades. The fact that the Konithae's doyenne and Mother were sisters merely added a personal, bitter edge to the contest. Cassie sipped her wine, leaving Xeran to ask the questions.

"Do we know who that will be?"

"According to reliable sources, Magistra Vessia Gallina ado Prefectae."

"What do we know about her?"

"Branius." Mother indicated for him to take over.

"She's been a regional magistrate in Basalonia province for five years. Before that, she worked her way up through the ranks here in Kavilli, mostly keeping her nose clean. There are stories about evidence going missing in several trials, but nothing ever pinned on her. A couple of unorthodox judgments, but again, nothing she couldn't deflect. She was born into the Helvicae family. Obviously, she swore her oath of impartiality and renounced family allegiance when she joined the prefecture, but we all know that doesn't count for much."

"Especially with the way the Helvicae have been sucking up to the Konithae recently." Xeran sighed and rubbed his head. "Is there any good news? Anything we can use?"

"She has expensive tastes and is known to be bribable."

"Who isn't?"

Bran shrugged. "It's a question of prudence. Lining your own pocket is one thing, harming the empire is another. One of my agents picked up a suggestion of potentially treasonable bribes she's taken, but no details. To date, she's been careful. But I'll be sending instructions to my people in Basalonia. Something might turn up."

"If she's not fussy about the bribes she takes, can't we work with her?" Xeran turned to Mother.

"That will become very expensive, very quickly, and will play into the hands of whoever has the deepest purse. I don't want to get into that sort of contest with the Konithae." Mother shook her head. "We need to make sure our candidate wins the vote. Which means putting pressure on people. That's why I've called you here."

Cassie put down her wineglass. "Who are we targeting?"

"For starters, Primus Tribonus Albanis pars Laurentinae dom Drusae."

The leader of the Senate. Mother was aiming high. "Do you think we can crack him?" Cassie asked.

"Oh yes." Mother even allowed herself a smile. "In fact he's the easy one. We already have everything we need, thanks to your brother."

Jadio! "What on earth has he done?"

"He slipped a couple of army reports to me," Mother said. "The documents have been in my safekeeping for a while, waiting for the right moment. They relate to the battle where Tribonus's youngest son lost his life. The official story is that his son was in command of one wing, when they were outflanked by a surprise manoeuvre. Supposedly, he rallied his men in a heroic, but doomed defence, until he fell, fighting the enemy to the last."

"I take it that isn't what happened," Xeran said.

"Quite. As I understand it, his wing was deliberately weakened to lure the enemy into committing their entire cavalry there. He wasn't expected to win, merely to pin down the enemy long enough for our main force to punch through in the centre. However, as soon as his wing started to give way, he fled, abandoning his men. If his second-in-command hadn't stepped in and rallied the troops, it would have been a complete rout. Tribonus's son was found afterwards, cowering in the baggage train."

"Had he never been in battle before?" Xeran asked.

"Apparently not. Tribonus had used his influence to get his son promoted. But the boy didn't have the experience or the character for command."

"It happens." Xeran shrugged. "I came across some like that during my service. How did Tribonus keep the story hidden?"

"The soldiers who found him were so disgusted they killed him on the spot. No court martial, no record, and Tribonus paid a lot of money to keep it that way. Except, the legate and his senior officers sent their own, uncensored reports to army headquarters, where they landed in Jadio's hands." For a moment, Mother's face held a hint of exasperation. "I'd like to think even he couldn't miss their potential usefulness."

But it was more likely Jadio had simply been outraged at the abject cowardice and appalled by the army's willingness to cover it up. Jadio was undoubtedly a capable officer, but with political instincts that would shame a senile hamster.

"Didn't the surviving troops have something to say about it?" Xeran asked.

"I'm sure they did. But Tribonus has made sure they've been stationed at the far borders of the empire. However, with the reports as evidence…" Mother pursed her lips. "Let's say, I think we can count on Tribonus's vote. And as leader of the Senate, he'll carry others with him."

"Who else is on our list?" Cassie asked. Mother would not have summoned them if there was nothing more to do.

"Doyen Bellorion Thracius pars Tribonae dom Marcustae. The death of his second wife was far too convenient."

"She was obviously murdered," Xeran said. "I think most people agree about that, but nobody has had any luck proving it. Her family wouldn't let it drop for ages, but even they've given up." His expression became more thoughtful. "Unless you've got new information."

"After all this time, we're not going to prove murder, but Branius has something." Mother indicated for him to take over again.

"We're in contact with a former Marcustae housemaid who's taken to drinking too much, and then talking too much afterwards. I fear neither activity is good for her health. If word gets back to Doyen Bellorion, she won't survive long enough to give a sworn statement. But she's told one of my agents about an argument between Bellorion and his wife. The wife lost her temper, took a document from her strongbox, ripped it into pieces, and literally threw it in his face, followed by a hairbrush, a pottery vase, and then anything else that came to hand." Bran paused. "The maid doesn't think it's a coincidence his wife died just two days later."

"Do we know what the document was?" Cassie asked.

"The housemaid had to tidy up the mess afterward. She can't read, which is probably why Bellorion thought it safe to let her do the job unsupervised. However, she was nosy enough to keep the pieces and show it to a friend. This friend claimed the document was the wife's will, the one she'd signed on her wedding day, leaving the bulk of her money to Doyen Bellorion."

"Have you tracked down this friend?" Cassie asked.

Bran shook his head. "He vanished years ago."

"Then all we have is hearsay."

"Not entirely. According to the records, the original marriage contract and all associated papers were submitted to the Senate archives when settling the wife's estate, including her will. It means either the housemaid and her friend are wrong, or the will in the archives is a forgery."

"Hopefully it's the latter," Mother said. "Xeran, that's what I want you to look into. You still have your contact in the archives?"

Xeran nodded. "Yes."

"We want sight of the will. If we can show it's a forgery, not only will we have Bellorion on a string, we'll have Scribe Ellonius Nonus ado Prefectae as well, since he was the one who certified the will as genuine."

"Ellonius doesn't have a vote in the Senate," Xeran said.

"No. But his wife does." Mother turned to Cassie. "The last name on my list is Juliana, the Nerinae family's doyenne. She's the one I want you to chase down."

"What do we have on her?"

"Not a lot. Just an old rumour. The cult of Olliarus. It was years before you were born, but I take it you've heard the name?"

Cassie dug into her memory. "Human sacrifice?"

"Yes. That one."

"Doyenne Juliana was a cult member?"

"That was the rumour. A very quiet rumour, but I have reason to believe there might be truth to it. Obviously, she wasn't doyenne back then. She'd have been no more than seventeen, a few years older than me."

Across the empire, countless gods were worshiped, each with their own peculiar rites. The nearest thing to an established, empire-wide religion was the assertion that all gods were merely aspects of a single divine spirit—a spirit so immense as to be incomprehensible to the mortal mind. It therefore presented itself in multiple forms, differing from place to place, according to the needs of the local population. Any perceived contradictions were a result of imperfect human understanding.

This meant all gods were equally valid. All could be worshipped in whatever way their followers thought right, with just one exception. Human sacrifice was outlawed, even with willing victims. The taboo was not just a question of morality. Once religion got involved, people lost all sense of proportion. The whole empire would go up in flames if fanatics launched murderous rampages whenever a priest with a glib tongue claimed their god commanded it.

Yet Doyenne Juliana had been caught up in one such cult. From what Cassie knew of her, it was the last thing anyone would expect. "Any idea how I'm going to get proof?"

Mother smiled. "No. I'm leaving it to your initiative. Be imaginative."

Thanks. "I'll see what I can turn up."

"Anyone else on your hit list?" Xeran asked.

"No definite names. Branius will be working with me on a fishing exercise." Mother pointed to him. "Gambling debts. Start with that. Some of the big players have been getting very wealthy recently, which means dupes are going into debt. I don't want to pay out a fortune, but if someone is in desperate need of money we might be able to turn it to our advantage."

Bran nodded. "Yes, Doyenne. I'll see what I can dig up."

"Good." Mother pushed back from the table and stood. "And that concludes all we need to discuss for now. Branius, I think you have something for me."

"Yes. Here." He pulled a wad of paper from the dispatch wallet. "This is what you asked for."

Mother flipped though the pages. "Perfect." She looked up. "I need to study these in detail. Branius, Xeran, you can stay for lunch, or return to Kavilli, as you wish. But, Cassie…" Mother glanced in her direction. "There's another issue I need to discuss with you. I'll be back as soon as I've finished with this."

Mother showed no trace of annoyance, so the issue was unlikely to be a reprimand—not that Cassie could think of anything she had done recently to earn one.

After Mother left the salon, Xeran drained his wineglass and stood. "I'll be off. Will you be at Fabrica's for her birthday?"

"Probably," Cassie replied. Fabrica threw the most interesting parties.

"I'll see you there then." He nodded to Cassie and patted Bran on the shoulder. "Good hunting."

Bran remained seated after Xeran had gone.

"Are you staying for lunch?" Cassie asked.

"No. I've got too much to do back in town, but…" A broad grin split his face. "I wanted to tell you Tessa is pregnant."

"Congratulations."

"Whoever thought I'd be a father?"

"Nobody back in Lycanthia. That's for certain."

The matrilineal Lycanthian families did not even recognise the existence of fatherhood. A man's heirs were his maternal sisters' sons. This was peculiar from an empire viewpoint. However, since births were witnessed, it carried the advantage a man could always be absolutely certain his heirs were genuine blood relatives, unlike men in the empire, who had to trust their wives on the matter.

A faint blush reddened Bran's face. "I just wanted to say, thank you, my lady."

"I can't take any credit." Cassie laughed. "That's definitely one thing you did on your own."

"No. Without you I'd be working in a mine somewhere, or dead, or wishing I was. Everything good in my life has come about because I met you."

"I bought you."

"And freed me."

Cassie smiled. "And got the best spymaster in Kavilli. I think I'm ahead on the deal."

"It's good of you to say so." Bran got to his feet. "I have to go."

"Pass on my best wishes to Tessa."

"Will do." Bran collected his now empty wallet and left.

Alone in the room, Cassie wandered to the window where Mother had been standing. The ground fell away sharply on this side of the lodge, dropping six hundred feet to the lowlands. The thick glass turned the world outside green. Circular whirls made the scene ripple as she moved, as if it were underwater. Ten miles away, the city of Kavilli was laid out, like a child's toy.

Arian was down there.

Depending on what Bran's papers contained, Mother might be back in ten minutes, or some time past midnight. Cassie rested her forehead on the glass and closed her eyes. She wanted to be back in Kavilli, with Arian, right now.

She could not shake the idea that their time together was measured in days, and she dare not waste a moment. The sense of urgency was ridiculous. Nothing was going to happen until she was back in Kavilli. They needed to be in the same room to have an argument. As long as they were not in speaking distance, the funeral rites for their love affair were safely on hold.

❖

Dusk was settling in by the time Mother reappeared in the salon. There would be no return to Kavilli that day. Sleet rattled on the windows. A footman added logs to the fire and lit the lamps while a pair of housemaids delivered food and wine.

After the servants left, Mother poured herself a large glass and reclined on one of the dining couches. Both actions were unusual and disconcerting. It was so rare to see Mother relaxed. "I'm sorry to have kept you hanging around all day. I had unexpected matters to deal with."

Apologies were also rare. Maybe there was cause for concern after all. "That's all right. I had plenty to think about."

"Did you reach any conclusions?"

"I was trying to work out where I could go for information about the Olliarus cult." *When not worrying about Arian.* "Who would be a likely source, after all this time? You said you thought Doyenne Juliana was involved. Is there anything more you can tell me?"

"It's a case of spotting what wasn't there, rather than what was." Mother shifted around on her couch. "The cult should have stuck to sacrificing people who wouldn't be missed. There's enough of them around. But they became overconfident, and once they'd got the prefects' attention, it was over for them. The first arrest led to others, and then more. About twenty people were executed in all. But the pattern of arrests had holes. There were known associates of the cultists who the prefects ignored."

"Juliana was one of the holes?"

"Yes. Her lover and two of her friends were among those executed. But her family was influential enough to shield her."

"Even so, there must have been gossip."

Mother laughed. "There certainly was, but mainly about the high-profile people under suspicion, Juliana was overlooked. She was young and unimportant back then, and not many knew about her lover. She'd been very discreet. Her husband at the time wouldn't have taken it at all well."

"You know who the lover was."

"A centurion in the Senate guard." Mother frowned. "Calvus. That was his name. Juliana's husband's family had sponsored his promotion, since both his parents were employees. He had no links to any other family of note. However, he was extremely handsome, and visiting his parents gave plenty of opportunity to meet with Juliana."

"How do you know about their affair?"

Mother laughed. "One of my schoolmates had a crush on Calvus and used to follow him around. We were only eleven or so at the time. She was the one who saw them together."

None of which was much help. "Do you have any ideas about where I should start hunting for evidence?"

"I'm afraid not. Your task is far less straightforward than Xeran's." Mother swirled the wine in her glass thoughtfully. "His contact in the Senate archives made him an obvious choice to include in the meeting today, and I wanted to get the pair of you working together. Xeran has a lot of ability and some significant limitations." Mother looked up, meeting Cassie's eyes. "You need to know how to use the tools at your disposal when I'm no longer here."

"Hopefully, that's a long way off."

"I won't argue with that." Mother put down her glass and dipped a stuffed vine leaf in sauce.

Cassie selected spiced pork wrapped in pastry. "There was something else you wanted to talk to me about."

"You've received a marriage proposal."

Arian. How am I going to tell her? Or was it a ploy in pursuit of another goal? "Am I going to accept?"

"Yes. It's a good offer."

Cassie concentrated on chewing and swallowing, taking time to ensure she was fully in control of her voice before asking, "Who is he?" Her third husband.

"Master Antonius Vitus par Salvinae dom Egantae."

The Egantae. An established family, but with no permanent seat in the Imperial Senate. Based in the south. Most of their money from... Cassie's thoughts raced. "What's the offer?"

"The Egantae are an old provincial family, but not a wealthy one. Their biggest asset is the port at Navolle. At the moment, it's woefully underdeveloped, but a moderate financial investment would change that. If we put up the capital in return for privileged access, we could shift our textile imports there. It would be highly profitable. The marriage contract will bind both families to the deal."

Was there any chance she could get Arian to see the marriage primarily as a commercial arrangement? Cassie took a sip of wine to ease the dryness in her throat. "Have you been planning this for long?" *And why didn't you let me know?*

"I put out feelers a few months ago to Doyen Valerius of the Egantae. I wanted to be sure your fiasco with Senator Flavinus's wife wouldn't still be a problem. However, enough time has passed. So while I doubt Valerius has forgotten about it, he's not seen fit to raise the subject."

Not when there was money involved. "What else is in the contract?"

"You'll be going down to Navolle to finalise the details with Doyen Valerius in person. I'll give you copies of the documents you'll need to read. The most important thing is that you will retain allegiance to our family. Your husband will take the name Antonius Vitus dom Egantae con Passurae. It's up to you whether you want to acknowledge his family, though it would be polite."

Cassie nodded. Her name was the last thing she was worried about.

Mother dipped another stuffed vine leaf in the sauce. "I'm not about to lose you from the Passurae. You're the future of this family. You'll be doyenne after me. You know that, don't you? There's no other candidate who comes close to matching your talents."

Again, Cassie nodded. There was no point indulging in false modesty.

Mother slipped off the couch and wandered to the window. "Do you ever wonder why I spend so much time up here at the lodge?"

"The peace and quiet helps you think?"

"There's that, of course." Mother's smile was reflected in the window glass. "But no. Mainly it's perspective. From here it's much easier to sift fact from fiction. Discrepancies between what people say and what they do are so much sharper when you take a step back. Branius keeps me up to date with all that's going on, although I never rely on a single source. I get to witness everything I need when I attend sessions at the Senate and I avoid all the social fluff that's just a distraction. And when anyone wants to talk to me, they must come here, onto my home ground, where I'm in complete control."

And every servant at the lodge had been hand-picked for loyalty. No spy or thief could get close.

"The reason I'm telling you this," Mother continued, "when you're doyenne, you will also need to keep your distance. It doesn't have to be a physical separation, such as I have at the lodge, but you must maintain your emotional detachment. You need to keep the world at arm's length. You cannot let anyone inside your guard. Husband, friend, or lover. It's a weakness you cannot afford. This marriage should help you along the path. It is, to be honest, overdue. I'm concerned your objectivity is slipping."

Arian. No need to say her name. It was obvious who and what Mother was referring to. Nor was there any point claiming Arian was not really that important, not least because making the appeal would merely prove just how important she truly was. Cassie clenched her jaw, trying not to show any emotion. She always knew one day would bring an irreconcilable conflict between her family and their relationship, and there was absolutely no satisfaction in being proved right.

Cassie joined Mother at the window. Thick cloud blanketed the sky. Kavilli was lost in the gloom. No more than a few pinpricks of lamplight showed where the city lay.

Arian was going to be furious.

❖

"Lady Arian has arrived," the housemaid announced.

A fist of ice tightened around Cassie's stomach. She pushed away from her writing desk. Outside the window, night had fallen over the city. A page covered in meaningless doodles was all she had to show for her day.

Arian stood in the doorway. Her cheerful smile was nothing short of heartbreaking. Cassie wrapped her in a hug, burying her own face in Arian's shoulder. Arian's body was firm and warm in her arms. When they kissed, her lips were soft. Cassie tried to imprint the moment in her memory, so she would be able to recall it in the months and years to come—every touch, every scent, every sound.

"Will you be wanting dinner now, my lady?" the housemaid asked. Cassie had forgotten her existence.

"No. You can go. I'll call when we're ready."

Delaying things until after the meal was futile. Eating was impossible. The mere thought of putting food in her mouth gave Cassie indigestion. Nor was there any point scrapping dinner and suggesting they go straight to bed. She would not be able to enjoy that either.

She gestured Arian to a chair, then sat facing her, although her legs ached from the urge to pace the room. "Thanks for coming over. I'm sorry it was so late when I sent the messenger." More pointless procrastination. Hours spent running excuses and explanations through her head, and still no idea how to spin the news in a way Arian might find acceptable.

"That's all right. When did you get back?"

"Mid morning. But I've been tied up all day." Which was the truth. Her head was a mass of knots. "Mother had some new assignments for me."

"How is she?"

"Same as usual."

"Devious and controlling?" Arian's smile did not conceal the bite in her tone.

More than you know. Cassie gave a noncommittal shrug. "I'm going to be away for a few days. I've got things to attend to in Navolle."

"Is that one of your new assignments?"

"In part."

"How long will you be away?"

"Ten days. We're working out a deal to expand the port there. We're hoping to use it for importing textiles. The family who own the land have a long history in the empire, although they don't have a seat on the Senate, and they aren't..."

Arian's eyes had glazed over. She had a low tolerance for imperial wrangling, and it was not as if skirting around the issue was going to help.

"...and I'll be arranging a marriage contract while I'm there."

A confused frown solidified on Arian's face. "Who's getting married?"

"Me."

"What?"

"Mother has selected a new husband for me."

"Tell her no."

"I can't."

"Why not?"

"Because that's not how the world works."

Arian lurched to her feet and stabbed a finger at her. "Maybe that's how your world works. Not mine."

Cassie forced her voice to stay calm and reasonable. "It's purely a business deal. The port is the most important part."

"You'll share his bed."

"No more than I have to." Cassie drew a breath. "Both our families will want children. But once I've had one or two, that'll be an end to it." If she had any say in the matter. "You and I can still be lovers. We'll need to be a little more discreet, but—"

"NO!" Arian's hands had formed fists. "No, no, no. I am not living my life like that."

"We can go on the same as now. The Passurae are the dominant family, so I get to dictate terms. We just need to maintain a suitable façade for society."

Arian's voice went up a notch. "You can shove your suitable façade up your arse. I'm not dancing to that tune. And I can't believe you're asking me to."

Cassie closed her eyes. The conversation was going exactly as anticipated. The irony being that the marriage really was less significant than the port. Antonius would be her third husband, and most likely, in a few years, her third divorce.

"I'm not asking you to do anything. I'm just explaining what our options are."

"No, you're not. You're telling me what you're going to do, and tough shit if I don't like it."

"Do you think I'm happy about this? Do you think I want to get married? I don't have a choice."

"You're the one who's chosen to go along with it. You're the one making decisions. So I'll give you another pair of options you can choose between. Me or him. One or the other."

"Please, Arian. I can't—"

"Yes, you can. You're going to." Arian folded her arms. "Go on. Pick one of us."

Cassie covered her eyes with her hand. "He means nothing to me. But I have to follow—"

"Pick."

"You're being—"

"Childish? Irresponsible? A stupid barbarian?" Arian's voice dripped sarcasm. "I'm being honest. I know it's a concept you struggle with."

"You want honesty?" A spike of anger drove Cassie to her feet. She faced Arian. "I don't want to marry him, but I'm going to. Because crying and stamping my feet isn't going to get me anywhere. The world isn't going to turn upside down just to make me happy. And yes, it is childish to think otherwise."

For the space of a dozen heartbeats, they glared at each other. "So that's your answer. You pick him."

"No. It's…" *You I want. Only you.* The words died on Cassie's lips, along with her anger. "It's the only sensible option I have."

Arian stared down at her hands, as if wishing she could magic a throwable object into them. Long seconds passed before she looked up. "Fine. Enjoy being sensible." She turned away. "Don't bother contacting me again."

"Please."

Arian did not look back. "Goodbye." The door closed behind her.

Cassie sank onto her chair. There had never been the slightest hope Arian would accept the marriage, and even less that she would ever now change her mind. The goodbye was final. No need to consult an oracle. Their love affair had been hopeless from the start.

Arian wanted commitment, and all Cassie could offer was fidelity. The three years they had been lovers was by far the longest period Cassie had ever remained true to one person. Now even that was off the table. She had nothing to give Arian as proof she mattered, and Arian deserved so much more. Maybe now Arian would be able to find someone who could put her first, someone who could match her for honesty and courage.

The room blurred as tears stung Cassie's eyes. Arian was gone, and it hurt every bit as much as she had always known it would.

ARIAN

The garden lining the river embankment was one of the rare patches of public greenery in Kavilli. Stunted trees formed twin rows separated by a strip of grass. Or it would be grass, if children had not worn it bare, playing games that involved a leather ball and screeching at the top of their lungs.

The garden ended at a busy thoroughfare leading to a bridge over the river. The road was crowded with carts, horses, and people, making a loud enough racket to almost drown out the sound of children yelling. Arian turned to walk back between the trees, as she had been doing all morning. To and fro, trying to make the rhythm of her steps impose order on the chaos ripping up her insides.

It was not working.

She stopped midway along the row and leaned against a tree trunk. In a sudden flare of anger, she formed her hand into a fist. But punching the tree would be unfair. It was just as out of place as herself, and even more trapped. At least she could hope to escape the city one day and return to the forests of home. The tree was doomed to stay throughout the decades, forever captive. Arian closed her eyes and rested her forehead on the ragged bark. If only she could draw on the tree's strength, its power to endure.

"Damn her. Damn her to hell and back."

Something thumped into her calf.

"Sorry, lady." A scrawny urchin reclaimed the ball and scurried away.

Arian continued walking. This time, when she reached the other end of the garden, she carried on, entering the maze of cobbled streets and rubbish-filled alleyways. Marble mansions and ornate temples lined the widest avenues, while crammed behind them were warrens of squalid tenements. Open plazas were busy with clusters of slaves and soldiers, merchants and mothers, passed out drunkards and the retinues of senators. All of them rubbing shoulders, getting on with their lives, and keeping the empire going. And all of them creating so much commotion while they did it.

With relief, Arian reached the entrance to her house. She closed the heavy outer gate, muffling the sounds of the street, and rested her back against the timbers. She was alone in the courtyard, with just the stone wolf for company, frozen in the sunlight. But peace was a two-edged sword. Now there was nothing to distract her from the gut-wrenching, soul-shredding—

"I've been looking for you." Ulfgar strode into the courtyard. Obviously, he had been keeping watch.

"Whatever it is, it can wait." She was most definitely not in the mood to deal with him, or anything else.

"No, it can't." Ulfgar planted his feet in front of her, arms folded across his chest, blocking her in. "We have to return to Breninbury immediately."

Arian sighed. "What's Feran been saying?"

"The same childish nonsense. That isn't the point."

"Then what is?"

Ulfgar's expression wavered for a moment, a twitch of his lips, a narrowing of his eyes, then he jutted out his chin. "Feran needs to be back with his people."

The idea of packing their belongings without delay and leaving Kavilli was so very tempting. Just put a thousand miles between herself and Cassie, and never set eyes on her again. The temptation was not one Arian could surrender to.

"He goes back when it's safe. Not before. I've sent a message to Earl Kendric. We'll stay in Kavilli until we hear back, saying whether he agrees the time is right for Feran's return."

"We cannot stay here another three months."

Three months. How would she bear it? "Yes, we can."

"I've warned you of the consequences."

And I've been too polite to tell you to go fuck yourself. "You must do as you see fit."

Arian pushed past Ulfgar and approached the wolf statue. She rubbed a hand over its neck, as if she were stroking a pet dog. They were both prisoners, trapped in the city. How much easier it would be if she too had a heart of stone.

The silence drew out. Eventually, Arian turned around, half hoping Ulfgar had gone. However, he had not moved, except his eyes were downcast, and his expression had become uncharacteristically hesitant. If there was one thing about a priest you could rely on, it was unshakable conviction, born of faith. It was a common platitude that, across the empire, there were countless gods of love and war, but not a single god of indecision.

As if sensing her eyes on him, Ulfgar looked up. His face hardened and his normal assertive manner returned. "This is not the end of the matter."

"It is for me."

The last hint of doubt vanished. "In that case, I have another request to make of you."

"If it affects my children's safety, my answer is the same."

"No. Neither child is directly involved. I…" He drew a deep breath. "I wish to make a sacrifice to the gods, to beseech them to guide us all on the path of true wisdom."

"What sort of sacrifice?"

"A bull."

The sacrifice of animals, while not unheard of, played a small part in Lycanthian religion. Normally, it was only done in the most extreme of circumstances. The land, and all its riches, was a gift from the gods. Sending bits of it back to them unused could be viewed as ungrateful. However, Ulfgar was the priest, and the judgment lay with him.

"If you think it will help, I have no objection."

"I'll need resources to purchase the animal."

"You want money?" Was Ulfgar really being that crass?

"Yes."

"Would you like me to attend the ceremony?"

"That won't be necessary."

There's a surprise. Such a blatant and amateurish attempt at extorting money was not expected behaviour in a priest. Feran and Eilwen were not the only ones picking up more Kavillian culture than was desirable. Undoubtedly, the bull would neither be bought nor sacrificed, and normally Arian would not dream of giving in to the demand. However, in the context of her other problems, the price of one bull to make Ulfgar go away and leave her alone was money well spent. Just as long as he did not make a habit of it. The money itself was not an issue. The Imperial Senate had granted a generous stipend to cover Feran's upkeep.

"I'll arrange for adequate funds to be made available to you."

"Good." Thankfully, Ulfgar turned on his heel and left.

Arian sat on the plinth and met the wolf's eyes. That fixed stare. What could she read into it today? Fear, doubt, regret? But for once, she did not empathise. She refused to look back.

"Excuse me, my lady." Her Kavillian housemaid, Laelia, appeared in the courtyard.

"What is it?"

"A messenger has arrived to see you."

Cassie. She could go fuck herself as well.

But before Arian could put the thought into words, Laelia continued. "He's from Doyenne Lilliana Tacita con Avitae dom Konithae. Shall I show him in?"

"Er…yes."

Somewhere amid the surprise was a twinge of disappointment. Arian closed her eyes. *Damn her to hell and back.* Cassie had played games with her since the day they met, but it was over. No matter how much it hurt, she refused to be a plaything ever again.

A polite cough recalled Arian to the courtyard.

The messenger gave a formal bow. "Doyenne Lilliana invites you to dinner at her home, tomorrow night. Can I report you'll be able to attend?"

How quickly the news had spread. The most likely source was a paid informer in the Passurae household. Cassie had warned her not all servants could be trusted. Doyenne Lilliana must have heard about both Cassie's forthcoming marriage and the end of the relationship. Previous arguments between her and Cassie had not produced an overture from the Passurae family's biggest rival. Clearly, this time, Doyenne Lilliana felt it worth testing the water.

More games. Yet, permission for Feran to leave Kavilli would only be possible with support inside the Senate, and asking Cassie for help was unthinkable. Rejecting Lilliana's invitation was both short-sighted and pointless.

"Tell Doyenne Lilliana I will be delighted to attend, and please thank her for her kind consideration."

And no doubt, even before she set foot inside the Konithae mansion, news of the invitation and acceptance would have made its way back through the Passurae network of spies. Something else for Cassie to shove in with her nice, sensible, suitable façade.

Damn her.

Experimenting with food at Kavillian dinner parties was risky. Arian had learned this the hard way. Not that it was all bad. Most dishes fell somewhere between good and acceptable. But the chefs would not leave anything alone. Half the food ended up too sweet, too salty, too oily, or with a combination of flavours that simply did not work together. As a general guideline, the more elaborate it looked, the worse it tasted. Anything classified as "regional cuisine" would either be utterly bland, or so spicy it set her mouth on fire and turned her face numb.

As a guest at the Konithae mansion, spitting out food would create an unacceptable first impression. Arian stuck to the safe options of cheese, olives, bread, and fruit. All were reliably edible. Best of all were the sweet cinnamon pastries with almonds. These were far and away her favourite Kavillian food offering. Arian helped herself to a third.

Cassie used to encourage her to try new dishes when they were alone together, working out what she liked, and what to avoid. The cinnamon pastries were a notable success. More often, Cassie had been reduced to uncontrollable laughter at Arian's expression when she put whatever it was in her mouth. Arian's eyes prickled at the memory. She would laugh as well, in-between choking—*People actually like this?*—while Cassie held her sides, whimpering.

Arian slammed shut her mental doors on the past.

"...then he said to me, if you don't like it you can leave. So I left."

Presumably, the dinner guest's story was humorous, since most of the audience laughed. Arian smiled and took a bite of the pastry.

A total of eighteen people were at the meal, including herself and Doyenne Lilliana. The layout of the room was identical to similar dinners in the Passurae household. Guests semi-reclined on couches. A musician with a harp played a soothing melody in the background. Unobtrusive attendants delivered food and wine to conveniently placed side tables. Couples might choose to share a couch, as she and Cassie had often done in the past. Two juveniles were making a show of feeding each other. The more mature kept such displays for in private.

Being alone felt vulnerable. Kavillian politics were brutal, and Arian knew she was ill-equipped to play the game. Had Cassie been present, she would be adding up the telltale signs. In whispers, she might explain the significance of lapses in protocol, point out attempts at intrigue and seduction, give her analysis of the players.

Arian used to listen with only half an ear, impatient and contemptuous. She should have paid more attention. The man who had just spoken, why had he chosen that story to tell, rather than another? Of the listeners, whose laughter had been forced? Who had whispered into their partner's ear? Who was waiting to jump in with their own story? Who was silently watching?

This last group was the most dangerous. Unsurprisingly, it included Doyenne Lilliana. The elderly matriarch met Arian's eyes and smiled—a smile that was superficially warm and gracious, but behind it lay a maze of plots, tricks, and calculations. Arian did not need Cassie to point out the obvious. It was easy to believe Lilliana and Cassie's mother were true sisters in the Lycanthian way of thinking, born of the same mother, coming into the world covered in the same blood.

For the Lycanthi, blood was family, and family was everything. Whatever part men played in creating children, it was restricted to semen, which contained no blood. And since they contributed no blood to the child, the children their bedfellow gave birth to could not be called their blood-kin.

For the Kavillians, family was everything, but they felt free to make it up as they went along. Cassie's mother, Pellonia, had been adopted by the Passurae, and for them, somehow signatures on a piece of paper counted for more than the blood she shared with her sister. It made absolutely no sense.

Meanwhile, another guest was talking, but he had either drunk too much, or was pretending he had. This was a trick Cassie occasionally employed, to see who might let their guard down. The man's story jumped around, missing out steps. Several people were clearly getting ready to interrupt.

Lilliana signalled to the attendants. "We've finished eating. You can clear the rest away."

"I…oh…yes." The speaker picked up something from a dish and pushed it into his mouth, bringing his rambling to an end.

Around the room, guests left their couches to gather in small groups. This was where things got really interesting. Arian could imagine Cassie's voice, whispering in her ear. Like a hunter, reading tracks made by game, Cassie would be reading the room.

And how long would it take before Arian could go five minutes without thinking about her? Again, tears stung her eyes. She needed fresh air, although with winter on the way, it would be too cold to stay outside for long. Arian grabbed her wine glass and slipped off the couch. At the rear of the room, a doorway led to a balcony.

The sun was setting over Kavilli. Bands of red and orange lined the horizon. A swirl of birds swooped past, heading home to roost. Unlike the Passurae residence in the centre of the city, the Konithae mansion was sited in the eastern outskirts. It was surrounded by private gardens and a high wall. Sounds from beyond were muted. Arian rested her forearms on the stone balustrade and closed her eyes, trying to draw on inner peace, trying to clear her mind.

Footsteps sounded on the tiles. "I wanted to thank you for coming." Lilliana joined her.

"Thank you for inviting me."

"Oh, no need to thank me. It's been what…three years you've been living in Kavilli? I really don't know why I haven't invited you here before."

Arian's pulse rate spiked. Verbal duelling with Pellonia was a game for the foolhardy. Arian had let Cassie handle her mother whenever possible. Fortunately, Pellonia had taken to spending all her time at the old hunting lodge where Arian never went. Lilliana was clearly every bit as dangerous as her sister, but Arian was in her home as a guest and had no polite way to dodge the conversation.

"It'll be because I was involved in a love affair with your niece who's in a rival family." Arian pitched her tone to suggest a serious explanation was required.

Lilliana laughed, sounding unexpectedly genuine. "Honesty. Now there's an unusual tactic."

"So I've been told. I've also been told that while it can have surprise value, you can end up digging yourself into a hole."

"I see you've been taking lessons."

Whether I wanted them or not. "Honesty is valued by my people. I like to keep true to my roots."

"You must find life in Kavilli a strain."

"At times."

"But not all the time?"

"Of course not. Kavilli isn't without its good side."

"Such as cinnamon cakes?"

That's to let you know she was watching you. Cassie's voice in her ear. Arian forced an innocuous smile. "Oh, those cakes. They're wonderful."

"Do you have anything like them in your homeland?"

"No. You could make a fortune selling them. My people would give their weight in gold."

"Literally?"

"Maybe an exaggeration. Let's say half their weight."

Lilliana nodded slowly. "It's interesting you mention trade. The subject has been on my mind recently. Although up until now, cakes and pastries haven't figured strongly."

"It's a missed opportunity."

"Some families get more opportunities than others. It's a shame, when there's so much profit to be made from iron ore." Lilliana's tone was neutral—too neutral, which was in itself a giveaway.

So that's why I'm here. Lilliana wanted to talk about trade concessions. She had steered the conversation that way. But was there any reason to avoid the subject? Arian took a sip of wine while she thought.

"You think the Konithae aren't getting fair access to the new Lycanthian mines?"

"It could be better." Lilliana's smile did not waver. "I note that, as yet, there's no official Lycanthian ambassador to the Senate. Is this something you might be interested in taking on? It could be highly advantageous for all concerned."

Arian shook her head, trying not to laugh. The concepts of embassies and ambassadors would first need explaining to those back home, but once it had been done, there was not the slightest chance of her being entrusted with the role. "My people wouldn't think it appropriate to have a woman speak for them."

"Really? How…" For a moment, Lilliana looked genuinely confused, but then her smile returned. "So you couldn't sign trade contracts on their behalf?"

"No. Any proposal would have to go to Earl Kendric, who's acting as regent for my son."

"You can't make decisions on your son's behalf?"

"I'm just his mother. And he's too young to care about trade deals—even if they include cake."

"How was Earl Kendric selected as regent?"

"He's a respected warrior, related to me and my son by blood." *And Cassie picked him.*

"Do you get on well with him, on a personal level?"

"Yes. We always have." Kendric had been her favourite adult when she was growing up.

Lilliana looked thoughtful. "He's a long way from here and must rely on the advice he receives. I think a good word from you could prove helpful. Equally, your son is recognised by the Senate as your people's king."

A client king of a semi-autonomous protectorate. The concession was the price of peace and free trade. Arian said nothing.

"I'm sure your son would take advice from his mother. If he were to give his approval to an advantageous contract, what's the chance Earl Kendric would overturn it?"

"That would depend on how advantageous the contract truly was."

"Of course. But it's getting cold out here." Lilliana stepped back as if to return to the dining room, but stopped. "I understand my niece left town today to visit her prospective husband in Navolle. A good marriage is such a blessing. I wish her well."

"If I see her, I'll pass on your kind words." *Not as if there's the first frigging chance of that happening.* Somehow Arian's voice held steady.

"It's been lovely talking to you." Lilliana left the balcony.

Despite the cold, Arian stayed on, staring over the rooftops. The sun had set and the first stars speckled the sky. Darkness invaded the city, swallowing houses.

She was adrift and alone in dangerous currents. Cassie had been her helmsman, her pilot. Now, for the sake of herself and her children, she must learn to navigate her own passage. The first step was finding a star to guide them. In Kavillian politics, the Konithae family was a very bright star. She could do worse.

CASSIE

Mother was right about the port at Navolle, which was hardly cause for surprise.

Cassie stood on the quayside and looked at seagulls wheeling overhead. The sound of their raucous arguments contrasted with the gentle lap of waves against the timber pylons. Further along the waterfront, a few small boats were docked while fishermen unloaded their catch. Currently, these were the only vessels using the dock, but it need not be so.

The natural harbour was deep enough for cargo ships. The main obstacles were the poor state of the lighthouse, the length of the quay, and the lack of warehouse space. None of these were a major problem. Add new housing for an increased workforce and improve the roads to take heavy wagons, and the port would be transformed from a ramshackle fishing village into a trading hub. The only things to haggle over were who was going to pay for which bits and the size of the discount once everything was completed.

Doyen Valerius stood beside her, giving his own thoughts about upgrading the port. Some ideas were practical; some were not. He was in his mid-fifties, on the chubby side, and prone to talking too much. He had recently been elected doyen of the Egantae family and was clearly ambitious but lacking experience. Allying with one of the major imperial families was his predictable first step.

"My uncle thought trade beneath him. He wouldn't know an opportunity if it hit him in the face. The old fool and his cronies held the family back for decades." Valerius was not hiding his opinion of the previous doyen.

Cassie made a mental note to identify the cronies in question. A rival faction in the family could provide a useful lever, should the deal with Valerius turn sour. But for now, he was proving easy enough to handle. She shielded her eyes from the oblique winter sunlight and pointed to the headland on the other side of the bay.

"The lighthouse up there. If the Passurae pay for all repairs and upkeep, would you be willing to drop import fees for raw textiles?"

"I'd take a sixth off."

"A quarter?"

Valerius scratched his chin. "A quarter. And you pay the lighthouse keepers' salaries."

"I…well…" Cassie gave the impression of thinking it over. "All right. Agreed."

In truth, no inducement was needed. Whoever controlled the lighthouse controlled the port. Valerius's inexperience was showing. Furthermore, Cassie would not put it past him to make false economies by skimping on maintenance. One shipwreck would wipe out any savings.

"Shall we go back to the villa?"

Cassie nodded. "Yes. I've seen all I need to."

The housekeeper in the foyer took their cloaks and ducked a curtsy. "Master Antonius has arrived. He's waiting for you in the salon."

Valerius gave Cassie a broad smile. "I guess you're eager to meet your husband-to-be."

Eager was not quite the word she would have picked, but there was no point putting things off. She might as well learn the worst. "Please. Lead the way."

Bran's report on Antonius had been unusually lacking in detail. There simply did not appear to be much of note about him.

Like all noble Kavillian boys, Antonius had gone to the academy when he turned seven. After leaving at fifteen, he completed his mandated twelve years in the legions. His military record was utterly unremarkable, never cited for anything either good or bad. When he left the army, three months ago, he had reached the very average rank of auxiliary tribune.

Cassie would be his first wife. As far as Bran could discover, there were no mistresses or illegitimate children hiding in the background. He appeared to be generally well liked by his comrades. The only gossip of note was that Antonius had wanted to stay in the army but had been ordered to resign to expand his appeal on the marriage market. Army wives had to follow their husband's postings, which ruled out any woman with senior status in her own family.

Valerius ushered Cassie into the salon. Three men were waiting, attended by a couple of housemaids. One man was too old to be Antonius, and one had a band around his neck that, although ornate and blatantly expensive, marked him as a slave. The remaining man, her soon-to-be husband, was a perfect fit for the traditional formula of tall, dark, and handsome.

At least he'll be ornamental. The first thought to shoot through Cassie's head.

Antonius bowed low as he kissed her hand. "You have done me too much honour in accepting me as your husband. From this day forth, I will devote my life to your happiness and well-being. And I shall count myself the luckiest of men for the privilege of doing so."

His voice matched his looks, deep and firm. He even managed to put a semblance of emotion into reciting the hackneyed phrases, as though he might possibly mean them. *He can act the part as well.*

Cassie stood on tiptoe to plant a countering kiss on his cheek. He had washed recently, and smelled of sweet herbs. "The honour is all mine. It's my pleasure to welcome you into my family, my home, and my heart. I thank the gods that they have blessed me to be your wife."

Valerius was beaming. "May your life together be long and fruitful. And may our two families grow ever closer." He snapped his fingers at the housemaids. "Wine, and summon the rest of the family. We need to toast the happy couple."

Good idea. She could do with a drink.

With a glass of wine in her hand and enough people to create a background hum, Cassie felt more relaxed, though she needed to keep a close watch on how much she drank. This was not a good occasion to make a spectacle of herself.

Antonius was not so cautious. He knocked back his wine and held his glass out to a housemaid for a refill. A cluster of younger relatives surrounded him, listening to a series of anecdotes, ranging from tragedy to farce. He knew how to hold a crowd and was happy as the centre of attention. The talent would come in useful when she needed a distraction created. Mother could have made a worse pick. He even remembered to smile in Cassie's direction from time to time.

The older man who had accompanied Antonius signalled to her, clearly wanting a private word.

Cassie joined him at the side of the room. She smiled. "We haven't been introduced." An oversight on Valerius's part. "But you are…"

"Quintilius Naevius con Salvinae dom Egantae. I'm Antonius's father. Welcome to our family."

"Thank you." Although, more accurately, Antonius was joining her family.

"Has a date been set for the wedding?"

"Ten days from now." A somewhat more rushed schedule than normal. However, work on the port would not start until the contracts were signed.

"Right. Well, um…I just wanted to say…" Quintilius stared at the floor, clearly ill at ease. "I hope Antonius is never a disappointment to you."

Which was an unusual thing for a father to volunteer about his son.

A burst of laughter from the centre of the room marked the end of another anecdote. Cassie turned to look. Again, Antonius smiled in her direction, but his eyes did not linger on her. Instead they latched onto the third man who had arrived with him.

The slave was standing inconspicuously in a corner. Cassie had not before registered much more than the band around his neck. Now she considered the man wearing it. If Antonius was handsome, the slave could only be classed as utterly stunning. His chiselled cheekbones, firm jaw, and light bronze skin were all perfect. Had he been a stage actor, he would have been playing the role of a god. From the way he stood, it was obvious that, under the expensive clothes, his body was lean and muscular. The hunger in Antonius's eyes was equally obvious.

Cassie turned back to Quintilius and smiled. "I'm sure your son won't be a disappointment."

Quite the opposite. Children were a requirement of marriage, but once this duty was fulfilled, Antonius would not be bothering her, or objecting to her own affairs. Mother truly could have made a far, far worse pick for her. All that was needed was to get over Arian and move on.

Unexpectedly, the room blurred as tears threatened. Of course, that last part was the hard bit.

With each marriage the contract had grown more complex. Cassie's first, when she was sixteen, had required a scroll less than a foot in length. This one, twenty years later, was easily five times as long. Unsurprisingly, the upgrades, costs, and import duties for the Navolle port took up a large chunk of the space.

Cassie worked her way down the articles, considering each one carefully. Regardless of the circumstances, never commit to anything without reading every word three times. Mother had drilled that lesson into her even before she fully mastered the alphabet.

She finished the sections relating to the port. The contract was correct in all details as agreed, including several points which might come as an unpleasant surprise to Doyen Valerius in the years ahead, but that was his problem, not hers.

At the other end of the table, Antonius was gazing vacantly into space. His face was a blank mask, giving no clue as to his thoughts. Seated between them, the rotund scribe wore a fixed, professional smile, although the way she was tapping her fingertips together suggested the onset of impatience. Meanwhile, sounds of revelry from the adjoining room were growing. The guests had started on the wedding feast without waiting for her and Antonius.

Cassie returned to the contract. The final section covered family issues. Her husband would become a member of the Passurae family, as would any children of the marriage. The size of their allowance and other fiscal matters were laid out, as were the protocols for initiating and finalising a divorce, amending wills, and settling estates. Everything was ready to be signed and sealed.

Cassie dripped wax onto the bottom of the scroll and made an impression with her signet ring. After a moment of hesitation, she wrote beneath it, Cassilania Marciana con Egantae dom Passurae. As Mother said, acknowledging her husband's family was the polite thing to do. She handed the contract to the scribe, who passed it to Antonius for his assent.

There was one more document in need of approval. Her will. At the moment, it contained only her promise to abide by their agreed terms. Unlike the marriage contract, which would be held in the Senate archives, she would keep possession of the will, adding codicils and redactions to modify the contract by agreement with Antonius, as their circumstances changed.

On her death or divorce it would go to the archives to help settle her estate. Alternately, she could tear it up, as Doyen Bellorion's wife had allegedly done. It was an overly dramatic, and generally inadvisable way to start divorce proceedings. Sorting out the resulting legal mess would be costly, time-consuming, and doomed to arrive at a worse settlement. Of course, this was not an issue if you had the misfortune to be murdered before taking the matter further.

Cassie finished with the will and put the pen down. Antonius was staring intently at the contract, but his lack of eye movement made it clear he was not reading. Was this down to disinterest or anxiety? Regardless, he should be more cautious. Although if Doyen Valerius had not spotted the potential pitfalls, there was no reason to think Antonius would.

To be fair, as a junior member of his family, he had even less control over his situation than she did, and less to be happy about. At least she enjoyed playing Mother's games of politics and intrigue. Antonius had not wanted to leave the army, had not wanted to move to Kavilli, and no doubt, had not wanted to get married. The life he was about to embark on was not one he would have chosen.

Eventually, Antonius gave a small nod and added his name and seal.

The scribe beamed while rolling up the completed contract. "May your life together be long and fruitful." She bustled from the room.

They were married, and alone together for the first time. Antonius was staring at the table where the contract had lain, his face still set in its mask. What was he thinking? What sort of man was her husband?

"How are you feeling?"

Antonius looked up and gave a weak smile. "That I could do with a drink and the chance to relax."

Cassie pointed to the door. "I'll agree with you about the drink, and there's no shortage of wine through there. But I don't rate your chances of relaxing. Over a hundred wedding guests are waiting for us, and every one of them will want to congratulate you and drop hints about children."

"You've been married before." He spoke as if uncertain. Had he really not checked up on her history?

"Twice. Wedding feasts are much more fun when they're someone else's wedding. You're about to be bombarded by people wanting to talk to you. They have to pretend the marriage is all about love, even though they know it isn't. This means they'll struggle to say anything sensible, and you'll have to agree with them. After an hour of it you'll be ready to..." Cassie mimed a face-slapping gesture.

"Maybe we should have held the feast on the dock at Navolle." So he had a sense of humour.

Cassie stood. "Shall we go?" There would be plenty of time to talk thereafter.

"Oh, why not?"

Ragged cheers and applause broke out around the banquet hall when they entered. Cassie gratefully accepted the first glass offered to her. Getting drunk would be a mistake, but neither did she intend to stay totally sober. Others were not so prudent. Fortunately, there was no risk the food and drink would run out.

The wedding feast took the form of an informal buffet, spread across the public reception suite of the Passurae mansion. Normally, this would be a prime opportunity to watch and gather gossip. Except, as the centre of attention, Cassie had no chance for surreptitious eavesdropping. A constant stream of well-wishers claimed her attention without one of them managing to say anything even remotely interesting.

Even so, she was faring marginally better than Antonius. He had been surrounded by a group of young men, who were giving him some very unsubtle advice, judging by their actions. He was smiling, taking the ribbing in good humour, but there was tension in the set of his shoulders. It matched the tightness in Cassie's gut.

"Such a handsome man." The elderly aunt had noticed the direction of her gaze. "You'll have beautiful children."

Cassie nodded and helped herself to another glass of wine.

❖

"Lastly, our thanks go to all of you. My husband and I are delighted you've come to celebrate this special day with us. Our hearts are filled with joy, that we've been able to start our lives together, surrounded by so many of our friends and family. May the gods bless you, as we have been blessed. Now it's time for us to take our leave. But please, stay here and enjoy yourselves. After all, it would be a shame if what's left of the wine went to waste."

On Cassie's previous marriages, she had been the junior party. This time, it was her turn to give the final speech. She ended on a light note and stepped down from the podium to a round of applause, including the predictable heckling from those who had already drunk too much. Her departure from the wedding feast ran a gauntlet of rose petals and grain showers.

Finally, she escaped to the peace of her own rooms. Cassie ran a hand through her hair, dislodging a cascade of petals, rice, and wheat. Worse were the errant husks that had gone down the front of her dress and were now scratching her more delicate parts. Fortunately, a pair of maidservants were on hand to help her undress, bathe, and get ready in her night robe.

When all was done, one asked, "Shall I summon your husband, my lady?"

"Yes. Do that." She could hardly say no. On both previous marriages, as the junior partner, she had been the one summoned. It made surprisingly little difference.

While waiting, Cassie walked to the window and looked out. The short winter's day was over and the sun had set. Lanterns lit the courtyard garden. Whoops and laughter came from the reception rooms, where the wedding feast was still in full swing. Stars hung over Kavilli, with the constellation Draconis, the imperial dragon, climbing in the northern sky. Somewhere out there was Arian, and that was one thought she dare not dwell on. Cassie closed her eyes, fighting to get her memories under control.

Sex with her previous husbands had been occasionally fun, usually forgettable, at times irksome. She had fallen pregnant quickly, resulting in three sons who were away, either in the army or the academy, and two daughters who now lay in the Passurae family crypt.

Marriage and childbirth were a duty, not one she would have chosen, but far from her worst assignment undertaken for the sake of her family. That accolade went to spending months in a shit-covered hovel and having to wash in ice cold water while someone was trying to murder her. And again, the memory led her back to Arian and the circumstances of their first meeting.

Cassie clenched her teeth and angrily slapped a hand on her thigh. Part of her wished she had drunk more, but that was its own trap. Controlling the direction of your thoughts was far easier when sober.

The door opened and Antonius entered. But he was not alone. The eye-catching male slave slipped in behind him. Antonius shuffled from foot to foot. The mask had slipped. He looked like an awkward, frightened boy, with an edge of desperation.

"Do you mind if Timmi is here?" he asked.

"Why?"

"I need him to raise my enthusiasm. If you know what I mean."

She did. "What do you want him to do?"

"Nothing. I just need to see him, and I think I'll be able to manage."

Cassie sighed. "If that's all."

Denying his request would be unfair, since for women, any sort of enthusiasm was optional. It was not as though this would be her first time with an audience, although on those previous occasions she had been considerably younger, drunker, and far more enthusiastic. She gestured Antonius toward her bed. Regardless of how things went, this was not going to be her finest hour.

ARIAN

If she had known how many people would be gathered at the Konithae mansion, Arian would have made an excuse not to attend. Admittedly, Doyenne Lilliana had been unusually insistent in her invitation. But why? The event concerned elections in the Senate and held absolutely no interest for Arian. Even if it did, she had no part to play in the cutthroat web of imperial politics.

Easily two hundred guests were already there, and more were arriving all the time, ramping up the noise. Any attempt at conversation turned into a shouting competition. Arian squeezed between knots of people, finally reaching a door to the garden. Even outside, she was far from alone. The hubbub drowned all sounds from beyond the estate walls, but at least the volume was at an acceptable level.

This was Arian's favourite time of year in the city. Winter was past, but they were not yet enduring the stifling heat of summer. Jasmine and hyacinths scented the air. The flower beds held a riot of spring flowers in every possible colour. Overhead, the sky was a tranquil washed blue.

While shadows lengthened, Arian drifted from group to group, giving half an ear to the conversations. Many faces were familiar from previous events at the Konithae mansion, but the gathering was not limited to friends and allies. Over half the people were from other factions, including some who could only be counted as rivals. Arian spotted a man named Xeranius, one of Cassie's cousins.

Would Cassie be here? The thought had not occurred before, given the hostility between the two families. Almost five months had passed since the day Arian walked out of the Passurae mansion and their relationship. It was the last time she had set eyes on Cassie, and that was how she wanted things to stay.

"I'll…um…see you later." She backed out of the group of young women.

They nodded at her and returned to their argument over the best name for a new puppy.

Arian hurried away, heading for the exit. She rounded a bush sculpted in the shape of a peacock and nearly collided with Doyenne Lilliana and another woman.

"Ah. There you are." Lilliana beamed at her.

"Were you looking for me? I'm sorry. I didn't know."

"No need to apologise." Lilliana indicated the woman beside her. "I want to introduce you to Magistra Vessia Gallina ado Prefectae. She's going to be our next principal magistrate."

That's nice for her. Arian smiled. "A pleasure to meet you."

"Likewise."

Magistra Vessia looked to be about forty years old. As with all Kavillians, her hair was dark, almost black, although in her case greying at the temples. She was a few inches shorter than Arian, which made her of average height for Kavillians. "Elegant" was the word that sprung to mind, her clothes, her hairstyle, her features, and also in some peculiar way, the look in her eye. She obviously put considerable effort into her appearance, and it paid off. She also had a warm smile that lit up her face.

Vessia continued. "Thank you for coming tonight, for the launch of my campaign."

"You need to thank Doyenne Lilliana for inviting me."

"I wanted the two of you to meet." Lilliana paused for a moment. "I thought you would get on well together." Her faint emphasis on the "well" was clearly supposed to mean something.

Arian could only nod in reply. "I don't think I've seen you around before," she said to Vessia.

"I only arrived in Kavilli yesterday. I've been in Basalonia for the last few years. But I've come here for the start of the election campaign. Doyenne Lilliana has been kind enough to put my name forward."

"I assure you I'm—" Lilliana's words were cut off by a large man barrelling down on them.

"Lilliana, Vessia, we need to talk."

Lilliana smiled at Arian. "Now I'm the one to apologise. Hopefully we'll speak again later." She walked away with the man.

Vessia started to follow, but then glanced back. "I really want to speak with you. Please say you'll make time for me later this evening."

"All right."

"Is that a promise? You won't leave until we've had a chance to talk?"

"If you want. Yes. You have my word."

Vessia gave another of her radiant smiles, then hurried to catch up with Lilliana.

Arian pinched the bridge of her nose. *Damn.* Why had Vessia made her promise to stay? What could she possibly need to talk about so desperately? Was Vessia really serious? Kavillians were always making promises with no intention of keeping them. Their word meant nothing to them. Arian looked around the garden. What was the chance of running into Cassie? But there was nothing she could do about it.

Food and drink were set out under a portico at the back of the main building. If she had to hang around, she might as well make the most of it. One of the servants handed her a small cup. Arian tasted the wine. It was not the highest quality, but close enough. Lilliana was clearly spending money to impress. The main concession to cost was the cheap pottery cups, rather than the hand-painted, ornate crystal glasses, used for dinner parties.

She took another sip. How to find out whether Cassie was expected to attend? And what to do if she was? The wine attendant was unlikely to know the guest list. Alternately, she could break her promise and leave. The temptation was worryingly attractive. Arian turned around.

Too late. Cassie stood less than twenty feet away, talking to a tall, clean-cut man a few years her junior.

Arian felt the blood drain from her face. Spikes of ice twisted in her gut. She tightened her grip on the cup, worried it might drop from her hand. Cassie looked the same as she always did in public—calm, aloof, and completely in control. Only in their intimate moments would it slip, and the passion, humour, and tenderness break through. Arian refused to give power to the memories. Cassie was out of her life, and that was how she wanted it.

Was the man with her the new husband? Neither was looking in her direction, but trying to slip away was pointless. Of course Cassie knew she was there, had most likely been watching her even before the encounter with Lilliana and Vessia. Cassie's ability to pick out her prey in a crowd put eagles to shame.

Arian squared her shoulders. She was not going to hide. With her best attempt at a nonchalant expression, she forced her legs to carry her forward.

"Lady Cassilania. I didn't expect to see you here." That much certainly was true.

Cassie turned to face her. "Arian. It's been a long time."

Not long enough. "Is this your husband?"

"Yes. Let me introduce you. Master Antonius Vitus dom Egantae con Passurae." Cassie gestured to him. "And this is Lady Arian dom Lycanthae. Her son is king of an outlying region. He's here for his protection, while some local unpleasantness is resolved."

A nonsense name and a half truth. Apart from reasons of safety, Feran was also part hostage and part trainee Kavillian. No matter how misguided Ulfgar's demands, it did not mean he was wrong about everything.

From the cheerful smile Antonius gave her, they might have been long lost friends, rather than two people who had never met before. Did he know about her previous relationship with Cassie? Did he care? Then his gaze drifted away, to fasten on a group of young men standing nearby.

A sip of wine eased the dryness in Arian's mouth. "I should have guessed you'd be here to meet the new principal magistrate."

"Who?"

"Magistra Vessia. I was talking to her just now." Which Cassie would be quite well aware of.

"Oh, her. She's getting a little ahead of things. The election is still months away."

"She didn't mention other candidates."

"She wouldn't. And her chances of winning are—" Cassie broke off with a smile. "Well. We'll see."

So that was it. Cassie's family were backing someone else in the election and she was here to check out the state of the competition. Cassie would be studying the crowd, working out who would be voting which way, and who she could influence or intimidate into changing their minds. She would be forming plans to undermine Vessia's campaign, spreading rumours, and listening for hints of scandal she could turn into a weapon. It was a stupid mistake for Lilliana to have invited her in the first place. But maybe there was no option. Perhaps the election gathering had to be open to all.

"Anyway, I won't keep you," Cassie said.

No. You threw me away. Arian's mouth dried up, beyond the ability of wine to ease. She could not speak.

"Hopefully we'll get a chance to talk again later."

Hopefully not.

Arian watched Cassie and Antonius stroll away through the gathering. Cassie slipped an arm around his waist, pulling him close. He responded by casually draping his own arm over her shoulders.

A scream tried to crawl up from the centre of Arian's chest. It lodged, unvoiced, at the back of her throat, choking her. She drained the wine and turned to the attendant for a refill.

Damn her. Damn her to the deepest pit of hell.

"For too long, corruption has been a cancer in the empire. If you select me for this honour, I swear to fight tirelessly to root it out."

Around the garden, people nodded. Some even clapped and whistled their approval. Arian had trouble keeping a straight face, though she had to admit Vessia sounded good. Passion and confidence resonated in her voice. However, if people truly believed she would do what she said, there was no way anyone would vote for her. But of course, by rooting out corruption, what she meant was making life difficult for people in factions opposed to the Konithae family.

Vessia stood beside Lilliana at the top of a short flight of steps, just high enough that the two women were visible above the tallest head in the audience. Too many people were at the meeting to fit into even the largest reception room. So everyone had moved to the garden, to hear Lilliana formally announce she was nominating Vessia for the post of principal magistrate. This was followed by Vessia's acceptance speech, which was now drawing to a close.

"I swear to be a faithful servant of the law. I swear to apply it impartially, without fear or favour. I swear to bring honesty and integrity back to Kavilli." Vessia bowed to the woman beside her. "Thank you once again, Doyenne Lilliana, for the amazing trust you've placed in me. I'll try to be worthy of it." She turned back to the crowd. "And thanks to everyone for being here tonight. May the gods watch over you all."

More applause and cheers rang out as Vessia descended the steps and disappeared into the throng. Around the grounds, servants were lighting torches. The sun had set during Vessia's speech, and dusk was thickening. A crescent moon hung in the sky. The audience drifted apart, forming small clumps in the last of the daylight. With the excitement over, some were heading for the exit, others for more wine.

What had Cassie made of it? Vessia's performance could only have amused her. Yet not everyone was so cynical. How would Cassie evaluate its effect on the gathering? Somewhere in the garden, she would be listening, watching, and drawing conclusions. Plans for twisting the vote would be forming in her head. This was the game she lived for.

Arian scanned the thinning crowd. No matter how little she wanted to see Cassie, she could not stop herself looking for her. Unfortunately, the search proved easier than expected. Cassie stood on the other side of an ornamental fountain with a clear line of sight between them. Even more unexpected, Cassie was staring at her, seemingly oblivious to everything else around. Their eyes locked and held for an eternity.

Cassie was the one to break contact, turning away. She looped arms with Antonius, who was standing beside her, and together, they strolled along the gravel path, towards one of the louder groups of Vessia's supporters. Cassie threw a last look back, and then was gone from sight.

Arian's heart pounded against her ribs. Her knees had turned to water. She felt physically sick. After months apart, did Cassie still care for her? Was it even possible Cassie was hurting a fraction as much as she was herself? That Cassie was not as calm, aloof, and completely in control as she pretended? Else why had Cassie fixated on her rather than the people with votes to cast in the Senate? Surely they were the ones Cassie had come to study.

Arian rubbed her forehead. Was that why Lilliana had been so insistent on her being at the meeting? Was Lilliana hoping her presence would upset Cassie's concentration? If so, Lilliana should have been more honest, but then, if Arian had known Cassie would attend with the new husband, there was no way she would have agreed to come.

Arian went to take another mouthful of wine, only to discover her cup was empty. Another refill was tempting, even though she had already drunk far more than normal. Before she could make her mind up, she was distracted by a minor disturbance, getting louder. Vessia was coming her way, although progress was slow due to the numerous well-wishers wanting to offer congratulations and advice.

At last Vessia reached Arian's side and slid an arm through hers—a surprisingly familiar gesture. "Thanks for waiting. Come on. We'll find somewhere quieter to talk."

Arian let herself be guided to a rose bower. Plant stems and wickerwork formed a dense lattice, giving a sense of privacy. Even the voices in the garden were muted. A torch at the flower-entwined entrance provided light, as darkness swallowed the world outside. The last of the well-wishers took the hint and left them alone.

Arian slipped her arm free and put her empty cup on the seat at the rear. She took a step back, which was all the distance possible in the enclosed bower. "You wanted to talk?"

"Yes. Right. Talk." The confidence was gone. Vessia placed a hand over her eyes, and stood motionless, like a monument to doubt and indecision. Eventually she let her hand drop and sighed loudly. "Oh...why not say it?" She stared directly into Arian's eyes. "Do you know you're an outrageously attractive woman?"

"I..." It was possibly the very last thing she had expected Vessia to say. "I'm what?"

Vessia laughed softly. "You. With your golden hair and white skin. Your eyes. I was told they were green and thought people were making things up. But they really are. You look like something from myth. A goddess." Her gaze dropped and she shook her head ruefully. "And I know I'm making a fool of myself. If you want to go, I'll understand, but..." Her voice grew wistful. "I hope you don't."

The ground wobbled under Arian's feet. Was it just the wine? She could leave. Maybe she should leave. Arian stared through the archway into the darkness beyond. Cassie was out there and was undoubtedly aware of where she was and who she was with. The privacy offered by the bower was nine-tenths illusion. Cassie might even be standing just outside the circle of lamplight, looking in. The image ignited a bonfire of conflicting emotions, fanned by memories of Cassie's arm around her husband's waist.

She had loved Cassie with all her heart, and what had she got in return? Arian's eyes threatened to fill with tears. She fought them back. Supposing Cassie was out there watching from the shadows? Supposing, somewhere deep inside, Cassie was upset and miserable and wanted her back?

Good.

In which case…

She met Vessia's eyes. "I'll stay."

"Really?"

"Do you see me moving?"

A smile spread across Vessia's face. "Well, now you mention it."

Vessia took a step closer, then reached out and clasped Arian's hand. Her thumb ran over Arian's knuckles. The touch set off a startling ripple effect. Out of nowhere, a flip in Arian's stomach radiated out, through her chest and down, ending as trembling in her knees.

Vessia moved closer still, until their bodies were touching from thigh to breast. Her free hand slipped behind Arian's neck, pulling her head down. Their lips met in a kiss. The flip in Arian's stomach increased a hundredfold. She had to lock her knees to save herself from collapse. She wrapped her arms around Vessia, partly for support, partly to pull them into even harder contact. Arian surrendered to the wildness, welling up inside. The kiss turned to raw hunger, an exploration of desire.

Cassie was out there. Cassie would know. And Arian did not care. She let herself melt into Vessia's embrace.

Arian awoke to darkness and disorientation. She grasped at scattered memories, trying to make sense of her surroundings. Where was the window? The door? Cassie lay beside her, breathing gently. And so…

Reality caught up. No. Not Cassie. Vessia.

Arian rolled onto her back and stared up at the shadows of trees dancing across the ceiling in the moonlight. How could she have got the rooms confused? The softness of the bed, the way the walls reflected sounds, the scent of wood wax and perfume were different. Everything was different. Including herself. And she was going to need a bit of time to work out how she felt about it all.

Vessia gave a half snore that turned into a sigh.

Arian scrunched her eyes shut. Did she want to be there? A jumble of emotions churned inside her. Making love with Vessia had been fun. Denying it would be dishonest. If her head would only shut up, Arian thought her body would be relaxed and content. So why worry? And why waste time wondering where she wanted to be? It was not as if she had much in the way of choice. Until she heard from Kendric, she had to stay in Kavilli.

In the meantime, there was no reason not to pursue an affair with Vessia. It might not displace her anger and pain over Cassie, but it could blunt them. Lilliana had used her as a weapon. Vessia might be doing the same thing, but it did not matter.

She was going into this affair with her eyes open and a shield around her heart. At the end of the day, Vessia was safe, because Vessia could never hurt her the way Cassie had done. Vessia was fun to be with, and if ever this changed, Arian could walk away. No harm done.

The awkward, churning, ill-defined emotions still refused to shut up. But they would have to wait. Tomorrow she would be sober and with as much time to think as she wanted.

Vessia lay on her side, facing away. Arian rolled over and slipped her arm around Vessia's waist. Their bodies melded together, matching the curve of back and legs. She planted a light kiss on Vessia's bare shoulder and was suddenly hit by an onslaught of memories. The action was so familiar. She had kissed Cassie like that a thousand times or more. The muscle memory had taken over and once again left her out of place. The room seemed to melt and flow around her, threatening to drag her back in time.

Arian forced the confusion to recede. Picking though the residue of a dead love affair could wait until daylight. She should take what she had, here and now. Holding someone at night was good—a woman's warm body in her arms. Arian drew on the peace that came from the touch of skin on skin. A wave of calm swept over her, carrying her gently back to sleep.

❖

When Arian woke again it was to the sound of soft voices in an adjoining room. The bed beside her was empty, but the sheets were rumpled and still warm. Dazzling light from the rising sun turned lace window drapes to a shimmering haze, obscuring whatever lay outside, although she had to be somewhere in the Konithae mansion, given how short the walk had been from the rose bower.

Vessia returned a few seconds later. "Good. You're awake. The housemaid has just brought breakfast. I'll carry it in."

Kavillian breakfasts could be every bit as unpalatable as their dinners. "I don't normally eat, um…"

Vessia laughed. "Don't worry. There's cinnamon rolls and warm milk. I've done my research." She left the room again.

Indeed she had. Arian raised herself on an elbow and plumped up her pillow while sorting out her thoughts. Cinnamon rolls did not appear on a breakfast tray by magic. Vessia must have given instructions to the cooks before going to the campaign meeting yesterday, since there had been no opportunity to do it afterwards. Which meant everything had been planned in advance, even before Vessia had set eyes on her.

The seduction was just a ploy, and she had walked right into it. Was she really so predictable, so easily manipulated, so gullible? Anger at Vessia came second to disgust at herself. With hindsight, Doyenne Lilliana was behind it, setting up their initial meeting. How much had she scripted? Suggesting lines for Vessia to recite? Picking the rose bower as the perfect romantic setting?

Arian gave the pillow a harder punch. She should have known better. She would have known better, if she had not drunk so much wine. For the sake of her self-respect, it would have been nice if she had not fallen into the entrapment quite so easily. She stifled a groan. Best case and a small salve for her pride would be if the seduction had been a suggestion from Lilliana, rather than an order, leaving Vessia free to back out if she felt disinclined once they met.

Admittedly, Vessia was easy on the eye and amusing—surprisingly so, compared to her outward persona of ambitious judge and lawyer. She even had a tendency to giggle like a young girl. And if her display of passion had been an act, it was a convincing one. Was anything Vessia had said to her the truth? Did she feel any genuine attraction, or had she simply been working to script? Was there any way to know?

Vessia reappeared, carrying a large breakfast tray which she set down on the bed. "There. Help yourself."

The idea of throwing the cinnamon rolls in Vessia's face was tempting, but it would not undo anything or make her feel better about herself. Wounded pride was not enough of a reason to break with the Konithae family.

Arian forced a smile and took a bite of cinnamon roll. It was good. And, to be fair, so was Vessia's lovemaking.

Lilliana and Vessia were making use of her. No surprises there. As for their reasons and goal? Almost certainly, they wanted to throw Cassie off balance, and upset her twisted, unending games of intrigue—games which had always been so much more important than their relationship.

Could Vessia be drawn into revealing more? There was no harm in trying. "I saw Lady Cassilania at the meeting last night."

"Her family are going to oppose my nomination. She'd have wanted to see what they're up against."

"You know we were having an affair before she got married?"

"You and half the women in Kavilli." Vessia held a hand over her mouth until she had swallowed. "Not all at the same time, of course. And when I say half the women, I mean half the women of the right status. As a junior member of the prefecture I wasn't good enough for her. Except for when—" Vessia broke off, looking guilty. "Forget I said that."

"Except for what?"

"It was nothing."

"You and she were lovers?"

"Only the once. Years ago. Soon after my first divorce. She probably won't remember me. She was very drunk, and I wasn't the only one there. It was quite a party."

The cinnamon roll became dry in Arian's mouth. She took a long drink of warm milk.

"Even before then, I knew of her by reputation. Who didn't?" Vessia giggled. "She'd been burning her way through women like it was a competition. There was always gossip going around about her. But she topped it all with the scandal over Senator Flavinus's wife. He actually caught them in bed together. I wasn't in Kavilli at the time, but the story made it all the way down to Basalonia. And of course she was—" Vessia cut off mid sentence. "Oh, sorry. I'm not being very tactful, am I? Are you still upset about her?"

"Yes." The truth was easy. Arian's eyes stung, but she refused to cry. She fixed on the shifting pattern of sunlight on the window drapes.

Vessia put down her food and shunted across the bed. She put an arm around Arian's shoulders. "Don't be. She's not worth it. Yes. I heard you were lovers for a long time. Well. A long time by her standards. But she was never faithful to anyone. She'll have been jumping from woman to woman behind your back. You do know that, don't you?"

Arian knew no such thing. Or thought she did. "I need to go."

However, Vessia held onto her. "No. Please. Stay." But then she released her grip. "Unless you have to get back for your children, or whatever."

Staying away all night had not formed part of her plans, but the house staff would get Feran ready for school, and Eilwen was quite capable of looking after herself. The routines were sorted out back when she started staying overnight with Cassie.

Arian sunk into Vessia's arms. "I…"

Vessia kissed her forehead. "Don't say anything."

That was convenient. There was absolutely nothing Arian wanted to say.

Vessia rubbed her back, gently massaging the tension from her shoulders. Fingertips brushed the nape of Arian's neck, sending a shiver down her spine. Despite everything, Arian felt a tingle of desire stir. Why could her body not stay on the same page as her head?

Did Vessia sense it? She moved away but kept her hand on the small of Arian's back. "Go on. Finish breakfast. Then I'll see if I can put a proper smile on your face."

Her face, maybe. Not her heart.

Arian picked up the discarded cinnamon roll. People said time could heal a heartache, People said all sorts of stupid things. Cassie still had a brutal grip on her. But why wallow in misery? Blocking Cassie out of her thoughts would take practice. She had to start somewhere. Arian turned her head and met Vessia's lips in a kiss. For now, this would have to do.

❖

A bath, a change of clothes, and a chance to get her thoughts in order. Arian adjusted the set of her robe on her shoulders. The material flowed around her as she moved, softer and finer than anything she had worn before coming to Kavilli. She had bathed in hot water, with scented soap, and dried herself with fluffy towels. All were unimaginable luxuries back in the Lycanthian homeland. Obviously, Eilwen did not want to return. Arian pursed her lip. More to the point, did she?

Her discarded clothes lay in a heap near the door, ready for the housemaid, Laelia, to collect. In Kavilli, Arian was merely an insignificant visitor from the fringes of the empire, a blond exotic novelty, a hanger-on for one senatorial family or another. In Breninbury she had been a princess, the king's sister, keeper of his bloodline. Yet she not only needed to wash her own clothes, she had to spin the raw wool they were made from as well.

Her necklace lay where she had dropped it on the bed. The onyx and amber beads had been handed down from before her great-great-grandmother. It was one of the few precious items she had brought with her from Breninbury. At least, it was precious to her. As a piece of jewellery, its value in the Kavillian marketplace was negligible.

But some things you could not put a price on. The necklace had once been her sister's. Arian studied the beads pensively. If Merial was watching from the afterlife, what must she be thinking? What advice would she give? Merial had never been one to cling to tradition. That had been Arian's role.

She placed the necklace in her jewellery case. If neither she nor Eilwen returned to Breninbury, the necklace should be sent back for Merial's daughters. Arian was about to shut the lid but paused. A gold-and-sapphire bracelet was missing. Eilwen had taken to borrowing her things recently. While this was no great problem in itself, asking permission first would be nice. Though maybe Eilwen was being tactful, since the bracelet had been a present from Cassie. For it to spontaneously vanish without a fuss was probably the best thing.

Arian walked to the window and stared at the wolf in the courtyard below. The house was silent. The small team of servants had their jobs, Feran would be at school, and Eilwen would be reading up on commercial law, or practicing speech making, or spying on someone. She had definitely latched onto Cassie as a role model.

Cassie.

Arian thumped the wall with the side of her fist. *Damn her.* The memory of seeing Cassie last night was like worms of fire, crawling through her mind, burning every thought they touched. She felt physically sick. And the memories would not stop. Cassie's arm around her husband's waist. Her smile. Her voice. The way she moved. Again, Arian punched the wall, this time hard enough to hurt. What would it take to get the woman out of her head?

Surely Vessia was a start. They had arranged to meet again the following day, and the thought was...

Arian chewed her lip. Exciting might be overstating the case, but she was looking forward to it. Vessia was not Cassie, and that could only be a good thing. Right? Except Arian's emotions on the subject were up and down, all over the place. One minute, bubbly anticipation, the next, brooding over cinnamon cakes for breakfast. Was she reading too much into them?

That was Cassie's fault as well. Expecting the worst of everyone, running schemes within schemes and taking it for granted everyone else was doing the same. Arian rested her forehead on the glass. If she had not spent three years listening to Cassie, it would never have occurred to her to question the fucking cakes.

A knock interrupted her thoughts.

"Come in."

Laelia entered, holding a packet, wrapped in a stained, waterproof skin. "This came for you last night, my lady. I think it's from Lycanthia."

At last, Kendric's response. Even allowing for winter delays, it was well overdue and Ulfgar was becoming increasingly impatient. Arian removed the outer covering. Lycanthian runes were written on two thin wooden strips using oak gall ink. Obviously, Kendric had dictated to a local scribe. Quite apart from convenience, anyone intercepting the letter would be unable to read it. The question was, could she? As a priest, Ulfgar would undoubtedly do better, but Arian wanted to know what it said before letting him see.

Her familiarity with runes had never gone much beyond making out a name on a boundary post. After three years away, she was now more adept at Kavillian script, although she could not match the effortless way Cassie committed her thoughts to paper. The image of Cassie, sitting at her writing desk, was yet one more burning memory to shove aside.

Arian sat at the sunlit window, sounding out the runes one at a time, under her breath. Between hazy recall and guesswork, she put together the first words. Kendric's message did not start well.

I didn't want to alarm you, so I delayed sending this letter in the hope of better news. Alas, it'll take longer to deal with the troublemakers than I expected. After grumbling for three years, Rhys and his supporters have made their move. They ambushed the guard escorting Perrith to see his sister and are now holding him prisoner in their stronghold at Drusbury.

Arian shook her head. Her nephew, Perrith, Merial's only son, was barely four years old. He was too young to be anything other than a bargaining piece. After Feran, he was next in line to be king, which was exactly the direction Kendric's letter took.

They've spread the story Feran is dead and declared Perrith the lawful king. To date, Rhys and his friends have had no luck selling their lies to anyone outside their circle. I suspect their goal is for you to bring Feran to Breninbury to prove them wrong. They'd then hope for a chance to turn their fiction into fact. I don't need to say how important it is to keep Feran safe. If anything happened to him, Rhys would have the new king in his hands.

A sick feeling blossomed in Arian's stomach. Before, the risk to Feran had been without focus.

You needn't worry overmuch. Rhys and his friends have stuck their heads over the palisade. I now have a target to aim at, but I don't want to rush my move. Better to wait and see how many more rats will crawl out of the cesspit, so I may remove them all with the same blow, but I cannot guess how long this will take. Much as I would like to see you again, it's vital that, for now, you stay where you are.

So much for Ulfgar's desire to return. In no way would she allow it. In fact, sending Feran to the academy might even be the best thing. Embedding him in the Kavillian military would surely be safe. Feran had bodyguards when he walked through the streets, to and from school, but there was always the risk of a surprise ambush, the knife-wielding stranger in the crowd.

Someone's going to end up unhappy. Cassie's words from way back, when Arian first mentioned it to her. At the moment, that someone looked like Ulfgar.

CASSIE

What could be more boring than watching horses run round and round in a loop? Unfortunately, the person Cassie needed to question was a racing enthusiast who never left home to go anywhere other than the track. Magister Helvius Aelanus ado Prefectae had reached an age where he no longer felt any need to socialise, and an invitation to his villa was not in the cards. As a member of the prefecture, Helvius was supposedly detached from senatorial politics, but his wife was not. Relations between her family and the Passurae could not be described as warm.

Cassie's only option was to waylay him at the racetrack, but in this she was handicapped by her lack of interest in horses, chariots, riders, and everything else equestrian. Cultivating contacts who could help took months of careful manoeuvring, as well as threats and bribery. Finally, a small fire in the section of the terraces reserved for the prefecture placed Helvius somewhere she could contrive an encounter. The seat and steps themselves were stone, but the struts supporting the awning over them were wood and had come crashing down. Clearing the area and repairing the damage would take several days.

Cassie, with Antonius beside her, passed the guards on duty at the entrance to the privately owned stands. They climbed a flight of stairs and emerged onto a luxurious balcony overlooking the start and finish line. It had to be one of the most expensive areas in the stadium, yet the young occupants were clearly there to be seen, rather than watch. They were showing far more interest in each other than the race in progress. Although, given the way they were knocking back wine, most would have trouble focusing on the horses anyway.

The owner of the balcony, Ovidia, staggered over and slurred, "Cassilania. It's so good of you to come." She turned to Antonius. "And you've brought your hunk of a husband with you."

"Thank you for inviting us." Cassie nudged Antonius. "I know he's dying to chat with you."

Ovidia latched onto his arm, possibly to prevent herself falling, and allowed Antonius to guide her to a chair in the centre of the balcony.

After six months of marriage, Cassie knew the full extent of Antonius's strengths and weaknesses. He was easygoing, charismatic, compliant, and not overly bright, relying on charm to carry him through life—all of which explained his military career. He would do exactly what he was told because it saved him having to think for himself. It limited his usefulness in many ways, but on the other hand, he would never accidentally disrupt a plan due to misguided initiative. Best of all, he could be relied on to create a distraction, leaving Cassie to work undisturbed. True charisma was such a rare talent. Already, the drunken guests were forming a ring around him.

However, Magister Helvius was not among them. Had he already given up in disgust and left? Ovidia had been persuaded to invite him, after his normal seat was ruined by the fire, but her friends were blatantly not the sort of company any racing devotee would choose.

Cassie shifted to the side of the balcony for a better view. There was her target. Helvius sat hunched over the low wall at the front, clearly doing his best to ignore the racket behind him. Cassie sidled around the revellers and slipped into the seat beside him. On the track below, the race had just ended. Horses and riders were leaving through the tunnel.

"What's coming up next?"

Helvius scowled at her. "If you need to ask then you've not been paying attention."

"I've only just arrived."

"And if you were genuinely interested in racing, you'd have got here earlier."

Even though he was in his mid-seventies, Helvius was clearly still sharp, which was both a challenge, and good news. Cassie would need to raise her game, but the chance he had worthwhile information was better.

She held up her hands in mock surrender. "You have me there."

"So, what do you really want to talk about?"

"To dig into your memory."

"Concerning what?"

"The cult of Olliarus."

"Ha." Helvius leaned back and scowled at her. "What makes you think I know anything about that shit-show?"

"You were part of the team of prefects who investigated them."

"Back then, I was only a couple of years out of the army. My role was junior dogsbody. There's nothing I know that wasn't made public."

"Not wishing to be rude, but I don't believe you."

"You can believe what you want." Despite the dismissive words, his tone held a hint of amusement. Helvius was clearly willing to take part in a duel of words.

"How about you tell me what you think was public knowledge, and I'll see which bits are news to me."

"You've come to the wrong person for gossip."

"Good. Because what I want are facts."

"Facts, eh?" Helvius rubbed his chin. "That's easy enough. Centurion Calvus dom Brutenthae claimed to have found an ancient text describing a ritual for the god Olliarus. In return for human sacrifice, Olliarus would bestow magical powers on his followers. Calvus was a handsome bastard and had a way with words. He talked a group of idiots into going along with it. They started grabbing beggars off the street, which didn't attract much notice. It also didn't produce any magical results. Calvus then claimed Olliarus wasn't satisfied with riffraff. He needed a sacrifice of importance. So they abducted a member of the Querillae family. And that got attention."

"But still no magical powers?"

"Of course not." Helvius gave a snort of derision. "Are they enough facts for you?"

"I'm more interested in the investigation. How did that go?"

"We caught two idiots as they were trying to get rid of the body. Calvus had given the job to a pair of clowns."

"That was a mistake." Hiding bodies was far more difficult than generally realised.

"I think he saw them as expendable. But once we had that pair, they were quick enough to name the others. We reeled in the whole cult and executed the lot."

"I heard there were nineteen in total."

Helvius laughed. "There you go. You already knew it all. I told you everything I had was public knowledge."

"How about people you suspected of being in the cult, but weren't able to prove? There must have been a few."

"Maybe."

"Do you have any names?"

"None that I'm going to tell you." So Helvius did know the identity of more cultists.

"Supposing I make a few suggestions. Would you be willing to give a yea or nay?"

"Why would I do that?"

"Why wouldn't you?"

"Because only a fool gives away bargaining chips for free."

"You've got something worth bargaining with? That's got to be more than just unsupported guesswork." Cassie met his eyes and smiled. "I think you've got solid evidence, squirreled away somewhere."

Helvius shrugged, neither denying nor confirming.

But of course he did. Everyone who played the great game of imperial politics had a safe place, usually a locked strongbox, filled with dossiers for use in blackmail and extortion. Magister Helvius Aelanus ado Prefectae was clearly a player. If he had undisclosed evidence against a member of a powerful family, he would not let go of it readily. The question was, did it implicate Doyenne Juliana? And if so, how to persuade Helvius to hand it over?

Cassie leaned closer and lowered her voice, although with Antonius in full flow no one in the balcony was paying them the slightest attention. "I heard Calvus was having an affair with a junior member of a senatorial family. This woman, apart from being his lover, was also close friends with a couple of executed cultists. Yet somehow, the finger of the blame never pointed her way."

"Do you want to give this supposed lover a name?"

"Do I need to?"

Helvius held Cassie's gaze for the space of a dozen heartbeats, then looked away. "So that's who you're after." He shook his head. "She's not a junior member of her family anymore. Why should I risk making enemies like that?"

"You have something on her?"

This time, his shrug said yes.

"If you give it to me, I swear she'll never know where it came from," Cassie said.

"Still don't see how I benefit."

"Supposing I offer a deal you'll find interesting."

"Such as?"

How much did she need to put on the table? What would be most tempting? "I've heard a rumour your son is looking for a divorce, but his wife's family are demanding concessions."

"And?"

"I have information that could get your son a very favourable settlement."

"That's what you're proposing? Swapping dirty laundry."

"I promise what I've got is good. I'll even let you have sight of it before we make the exchange."

"How about I make an alternate suggestion?"

"What?"

Helvius pointed at the racetrack. While they had been talking, track officials had made ready for the next race. A row of two-horse chariots were drawn up at the start. Grooms were finishing the harness adjustments while awaiting the drivers.

"Let's do it as a bet. You choose one chariot, and I'll take another. Whoever's chariot is best placed at the finish gets the loser's stake."

"I'd prefer a straight swap."

"I'm sure you would, but those are my terms." He smiled. "I'll even let you pick first."

Because you like your chances against someone who arrived late and doesn't know the order of races.

Cassie looked down at the racecourse. Five chariots would be taking part, which meant the odds were stacked against a random pick. She needed to shift things in her favour.

Immediately beneath the balcony was a wide walkway where the bookmakers set out their stalls. Business was brisk. An excited crowd of punters milled up and down, eager to throw their money away. The bookies were the only ones who were going to win, most of the time. But not always.

"All right." She might not know the first thing about horses, but she knew people. She just needed to spot the right one.

Cassie scanned the crowd below. A blond head appeared, squirming through the sea of black. The hair was too long for a man, and could not belong to a slave, since they were not allowed to gamble at the racecourse. Cassie's stomach kicked and she felt the blood drain from her face. It was ridiculous. Over half a year had passed since Arian walked out, and still the sight of her could scramble all coherent thought.

Yet surely it was not Arian. She would not be down there with the rabble. The election for principal magistrate was less than a month away, and Kavilli had no shortage of rich people who wanted to curry favour with the Konithae candidate. If Arian had expressed the slightest interest in attending the races, folk would have fallen over themselves offering her a seat in their private stands. In fact, it was quite possible she was nearby, sitting on a balcony with Vessia.

Oh, Arian. You were supposed to find someone better than me. Not a two-faced shyster like her. Cassie clenched her teeth, trying to clear her mind. This was not the time for self-indulgence, wallowing in regret. She had work to do. Yet it was so hard to drag her eyes from the blond head below.

The person reached a clear spot and turned around, revealing an equally long beard. A man after all! One of the Lycanthi, retaining their traditional tribal hairstyle. Kavillian men clipped their hair short and usually shaved. This man looked like Feran's tutor, although the facial hair made it hard to be sure.

Cassie's pulse slowed. The race would be starting soon, and she did not have time to waste. She returned to searching the punters for the one she wanted, hoping he would be there, hoping this was a race to catch his interest.

And there he was.

Cassie did not know his name. To the best of her knowledge, she had never set eyes on him before. But she knew what he was. Unlike the fevered excitement around him, this man had a look of studied indifference. The bookies hailed him as he strolled by. Clearly, they were on familiar terms. Yet, the faint grin of relief after he passed was unmistakable.

The owner of the stall he settled on gave a broad smile, while his eyes tightened ever so slightly. No doubt, off the racecourse, they were friends, drank in the same taverns, knew the same people, shared the same interests, maybe even came from the same family. But here they were bitter rivals—a bookmaker and a professional gambler.

The gambler was Cassie's best guide. He still might lose on this race, but when the day was over, he would go home with more coins in his pocket than when he arrived. The gambler passed over his bet, took a token in exchange, and walked away from the stall. Ten steps, and then, as Cassie had known he would, he glanced back over his shoulder. This was the moment she was waiting for. The gambler's final look at the chariot of his choice—which, judging from the angle of his head, was second to last on the starting line.

Unlike most others, this pair did not match in colour. One was a dappled grey, the other a warm brown with white legs. An interesting choice. Did this mean that, rather than looking pretty to flatter the owner, they had been chosen because they worked well together on the circular track? Cassie made a mental note, in case she should ever find herself in a similar situation again.

"Well. Have you made your mind up yet? The race is about to start." Even as Helvius spoke, down below, the first driver stepped into his chariot and scooped up the reins.

"Yes. The brown and the grey pair, second from the far end."

Helvius's face dropped. "Hmmmp. So you know more about horses than you let on." He slumped back in his seat. "I should have guessed."

A knock at the door. Cassie looked up from her desk. "Yes?"

Bran stuck his head in. "Do you have time to talk, my lady?"

"Of course. I've nearly finished for the day. Come in. Sit down."

He hooked a stool over with his foot. "I was wondering how things went at the racetrack, yesterday."

"I turned out a winner." Cassie gestured to the documents. "Best of all, it didn't cost me a brass minim. I won them on a bet."

"Magister Helvius had the goods?"

"And more. I think we can count on Doyenne Juliana's vote." She smiled at Bran. "I was worrying I wouldn't get anything on her in time for the election. Thanks for your help with the seating. It worked out perfectly."

"I struck lucky finding a track employee with a grudge against the prefects. He didn't require much prompting. Once I'd put the idea in his head, I think he'd have started the fire just for the fun of it."

"Is there any danger of him shooting his mouth off now?"

"I doubt it. He's the sort who like to let their actions speak for him, and I made sure there's no evidence linking him to us."

"Did he say what the prefects had done to upset him?"

"Something to do with his sister. As I said, he doesn't like to talk about himself."

Which possibly meant his sister's misfortune had taught him the danger of careless gossip. "It sounds like he could become an asset. See what else you can learn about him." Common folk with a grudge against the prefects could be found on every street corner in Kavilli. Those willing to stage accidents and keep their mouths shut afterward were far rarer.

"Do you have anything in mind?"

"Not at the moment. But it won't hurt to know the extent of his skills, and weaknesses."

"I'll see to it." Bran indicated the pile of papers on the desk. "I'm going up to the lodge tomorrow. Do you want me to report on your progress?"

"Yes. Let her know we have Juliana in the bag." Keeping Mother informed was always a wise choice. "How about you? Any news?"

"That's what I need to see your mother about." Bran pulled out a key and held it up. "I've acquired a duplicate to Magistra Vessia's strongbox."

Now that was impressive. Vessia had taken more than her share of bribes over the years and would have hung onto as much evidence as she could, just in case anyone ever tried to double-cross her. Her strongbox would be a treasure trove.

"The box is in Kavilli?" Cassie asked.

"No. Back at her villa in Basalonia. Her husband is still there, but half her staff have come here to help with the election."

"A perfect time for a break-in."

Bran smiled. "I've picked a team for the job, but I want to run it past your mother first."

"Wise." No matter how the burglary turned out, Mother would not want to hear about it second hand. She had never been keen on surprises, even when they were good. She would also want to be involved in the planning. The potential benefits easily outweighed the risk, which was all the more reason to make sure nothing went awry. "Do you have any idea what might be in the strongbox?"

"I know what your mother is going to hope for. Vessia will have brought anything she can use to twist arms with her. But she's staying in the Konithae mansion, so she'll have to rely on Doyenne Lilliana to keep the evidence secure."

Bran did not need to add this meant, should Vessia possess anything incriminating about the Konithae family, it was certainly still back in Basalonia.

Cassie laughed. "So Mother might finally get to put the screws on her sister."

"I'd say there's a good chance of it. Magistra Vessia has done the Konithae a lot of favours over the years. I'm sure they weren't due to affection for Doyenne Lilliana."

Cassie interlaced her fingers and rested her elbows on her desk, mulling it over. The sisters were a match for each other when it came to games of intrigue. Would Mother ever have been so careless as to leave herself open to blackmail? Was Vessia sharp enough to have tricked Lilliana into a slip up? Regardless, the possibility was too good to ignore, as Mother was certain to agree.

"Anything else?" Cassie asked.

"No. At least, not regarding work, but…" Bran ducked his head, looking unexpectedly bashful. "My son was born this morning."

"Congratulations. You should have said earlier."

"The whole thing with being a father. I'm not sure what I'm supposed to do." He rubbed a hand over his head. "I guess I'm feeling dazed."

"Are Tessa and the baby all right?"

"They're both fine. We've…" He shrugged awkwardly. "We've been talking about names, and we both thought, if you didn't mind, we'd like to name him after you. Cassilanius."

"I don't mind at all. If you're sure it's wise." Cassie laughed. "Some might see my reputation as a handicap to saddle a child with."

"I'd hope any child of mine would be up to dealing with nonsense like that. And thank you, my lady, for everything."

"Go on. Get back to Tessa and the baby. I'm sure you want to be with them."

After Bran left, Cassie rose from the desk and went to stare out at the garden. The request concerning his baby's name left her feeling flattered, and surprisingly envious. Her own choice, in a perfect world, would be to name a baby after Arian. Unfortunately, the world was most definitely not perfect.

Cassie closed her eyes and leaned her head against the glass. "Oh, Arian, I..."

Despite the months that had passed since Arian walked out of that very room, the pain was showing no sign of easing. Talking about Vessia only made it worse, adding a corrosive dose of jealousy and anger to the mix.

With any luck, Bran's burglars would return with enough fuel to set a fire under the bitch's arse and have her running back to Basalonia, with Lilliana in pursuit.

ARIAN

"A rios gom tossy gams forris burffy." Feran's words were garbled as he pulled his clothes over his head.

"What did you say?" Arian picked up the discarded tunic from the floor.

"Kario's going to the games for his birthday. His parents are taking him, and he's asked me to go with him." Feran looked up at her hopefully. "Can I, please?"

"Do his parents agree?"

"I think so. Maybe."

Arian sighed. "I'll contact them. As long as they say yes, you can go."

Happily, Feran scrambled into bed, but then his smile crumpled. "Afterwards, I'll never see him again. Just like Daril and Luce. They've all gone and I'll be the only one left." His eyes fixed on the blankets, while his lower lip quivered.

"There's other boys." Unlike the academy for sons of the aristocracy, the school was open to any family who could afford the fees.

"Only stupid ones who won't ever count for anything."

"Just because they don't come from noble families doesn't mean they're stupid. You can still be friends"

"I don't want to be friends with them."

Ever since the subject of the military academy was first raised, Feran's tactics had switched between heated arguments and emotional blackmail. Neither was working in his favour. Of more concern was the news from Lycanthia that had arrived an hour earlier. Arian had only just finished reading it.

The tide is flowing in our direction, although events are proving thornier than I'd hoped. We dislodged Rhys and his rebels from their stronghold, only for them to go into hiding. Alas, they still hold Perrith captive. Yet I'm sure we'll have the matter sorted by the year's end.

The rebels haven't abandoned their claim that Feran is dead, but few believe it. I'm certain they've given up any hope of making Perrith king, and are holding him merely with the aim of trading his life for their freedom. We should not though, disregard the threat they pose. They're running out of options, and desperate men will try desperate means.

The greatest threat is always that they will try to make their lie become true. Even though showing Feran here in Breninbury would put an end to their story, he's much safer where he is. But I must ask you to take extra care. I don't think Rhys has the reach to strike Feran in Kavilli, but he may yet surprise us. If you have another, more secure, location, it would be as well to move your son.

Just how safe was Feran? Surely their home was secure. Every member of staff had been vetted, and even if one was in the pay of rival families, it was all part of everyday intrigue and political games in Kavilli. Nobody in the Senate stood to gain from replacing Feran with an unfamiliar infant who was currently in the hands of anti-empire rebels.

The time Feran spent at school or in his friends' homes was not under Arian's control, but he was still well protected. The children of wealthy parents were prime candidates for kidnap, and considerable effort went into guarding them.

As ever, the greatest danger was his journey to and from school. Feran's routine was fixed. Anyone could work out when he would be walking through the rowdy streets packed with everything from illustrious dignitaries to lowlife thugs. He was always accompanied by Olric and Durwyn, but were two bodyguards enough to stop a lunge attack from the crowd? A knife in the back? An arrow from an upper story window?

Much as Arian hated to admit it, there was no disputing that Feran would be safer at the academy, embedded at the heart of the greatest military force in the world. Was it really necessary?

"How was your walk home from school?" Arian asked.

"All right. Same as normal."

"You didn't see anyone acting strangely?"

"You mean the creepy man?" Feran snuggled down in his bed, clearly unconcerned.

Arian's guts turned to ice. "What creepy man?"

"The one who follows me, asking to stroke my hair."

"Do Olric and Durwyn let him?"

"No. Of course not." He sounded disgusted. "They tell him to go away. But he won't."

Arian pulled the blankets over Feran, forcing her face and voice to remain calm. "What does he look like?"

"Dirty."

"What colour is his hair?" Was he a Lycanthian assassin?

"Can't tell. He's bald."

Arian bit back any further questions. The bodyguards would be far more informative. Summoning all her resolve, she remained at the bedside, singing a familiar lullaby from their homeland until Feran was asleep. But as soon as his breathing changed to gentle snores Arian hurried away, praying Olric and Durwyn would not yet have left for one of the local taverns. Luckily, she found them sitting on the shady side of the courtyard, sharing a flagon of beer.

Both men had volunteered to leave Breninbury and follow Feran into the heart of the empire. As Lycanthian warriors, their faces bore the blue tribal tattoos. The stylised wolves were all the more evident because, unlike Ulfgar, they had adopted Kavillian fashions, shaving their beards and trimming their hair. Also, while escorting Feran through the city, they wore leather armour and helmets, rejecting the bravado of warriors back home, who stripped off their clothes to face their enemies bare-chested. Was it any wonder the empire legions had triumphed in battle?

However, despite changes in hairstyle, their social outlook was unaltered. When Arian arrived, neither sprung to attention, or deferred to her as "my lady." Instead Durwyn merely smiled and held out the flagon to her. Back home, warriors outranked women, even princesses.

Arian shook her head to the beer and got straight to the point. "While he was getting ready for bed, Feran talked about a strange man who's been following him on the way home from school, wanting to touch him."

"The wino?" Olric snorted. "He's a pain in the arse, but harmless."

"You're sure?"

"Yes. It's our hair. Half the people here want to play with it." Durwyn ran a hand over his own short blond crop. "You must get it as well."

She did.

"Don't worry." Olric said. "We make sure the old sot keeps his hands to himself."

"He might be more dangerous than he appears."

Durwyn rolled his eyes. "You don't need to concern yourself with this jackass. We can handle him."

Which sounded like a worrying display of overconfidence. "Earl Kendric is concerned someone might try to harm Feran, either an assassin sent from home, or a paid agent here. I want you to be on the alert for danger at all times."

"That's what we're here for." Durwyn's disdain was unmistakable—a Lycanthian warrior's response to a woman telling him his job.

Olric was more supportive. "We'll keep an extra lookout for trouble."

Arian chewed her lip. "Has Feran said anything to you about going to the military academy with his friends?"

Both men laughed. "Only three or four times a day."

"If not more."

No surprise there. "What do you think about the idea?"

"He should go." Durwyn answered without a trace of doubt.

Arian had not expected such an unequivocal response. "Why do you say that?"

"Because, as our king, he needs to know how to lead warriors in battle. There's no point him learning the old ways."

Olric nodded. "I was on the walls at Yanto's Leap. I saw what happened to Leirmond, and the men who followed him. Feran needs to learn the new way of war. Siege engines and cavalry charges. How to command tight formations. We can't teach him that."

"Ulfgar won't like it, and I know, as a priest, he gets more say than we do." Durwyn shrugged. "But you asked our opinion."

"Ulfgar is stuck on tradition." Olric spoke with unusual vehemence. "For me, tradition died on the fields below Yanto's Leap."

"What would you do, if Feran did go to the academy?" Arian asked.

"Feran is our king. It's our honour and duty to serve him. But if he's not here, there's no shortage of work around for us in Kavilli." Olric shrugged.

"Right. Well. I don't have any plans to send him, but I'm not ruling it out either." The men's thoughts gave a new angle, and one more thing to consider. "Please don't say anything to anyone, certainly not Feran or Ulfgar."

Arian returned to her own quarters. The long summer's day was drawing to a close. Sunlight through the open window struck the walls obliquely, casting amber shadows. First thing tomorrow, she would visit the Konithae mansion. Permission for Feran to attend the academy would require sponsorship in the Senate. She would start by getting advice from Vessia, before making an appeal to Doyenne Lilliana.

A shadow by the window moved. "Are you really going to send Feran to the academy?" Eilwen leaned forward so her face caught the light.

"How did you know?"

"I was listening, of course. You were right below me."

Arian slumped onto a couch. "It's not polite to eavesdrop."

The look Eilwen treated her to could only be described as pitying.

"I'm thinking about it." Arian answered the initial question. "But don't say anything to Feran yet."

Eilwen came to sit beside her. "You ought to send him."

"Won't you miss your brother?"

"A bit. But this way, we'll all get what we want. Feran will be with his friends, and you and I can stay in Kavilli. Olric and Durwyn won't mind, as long as they can still drink beer together."

Eilwen's nose wrinkled in thought. "Ulfgar will be unhappy. But I don't care what he wants." Her frown deepened. "I don't trust him."

"He's a priest."

"So? He's up to something. Something he shouldn't be doing. I know it."

"You shouldn't make accusations like that without proof."

"How about the way he acts when he thinks nobody's watching. He fidgets. Can't sit still. And he mumbles to himself."

"Which means nothing."

"Cassie would agree with me."

"Cassie's not here." *Thankfully.*

Eilwen was silent for a while. "You know he goes through your things when you're not around?"

"Have you seen him do that?"

"Why else would he sneak into your room? He's probably looking for stuff to steal."

"Eilwen! You can't just make accusations about people. Ulfgar is a priest, and priests don't steal." Far more likely he was looking for the reports from Kendric, to make sure he was being told the truth about their contents.

The pitying look returned. "He's avoiding people. You watch him. He always checks who's in the street before he leaves the villa."

"That's a very sensible precaution. There are thieves around."

"It's not the sort of—"

"NO! I don't want to hear any more."

Eilwen stood. "Then don't blame me if he steals all your stuff and sells it to the riffraff he meets up with, when he thinks no one is watching." She flounced from the room.

The door closed before Arian had a chance to marshal her thoughts. What sort of riffraff? The bald man who was following Feran? Agents working for the rebels? Was it in any way even remotely possible Ulfgar was in league with them? Was this why he was so keen for Feran to return to Breninbury? Did he want Feran dead and his cousin Perrith made king?

Arian went to the window and stared down at the wolf statue in the courtyard. The last shred of doubt was blown away. Feran was going to the academy, and she would make sure Ulfgar knew nothing about it until her son was safely away.

If Ulfgar was innocent and she was wronging the man? Then no harm done. She could apologise afterwards. But no matter what, she would not take risks with Feran's life.

❖

The nervous housemaid pointed to the door and stepped back. "These are the magistra's rooms, my lady."

Not that Arian needed to be told. "Thank you." Apparently, her arrival would not be announced. Already the housemaid had scurried away. Arian opened the door herself.

Vessia was alone, standing by the window. She flinched at the sound and jerked around. Her expression spun through a series of reactions, of which surprise was the most easily identified. Clearly, another visitor was expected, and not one either Vessia or the housemaid was happy about.

"Oh. I didn't…" Vessia looked down and drew a deep breath. After a moment to compose herself she raised her head and offered a smile. "Arian, it's good to see you." She almost managed to sound as if she meant it.

Vessia had a ground floor suite in a wing of the Konithae mansion. The large reception room was light and airy, overlooking a small garden. This was where Vessia carried on the business of browbeating, bribing, and flattering various members of the Senate. The smallest room was used as a store, and normally locked. Next to it, the bedroom door was ajar.

Was somebody in there? Was this what had Vessia so ill at ease? She was obviously expecting an unwelcome visitor. Might it be a jealous husband or lover? Arian was surprised at how little the idea of infidelity on Vessia's part bothered her, but it would be nice to know exactly how things stood.

Her affair with Vessia was on its last legs. It had been fun, but was going nowhere, Arian had no illusions of it continuing much past the election for principal magistrate, in just four days' time. As long as everyone acted like an adult, there was no reason they could not remain friends. Yet it would be prudent to get Feran's admission to the academy agreed and sorted as quickly as possible.

Arian crossed the room to join Vessia by the window. "You're obviously busy. I won't stay long."

"No, no. It's always lovely to see you." She planted a brief kiss on Arian's lips.

"I just have a quick request about Feran."

Vessia nodded, but her eyes were glazed, as if she had no idea what Arian was talking about.

"My son. Feran."

"Oh yes. He's well, I hope."

"He's fine. But he's missing his friends who've gone to the military academy."

"Boys are so—"

Her words were cut off by a knock.

"My lady. Doyenne Lilliana is coming," the housemaid called from the corridor.

Vessia stiffened. "Arian, I…I'm sorry. I…" Her voice held an edge of desperation. A nearby door gave access to the garden. Vessia wrenched it open. "I can't talk now. Please, you know your way out. Later. Come and see me later." She gave a firm push.

Arian found herself standing outside, staring in bewilderment at a closed door. *So. Not a jealous husband then.* Clearly, Vessia had done something to get on Lilliana's bad side. Did it relate to the election campaign, or was it personal? Would the problem sour her own standing with the Konithae family? Talking to Lilliana about the academy was better left until she knew just how serious things were.

The route to the mansion's main gates led around the end of the building. Arian glanced up as she passed Vessia's open bedroom window. Bees going from flower to flower and the distant rumble from the city beyond the walls were the only sounds. Then she heard a door open and close inside.

"When did you plan on telling me the news?" Lilliana's voice was muffled by the intervening room.

"I wanted to get all the facts, first." Vessia was clearly fighting to sound confident.

"And then you'd have let me know?" Lilliana, at her most sarcastic.

Arian hesitated. Nobody was in sight, and if she sat on the bench under the window she would be further hidden by rose bushes. Yet, eavesdropping was dishonourable, the first step towards lying and cheating. If the matter was any of her business, either Vessia or Lilliana would tell her. And if it did not concern her, better to stay aloof from all the petty infighting and intrigue. On the other hand, Feran's safety was at stake if she could no longer seek Lilliana's help with the academy. Arian slid onto the shady end of the bench and tucked her feet back.

"Of course," Vessia replied.

"Truly?"

"Yes."

"Either you're lying or..." Lilliana's voice faded briefly before coming back. "...tell me. Which is it?"

"I need a full report from my people in Basalonia. Give me another—"

"If you want to maintain any hope of becoming principal magistrate you'll tell me the truth. Now." Lilliana snapped out the words. "What did they take?"

A long silence followed. When Vessia finally spoke, her voice was so soft Arian had to strain to hear it. "Papers relating to the Roldanian contract."

"You didn't trust me to keep my side of the bargain."

"Would you, in my place?" Defiance from Vessia.

Lilliana gave a harsh bark of laughter. "No. But you may consider your bid for principal magistrate is over."

"We shouldn't do anything until we know for certain who broke into my home."

"That's not a gamble I'm willing to take."

"Even so. Our best hope of burying the Roldanian story is with me as principal magistrate. There's just four days to go, and we still have the votes we need."

Politics. Someone had taken something from Vessia, and now the election campaign was in trouble. One family was up and another down. Back in Lycanthia, such matters would be settled by two warriors fighting a duel. It would all be out in the open, settled quickly, with far less fuss, and probably less bloodshed as well. Arian got to her feet.

"Not any more. We're out of time and luck," Lilliana said. "Lady Cassilania has found the means to pressure Doyenne Juliana and take the Nerinae family vote."

Cassie.

Arian sunk back on the bench.

"What pressure? How?" Vessia asked.

"I could make a guess. And if it's what I think, my niece has been very enterprising."

"You're sure Cassilania can swing Juliana's vote? We've got plenty on the Nerinae as well." Vessia was insistent.

"Not enough, I fear."

"We still have Arian in our pocket. Can't we—"

"By now, Arian is a very blunt weapon. And it's not just Juliana. Our vote is under threat on other counts. Tomorrow afternoon, Doyenne Pellonia has invited four of our supporters to a meeting at her hunting lodge. I think we can assume my sister is hoping to take all their votes."

"Juliana is one of them?"

"Yes."

"We can still fight."

"That bird has flown. Do I really need to explain what will happen if the truth about the Roldan Pass becomes public?" Lilliana sounded as though she were talking to an unruly child. "I could overlook you keeping the evidence. I might have done the same thing, in your place. But being so careless with it?"

"What can we do?" Vessia sounded defeated.

"We start by joining this meeting at the lodge, and find out if the Passurae were behind the break-in."

"If it was them?"

"We're out of luck. It'll be up to my sister and how hard a bargain she wants to strike. Best case, we withdraw your candidacy in return for the documents."

"Best? What's worst?"

"A trial for treason. And be assured, I've no intention of joining you on the scaffold."

"It won't come to that, surely." Now Vessia was frightened.

"It will depend on what mood Pellonia is in."

"Supposing she demands both our heads?"

"Then we have to take a chance on a high stakes play. I'd rather avoid it, but we need to be prepared for all eventualities."

Arian tiptoed away. Was there anyone in Kavilli who understood the meaning of honour? Vessia viewed her as a weapon to use against Cassie. No news there. And whatever treasonable act Vessia and Lilliana had committed, neither had the slightest trace of guilt, merely concern they might be found out and punished. It was all one grotesque, vicious, scandal-wracked game.

Now Lilliana wanted to concoct a scheme to outwit Cassie and her mother. Arian did not rate her chances.

CASSIE

The carriage shook as Scribe Ellonius Nonus ado Prefectae climbed in, rain trickling down his face in rivulets. His hair was plastered to his head, making him look even more like an animated skull than usual. The caricature of a lawyer—dead but refusing to concede on a point of order.

He froze at the sight of Doyenne Juliana, huddled in a corner. "Why's she here?"

"Same reason as you." Cassie gave her brightest, insincere smile. "A regrettable lapse in judgment on her part."

"It was a long, long time ago." Juliana sounded more like a lost child than a doyenne. She looked like an immature girl as well, if you ignored the grey hair and wrinkles. The Nerinae family really needed to find a better method of selecting its leader.

"What did she do? Write rude words in her schoolbooks?" Ellonius evidently shared Cassie's opinion.

Cassie merely rapped on the carriage wall for the driver to continue. For now, her role was to look smugly confident and say as little as possible.

The rest of the journey passed in silence. Neither extortee showed any desire to talk. They spent their time staring out through opposite windows, at rain falling on sodden scenery. No doubt they were trying to assess just how much trouble they were in, and which route provided their easiest way out.

The meeting at the lodge was the final step in securing the election. Over the previous few days, the four candidates for blackmail had been contacted, with details of the relevant evidence against them, and invited to attend. None had dared say no. From here on, things might play out in various ways, and Mother had plans for all eventualities.

The rain stopped as the carriage rolled into the stable yard at the lodge. Cassie followed her two extortees, dodging puddles, and up the steps to the foyer. The housekeeper, Marcella, was waiting to greet them and take their damp cloaks. Cassie reattached the ornate brooch before passing hers over.

"Doyenne Pellonia is waiting for you in the salon." Marcella bobbed a curtsey.

"Are the others here?" Cassie asked.

"Yes, my lady." Marcella retreated to the housekeeper's office, her arms full of soggy cloaks to hang up.

"Who else have you dragged into this?" Ellonius demanded.

Cassie merely smiled. "Shall we go and find out?"

The scene in the salon was reassuringly predictable. Mother was sitting in her favourite chair, serenely ignoring everyone. Four maidservants were on hand, two with food platters and two with wine jugs, although Xeran was the only person showing any interest. A harpist in the corner provided a gentle background melody. Bran was playing the role of butler in a manner designed to convince nobody. The guests would undoubtedly recognise him as the Passurae spymaster.

Primus Tribonus Albanis pars Laurentinae dom Drusae was standing by the fireplace which, during the summer months, held an artistic arrangement of pinecones and thistles. Some had voted for him as leader of the Senate because he looked the part, dignified and stern. However, most votes had come because he was far too easy to outwit. The last thing most Senate members wanted was a leader capable of pushing his own agenda.

Tribonus's scowl could not have been more pronounced had he just been forced to eat one of the thistles. Whereas Doyen Bellorion was shifting about as though he was sitting on one.

He half stood when he saw Ellonius, and then slumped back on his couch, balding head in hands. His shape and posture were reminiscent of a large sack of potatoes.

Xeran got to his feet and gave a broad smile. "Cassilania. Cousin. It's good to see you." He wandered over to the window, grabbing a pastry from a maidservant's tray on the way.

"Likewise." Cassie joined him.

"What do you think? Will the rain stop by tomorrow? I was hoping to go to the games."

Cassie studied the sky. "You might be in luck."

"It's been miserably wet for the time of year."

"Cold as well. Who'd think it was supposed to be midsummer?"

The rising tension in the room behind her was so thick Cassie could almost feel it. How long before one of the extortees snapped? Although there was little doubt as to which one it would be.

"I've heard it might snow befo—"

"Have you two idiots finished discussing the weather?" Primus Tribonus, of course.

Mother spoke. "Why? Is there something else you wish to talk about?"

"I want to know why you've called us here."

"Didn't Lord Xeranius explain? I assumed you knew."

"I know you're playing stupid games."

"I assure you they aren't games, and as for being stupid, if you prefer, we can have a serious discussion. We could talk about your family. Your unfortunate son, for instance."

Tribonus's mouth flapped open, although nothing came out.

Oh, Tribonus, you really shouldn't try sparring with Mother.

Ellonius was the only extortee managing a façade of calm. He had even taken a glass of wine. "I assume you want to discuss the election of principal magistrate in two days' time."

Mother looked at him. "Is there anything to discuss?"

"Maybe not. But there's a lot to think about."

Mother raised her glass to Ellonius in a toast. "Hopefully, this gathering will give you plenty of opportunity for thought."

"I don't need to think. I just want this nonsense to stop." Tribonus had regained his voice. "Why don't you—"

A disturbance in the courtyard interrupted him, the sounds of multiple footsteps overlain with a high, pleading voice. Then the door of the salon opened and Doyenne Lilliana sailed in, with Marcella trailing in her wake.

The visibly upset housekeeper bobbed a curtsy. "I'm sorry, Doyenne. I asked her to wait in the foyer, until I could send word to you, but she wouldn't."

"That's quite all right." Mother did not look concerned. "I was hoping my sister would join us."

"Really? You should have sent an invitation." Lilliana also appeared completely at ease.

"I didn't think it was necessary. You'd show up without one if you were interested." Mother smiled. "And I was right." She nodded to Marcella. "You may leave us."

"Yes, Doyenne." Marcella again curtsied and turned to go, colliding in the doorway with Magistra Vessia who had just arrived, lagging well behind the others. Presumably, she had been in no hurry to reach the salon. After an awkward moment of shuffling sidesteps, the door closed after Marcella. The harpist began playing again, having stopped at Lilliana's surprise arrival.

While Cassie normally preferred to see as little of Vessia as possible, the current situation was sure to prove entertaining. Of course Konithae informants would have passed on news of the planned meeting. Mother had thought it highly likely her sister would choose to gatecrash the party. Vessia's presence was less certain, and indicated Lilliana was not fully committed to throwing her to the wolves. However, Lilliana had been forced onto Mother's home turf, in front of an audience of her former supporters. Nothing could be a clearer acknowledgment of just how precarious Lilliana's situation was.

In the swamp of imperial politics, nobody's hands were clean, but even so, some crimes could not be overlooked. The loss of Verilla province, ten years before, came into this category. The defeat was largely a result of the army's failure to hold the Roldan

Pass, which was, in turn, due to inadequate food stocks. The garrison had received only half the supplies the army paid for.

To be fair, the supplier might have got away with the fraud. The soldiers would have been on short rations for a month or two, and would have complained furiously, but no permanent harm would have come about, were it not for the unexpected invasion.

The food situation became critical when extra troops rushed to bolster those guarding the pass, only to discover the grain sacks in the stores were filled with sand and straw, not wheat. The starving soldiers had been forced to retreat, allowing the invaders to complete a pincer movement and claim the province.

The prefecture's investigation into the disaster had named the garrison commander as culprit, accusing him of selling the grain and pocketing the money. However, since he had died in the fighting, his side of the story went unheard. The merchant who delivered the bogus food supplies vanished.

However, the judge tasked with the investigation had produced an initial report telling a different story. This version was currently in Mother's hands. It proved the cheating merchant had been working on instructions from Doyenne Lilliana herself, as part of a wider fraud. The report was signed and stamped with the official seal of Magistra Vessia Gallina ado Prefectae, and as a bonus, Mother had other papers detailing the bribe Vessia had accepted to keep the truth hidden.

And now the fun begins. Cassie concentrated on projecting an air of nonchalance.

None of the extortees appeared forewarned of Lilliana's arrival. Their reactions were of surprise and dread, covered to varying degrees. Ellonius retreated further behind his blank, lawyer's mask. He put down his glass, possibly so ripples on the surface of the wine would not betray his shaking hands. Tribonus's expression said he wanted to bluster his way out but lacked the nerve to try. Bellorion was staring at Lilliana as though she were a particularly macabre ghost. Juliana looked ready to cry.

Meanwhile, Mother and Lilliana continued smiling at each other. Their age and attire notwithstanding, they were reminiscent of two gladiators, sizing up their opponent before the combat started in earnest.

Vessia had stopped just inside the door. She had her own version of a lawyer's impassive expression which, as befitting a judge, held an additional disapproving pout to motivate uncooperative witnesses. The four extortees had reacted with even more unease when she entered, although she was surely not there to intimidate. Lilliana was more than capable of handling that role on her own. For all the good it would do her.

Lilliana treated the room to a measured appraisal. "This has the makings of an entertaining party. I'm pleased I was able to attend."

"As am I." Mother indicated the maidservants. "Please, help yourself to food and drink. I made sure the supplies were in good order in case additional guests turned up. There's no risk of us running out."

The innocent seeming words struck home, skewering their prey. Mother had them in her hands, and they knew it. Lilliana's eyes dropped briefly to the floor before she regained her air of confidence. Vessia's reaction was more marked. A flash of anger bunched the muscles in her jaw. The corners of her mouth twitched in anxiety. She moved a half step closer to Lilliana, as if hoping to use her as a shield.

"Yessss." Lilliana drew out the word. "I would have expected nothing less from you. Which is why I've come to make my own proposal. Perhaps we could go somewhere quieter to discuss it."

"Of course. My study is upstairs."

Mother rose from her chair. Before following her out, Lilliana paused to whisper briefly with Vessia. Nobody else moved until the door closed behind the two sisters. Tribonus shuffled closer to Vessia although, judging by his face, he had no idea what he was going to say.

Bran strolled over. "Do you think she's going to withdraw Vessia's nomination?" His voice was pitched low so only Cassie could hear him over the harp music.

"What other option does she have?"

"I don't know. But Doyenne Lilliana doesn't give up easily."
Which was akin to saying the ocean was damp at times.

"True. But after what you got from Vessia's strongbox?"
Cassie shook her head. "She can't brazen this one out."

"Do you think your mother will be satisfied with just Vessia's
withdrawal?" Bran asked.

"I don't know. Probably not."

If the truth about the grain fraud came out, heads would roll,
quite literally, and Lilliana would do whatever it took to make sure
hers was not one of them. Vessia had no hope of seeing the year out
if Mother demanded her life rather than just the election. Luckily
for Vessia, Mother was unlikely to be so vindictive. Far better to
negotiate concessions that were of practical benefit to the family.

In fact, considering the amount of money sunk into the
campaign, Lilliana was more likely to dispatch Vessia on her
own account, as payback for incompetence. Cassie could think
of no more deserving a candidate. Hanging on to evidence about
the Roldanian fraud could be seen as prudent. Lilliana would
undoubtedly have done the same thing, were their positions
reversed. But taking such poor care of it was shockingly negligent.
No matter how good Bran might be, he should never have been
able to get a copy of Vessia's strongbox key.

Xeran joined them. "Lilliana is here to concede the election?
Is that how you read it?"

Cassie nodded.

"That's why she dragged Vessia along? To put her seal on the
notice?"

"I think so, but…" Cassie paused. Could another game be in
play? She turned to Bran. "Stick by Vessia. Don't let her as much
as fart without you knowing."

"Right."

On the other side of the room, Tribonus had finally worked
out what he wanted to say. "I'm pleased you showed up. I heard
what was going on here and came to put an end to it. But support
is always helpful when you're dealing with someone like Doyenne
Pellonia."

Xeran rolled his eyes. Tribonus was not going to convince anyone he was there in a policing role. Vessia was certainly unimpressed. She even looked relieved when Bran approached.

"Excuse me, Magistra. I see you're not drinking. If there's nothing here to your liking, I could send for another bottle. We have a well stocked cellar at the lodge."

"No, I…I…" For a moment, Vessia's expression wavered. Dejection fuelled by anger slipped through, before being hidden again. "I'm sure whatever you have out will be perfect."

Bran beckoned to a servant, then stepped away a discreet distance, while staying close enough to prevent private conversation. Tribonus scowled at him, but then also took a glass of wine from the tray. His gulp was considerably larger than Vessia's cautious sip.

The voices and movement released the other extortees from their daze. Bellorion heaved his bulk from his seat. He gestured for Ellonius to join him in a corner.

"I won't let you ditch me on this one. If I go—" Bellorion probably thought his hissed whisper too quiet for anyone else to hear.

Ellonius grabbed his elbow. "By the gods, man. Don't you ever…" He glanced over his shoulder. Briefly, his eyes met Cassie's, before returning to his co-conspirator. "Come on." He shepherded Bellorion out through the door.

Xeran kept his back to the room to hide his grin. "Isn't it sad when friends fall out. Ellonius doesn't want to play with him any more." His volume level was far better judged.

"Let's hope Bellorion was bright enough to keep evidence of the bribe he paid."

"Would it make any difference? If Lilliana's here to admit defeat, then it's all over."

"That's a big if. Until we know for certain, we need a tight grip on everyone. The forgery was just about good enough for Ellonius to argue he certified the will in good faith. If he can wheedle his way out, the situation gets harder to manage."

Xeran shrugged. "We still have the others. Bellorion can hardly claim he didn't know he'd forged the will, after his wife died so conveniently. We've got enough proof about Juliana and the cult to send her to the block. And Tribonus would rather die than have everyone learn about his son's cowardice."

"I think you're right, but until Mother returns it's best not to assume anything."

Doyenne Juliana was sitting as far away as the room allowed, head down, shoulders hunched, as if by ignoring everyone she could make herself disappear. Now she squirmed to her feet and skirted the edge of the room, in the manner of a mouse, hoping the cat was asleep. Xeran gave Cassie a wink and strolled away, relieving a maidservant of yet another pastry as he passed.

"Please can we talk, somewhere else." Juliana's mumbled words were hard to make out. "Please."

Why not? Cassie could do with a break from looking at Vessia's insipid face. *Arian, haven't you found anyone better yet? It's been months.* Though surely their affair would not last long, once the election was over.

Puddles in the courtyard reflected a grey, leaden sky. The rain was holding off for now, although a layer of dense cloud threatened its return. A damp breeze carried the scent of wet soil and vegetation. Ellonius and Bellorion were huddled close by the door, clearly partway through a lively exchange of views. Both looked around and glared at the disruption. Bellorion made as if to stalk back to the salon, but Ellonius grabbed his sleeve and towed him across the garden.

They recommenced their squabble at the opposite end of the foyer from the housekeeper's office. Would there be anything new in what they were saying? Marcella was not in sight, but sound echoed in the foyer. Checking with her later might prove worthwhile. For now, Cassie led the way to a guest room. Juliana tottered after her, moving as someone far older than her sixty-four years.

Accommodation for visitors to the lodge was basic, although adequate for a night or two. Cassie had stayed on numerous occasions. Furniture was minimal. A log burning stove was the only heating in winter. The window was set with poor quality, green glass, allowing light in and a distorted view of the courtyard outside.

Once the door closed, Juliana abandoned any trace of composure and collapsed, sobbing, on the bed. What possible method could the Nerinae family use to pick their leader? According to rumour, a few diehard traditionalists still consulted oracles. It could be the explanation. No matter how unsuitable the outcome, who could argue with chicken entrails?

Cassie waited for the sobs to subside. "You wanted to talk to me?"

Juliana levered herself into a sitting position. "I didn't know what I was doing. I was so young."

"Are you saying you didn't realise you were taking part in human sacrifice? Or that you were too young to know it was illegal?"

"No. But...but, it wasn't my fault. I haven't ever... It was so long ago. Why are you bringing it up now?"

Cassie sighed. "You know why. It's very simple. We don't want you to vote for Magistra Vessia." She spoke as if addressing a young, and not very bright, child.

"If I do that, Doyenne Lilliana will...she'll..." The sobs took over again. "I can't." Juliana's voice was a hopeless wail.

"When it comes to the vote, you'll do as you see fit. However, Doyenne Lilliana doesn't have the evidence about the cult of Olliarus." Cassie paused for emphasis. "And we do. Or does she have something else on you, equally serious?"

"No. I've been so careful ever since. When I realised the risk I'd..." Juliana shook her head.

"Then it would seem you have a simple choice to make." Of course, if Doyenne Lilliana was about to concede the nomination it was all moot, but there was no need to let Juliana off the hook just yet.

"The Konithae control import duties. They can cut us out of the southern spice market."

So that was their hold. Over the previous decade, Lilliana had been diligently packing several city councils with her appointees. Obviously, the effort was paying off. It was something worth bringing up with Mother.

"I can't defy her. It will cost my family a fortune." Juliana's voice was no more than a despairing whisper.

"Money is no use to you after your head is cut off."

This set off another fit of sobbing. While waiting for Juliana to stop, Cassie peered through the window at the warped and discoloured scene in the courtyard. Someone in female clothing was coming down the stairs, her identity uncertain through the thick glass. Cassie cracked open the door for a clearer view.

It was Lilliana. Mother must still be in the study, since there was no way she would have gone first, leaving her sister alone up there. Lilliana reached the bottom step and turned towards the salon. Even in an unguarded moment, her expression was hard to read.

Regret? Maybe.

Anger? Yes, at least in part.

And something else. Determination. Lilliana may have lost this battle, but she was not about to give up on the war.

Cassie opened the door fully. "The meeting in my mother's study is over. I'm going to hear what Lilliana has to say."

Juliana threw herself face down on the bed. "I don't want to see her." Her voice was muffled by the pillow.

"Your choice." Cassie left Juliana to her misery. She slipped into the salon behind Lilliana.

"Doyenne Pellonia and I have finished our discussion. She'll be rejoining us shortly, after she's reviewed the proposal I left with her." Lilliana delivered a general announcement to the room. Her tone gave nothing away. She accepted a glass of wine from a maidservant and took a seat in the same chair Mother had previously occupied.

After getting a glass for herself, Cassie returned to the window, with its view of Kavilli. How had the negotiations gone? What had Mother demanded? What concessions had she won? The proposal mentioned, did it merely announce Vessia's withdrawal from the election, or did it go beyond that? Was there any chance Mother had demanded Vessia's permanent removal?

Cassie focused on the distant city, imagining how the news would be received, if Vessia went overnight from prospective principal magistrate to condemned criminal. It would certainly liven up the dinner party gossip. Yet, no matter how unworthy Vessia might be, she was the lover Arian had chosen. How much would it upset her if Vessia was sentenced to exile, or even death? *Arian, I'm so sorry I hurt you. I never meant to.* Yet here she was, doing it again.

A familiar flutter rippled in the pit of Cassie's stomach. Life was created so haphazardly, and so easily forfeited. When her own life was over and she faced her final judgment before the throne of whichever god wanted to claim her soul, her greatest regrets were not in doubt—the two little coffins in the family crypt, and losing Arian. Cassie forced a wry smile to her lips. Of course, there was plenty of time left to add more painful disasters to the list.

The door opened again but, rather than Mother, Bellorion and Ellonius entered. They immediately went to opposite ends of the salon, clearly wanting to get as far from each other as possible. Both looked furious, although from the absence of blood, bruises, and torn clothes, they had not been reduced to blows. They must have seen Lilliana return and were anxious to learn what was going on.

Xeran joined Cassie at the window. "Shall I check on Juliana? We don't want her doing something stupid."

"Does she know how to do anything else?"

"I meant like committing suicide. It'll be so awkward to explain to her family."

He had a point. "Yes. See if you can get her to stop sobbing and come back here. I left her in the nearest guest bedroom. We ought to have everyone together for when Mother returns."

Xeran nodded. After he went, Cassie considered those gathered in the room.

The maidservants looked politely bored, whereas Bran might be enjoying himself, although he covered it well. His attentive manner mimicked a diligent servant, alert to the needs of the guests, but his eyes were those of a hunter. The seething undercurrents, unspoken recriminations, and gut-level tensions made a psychological playground for the spymaster. Bran had always shown talent, and it had blossomed since taking on his new role.

Bellorion had gone back to sitting slumped on a couch. He stared at the floor between his feet while wringing his hands, as though practicing how to wash them the next time he encountered soap and water.

Ellonius knocked back his glass of wine and immediately got a refill. If he kept it up, he would be drunk before Mother returned. The behaviour was so unexpected from the dry, impassive lawyer it left huge questions about exactly what Bellorion had said, or threatened him with. Could there be more scandal to dig up? It was certainly worth putting Bran on the scent.

Tribonus's face was turning ever redder as he muttered under his breath about leaving. Not that he could get far. One reason she and Xeran had collected the extortees, rather than letting them arrive on their own, was so they would not have independent means of departing. The stable hands were under strict orders to deny the riding horses to the visitors. Only Lilliana and Vessia came to the lodge using their own transport, but they were showing no sign of cutting short their visit.

Lilliana sat regally on her chair and was impossible to read. Vessia stood behind her, bending forward to whisper in her ear. Was Bran able to overhear or read signals passing between them? Vessia's expression was sombre, but not fearful. Assuming Lilliana had passed on details of the deal agreed, it involved nothing too extreme from Vessia's viewpoint.

Cassie returned to staring out the window, while conflicting emotions erupted into full-scale battle. She wanted Arian to be happy—honestly, truly she did. And Arian would be much better off without the cheap, scheming, shyster. However, Vessia and Lilliana had blatantly used Arian as a weapon against her, and with far more effect than Cassie cared to admit. Surely Arian knew what was going on. Did she care?

Now the election was effectively over, would Arian still be dragged along to every event where their paths might cross? Cassie caught her lower lip in her teeth. If these contrived encounters stopped, would it be cause for relief or regret? Or a miserable combination of the two? No matter how much seeing Arian with Vessia hurt, not seeing her at all was worse.

Cassie drained her wineglass, but decided against another. Getting drunk was a bad idea. Long minutes passed before the door opened again and Xeran ushered in Juliana. Curls of wet hair stuck to her forehead and cheeks. The front of her gown was splattered in a way that spoke of washing her face, rather than rain. It had not helped. Her eyes were red-rimmed and her complexion blotchy.

Xeran left Juliana to cower amid the cushions and rejoined Cassie. "Can you believe she didn't know how to work the pump in the kitchen yard and needed help?"

"Yes." Easily.

"I wouldn't have minded, except she mistook my shirt for a towel." He grinned, holding up his arm, displaying a soaking wet sleeve. "Have I missed anything?"

"No. Lilliana has announced nothing new, but I think she's passed information to Vessia. By the look of things, they're both keeping their heads. That's about it. Bran might have picked up more."

"Right. Hopefully, your mother won't be much longer. While we wait, I'm getting another drink." Xeran strolled over to a maidservant.

Cassie returned to staring out the window. Time crawled by to the accompaniment of the harp music. Surely Mother did not need so long to review Lilliana's proposal. Which left the possibility she was making everyone wait to ratchet up the tension.

If so, it was working. Juliana was trying to wipe her eyes discreetly and Ellonius was on his seventh glass of wine. Bellorion was running out of fingernails to chew. It could not be much longer before someone snapped.

Predictably, the someone was Tribonus. "This is ridiculous. I'm not staying here a moment longer."

"Please, my lord, I'm sure Doyenne Pellonia will be with us shortly." Bran's calm voice.

"Someone should go and see her. I bet the old biddy has fallen asleep."

Cassie kept her face to the window to hide her smile. Old biddy! That was a new term for Mother.

"It's…it's…bah! I won't stand for it."

The stamp of feet was followed by sounds of the salon door opening and then slamming shut. The window glass rattled in its frame. The leader of the Imperial Senate had made his exit with all the poise of a two-year-old throwing a tantrum.

Cassie turned around. Nobody else showed signs of following Tribonus's lead, although they were clearly keen to see how it would play out. Both Bellorion and Juliana had their eyes fixed on the closed door. Ellonius drained his glass, but for the first time did not get an immediate refill. Vessia again bent down to whisper something in Lilliana's ear.

Xeran left the couch where he had been sitting and wandered over. "Do you think you should warn your mother?"

"Tribonus can't go anywhere."

"True. But after he's finished shouting at the stablehands, she'll be next in line."

"I'm sure Mother can handle him."

"Well, yes. But…" He shrugged. "You know her best."

"I know she doesn't like being disturbed in her study."

Xeran's grin returned. "Why do you think I asked you to do it?"

"Coward."

"Guilty as charged."

To be honest, Mother had been gone far longer than expected. What best to do? Tribonus was all bark and no bite, but Mother hated surprises. Maybe it was a good idea to warn her and find out how she wanted things to proceed. Cassie put down her empty wineglass.

She paused outside the salon. Tribonus was shouting obscenities at the stablehands in the outer yard, audible even from where she stood. Marcella and one of the housemaids were visible, standing in the foyer, with their backs to the courtyard, watching his performance. Cassie thought about joining them, partly for the entertainment value, partly in case Tribonus tried assaulting lodge employees. He was not the sort of man to react well when lesser mortals refused to follow his orders.

As she stood there, Tribonus's voice stuttered into silence and Marcella retreated to her housekeeper's office. Clearly, Tribonus had given up threatening the stablehands and was on his way back. Cassie made haste to beat him to Mother's study.

The wooden steps were dark and slick from the rain, and the handrail cold to the touch. Cassie reached the balcony overlooking the courtyard. Mother's study was the first door along. A cautious knock received no answer. Cassie tried again, louder and more insistent, before turning the handle.

The cone of daylight from the doorway cut through a watery haze filtering through the window opposite. The room's layout was unchanged from the last time Cassie had been there. The large desk stood in the middle of the floor, facing the doorway. Mother was half sprawled across the top, as if she had fallen asleep in her chair. Her right cheek was cradled in the curve of her arm.

"Mother?" Cassie hurried around the desk and put a hand on her shoulder. "Mo—"

The absence of muscle tension told Cassie the news. She did not need, did not want, to see the pallor of Mother's face, in stark contrast to the pool of red covering the papers on her desk. Even so, she pressed her fingertips on either side of Mother's throat, checking for a pulse.

Nothing.

Cassie's hands came away, smeared in blood.

"What's going on?" Tribonus stood in the doorway.

"Mother she's…she's dead. Someone's murdered her."

"Who?"

"How would I know?" But she would find out. And once she knew the murderer's name, their life could be counted in days, if not hours.

Tribonus cautiously took a step into the room. "How?"

"Stabbed or bludgeoned. Look at the blood." As gently as possible, as if Mother were still capable of feeling pain, Cassie eased her upright. The fatal wound did not require a search. The ornate hilt of a knife protruded from Mother's right ear.

"I...I'm going to summon..." Tribonus backed onto the balcony. "HELP! MURDER! HELP! COME HERE!"

Cassie did not move, unable to drag her eyes from the familiar design, a silver-and-onyx fox, five inches long, with a diamond for its eye. Someone had taken the brooch from her cloak, twisted the pin to turn it into a stiletto, and used it to murder Mother. Was it an insult or, more likely, a clumsy attempt at framing her?

They would not get away with it. By all the gods, they would not get away with it. In a blaze of white-hot anger, Cassie reached for the knife. But Tribonus had seen the ornate design, and removing it might be taken as proof of guilt. She had to stay a step ahead of the murderer because that was the only way to make the bastard pay for what they had done.

Feet pounded on the stairs.

Xeran was first to arrive. "Cassie, what's happened? Who's..."

His words died amid a babble of muted exclamations as more people jostled through the doorway, spilling around the edges of the room.

"My lady, are you all right?" Bran reached her side.

"Yes. I'm fine." Was she?

Xeran joined them. "Who did it?"

"I don't know. She was dead when I..." Cassie's voice failed her. She swallowed, biting back on grief. "But when I find out, they'll regret it. I swear. They will regret it." Unexpectedly, tears trickled down her face. Still she could not drag her eyes from Mother's lifeless body.

"I'm going to Kavilli. I'll summon the prefects. They need to be here." Xeran put a hand on Cassie's shoulder, giving a squeeze.

"We'll get the bastard. I promise." His hand dropped. "I'm going. Right away."

Xeran barged his way through the crowd by the door. His footsteps thumped loudly on the stairs, going down them two or three at a time.

Ellonius lurched forward. Even with both hands braced on the desk he was swaying visibly, and his slurred words ran together. "Asha member of the prefa…prefechure…"

"I'll be overseeing the crime site until the prefects arrive." Vessia moved him aside, firmly. "In the meantime, we need to vacate this room and secure it. Is there a key for the door?"

"Yes. Here." Cassie took it from the drawer where Mother kept it.

"Thank you. While we wait for the prefects, Primus Tribonus will be entrusted with its safekeeping." Vessia took the key. "And in case someone has a duplicate, Doyenne Lilliana's driver will stand watch outside."

Vessia locked eyes with Cassie. Her lips curled in a smile of triumph. With clear evidence of murder, a judge had the unquestionable right to take control, and it was not as if Vessia's instructions were, on the surface, unreasonable. But they both knew her eagerness had nothing to do with the pursuit of justice or the rule of law.

Mother's strongbox was hidden behind a false panel in the study. It contained evidence of the Roldanian grain fraud, as well as documents incriminating the other extortees, and who knew what else. Without a doubt, this was Vessia's goal. She could rely on Lilliana delaying the murder investigation until after the election, when she, as principal magistrate, could declare the crime scene off limits. Her underlings then had as long as they wanted to tear the room apart.

Cassie dared not allow events to follow that path. The treasure trove of dossiers Mother had amassed over her lifetime was a family asset. Losing it would be bad enough. Letting it fall into rival hands would be a disaster. More than anything else, she owed it to Mother to keep the strongbox contents safe with the family.

Vessia ushered everyone from the room, locked the door, and handed the key to Tribonus.

Marcella was waiting at the bottom of the stairs. "Oh, my lady, I heard about the doyenne. It can't be true, can it?"

"Yes. It's true." The weight of events crashed down on Cassie, threatening to destroy her composure. She wanted to cry like a baby. "Mother's dead. Someone murdered her."

"And I know who that someone was." Tribonus elbowed Marcella aside and stabbed a finger towards Cassie's chest. "It was you. I saw you."

"No, you didn't. I don't know what you imagined, but she was dead before I got to the study."

"I caught you at it. You were standing over her with your hands around her throat."

"She was stabbed, not strangled,"

"Yes. Stabbed." Tribonus did not miss a beat in contradicting himself. "With your brooch. Do you think I didn't recognise it?"

"I left it on my cloak in the foyer. Somebody stole it from there."

"So you admit it was yours."

"It's not a secret. Anyone in Kavilli wou—"

"Enough." Vessia cut through the argument. She faced Cassie. The triumphant smile returned. "Lady Cassilania, by the authority of the prefecture, I am placing you under arrest for the murder of your mother, Doyenne Pellonia Valeria dom Konithae ado Passurae."

ARIAN

"My lady, a messenger has arrived. Magistra Vessia Gallina ado Prefectae has invited you to an informal gathering at her apartment." Laelia accosted Arian as she was coming down the stairs after putting Feran to bed.

"Did she give a date and time?"

"Tonight. She asks for you to go over immediately."

Arian stopped on the bottom step, one foot hovering midair. "Now?" What could be so urgent?

"Yes, my lady. The magistra apologises for any inconvenience but adds that she would take your attendance as a personal favour."

Convenience was not the issue. The rain that had been falling on and off all day had returned in force. The sound of it drumming on the roof was a background roar. Water gushed from overflowing gutters.

"I'd have to summon a sedan chair." If one was available at such short notice.

"There's no need. The magistra has sent one for you. The crew's waiting in the courtyard."

Vessia was clearly desperate to see her and, given the cooling state of their relationship, it must be for more than a night of passion. A problem with the election would fit the bill, though it was difficult to think of any help Vessia might expect from her.

Voting in the Senate was due to take place the day after tomorrow. If a crisis had erupted, Vessia and Lilliana did not have long to fix it. Which would make it all the more surprising if Vessia wanted to use up precious time with her. However, if Vessia was hoping for help, it presented a good opportunity to ask a favour in return, such as permission for Feran to attend the academy.

"I need to change clothes. Tell the sedan crew I'll be with them shortly."

Arian turned and hurried back up the stairs.

❖

Vessia enveloped Arian in a hug the moment she stepped through the door. "Thank you so much for coming."

"Thank you for sending the sedan chair."

More than three dozen people formed clusters around the reception room. Most were familiar faces, Vessia's friends and employees. A celebration was in progress, judging by the abundant wine, laughter, and smiling faces. The babble of cheerful voices had been audible halfway down the corridor outside.

Not a setback with the election campaign then. Which only left her with more questions. What could Vessia possibly want?

Before Arian could ask, Vessia linked arms with her. "Come on. I need to talk to you. It's too noisy out here."

Arian let herself be towed to the adjoining bedroom and guided to a seat on the side of the bed. "Everyone seems happy. Can I take it you've had good news?"

Vessia remained standing, shifting her feet as though she was on the point of breaking into a dance. "You could say that."

"The election?" An easy guess.

"Yes." Vessia laughed. "It's been handed to me on a platter."

"They're just giving the appointment to you? Isn't the Senate going to vote on it?"

"Oh, they'll vote. But the result isn't in question."

"You've said that before." Whatever personal shortfalls Vessia might have, she did not lack confidence.

"This is different." Abruptly, Vessia sat down beside Arian and drew a deep breath. "But first, the reason I asked you here tonight. Well, obviously, I like your company." She scooped up Arian's hand and planted a row of kisses across her knuckles. "You being here means a lot to me. But, umm..." Vessia broke off in an uncharacteristic struggle to find words. "I know this isn't going to make much sense, but believe me, I have my reasons for asking."

"What?" How long would Vessia take to get to the point?

"Lady Cassilania."

Or maybe some points were better avoided. "What about her?"

"Her brooch. The one she uses to fasten her cloak. You know the one I'm talking about?"

"Yes." *Of course.*

"What can you tell me about it?"

"It's shaped like a silver fox, with a diamond for an eye."

"I know what it looks like."

Then why ask?

Vessia continued. "Do you know anything else about it?"

You could kill someone with it. "In what way?" If Vessia would only give a few clues about what she was after, answering her questions wouldn't take a lot less guesswork.

"Do you know where she got it?"

"It was a gift from her mother, some years ago. A birthday present, or marriage, or something. I'm not sure which."

"Do you know where her mother got it?"

"Why do you want to know?" Surely it was not as simple as Vessia wanting to buy one for herself.

"I'm sorry. I know it must seem odd. I'll explain, I promise. But first, humour me, please?" Vessia gave one of her most encouraging smiles.

"Her mother had it made for her."

"Who designed it? Who made it?"

Where was this going? Arian shrugged. "A jeweller in the city. I've no idea which one. I don't even think Cassie knows herself."

"And the fox design?"

"It's her family emblem." Why ask? Vessia must know.

"I mean the exact form it takes. It's very unusual. Sort of old-fashioned, in the style of the temple carvings you'll find deep in the southern provinces."

Dredging up memories of time with Cassie was not a favourite form of entertainment, but Vessia was not going to give up until she got whatever she was after. "Cassie told me about an old mosaic she'd been fond of as a girl. There was a fox in the middle. It was in her…" Arian frowned. "Nursery? Maybe? Anyway, the floor was dug up when a new bathhouse was built in the mansion. As a surprise, her mother got someone to sketch the fox before it was lost forever, and then sent the drawing to the jeweller to base the design on."

"So it's unique? The only one like it in the world?"

"That's what Cassie told me."

Vessia closed her eyes and flopped back on the bed. "I've got her. I've…" Her words got lost in a fit of giggles.

"You've got what?" When would this start making sense?

Vessia stifled her laughter and sat up. "The brooch isn't as innocent as it appears."

"You mean the way the pin can lock into place?"

"You knew it could turn into a knife?"

"Cassie showed me. But you can't cut anything with it."

"But you can stab someone." Despite the glee on her face, Vessia's voice held a serious edge. Deadly serious.

The implication hit like a punch to the gut. *No. She couldn't have.* Arian's skin prickled. Her voice refused to obey her, but at last she managed, "Has she?"

"Stabbed someone?" Vessia nodded. "Yes."

"Someone attacked her?" Was Cassie all right?

"No. It's a blatant case of murder."

"Who?" Not that the victim's identity mattered.

"Her mother."

"No. Never." Vessia had to be wrong. "She wouldn't."

"Oh yes she would."

"When?"

"This afternoon. At her mother's villa in the hills."

"I don't believe you."

Vessia slid closer and put her arm around Arian's waist. Her expression changed to one of sympathy. "I know. I understand. It's shocking, but there's no doubt. I was there when it happened."

"You saw her do it?"

"I wasn't in the room at the time, but I was at the villa."

"You were..." None of this made sense. Why would Vessia be invited to the lodge? Why would Cassie murder her mother? Why would Cassie pick a weapon so uniquely linked to herself? "Tell me everything."

"I'm not allowed to say much. The prefects are there at the moment, interviewing the staff, checking everyone's stories, examining the scene, taking care of the body. It'll all come out in due course. For now, let's celebrate. The Passurae can't now force senators into voting their way, and no other candidate stands a chance."

Arian struggled to pull her thoughts together. Was it really unbelievable? Cassie was ruthless, resolute, and willing to do whatever was needed. She had more or less admitted ordering her agents to eliminate rival spies, assassins, and other threats to her family. But this had always felt remote, an abstract part of the war the imperial families fought among themselves. Not a crime committed with her own hands, not her own mother. Plus, Cassie was neither crazy nor incompetent—far from it. If she decided to kill someone, she would have a watertight alibi and a stooge lined up to take the blame. She would never do it in such a crass, idiotic way with Vessia standing around as a witness.

On the other hand...

"What were you doing there?"

"Doyenne Pellonia wanted to pressure a group of my supporters into switching sides. She bullied them into attending a meeting at the old hunting lodge. Luckily, Doyenne Lilliana got wind of it. She and I went to put a stop to the game. While we were there, Lady Cassilania murdered her mother. I suspect she planned to frame one of us for it."

"How?"

"I don't know. But it hasn't worked."

"No." Arian shook her head. It was all wrong. Any plot Cassie made to frame someone would take more than one afternoon to unpick. "Using her own brooch? Cassie wouldn't be so—"

Vessia put a hand on Arian's arm. "We don't want rumours spreading. I had to ask you about the weapon. I was hoping you'd know more about its origin. But for now, I'll have to ask you to keep the information secret. It's part of the case against her. We need to let the evidence come out at the trial."

The trial. Obviously, Cassie was going to be tried for the murder. And if she was found guilty? Ice formed in Arian's stomach. "Do you know when that will be?"

"Soon." While still appearing sympathetic, Vessia's expression held a hint of triumph. "Very soon. In fact, I expect it to be the first case I judge as principal magistrate. The murder of a doyenne must be tried in the highest court." She stood and pulled Arian to her feet. "Come on. Let's join the others. The election had been more in doubt than I was happy to admit. But it's over. We've won."

Won? It did not feel like a victory, certainly not one Arian was in the mood to celebrate. Ideally she would like to go home, but the sedan crew had left her at the Konithae mansion and hurried away in search of shelter. The rain was, if anything getting harder. Clearly, Vessia expected her to stay the night—something else she was not in the mood for.

"Just one thing."

Vessia stopped with her hand reaching to open the door. "What?"

"The trial. Can you get me a seat in the courtroom? I want to see it through."

"Are you sure?"

"Yes."

In truth, "want" was not the right word, but she had to be there. Maybe hearing the evidence would clear up her misgivings about Vessia's role. Maybe Cassie really was guilty. Maybe it would strengthen her faith in Kavillian justice. Maybe it would answer all her questions and put her mind at rest.

Vessia gently held Arian's shoulders and looked directly into her eyes. "Of course I can get you a seat in the court. But I warn you, there's no doubt of her guilt and only one possible sentence I can give. You were lovers for a long time. Even though it's ended,

I know you're not fully over her. You need to be sure. Do you really want to attend?"

"Yes."

Maybe it would be her last chance to see Cassie.

The courtroom took the form of a small, roofed amphitheatre. The three tiers of semicircular seats had enough space for an audience of possibly two hundred, as long as everyone was willing to squash up close. Windows in the domed roof created sparkling bands of afternoon sunlight on the white tiled floor. In place of a stage, the judge's imposing throne stood on its dais. Directly facing it was a much smaller chair for the accused. A lectern was positioned to one side, so a person standing there could see and be seen by both parties.

Arian took a top tier seat on the shady side of the room, directly opposite the lectern, where she would be able to study the faces of those giving testimony. She slunk down as much as possible, attempting to hide behind two heavyset senators in front. Unsurprisingly, the Kavilli social scene was bubbling over with gossip, placing her in a salacious triangle with her ex-lover, the defendant, and her current one, the judge. She did not want to deal with questions from scandalmongers.

Was it possible Cassie might be guilty? She had never spoken about loving her mother, Arian simply assumed she did. Cassie certainly still grieved for her two daughters. The mother-daughter bond was central to most women. Even though Arian had never known her own mother, who had died the day after giving birth to her, the absence was a constant source of pain and regret.

Yet, in the end analysis, the depth of Cassie's feelings for her mother was irrelevant. Cassie was utterly dedicated to her family and would never do anything to weaken it. The loss of her mother was a devastating blow to the Passurae family fortunes. Cassie would never have murdered her.

"Do you think she did it?" one of the senators asked his companion.

"Who knows? Either way, it won't make any difference."

"You think she'll be found guilty?"

"With the Konithae's hand-picked judge running the trial?" The senator sounded incredulous that his friend needed to ask. "Lady Cassilania could bring in a hundred witnesses to swear she was miles away at the time, and she'd still be condemned."

Arian fought a childish urge to stick her fingers in her ears and block out their voices. It would not silence the far worse dialogue going on in her head. Supposing the evidence showed Cassie to be innocent, would Vessia still find her guilty? Supposing Vessia herself had played a part in the murder, could she really be so cynical? Supposing, against all reason, it was proved Cassie had committed the murder, would that make it easier to accept the outcome? Arian bit her finger to stifle a groan. Supposing Vessia wanted to continue their affair after the trail, would she agree? How would it feel, kissing lips that had condemned Cassie to death?

Starting by the entrance passage, a disturbance spread through the audience. Heads turned. Conversations stopped. People leaned forward for a better view as a column of imperial guards marched in, escorting Vessia and other trial officials, members of the prefecture. And then, at the rear, was Cassie, looking as serene as ever, despite her bound wrists and the armed men holding her.

Arian's stomach tried to jump up her throat. Her hands grew sticky. For a moment, the urge to flee the court threatened to overwhelm her. It was all far too painful. But she had to stay, because she would never be able to live with herself if she did not witness the trial. She had to know the truth.

The guards took up position around the edge of the courtroom, with extra ones stationed across the entrance, presumably on the chance Cassie might attempt to flee. Vessia settled on the magistrate's throne, then signalled for the guards to let Cassie also sit.

A man in black robes approached the lectern and carefully arranged a bundle of rolled scrolls on the angled top. "Silence in court."

The order was unnecessary. The room was so quiet, Arian could hear birds chirping outside.

The man continued, "In the sight of the gods, this court is convened to hear the case against Lady Cassilania Marciana con Egantae dom Passurae. As prosecutor on behalf of the prefecture, I will present evidence she murdered her mother, Doyenne Pellonia Valeria dom Konithae ado Passurae."

Now a murmur ran around the courtroom. The black-robed prosecutor waited for it to subside before unrolling the first scroll. "The undisputed events surrounding the murder are these. Five days ago, Doyenne Pellonia invited several leading members of the Senate to a meeting at her villa in the hills above Kavilli. Among them was her sister, Doyenne Lilliana Tacita con Avitae dom Konithae. The two doyennes left the others in the salon of the villa, while they discussed certain issues in private. Doyenne Lilliana then returned to the salon, with the understanding Doyenne Pellonia would rejoin them shortly. After considerable time passed without Doyenne Pellonia's return, Primus Tribonus went to make enquiries. He discovered Doyenne Pellonia lying dead in her study upstairs. The accused was standing over her with blood, quite literally, on her hands. The cause of death was this"—he held up Cassie's cloak pin—"a brooch belonging to the accused, which can be converted into a stiletto. Doyenne Pellonia had been stabbed in the head with it, resulting in her death."

Arian shook her head. Already things sounded wrong. Not only would any murder Cassie committed be more sophisticated, better planned, and with fewer witnesses, she would also never be caught by anyone as inept as Tribonus. Arian had met the leader of the Senate on several occasions at the Konithae mansion and had been decidedly unimpressed.

"I'll start with testimony from Primus Tribonus Albanis pars Laurentinae dom Drusae." The prosecutor stepped back, indicating for the witness to take over.

Tribonus marched up to the lectern. "I don't want to waste the court's time, repeating what's just been said, and to be honest, I don't have much to add."

Despite his stated intention, Tribonus went on to rephrase the prosecutor's summary in several different ways. His monologue ran to a considerable length, but Tribonus was correct in saying he would add nothing of note—except by omission. His well-modulated delivery could not disguise that he was skirting around details, although what these were had be a matter for guesswork. Finally, he rambled to the end of his testimony.

The prosecutor turned to Vessia. "Do you have questions for the witness?"

"No. I think Primus Tribonus's evidence is clear enough."

"Lady Cassilania?"

"Yes. I do."

A buzz of excitement rippled through the audience. Tribonus looked apprehensive. "What do you want to know?"

"For starters, why did you accept my mother's invitation to the lodge? It's no secret the two of you weren't on friendly terms."

"Just because we clashed from time to time, was no reason to snub her."

Cassie pursed her lips and nodded, as if giving his words serious consideration. "It wasn't that she'd pressured you in some way? Maybe threatened to reveal information you'd rather stayed hidden?"

Tribonus's apprehension blossomed into fully fledged alarm. "No. No. Of course not. Why should you suggest it?" He was blatantly lying. Anyone could see it.

The prosecutor came to his rescue. "This court needs to deal in facts, not conjecture. Lady Cassilania, do you have anything to back up your insinuations?"

"No. I just wanted to give Primus Tribonus the chance to clear up a point which might have been puzzling people." Cassie gave an innocent smile and turned back to Tribonus. "I would also like to clarify the issue of who was where and when. From the way details have been presented to the court, it might appear you left the salon, and went straight to my mother's study. But that isn't correct, is it?"

"No." Tribonus still looked ill at ease. "I first went to ask the carriage driver about arrangements for returning to Kavilli."

"Where was the carriage driver?"

"In the outer stable yard."

"Can you confirm everyone else at the meeting, including myself, was present in the salon when you left?"

"Yes."

"You're sure? No one accompanied you to the stable yard?"

"Of course I'm sure."

"So you have no witnesses to attest that you didn't stop by my mother's study on the way to see the carriage driver?"

"What?" Tribonus scowled. "Where's this going?"

Did he really need it explained? *Cassie has turned you into an alternate candidate for murderer.* As should be obvious to everyone in the courtroom, Tribonus was being blackmailed by Pellonia, and had been wandering around the villa on his own. Whether or not it affected the outcome of the trial, it would set the dinner party gossip ablaze for months to come.

Cassie did not bother answering. "One last thing. You mentioned seeing blood."

"On your hands. And I caught you standing over her."

"I was checking for my mother's pulse. Did…" Cassie stopped and looked down. For a moment, her face twisted in expression of grief. It looked genuine, although she was too good an actress for Arian to be certain. Cassie drew a breath and continued. "Did you also notice the pool of blood covering the desk?"

"Of course."

"Then you would have seen it had soaked into the wood and was drying at the edges. My mother had been dead a while when you arrived."

"Well. I don't know, I…" Tribonus looked to the prosecutor for guidance. "I, um…maybe."

Cassie waited for his mumbling to end. "Yet you're here to swear to the court you saw me murder my mother." She gestured to the prosecutor. "I have nothing more to ask this witness."

Tribonus returned to his seat on the lowest tier.

Cassie had definitely come out on top in this first foray, but would it help? She looked relaxed and completely untroubled. No one would guess her life was at stake. Or maybe she had worked out nothing would change the outcome and was enjoying one final round of gamesmanship. Cassie was cool, calm, composed, and easily the most beautiful woman Arian had ever set eyes on.

The prosecutor returned to the lectern. The next witness called was Doyenne Lilliana. Her evidence amounted to no more than confirming her presence at the villa, and asserting her sister had been alive when they finished their conversation in the study.

Again, Cassie took the chance to ask questions, although her manner was more guarded. Lilliana was a far more formidable opponent than Tribonus.

"Doyenne Lilliana. You weren't invited to the meeting at the lodge but chose to attend anyway."

"Doyenne Pellonia assured me it was an oversight on her part."

"Regardless, you had your own urgent business to discuss. Your request for a confidential talk with my mother was the first thing you said on your arrival."

"I wanted to get it out of the way."

"You can't offer any hints as to the subject matter?"

"No. As you said. It was confidential."

"You were the last person to see her alive."

"Apart from the murderer." Lilliana tilted her head to one side. "Are you going to ask if I invited myself to the villa with the intention of murdering my sister, and my request to talk was a ruse to get us alone together?"

"Would you admit it if you did?"

Lilliana paused for the briefest moment. "There's no answer to that."

Because, guilty or innocent, the only response is a meaningless no. Another win for Cassie, although less emphatic than before.

Lilliana's place at the lectern was taken by an elderly woman, Doyenne Juliana Balbina pars Drusae dom Nerinae. The name was familiar to Arian, although they had never met. Vessia had mentioned her a few times as a reliable supporter.

Juliana appeared so nervous you could be forgiven for thinking she was the one on trial. Her testimony amounted to a few mumbled sentences, adding nothing to what had already been said.

The prosecutor had to prompt her for information. "Doyenne Juliana, you told the prefects you and the accused left the salon for a while to talk in private."

Juliana nodded.

"This conversation took place in a side room off the courtyard. Correct?"

"Yes." The word was barely a whisper.

"And when you finished, the accused left you, claiming she was going to return to the salon?"

"Yes."

"Did you actually see where she went?"

"No."

"So—and I want to be clear on this—Lady Cassilania could have gone up to her mother's study after leaving you?"

"I…" Juliana hesitated, and then nodded. "Yes."

The prosecutor looked pleased. "One other thing. You were in the carriage with Lady Cassilania on the journey to the villa."

"Yes."

The prosecutor held up the brooch. "Did you notice whether she was wearing this?"

"Yes."

"Yes you noticed, or yes she was wearing it?"

"She was wearing it." Juliana was forced into giving more than a yes-no answer, although she sounded far from convincing.

Cassie's turn came to ask questions. "Isn't it true you were the one who asked to speak in private, and we left the salon at your request?"

Juliana's eyes darted left and right, as if hunting for an escape, but then she nodded.

"It wasn't the other way round?"

"No."

"So I couldn't have planned the conversation as a way to sneak up to see my mother?"

"No."

"As to the subject we discussed, I'm sure you'd rather it remained private."

Juliana opened her mouth although no sound came out.

"But can we agree, just as you can't say for certain whether I returned straight to the salon, I can't say where you went after we parted. You might have gone up to visit my mother once I left."

"No. No I didn't."

"You're sure? You would only need to sacrifice a few seconds to commit the murder."

The look of terror on Juliana's face was the unmistakable result of a guilty conscience. She clutched the lectern like a drunkard needing support.

Cassie smiled at her. "That's all."

The next two witnesses were Doyen Bellorion of the Marcustae family, followed by Scribe Ellonius, a member of the prefecture. The men's testimony appeared primarily constructed to provide an alibi for the other. Both swore they had been together from the time they arrived at the lodge to the time the body was discovered.

Although neither man added any new information, Ellonius sounded far more confident than Juliana in asserting Cassie had been wearing her brooch on the journey to the lodge. In response to Cassie's questions, both men were vague about their reasons for attending the meeting. There was an obscure reference to a will, which meant nothing to Arian, although it set off a flurry of whispers in the audience.

The prosecutor called the next witness. "Master Domitian dom Navicae." The name was not one Arian recognised.

A middle-aged man with a receding hairline came to the lectern.

"Master Domitian. You were the court-appointed physician who examined the body," the prosecutor said.

"Yes."

"Could you describe the injury?"

"Doyenne Pellonia had been stabbed in the right side of her head by a narrow, stiletto-style weapon. The point of the blade entered through her ear, causing instantaneous death."

"This was the knife used?" The prosecutor again displayed the brooch.

"It looks like it."

"Would the blow have required much strength?"

"No. The tip's sharp, and the thrust avoided the thickest bones in the skull."

"Could a woman have done it?"

"I'd say so."

"How easy would it be?"

Domitian's face scrunched in thought. "The angle had to be just right. And the brooch isn't ideal. The handle doesn't fit in the hand as comfortably as a purpose made dagger."

"Would you say the murderer needed to practice before attempting to use it?"

"Either that or get lucky on their first attempt."

The prosecutor smiled. "Is there anything else you can add? Where was the murderer in relation to the victim, for instance?"

"From the angle, they had to be standing right behind Doyenne Pellonia. She can't have seen the knife coming, else she'd have ducked."

"Would this mean the attacker had to be someone she trusted?"

"I never met Doyenne Pellonia, so I can't say for sure." He paused. "But I'd doubt it was a complete stranger, unless they were able to sneak up behind her."

The prosecutor turned to Cassie. "Do you have any questions for this witness?"

For the first time, Cassie shook her head. "No. No questions."

"Then finally, I wish to take evidence from Civis Marcella dom Rissanilae."

Another name Arian did not recognise, and not someone of rank. A stout elderly woman took the physician's place at the lectern. She scowled at the prosecutor with poorly disguised resentment. Clearly, she was there against her will.

"Civis Marcella, you are the housekeeper at the villa where the murder took place," the prosecutor said.

"Yes."

"How long have you had this role?"

"Nine years. Before that I was a housemaid."

Arian leaned forward. This should be interesting. Servants generally knew more about what was going on in a household than family members did. Although Doyenne Pellonia had probably been an exception to this rule.

"Could you give the court your account of the events on that day."

From Marcella's expression, there was little doubt she would have liked to refuse. "I was on duty in the foyer, welcoming guests to the lodge. The first to arrive was a carriage with Lord Xeranius bringing Primus Tribonus and Doyen Bellorion. Next came Lady Cassilania with Doyenne Juliana and Scribe Ellonius."

"I believe you took their cloaks from guests as they arrived."

"Of course." Marcella sounded offended, as if the prosecutor was implying she was not doing her job. "It had been raining all day and they were wet."

"What happened next?"

"They all went to the salon to meet Doyenne Pellonia. A short while later, a third carriage arrived with Doyenne Lilliana and someone I'm not supposed to name." The scowl Marcella directed at Vessia left no doubt as to the anonymous person's identity.

The prosecutor held up a hand to claim the court's attention. "I can confirm a senior member of the prefecture was present at the villa. This person played no part in the events that took place, and is not giving evidence, in order to ensure the impartiality of these proceedings."

As if that was going to work. But even had Vessia been a hundred miles from the lodge when the murder happened, would she be able to give an unbiased judgment? She had been certain of Cassie's guilt from the day it happened.

"Carry on." The prosecutor indicated to Marcella.

"These two weren't on the guest list, so I followed them to the salon. Once Doyenne Pellonia said they could stay, I went back to the foyer. I was there until Lord Xeranius came with word the doyenne had been murdered. He went to get a horse to ride to Kavilli for the prefects, and I went to see what help I could give. And that's it."

"I'd like a few more details relating to Lady Cassilania's brooch."

Marcella eyed the prosecutor cagily. "Such as?"

"Was it pinned to her cloak when she handed it to you?"

"I imagine so."

"You imagine? Did you see it?"

"I didn't look closely."

"So you didn't see it."

Marcella's shoulders slumped. "No."

"Thank you." The prosecutor nodded. "After the murder was discovered, I believe Primus Tribonus asked you to check the cloak, so there could be no doubt about the murder weapon."

"Yes."

"Was Lady Cassilania's brooch on her cloak when you examined it?"

"No."

The prosecutor faced Vessia. "At this point, I call the court's attention to the testimonies from both Doyenne Juliana and Scribe Ellonius, stating Lady Cassilania was wearing her brooch in the carriage on the journey to the villa." He returned to Marcella. "From the time she passed her cloak to you, to the time you confirmed the brooch was missing, did anyone other than you enter the office where the cloaks were hanging?"

"Only Lord Xeranius, when he came to tell me the news."

The prosecutor walked to the front of the lectern, so he was facing Marcella. "I want you to think about this very carefully. Is there any possible way someone could have entered your office and taken the brooch from Lady Cassilania's cloak without you seeing them?"

The courtroom was in utter silence while Marcella and the prosecutor locked eyes, but at last she said, "No."

The prosecutor turned around. "Lady Cassilania, you may question the witness if you wish."

Cassie smiled at the housekeeper. "Marcella. I'd like to thank you for the years of faithful service you've given my family."

"You're welcome, my lady."

"I believe you mentioned one time when you left the foyer. You accompanied Doyenne Lilliana and her companion to the salon on their arrival. Can you be sure nobody entered the office and took the brooch while you were gone?"

Marcella hesitated for a moment. "No, my lady. Of course I can't say what happened when I wasn't there."

"You're sure this was the only occasion when you left the office? Take your time. Think about it. Did anyone try to distract you? Is there anything else you can tell the court? Did you see anyone going up or down the stairs to my mother's study? Anyone acting strangely?"

"No. I...there was always..." Marcella's face contorted in confusion, or alarm, or fear. She shook her head. "I'm sorry. There's nothing more I can tell you."

Was she lying? There was something Marcella was not saying. However, after a few seconds to consider, Cassie merely smiled and said, "Thank you. That will be all."

The prosecutor reclaimed the lectern. "This concludes my list of witnesses. I would though, with the court's permission, like to question the accused about the murder weapon."

"That's up to Lady Cassilania. She's allowed to keep her own counsel, if she chooses," Vessia said.

Cassie did not wait to be asked. "I'm happy to answer your questions. In fact, I was hoping you'd give me the chance to speak."

The prosecutor consulted one of his scrolls. "Could you tell the court where you got the brooch."

"It was a gift from my mother, for my thirtieth birthday."

"Doyenne Pellonia had it custom made for you."

"Yes. As I'm sure you want to point out, it's quite unique."

"There's no doubt it was the weapon used to murder your mother?"

"Regrettably, no."

The prosecutor nodded, clearly pleased with the answer. "The unusual feature, the way the pin can lock into place. Whose idea was that?"

"My mother's." Cassie's expression was hard to read. "A joke of hers. No woman should ever find herself defenceless."

"You claim you left it pinned to your cloak when you arrived at the villa."

"I did."

"Can you explain how it ended up where it did?"

"Obviously, someone removed it, during the time while the housekeeper was away from the foyer."

"Any idea who that someone might be?"

"Yes." Cassie shrugged. "But unfortunately, no proof."

The prosecutor braced his hands on the lectern, drawing himself up to his full height. "I suggest you didn't leave the brooch attached to your cloak as you claim, but instead, kept hold of it. After concluding your conversation with Doyenne Juliana, you took the chance to go to your mother's study while nobody was watching. You murdered her, and then made a show of discovering her body later."

"No."

"Remember Master Domitian's testimony. You've had years to practice using the brooch as a knife. Also, Doyenne Pellonia would not have worried about her own daughter standing close behind her." He folded his arms across his chest. "What do you have to say?"

"That you can accuse me of all sorts of things, but please, don't insult me by making out I'm an idiot." Cassie sounded genuinely offended. "If I was going to murder someone, I'd plan it in advance, I'd make sure I wouldn't be a suspect, and I'd never be so stupid as to use a weapon which could only incriminate me."

"You admit the brooch is incriminating evidence."

"Of course. But the only possible reason the murderer used it, rather than a normal knife, is to frame me. What sort of fool would I be to commit a murder in such a way that I'm the obvious suspect?"

"I know your reputation. You're not any sort of fool." The prosecutor paused for emphasis. "In fact, you're known to have one of the most devious minds in Kavilli. And this is the game you're playing. It's a double-bluff, relying on your reputation. You laid a trail of clues pointing to yourself, which were so blatant you hoped to use it as evidence of innocence."

Cassie laughed. "Then why not a triple-bluff? The murderer knew you'd make the assumptions you're making at the moment and planned accordingly. You're trying to say 'heads I win, tails you lose.' By your logic, the evidence of my brooch means whatever you want it to mean. Which means it counts for nothing. And without the brooch, what evidence do you have against me?"

Under normal circumstances, the array of confused expressions around the courtroom would have been cause for amusement. Arian estimated less than a quarter of the audience were keeping up with the argument.

Even the prosecutor was struggling. He turned to Vessia. "This concludes the prefecture's case."

"And the accused, do you have more to say?" Vessia asked.

"If I thought it would do any good, but..." Cassie sighed. "Why waste more of the court's time? I'm sure you've made your mind up already."

"Then I will consider my verdict."

Vessia sat motionless on her throne for a long time. To be fair, she gave every impression of mulling over the testimonies she had heard. Her expression was sombre and thoughtful, her eyes focused beyond the confines of the room. As the minutes passed, sections of the audience began to fidget. Some exchanged whispers with the people beside them, earning angry glares from the guards.

Cassie also sat impassively. Her expression was every bit as thoughtful as Vessia's, although tinged with a very Cassie-like dash of amusement. Win or lose, she was playing the game she loved. The prosecutor was the one looking most worried. While his life was not at stake, his career might be, and Cassie had bested him at every point.

Finally, Vessia raised her head. "Lady Cassilania Marciana con Egantae dom Passurae, having considered the evidence, I find you guilty of the murder of your mother, Doyenne Pellonia Valeria dom Konithae ado Passurae."

Arian's insides turned to ice. The reaction was ridiculous, given that the outcome was never in doubt. Gasps rang out around the amphitheatre. Several voices were raised in shouts, both for and against the verdict. Cassie merely gave an ironic twitch of her eyebrows, along with a sardonic smile.

Vessia continued. "The murder of the doyenne of your family counts as an act of petty treason. The sentence is that you be taken from hence, and as soon as the authorities can make provision, you are to be executed in accordance with the law. Do you have anything else to say to the court?"

"Just one thing…well, two things actually." Cassie's voice was as clear and steady as ever. From her tone, she might have been exchanging gossip at a party. "The first is to thank the officers of the court, and you, for a well-organized trial, and for carrying out your duties in an even-handed and civilised manner." Cassie paused. "And the other thing is to say I am with child."

Vessia had to wait for the uproar to die down. "Has the infant quickened?" Both Vessia's expression and tone made her scepticism clear.

"Yes. I first felt it move nearly a month ago."

Vessia's face remained impassive, but her forefinger tapped out a rhythm on the arm of her throne. In Arian's experience, it was a sign of simmering irritation bordering on anger.

Over the months past, Arian had got used to the contrast between Vessia's public and private persona, yet never before had the difference between them been so harsh, so callous. Never before had Vessia's face looked so unappealing. Was this really the same woman Arian knew?

Eventually, Vessia drew a deep breath. "This must be confirmed by the midwives. If the infant has truly quickened, then sentence shall be postponed until after the birth. In the meantime, I charge the captain of prefects with keeping you secure." She got to her feet. "This concludes the business of the court for today. Guards, you may escort the condemned to her cell."

❖

The sun was sinking over Kavilli. The first blush of pink stained the sky above the rooftops. Arian sat at her bedroom window, staring at a flock of birds, coming home to roost. The scene rippled as tears filled her eyes. Again, she blew her nose. Trying to get her thoughts in order was a waste of time. Her head and heart were ripped into a thousand shreds and scattered to the winds.

She was left chasing images. The first time she had seen Cassie, walking into the great hall at Breninbury. The first time Cassie had kissed her. A warm lazy afternoon, lying naked in Cassie's arms. Cassie smiling as the verdict was delivered, as if nothing mattered. Cassie teasing her, and pulling strings, and turning her head around so she never knew where she was, or what she wanted. But at least that last part was answered. What she wanted was now so very clear.

Arian rested her forehead against the cool glass. The months of telling herself she never wanted to set eyes on Cassie again were revealed as a sham, an exercise in self-delusion. She had been lying to herself all along. A world without Cassie was not one worth living in.

"Damn her to the deepest pit of hell." Despite the words, Arian felt a sad, affectionate smile tug at her lips. "But only if I can go with her."

CASSIE

There. You felt that?"
The midwife nodded and lifted her hand from Cassie's abdomen. "Yes. The child is moving. I will make my report to Principal Magistrate Vessia."

"Thank you."

Cassie sat up and swivelled round to sit on the side of the bed. What a pity she would not get to see the bitch's face when she received the report. Vessia clearly hoped the claimed pregnancy was a fake. The midwife had arrived at the prison a few hours after Cassie's return from the trial.

"This child will be your what?" The midwife made conversation as she gathered up the few items she had brought with her.

"My sixth."

"Your other pregnancies went well?"

"Nothing out of the usual."

"And the children?"

"A couple of boys in the army, and a younger one who's still at the academy."

"The others?"

"Two daughters. But they both...they're..." Cassie swallowed. Some things did not get any easier with the passage of years.

The midwife looked sympathetic as she patted Cassie's shoulder. "For what it's worth, I think this one will be a girl."

Which only made it worse. One more daughter she would not see grow up.

After the midwife left, Cassie wandered over to the window. It was barred, as befitting a prison, but afforded her a panorama of the city. She was being held on the top floor of the prefecture headquarters, next to the Senate building in the heart of Kavilli.

Obviously, the accommodation was less luxurious than her apartment in the Passurae mansion, but all things considered, Cassie had no grounds for complaint. The conditions were vastly better than those at the common jail. The good-sized room was heated. She had a proper bed with clean blankets, a table to write at, access to sanitation, and a view. Best of all, she did not have to share it with anyone.

The cell was reserved for important detainees, usually political in nature. Thanks to the fiasco a few years back involving a former leader of the Senate, a circus performer turned prostitute, and a foreign spy, the room was guaranteed to be proofed against eavesdropping. As long as the door was closed, she could talk to herself in complete privacy. For the next four months it would be her home.

The sun had dropped behind the distant horizon. Bands of cloud flamed pink and orange, while the sky over Kavilli darkened. Cassie watched a flock of birds wheel across the sky, until they vanished behind the dome of the temple to Yelathi, goddess of justice. Was it worth offering up a few prayers? She could even arrange for a donation to temple funds. Except, in her experience, praying was the last resort of the desperate. The success rate never got above what might be achieved with random chance.

The gods best help those who help themselves.

If she was to avoid execution, it was up to her. The odds might not be on her side, but giving in to despair guaranteed failure. So, what were her options?

Cassie stared into the distance, letting her thoughts drift free. Vessia and the rest of the prefecture would be on the lookout for an escape attempt, a feat several prisoners had managed in the past—though, to the best of Cassie's knowledge, none had been five months pregnant at the time. Shimmying down a rope made from knotted sheets was out of the question.

Did anyone swallow the prosecutor's convoluted logic at the trial, using her reputation for deviousness to explain why she might have framed herself for the murder? In which case, doing the most predictable thing might catch her jailors out. Bribing the warders was an obvious first step, and one Vessia must anticipate. Surely such a blatant move could have no hope of success. Those guarding her would have been hand-picked for reliability.

She needed a scheme they were not expecting. And the last thing they would expect was—Cassie turned and paced across the room—not escaping? As an idea, it had limited appeal.

She returned to the view from her window. The temple dome again drew her eyes, silhouetted against the darkening sky. It was nearly time to sleep. According to the priests, Yelathi was gatekeeper to the eternal afterlife, who judged the souls of the departed. Were the followers right, or was it just wishful thinking? The evidence for their beliefs was decidedly lacking.

Considering the vast number and variety of priests to be found across the empire, they could not all be wrong, could they? Maybe she should have spent more time studying the different religions and found one that could provide more answers than questions. Perhaps then she might be able to muster confidence that, after death, she would be reunited with her mother and daughters.

Cassie shook her head ruefully. The odds were not on her side. But unless she could come up with a workable plan, in just four months, she would get to find out.

One of the worst things about being in prison was the food. Cassie forced herself to eat as much as she could stomach, for the baby's sake more than anything else. If there were just her own needs to consider, she would rather have gone hungry. Fortunately, her craving for blue cheese and pickled herrings had been fading, even before the murder and trial.

Cassie pushed the less palatable parts of her lunch around the plate, before setting the thing aside. With any luck, her family were negotiating with the authorities to supply her meals. It could not happen soon enough.

She could also request other items, the most pressing being pen and paper. Letters to her brother and three sons would not be easy, but had to be tackled, if only to stop Jadio doing something stupid, such as marching the legions under his command to Kavilli to rescue her. His chances of success were nonexistent. He would only end up getting himself and a host of his men killed. Cassie twirled the handle of her spoon pensively between her fingers. Or might the threat of him doing it work as a bluff in a wider scheme? The trick would be to make it sound plausible enough to cause worry, without being taken so seriously as to risk Jadio being arrested for treason.

The metallic clunk of the key in the lock interrupted her thoughts. One of the warders came in. "This has arrived for you." He put a wax sealed scroll on the table.

"Thank you." She smiled at the man. "I was thinking we should introduce ourselves, since we'll be seeing a lot of each other over the next few months."

"I know who you are." His tone was confident rather than surly.

"I assumed as much, but you have the advantage on me."

He hesitated. "Prefect Marcus Vitus ado Prefectae."

"Despite the situation, there's no need for us to be enemies."

"Neither can we be friends."

"True. Shall we aim for a polite and professional relationship?"

"My job is to keep you secure."

Cassie let her smile widen. "I'm sure Principal Magistrate Vessia wouldn't have picked you if she had doubts about your competence."

A slight jutting of the chin and straightening of the shoulders. "I…It's not for me to say." He indicated the plate. "Have you finished with that?"

"Yes, thank you."

He picked up the remains of lunch. "Your family will be providing your meals, starting with breakfast tomorrow."

"You won't believe how pleased I am to hear that. Could you ask them to provide writing materials as well."

Marcus nodded and closed the door.

The brief conversation confirmed Cassie's guesswork. Marcus had reacted with pride rather than surprise at the suggestion he had been personally selected by Vessia. Adding to his provincial accent, it was most likely he had accompanied her from Basalonia and was someone whose loyalty she felt assured of. All of which was exactly as expected and took any serious attempt at bribery off the table. Which did not mean it was not worth trying in the right circumstances, merely that it was unlikely to succeed.

Cassie turned her attention to the scroll. From the family crest on the seal, she could guess the contents without opening it. Using the handle of the spoon in place of a penknife, she split the wax and unrolled the document. More correct guesswork. Antonius wanted a divorce.

The terms offered were unusually generous. The Egantae family were understandably eager to distance themselves from her as soon as possible. Cassie placed the scroll back on the table to deal with later. Refusing would be churlish, yet ingrained habits would not let her sign anything without full consideration.

The timing of the divorce request was interesting, arriving the day after the trial. The Egantae must have drawn it up in advance but waited on the verdict. Did this mean Antonius would have been willing to stay married had she been found innocent? Or, more probably, the family had two documents prepared, one with fewer concessions if they felt they could afford spending a month or two negotiating terms. The marriage would be her shortest ever. Cassie allowed herself a wry smile. As things stood, it was not a record she would have any chance of beating.

How long before Antonius was forced to wed again? And how would his next wife feel about the slave, Timmi? Cassie shook her head. What was the appeal in having sex with someone who could not say no? As far as she was concerned, it held all the excitement of kissing a marble statue. No matter how sublime the artist's work, it would be cold and lifeless—unlike the fire burning in Arian, who did not settle for a simple no. From the day they met, Arian would not hesitate to tell her to fuck off, in two different languages. The proudest of Kavillian noblewomen did not present half as much of a challenge, or a quarter of the thrill.

Cassie turned her head to look through the window. The conviction she had carried, that one day Arian would walk out on her. Had it been truly inevitable, or just a game she played with herself, fuelling the flames of desire? If so, it was a bloody stupid and unnecessary game. No matter what, Arian would never turn into a doormat.

Cassie closed her eyes. She could have put up a fight over Arian—should have put up a fight. Fought Mother. Fought the whole world if need be. It might not have saved her from the current crap situation she was in, but at least she would have someone other than herself to blame.

❖

Breakfast the next morning, as provided by the kitchens in the Passurae mansion, was a huge improvement. Cassie finished off the pastries and licked the last of the honey from her fingers. Now for the hard part. As well as food, the basket also contained the requested paper, pen, and ink.

Most of the previous afternoon had been spent working out what she wanted to say in letters to her family. Her youngest son, eleven-year-old Derry, presented the greatest challenge. The overwhelming temptation was to wait another day or two, until she had her emotions firmly under control. But delay was not an option if she was to have any hope of the letters getting to Jadio and her sons before they heard the news from other sources.

Cassie sat at the desk, summoning the strength to dip the pen into the ink, when the key again sounded in the lock. Was it the housemaid returning to collect the food basket, or another message from her soon-to-be ex-husband's family, wanting to see if she had signed the divorce settlement?

Prefect Marcus stuck his head around the side of the door. "There's a visitor to see you from Magistra Vessia Gallina ado Prefectae. Shall I show her in?"

So neither guess was right. "Am I allowed to refuse?" Although the chance to play games with Vessia's lackey would provide a valid excuse to put off writing the letters a while longer, quite apart from any other entertainment value.

"No."

Cassie rose from the desk and took up position in front of the window, with the light behind her. "Then I would be delighted to see her."

Her tongue in cheek delivery was rewarded by a grin from Marcus. Although there was no chance of undermining his loyalty, getting the warders favourably disposed towards her could only bring benefits.

The door swung open wide, allowing Arian to enter.

Cassie's face prickled as the blood drained away. Her knees threatened to betray her by buckling. For her part, Arian looked ill at ease, as though she would rather be elsewhere. Was she visiting of her own volition, or had Vessia told her to? And if so, why?

Neither moved until Marcus left, closing and locking the door behind him.

Cassie's legs were trembling to the extent remaining upright was not easy. She shifted a step to the side, so she could lean back against the wall, praying her need for support was not obvious. "I didn't expect to see you here. Did Vessia send you?"

"No. I needed her permission to visit, but…" Arian bowed her head, pressing a hand over her eyes. "I had to see you."

"In that case, I'm afraid you're going to find me sadly lacking as a host. I'm completely out of wine and caviar, and there's not much in the way of home comforts. You can sit if you want, and I'll do my best with the social chitchat." Cassie indicated a chair.

"Please. I'm not here for an argument. I was in court. I heard all the testimonies."

"I didn't notice you." In truth, the audience had been a total blank. Dealing with the prosecutor and witnesses had taken every scrap of concentration.

Arian came over to stand at the window, but rather than face her, Arian's eyes were locked on the scene outside, staring in silence.

Cassie studied Arian's features in profile, close enough to touch, and yet so far out of reach. Sunshine caught in the gold of Arian's hair, glinted green in her eyes, and etched the elegant contours of her cheekbones. Calling on all her willpower, Cassie made herself look away. She had to get a grip. Could she make it to the chair without stumbling? Could she control her voice enough to talk normally?

At last, Arian spoke. "I was going to say I'm certain you're innocent. But do you know what? It doesn't matter whether you murdered your mother or not. I simply can't bear the thought of living without you."

Cassie's self-control teetered on the brink. Somehow she forced out the words, "You've managed it for the last eight months."

"Not really. You've been in my head, every hour of every day. I've been lying to myself. Pretending I could just carry on and eventually things would sort themselves out. But it isn't ever going to happen. I need you in my life, and always will."

"Bad luck for you then, becau—" Suddenly, the words refused to come.

Cassie swallowed and fixed her eyes on the ceiling, trying to make the muscles in her chest loosen, her legs stay firm, her face not crumple. But the room wobbled and blurred. Tears filled her eyes and then spilled down her cheeks. A sob shook her, destroying any hope of presenting a semblance of calm detachment.

Then Arian's arms were around her, holding her tight. Cassie dissolved into the embrace, burying her face in Arian's neck.

"Hush, hush." Arian's soft voice murmured in her ear. "I'll sort it out. I promise. I don't know how, but I'll do it."

Arian rubbed circles across her shoulders, then moved up to stroke the back of her head. Cassie reached around Arian's waist, pulling their bodies together, needing to feel Arian pressed hard against her, needing to feel Arian filling her arms. It was impossible to ever hold Arian close enough.

"It's not like you to make promises you can't keep." Cassie finally regained enough control of her breath to speak.

"There has to be a way to get the sentence reversed."

Why argue? Eyes closed, Cassie let herself draw on the scent of Arian, the sound of her breath, the rhythm of Arian's pulse beating in her throat, the warmth of her body.

Eventually, Arian pulled away. "I can't stay here too long. We need to talk."

They sat together on the side of the bed, holding hands. Cassie looked at Arian's fingers, interlaced with her own. "I've missed you." An absurd understatement.

Arian rubbed her thumb over Cassie's knuckles. "When you told me you were going to marry, I was so angry. I think I still am. But..." She leaned her head against Cassie's. "Now I'm sitting here thinking, if you hadn't married him we'd have just a day or so left. At least we've got more time." She shifted around so they were half facing. "When's the baby due?"

"Four months or thereabout. I'll have a few extra days while they sort out the wet nurse. The midwife confirmed the baby has quickened. She thought it would be a girl, but I'm not sure if that's a professional judgment or an even odds guess."

"A little baby Cassie."

"Actually, if it's a girl, I was going to call her Ariana."

Arian smiled, but then became more purposeful. "I heard what was said at the trial. Now tell me what you think happened. Who murdered your mother?"

"Would it really not matter if I said it was me?"

"It would matter, but I could..." Arian shook her head. "But you didn't, did you?"

"No."

"Who do you think it was? At the trial, you said you had an idea, but no proof."

Cassie drew a deep breath and let it out as a sigh. So much else they needed to talk about, things she ought to say. Yet this was safe, at least as far as her chaotic emotions went. The subject had certainly been at the forefront of her mind.

"As for who struck the blow, it could be almost anyone. But when it comes to who took the brooch from my cloak, that can only be Vessia. Nobody else was ever alone in the foyer. She and Lilliana were the last to arrive. Lilliana marched ahead, making poor Marcella chase after her, which gave Vessia the chance to duck into the office and grab the brooch before following. She must then have passed it to an accomplice."

"You don't think Vessia committed the murder?"

How much would it matter to you if she was the guilty one? What were Arian's current feelings for her lover? Was it over between them? When Arian said she had been lying to herself, was her affair with Vessia part of the self-deception? It was one of the unsafe, emotionally charged topics it was safer to avoid. Best not to ask unless she was sure she wanted to hear the answer. Feeding jealousy was not going to make anything better. Cassie raised Arian's hand to her lips as a cover, while waiting for the tightness in her chest to ease.

"No. In fact Vessia is the one person I can be sure didn't. Bran was watching her the whole time. She didn't leave the salon from when Mother went off with Lilliana until I found the body. But obviously she's working with the murderer."

"Why didn't you say so at the trial?"

"Accusing the judge of conspiring with an unknown person to commit murder! I can't see that working out well. Plus, Vessia wasn't supposed to be named in court, so everyone could pretend she was impartial."

"That was stupid. She wasn't impartial and everyone knows it. I don't understand how she could get away with it." Arian pouted. "What about justice? The whole point of a trial is to get to the truth."

"Have I ever told you I find your naivety one of the most endearing things about you?"

Arian batted their joined hands against Cassie's leg. "I'm being serious. It wasn't a fair trial."

"Maybe. But I prefer it to burning my feet with a hot iron until I confess."

"Don't say that, even as a joke."

In truth, this was a subject that risked getting into deeply unfunny territory. Cassie closed her eyes. Instead, they should talk about far more important things. She needed to say how sorry she was for her mistakes, and how much she truly cared. *I love you.* The words she had never voiced. But before she could work out where to start, Arian returned to the previous tack.

"If Vessia took the brooch and passed it to her accomplice. Who do you suspect?"

"Everyone."

"I'm being serious."

"So am I."

"From what you and Tribonus said at the trial, I realised your mother was blackmailing him."

"Not just him. Everyone we assembled at the lodge had their guilty secrets. As did Vessia and Lilliana, even though they weren't invited."

"You were blackmailing Vessia? I'd assumed the only reason she might want your mother dead was so she'd win the election."

"It's complicated. Lilliana was involved in a fraud that cost the empire a province. She didn't mean to. It's just the way events played out. Vessia had charge of the investigation. She took a bribe to cover up Lilliana's role."

"Your mother had proof of this?"

Cassie nodded. "She had Vessia's original report, signed and sealed."

"Do you know where it is now?"

"Either Vessia or Lilliana will have hold of it." Unless Bran had been able to take care of matters. "Mother kept her important documents in a strongbox at the lodge. Vessia had the room declared off limits. Supposedly so the prefects could investigate the crime scene. She'll have pulled the room apart. The strongbox was concealed and locked, but Mother always kept the key on her."

Arian shook her head. "I don't think Vessia has it yet."

"Why?"

"Something she said when I saw her last night."

Last night.

Arian must have noticed her stiffen. She slipped her hand free and put her arm around Cassie's shoulders. "I needed her permission to visit you. It was—"

"It's all right." Cassie did not want to hear more. "Anyway. It's not just evidence against her and Lilliana. Mother had dossiers on the others as well."

"You mean everyone had a motive to kill her?"

"Yes."

"Is there no one you can rule out?"

"Apart from Vessia?" Cassie shook her head. "Lilliana is the obvious suspect. She's the only one we know for certain was alone in the room with Mother. She could have come to the lodge with the sole intent of committing murder. She distracted Marcella to give Vessia a chance to take the brooch from my cloak. Then, before leaving the salon, she stopped for a brief word, which was Vessia's chance to hand the brooch over."

"Can we prove it?"

"Of course not." And it would not make any difference if they could.

Arian still would not let the subject drop. "How about the other people there? Can we dismiss any as suspects? What about the nervous doyenne for instance?"

"Juliana?"

"Yes, her. She doesn't strike me as a murderer. I know you said she could have slipped up to the study. But would she have the courage to do it? She looked terrified in court."

"I tend to agree. People like Juliana can lash out in a panic, but she's not someone Vessia would have picked as an accomplice for premeditated murder."

"What on earth did Juliana do that she could be blackmailed over?"

"Had an affair with a con artist and ended up helping him kill several people as part of a insane cult."

"She's been involved in murder before?"

"Only in a support role."

"And the others? What had they done?"

"Tribonus isn't guilty of any major crime as such. It's about his son, who gave such an appalling display of gutlessness on the battlefield he was executed on the spot. Tribonus arranged for the story to be buried. If the truth came out, he'd have to stand down as leader of the Senate, but that's about it." Although for someone like Tribonus, the shame would be more than he could bear. He might even feel he had to commit suicide to restore his family's honour.

"The other two? What had they done?"

"Bellorion murdered his wife, forged her will, and then bribed Ellonius to certify it as genuine."

"So, they could have conspired jointly to commit the murder?"

"Yes. They were together the entire time. They left the salon to have an argument over which one was going to backstab the other. But that could have been an act. In fact, if it wasn't Vessia who took the brooch, they're the next best bet. They were quarrelling in the courtyard for a long time. One might have distracted Marcella while the other snuck into her office."

"Your housekeeper was very certain nobody had gone near the cloaks. Except..." Arian frowned. "She got flustered when you pushed her about it. There was something she wasn't saying."

"True." That much had been obvious.

"Do you know what it was?"

"No."

"Then why didn't you press her for an answer?"

"Marcella has been with my family for decades. Before she moved to the lodge, she was a housemaid in the mansion. I've known her since I was a baby. Mother hand-picked her as housekeeper. If Marcella knew something she didn't want to tell the court, it's a good bet it was in the family's best interests to keep quiet."

"You don't know that for certain."

"True. But it wasn't going to make any difference to the outcome. Marcella could have testified she saw Lilliana coming down the stairs with blood dripping from her hands, and Vessia would still have found me guilty."

"We need to find out what Marcella knows. Supposing the murderer was blackmailing her, or threatening her family."

Arian was right, of course. "In that case, she could have taken my brooch and passed it to anyone. Or even placed it at the foot of the stairs for the murderer to collect on the way up." Cassie sighed.

"Another thing, are you absolutely certain your brooch is unique? The jeweller could have made a couple of copies."

"Mother was very definite on the matter."

"The jeweller might have done it anyway, if there was a profit to be made."

"Disobeying Mother's instructions was never wise. If a copy had shown up for sale, the jeweller would have come to regret it. Anyway, we know it wasn't a different brooch, because mine was missing from my cloak. I know I attached it properly, so it won't have dropped off. Somebody took it. And it's far too much of a coincidence if a thief happened to steal it on the very same afternoon that a murderer used a replica to kill my mother."

Having exhausted the topic of the murder, Arian fell silent. Now was the chance to talk about more important matters. But once again, before Cassie could formulate what she wanted to say, Arian got in first.

"How do we go about proving who the real murderer is?"

"We don't."

"What?" Arian's arm slipped down Cassie's back as she shifted around to face her. "We have to."

"There's no point."

Arian closed her eyes and pinched the bridge of her nose. "Am I missing something? You're going to be executed for a murder you didn't commit, and you're saying we just sit back and accept it? What was the point of going through the stuff you've just told me?"

"You asked."

"I wasn't just being nosy. I want to do something."

"There's nothing you can do."

"But…" Arian's voice died in bewilderment.

How to explain the situation to her in a way she would accept? Arian was not naïve enough to think what was right, fair, and truthful would always win, but she was innocent enough to think it ought to, and she would never surrender without a fight.

Cassie leaned forward and rested her head on Arian's shoulder. "I know you want to help. But even if you work out who killed Mother, you won't get the guilty verdict overturned. Not now. When I said I'd have been found guilty regardless of the evidence, I wasn't far from the truth. All they wanted was a plausible case against me. It wasn't about finding the murderer. It was about weakening my family."

"Then why did you bother at the trial, questioning the witnesses? What was the point?"

"People in the Senate get nervous when it looks like the law is being used in sham trials to get rid of rivals. That's why Vessia's supporters wanted to build a case against me. I was disrupting their story. Sowing doubt. Causing trouble for them down the line. It won't do me any good, but whoever becomes the next leader of the Passurae should reap the benefit, and I'm hoping for a favour in return."

"Could they get the verdict overturned?"

"No. It's not possible."

"Then what sort of favour?"

"Nothing." *Damn.* She should have thought before she spoke.

"Cassie!"

"It's not important."

"Tell me."

What did it matter? Arian would find out anyway. "Killing your family's doyenne counts as petty treason."

"Which means?"

"It means the Senate leaders take a dim view of their underlings trying to assassinate them and have passed laws to put people off trying. The penalty for petty treason is to be dressed in oil-soaked robes, chained to a post, and set on fire, but—"

"No."

"But," Cassie continued, "the new head of the family can request commuting the sentence to beheading. And I really would prefer that. I'm just hoping whoever becomes doyen is someone who likes me."

Arian slumped back. "That's it? You see no other chance?"

Cassie shook her head.

"How about if I find that report which proves Vessia took a bribe from Lilliana to cover up what she did. Would that get the sentence reversed?"

"Even then, Vessia can't simply say she's changed her mind and now thinks I'm innocent. If we really put the screws on her, best case…" Cassie shrugged. "She could accept a plea for clemency and commute the sentence to exile."

"Exile?"

"It would take the form of house-arrest, a long way from Kavilli. With luck, it could be somewhere nice, with decent weather." Actually, exile did not sound too bad, certainly by comparison with the alterative. But what was the point in raising false hopes? "Forget about it. There's no way you'll be able to obtain the evidence. Vessia isn't going to let anyone into Mother's study until she's found it."

"Then I'll take it off her afterwards."

"You think she'll just let you walk off with it?"

"I didn't plan on asking her permission."

"No."

"Why not?"

"I don't want you taking risks."

"You think I'm going to sit back and let you die?" Arian's voice resonated in its intensity. "I am going to do everything I can to save you."

"No." Why had she not seen where Arian's line of questions was leading? With hindsight, it was obvious. "It's not just Vessia. You'll be dealing with Lilliana as well, and she's far too dangerous to mess with." Cassie cupped Arian's face in her hand. "I need to know you're safe. And that's an end to it."

"No, it's not. I wo—"

The key sounded in the lock. Arian scrambled to her feet. "I have to go, but I'll be back."

"No. You can't. Please, Arian." Cassie caught Arian's hand and also stood, staring deep into her eyes. "More than anything else in this world, I want to see you again, but I imagine when you got permission from Vessia, you told her you wanted to find out whether I really was a cold-blooded murderer, or you had unfinished business with me, or stuff like that."

Arian's shrug said the guess was right.

"You can't play the same card twice. You can't let Vessia or Lilliana think you're no longer on their side. You must act as though you've decided I'm guilty."

"You think I'm going to accept that I'll never see you again?" Arian shook her head. "I love you."

"I—"

Cassie recoiled as the door opened. Her legs hit the side of the bed, causing her to drop back down onto it.

Prefect Marcus reappeared at the doorway. "A messenger is here, wanting to know if you've signed the divorce contract yet."

"It's on the table."

Marcus turned to Arian. "Have you finished with the prisoner?"

"Yes. I was just leaving."

Arian gave one last look back once before she went. Her expression held a mixture of love and resolve, that made Cassie want to cry on both accounts. Arian was going to do something stupid and dangerous, and there was nothing she could do to stop her.

Marcus picked up the divorce contract and followed Arian out.

Cassie remained sitting on the bed as tears again welled up in her eyes. "I love you too." Words spoken to the closed door. Words she would never have a chance to say to Arian's face.

❖

"Your dinner has arrived." A new warder, not Marcus, pushed the door open.

Cassie was lying on her bed. She looked up to see Bran enter the cell. "I wasn't expecting you. How did you get permission to visit?"

"It's official family business. They couldn't refuse." He smiled and held up a basket. "And I thought I'd make myself useful at the same time."

Cassie sat up. "It's good to see you."

"How are you feeling?"

"My back aches all the time."

Bran looked sympathetic. "Tessa had the same problem. She's glad that's over."

"How's the baby doing?"

"He's sleeping better now. We are too. Thanks for asking."

"What's the official business?" Although she could guess.

"Voting for the new doyen is complete."

"Who?"

"Lord Xeranius, or Doyen Xeranius as he is now."

Cassie nodded. With herself out of contention, the result was not a foregone conclusion, but hardly a surprise.

"He's sent a message," Bran said. "He'll be requesting your sentence is commuted to beheading."

"I guess it's time to be thankful I never went out of my way to piss him off."

"I think he likes you."

"That's nice to know."

Cassie levered herself off the bed and hobbled to the table. The baby was definitely making its presence felt. The basket held a loaf and a heavy pottery bowl, still radiating heat. She removed the lid and dunked a corner of bread in the stew. The flavour took her back. Someone had remembered one of her childhood favourites.

Bran leaned against a wall, arms crossed over his chest, watching her eat. "I took care of your mother's strongbox. There's nothing in it now but ash. I flipped the door catch while everyone was milling around so I could get back in. But I had to wait until after everyone left, taking your mother's body, so the key was gone. Pouring oil through the lid and dropping in a lit splint was the best I could do."

Cassie nodded. Regrettable, but better than the contents ending up with Lilliana or Vessia. "You did well." Apart from anything else, there was now no reason for Arian to take risks.

"I wish I could have done better. If we had the contents to bargain with, they wouldn't have dared put you on trial."

"Don't waste your life on ifs."

"It's hard not to." Bran glanced at the door, then reached inside his shirt. He pulled out a wad of paper. "There's just these left, though they're not much use. Your mother had them out on her desk when she was murdered."

Cassie wiped her hands on a cloth. Two documents were folded up together. She opened out the first. Blood had seeped along one edge, obscuring the end of lines. Even so, it was easy enough to fill in the missing words. It was the sworn declaration, signed and sealed by Lilliana, withdrawing Vessia as a candidate in the election.

The second, longer, document had presumably been on top. Whatever it had said was now lost in a coating of russet brown. Cassie tilted the paper to the light. Only the top few lines were clear.

Having concluded my investigation into the matter of the supply of wheat to the Roldan Pass garrison, it is my firm conclusion, supported by the evidence listed below, that the initial transgression was solely the work of

And that was it, except for the odd phrase here and there. Mother's blood had erased everything else. The imprint in the wax seal at the bottom was legible as that of Magistra Vessia Gallina ado Prefectae, but she was hardly likely to volunteer a full transcript.

Cassie held the sheet up to the window, hoping the light shining through might reveal what was hidden. Squinting? Holding the paper obliquely to the sun's rays? Moving it to within an inch of her nose? But nothing. Whatever had been written on the scroll was lost forever. It might as well have been burned, along with everything in Mother's strongbox.

"That's..." Cassie paused. "Unfortunate."

"That isn't the word I used when I saw it."

"I must admit, others did come to mind." She put down the ruined document. "I take it you didn't hang on to any of the stuff you got from Vessia's strongbox?"

"No. I handed everything over to your mother."

"Did you read it first?"

"I skimmed though quickly and made notes. But I assumed we'd get to work on it properly once the election was over."

"Were there any details Vessia would have wanted kept hidden from Lilliana?"

"Do you have anything particular in mind?"

"Just the beginning of an idea. Vessia has to be on shaky ground with Lilliana. Was there anything to widen the rift?"

Bran frowned. "A few things, maybe. I'll look at my notes and do a little digging."

"Thanks." Cassie returned to the stew. "I need you to do something else for me."

"Yes, my lady?"

"Watch out for Arian."

"In what way?"

"She was here earlier today." Which Bran doubtless already knew. Very little of note happened in Kavilli without catching the attention of his spies. "She's...we're..." Cassie waved vaguely, hunting for the word. "Reconciled. Now she wants to try prove me innocent. She thinks it will do some good. I've told her not to do anything stupid, but I don't think she's going to take any notice."

"Do you think she'll cause trouble?"

"Only for herself. I want you to make sure she stays safe."

"You don't think she could help us gather information? She's well placed to gain useful—"

"I don't care. She might end up getting herself hurt or killed."

"You're the one sitting there with the death sentence."

"I won't risk her life to save mine. And I won't have you do it either."

"Very good, my lady." Bran's expression was a polite mask, but Cassie could feel his disapproval.

The hostility between Bran and Arian was unmistakable and long-standing. Cassie had never got to the root of it, beyond deciding it was because of, rather than despite, them coming from the same barbarian tribe, albeit at opposite ends of the hierarchy. While this detail probably played a role, it could not be the entire story, since neither of them had any problems dealing with folk across the social spectrum in Kavilli.

"I know you aren't best friends, but Arian is important to me. I want her safe."

"I'll try, but if she won't take advice from you, there's little chance she'll listen to me."

"You have to work out something. I'm stuck in here, and powerless. I'm frightened Arian is going to end up in trouble with Vessia, or worse still, Lilliana. I want you to keep her away from them."

"I'll do my best, my lady."

"One more thing. How the murder happened. I think Vessia took my brooch from my cloak while Lilliana created a distraction."

Bran nodded. "It's a simple call."

"She passed the brooch to Lilliana, who was the one to actually commit the murder."

"That's where I disagree." Bran pointed to the blood-soaked report. "If Lilliana was the murderer, she wouldn't have left that behind on the desk. Admittedly, it's now useless, but she couldn't have guaranteed that would happen. She couldn't predict where the blood would flow. It would have been much safer to take both documents with her when she went back to the salon, and no reason why she shouldn't."

"Yes. Of course." Cassie pressed her hand to her forehead. Could she blame the pregnancy for making her so slow on the uptake? "The killer is someone who either didn't know what the documents were or didn't care who saw them."

"Obviously. Even if the murderer didn't want to risk being caught with them, there was a candle and tinder box by the door. It would only have taken a second to burn them."

Cassie let her hand drop. "Surely, Vessia's accomplice wouldn't have left the documents behind either."

"Unless whoever it is wanted to part ways and saw it as a means to get her into trouble."

"Ah, yes." Especially if Vessia had blackmailed the murderer into committing the crime to start with. "But there's one other possibility we must look into. Marcella could have taken the brooch, or is lying to protect the person who did."

"You don't trust her?"

"I want to. But she was holding back something at the trial."

"Any idea what?"

"No."

"Do you want me to question her?"

"Not straight off. First see if there's any chance someone has been putting pressure on her."

"You think she might have given in to bribery?"

"Or threats to her family. Either way, I want you to check her out."

"I'll see to it."

"I have one final request."

"Yes?"

"I want you to find out who was responsible for the murder and deal with them." Not because she had any hope it could earn her a reprieve, but because she owed it to Mother.

"You may count on me, my lady."

"Thank you."

Bran indicated the table. "Do you want to keep hold of those documents?"

"Better not. Just in case they search this room. You've also got more resources to try removing the blood."

"I don't hold out much hope, but I'll try." He picked up the documents and folded them together. "Any message for Xeranius?"

"Pass on my sincere congratulations and thank him for the offer to request beheading."

"I will, my lady."

After Bran had left, Cassie returned to her food, but her appetite was gone. She wanted to kick the door or pound the walls until her hands were bloody. Had she ever felt so helpless?

She left the table and went to stare out the window, although her eyes were unfocused. All the mistakes and regrets of her life rolled through her head in a miserable parade. If she could have her time again, there was much she would do differently. And some things were now far, far clearer.

I won't risk her life to save mine.

For people who knew her, it was surely one of the more unexpected things she had said. Cassie shook her head ruefully. She even surprised herself. Her life had been lived for the sake of her family, but if it came to a stark choice, Arian was the one she was willing to die for.

By evening, Cassie had names for all three warders who were guarding her in a two-on, one-off rotation. Marcus was the oldest and most senior. He was also the most forthcoming. The one called Orthias was the surliest, which possibly meant he was covering for a weakness she could exploit. She just needed to come up with a plan.

However, her thoughts kept snagging on memories of Arian's visit, a source of both happiness and despair. Cassie groaned and slid down in her chair. If she could avoid her appointment with the executioner, she and Arian might have a future together. Yet Arian was intent on taking pointless and dangerous risks. The most bitter irony would be if she escaped death, only to learn Arian had got herself killed.

Bran could normally be relied on to keep people safe. Unfortunately, given the friction between them, there was a worrying possibility Arian would do the exact opposite of whatever he suggested, and there was nothing Cassie could do about it.

She sat up straight. Wallowing in negativity was pointless. As long as she could draw breath she was still in the fight. Furthermore, while talking to Arian the first hint of an idea had occurred to her. The best option really did lie in not escaping.

After all, even if she broke out of prison, where would she go? She had seen what life was like outside the empire, and it was not on her list of experiences worth repeating. She was not going to live out her days cowering in a stinking, shit-covered hovel. Far better to get her sentence commuted to exile, preferably with a limited duration.

Cassie wandered to the window. Dusk was descending over Kavilli. Stars pricked the sky. At some stage, she needed to talk to Vessia, face to face. Asking for a meeting would only get refused. So Vessia needed to be goaded into visiting while thinking it was her own idea.

The first step was to get Vessia worried, which was an entertaining objective in its own right, without any other benefit attached. The warders would be on guard, anticipating an escape attempt. The last thing either they or Vessia would expect was for their prisoner to do nothing.

All she had to do was be a model prisoner for a month or so, while displaying the correct level of confidence to make them think she had a scheme in motion. Maybe she could throw in a few minor, random actions to set them off on a fool's pursuit, and tie them up in misplaced conjectures.

As the days slipped past, they would assume she was waiting for them to relax and drop their guard. Whereas she was really waiting for them to reach a state of hyper-vigilance, when a simple nudge would get them jumping the wrong way.

Cassie smiled. The prosecutor and his absurd claims of double bluffs and deviousness. None of them knew the first thing about how the game was played.

ARIAN

You would not believe how much I look forward to being with you again. Please let me know when I can come over so we can spend more time together. Having spoken to her, I now see how right you were about Cassi

No, no, no.

Arian groaned and crumpled the paper in her fist. She tossed it onto the floor to join the six other sheets. Her attempt to write a quick note to Vessia was becoming expensive and time-consuming. Arian would quite happily never set eyes on the woman again, and lying, even in the medium of writing, made her feel dirty. Yet if she was to get evidence to free Cassie she had to keep in contact.

Before she could start on her eighth attempt, a knock sounded at the door.

"Come in."

Laelia poked her head around the side. "My lady, there is a fuel merchant here. He wants to know if you'd consider him as a supplier."

At the moment, she needed neither fuel nor interruptions. "Tell him no."

Laelia hesitated. "He said he used to work for your uncle Maddock."

"What?"

"He said he used—"

"No. It's all right. I heard what you said."

Apart from members of her household, who else in the city would have the first idea about her uncle? The supposed fuel merchant must be Lycanthian, using Maddock's name as a code word. Which meant he was a clandestine messenger, a spy, or something else. Regardless, she had to know more. "Um. Send him in."

"Yes, my lady."

A dark-skinned, dark-haired man she had never seen before arrived at the door. "Thank you for seeing me."

However, the voice was familiar. Arian looked closer. "Bran?"

Had she known who it was she would never have told Laelia to admit him. The baseborn renegade left her ill at ease, and not just because of the way he had forsaken their people.

Bran smiled and strolled into the room. "Lady Cassilania asked me to visit you."

"Your hair…"

"Dye. It works on skin as well."

"Why the charade?"

"I thought it wiser, in case you're being watched."

A worrying idea, but how likely was it?

Bran sat down without being invited. "So. What are you up to?" His manner was challenging, verging on hostile.

"That's none of your business."

"Lady Cassilania's orders are to make it my business."

Easy enough to guess what Cassie had said. "She wants you to talk me out of trying to prove her innocent?"

"More a case of trying to stop you doing anything stupid." He wrinkled his nose. "Which is one of the tougher assignments she's given me over the years."

While being as insolent as possible? Bran was usually politely condescending towards her. The blatant insults were new. Arian ignored the temptation to match his rudeness. "I assume Cassie told you I went to see her yesterday morning."

"She did, though I already knew." His stare fixed on her face. "I also know you spent the night beforehand in Principal Magistrate Vessia's apartment, at the Konithae mansion."

"What's that to do with you?" The night was not something she wanted to be reminded of. Thankfully, Vessia had been so busy catching up with her new job that all they had done was sleep, but just being in the same bed as her felt sordid.

"You told Lady Cassilania you wanted to help her, but you're still f..." He paused. "Finding time for the woman who condemned her to death."

"I don't answer to you."

"You'll just let me figure out stuff on my own." Bran's smile vanished. He leaned forward, elbows braced on his knees. "Good. Because the thing I most need to figure out is whether you're going to betray her again."

"I've never betrayed her."

"Really? These last three months, you never once let slip anything when Vessia pumped you for information she could use against Lady Cassilania? Because you're not going to convince me the bitch didn't try. It won't all have been idle pillow talk.

"We..." *hardly ever mentioned Cassie.* But that would be a lie.

Bran seized on her uncertainty. "Do you want to swear you never let slip a single detail which was used by the prosecutor at the trial?"

Of course she had, on the night of the murder, when Vessia had been so insistent about the brooch and its origins. "I never meant any harm to come to her." Yet was even this much true? At some level, had she wanted revenge, to pay Cassie back for the pain?

Bran did not let up. "I don't care what you meant to happen. I'm not telling you a thing, until I'm convinced it won't get back to Vessia. Because, if it does, it won't matter whether it's due to you being in league with her, or merely because you're too dim-witted to know when to keep your mouth shut."

He was clearly going out of his way to be offensive. Arian bit back an angry retort. The man had the manners of a pig, and she was not going to sink to his level. "I'm sure, when Cassie asked you to visit me, she didn't mean you to do nothing but throw insults around."

Bran launched himself to his feet and stalked over to the window. He rested a shoulder on the frame and stood, staring down into the courtyard. "Lady Cassilania is great at reading people, but when it comes to you she's always had a blind spot. At the moment she's all alone at the bottom of a really shitty hole. If you went to see her, said nice things, gave her a kiss, maybe flashed your tits, then I ca—"

"Enough! Watch your tongue."

He shifted around to face her and gave a slow, sardonic smile. "So that's how it went? Have I touched a raw nerve? Or was it more than just your tits?"

"How dare you!"

Bran laughed. "How dare a lowborn serf like me say rude things about royalty like you? It's easy. We used to practice every night, down in our hovels by the farm."

He should have stayed there. "It's nothing to do with your rank. It's about you acting like an ill-mannered lout."

"Rather than kissing your arse, as I'm supposed to?" Bran shook his head. "I don't have to say a word. I just walk in the room and there's you, sneering down your nose at me. I was born a serf, and you think it gives you the right to treat me as less than dirt."

"It's not your birth. You've abandoned our people. You've gone over totally to the empire."

"Sleeping with the enemy? That's rich, coming from you. Not that I have any problem with you taking lovers here in Kavilli, but I don't think you're in any position to throw stones."

"I'm still loyal to our people, and our king."

"Well, you would, seeing how he's your son."

"And what do your family, back home, think of you?"

"They don't think much at all. They're dead. They were slaughtered by a raiding warband, while your lordly warriors hid in their hillforts."

Of course they were. Cassie had told her the story. "I'm sorry about that. It's not—"

"Really? You're sorry to hear about a bunch of dead serfs? Are you sure you weren't told about them before, but didn't find them important enough to remember?"

Which was uncomfortably close to the mark. "They were members of the Lycanthi. That makes them important to me."

"Being Lycanthian is important to you. I agree." Bran jerked a thumb towards the window. "Out there are hundreds of thousands of people from all over the empire. But you don't sneer at any of them the way you sneer at me. Because they're foreigners and don't count. But I'm Lycanthian, so you know where to put me. Right at the bottom of the pile, under your heel. And then I piss you off because I don't know my place."

He was right about pissing her off. Arian slammed her hands on the desk and stood up. "Look. Are you here just to pick a fight? Because I've had enough of this. Either say something useful or get the fuck out of here."

Bran's smile did not waver. He ducked down and scooped two crumpled pages from the floor. "What have we here?"

"They're nothing to do with you. Put them down."

He ignored her and flattened out the sheets, then picked up another. "Having trouble writing to your sweetheart?"

"She's not my sw…" Arian drew a deep breath. "Either get out, or I'll summon the bodyguards and have them throw you out."

"You'll rescue Lady Cassilania all on your own?"

"Yes. If I have to."

"Good luck with that."

Arian stared at the desk, trying to get her anger under control before saying more. She would not be drawn into screeching at him like a fishwife.

Silence made her look back up. Bran had not moved, but the intolerable smile had gone. "All right. I believe you." He dropped the papers and returned to his seat.

"What?"

"I believe you want to help Lady Cassilania. You're not a good enough actress to be lying. And your writing attempts show you no longer have an honest and frank relationship with Principal Bitch Vessia."

"You've been playing with me."

"I had to be sure you were on the level. I gave a few digs to see what you'd say."

"You're lowlife scum."

"And a serf who doesn't know his place. But I'm ready to put up with you treating me like shit, which you're going to do, because we need to work together."

"You think I'm going t—"

"I think we're Lady Cassilania's only hope. You'll just have to hold your nose for her sake."

Arian sank down on her chair. "You're a contemptible little arsehole."

"I've been told that before."

Which was easy to believe. Arian swallowed whatever else she was tempted to say. "I'm going to get her conviction overturned. If you're willing to work with me, then…" No matter how little she liked the idea. "I'd be grateful."

"Do you have a plan?" Bran's tone made it obvious he expected a no.

"Yes."

"Let's hear it then."

"Cassie told me about documents her mother had. They proved Vessia and Lilliana were involved in a serious fraud."

"The Roldan Pass scam? Screwing with army supplies and causing a military balls-up?"

"That sounds like it. Vessia is searching for it up at the lodge. Once she finds it, I—"

"She isn't going to find it."

"She won't stop until she does, and I know where she keeps her—"

"I've got it."

"What?"

"The evening of the murder, I got into Doyenne Pellonia's study without anyone seeing. I picked up the report, but it's useless."

"If we've got the evidence, we can force Vessia to change the verdict."

"I mean, it's unreadable. It was lying on Doyenne Pellonia's desk and got soaked in blood. The first couple of lines are clear, but the rest is…" Bran let a hand wave finish the sentence.

"Are there no other documents we can use?"

"There was another paper under it, which is in better condition. It's a signed declaration from Lilliana, withdrawing Vessia from the election. But it's irrelevant now the voting is over."

"Won't it look awkward for them if it comes out?"

"It'll take some explaining, but it's not enough on its own."

"That's all there is?"

"Apart from ash."

"Ash?"

"Doyenne Pellonia's orders. If ever things went to hell, I mustn't let the contents of her strongbox get into enemy hands. That's why I went to her study."

"What did you do?"

"I set fire to them."

"Why not take them?"

"Doyenne Pellonia had the key on her, but the prefects had already taken her body away. The box was cast iron and bolted to the wall. Getting the thing loose would have made too much noise, as would hammering off the lid. But there was a slit in the top to deposit documents when it was locked. I poured in lamp oil and set it alight. I'm sure, by now, Vessia has found both the strongbox and the key, but all she'll get out of it is ash."

Could things get any worse? "We have to find out who the real murderer is."

"That might help, depending on who it turns out to be."

"Is there anyone you suspect?"

"I suspect everyone. That's my job. I can provide a motive for all the people there, but as for which one's guilty?" Bran shrugged. "I need more information."

"From who, and how?"

"We need to interview the servants at the lodge. One of them might have seen something, or overheard something."

"Wouldn't they say? Aren't the servants picked for loyalty?"

"But not always for brains. They may not realise the importance of what they know."

"When will you talk to them?"

Bran shook his head. "I won't. I want you to."

"Why me?"

"Regardless of what part Lilliana played in the murder, things have turned out well for her. She won't be pleased if she hears I'm digging around. Not with the Roldanian affair hanging over her. If I go to the lodge and start questioning people, you can bet word will get back to her."

"How will it work any better if it's me?"

"The folk at the lodge know me. Even in disguise, I'd be recognised in an instant."

"It won't take much longer to work out who I am."

"Have you ever been there?"

"No. But they'll have heard about Lady Cassilania's blond barbarian lover. I'm sure they'll work out who I am."

"Probably, they would." Bran rubbed his head. "Which is where the dye comes in."

"You want me to dye my hair?"

"And your skin."

"Does it come off when you wash?"

"Eventually." He grinned. "But I have powder you mix with lemon juice which works much quicker."

"Even in disguise, I can't just wander up there and start asking questions."

"No. I'll arrange for three junior housemaids to be reassigned to the mansion in the city. I'll argue they aren't needed, now the doyenne is gone, which isn't true, since the building will take the same amount of upkeep. When the housekeeper complains about being short staffed—and she will—you can take their place as a temporary stand-in."

"You want me to pose as a housemaid?"

"For a few days. That's all it'll take. Servants love gossiping. It's their favourite hobby. Believe me, they'll be falling over themselves to tell you all about the murder. You'll have no trouble nailing down who was where and when. They'll volunteer stories to you it would take days for me to drag out of them. I make some people nervous, if you can believe it." Bran gave a crocodile smile.

That or throw up. And he was not telling her everything. Of that Arian was certain. "But why me? Can't someone else go? You must have people working for you who're used to this sort of thing."

"I do. But most of them are well known at the lodge, and the rest are busy on other missions. This is your chance to do something to help Lady Cassilania." Bran said it as a challenge. "Could you make an excuse to be out of town for a few days?"

"How many?"

"Ten at most."

"How soon would I have to leave?"

"Take your time. I need to recall the maids, then wait for the housekeeper to get pissed off about it. Let's say, twenty days."

"Why that long?"

"It won't hurt if things calm down, in case anyone is keeping an eye on the lodge. Lady Cassilania is safe for now. We need to make sure you are too. The murderer has killed a doyenne. They aren't going to think twice about offing a nobody from the barbarian fringes."

"As if you care."

"I know what Lady Cassilania will say if anything nasty happens to you, and I don't want to be on the receiving end of it." Bran got up. "I'll be in contact when I've got everything sorted."

As he reached the door, Arian said, "I still think you're an arsehole."

"But you have to admit I'm good at it."

"I can tell it comes naturally to you. When you said you knew about me visiting Vessia at the Konithae mansion. Have you been spying on me?"

"Of course. I spy on everyone."

❖

"What's your name?" Marcella barked the question. She was a completely different woman to the one who had appeared in court. Were it not for the identical appearance, Arian would have suspected an impostor.

"Ana."

Judging by the frown, this was not an acceptable answer. "I don't know where you've worked before, but here you call me ma'am, and you call Lucius, the butler, sir. The other staff will let you know how they wish to be addressed. Is that clear?"

"Yes, ma'am."

"Hmmmp. Do you have any belongings?"

"In that bag, ma'am. Do I need to br—"

"They'll be taken to the servants' bunkhouse." Marcella turned and stalked away. "Follow me."

Arian hurried to catch up, trying not to limp. The journey to the lodge, wedged between sacks on the back of a supply wagon, had been highly uncomfortable, and things were not getting better. After scrambling down from the tailboard, she had barely begun to work the cramps from her legs before being accosted by the housekeeper.

They climbed a short flight of steps and entered the villa through a wide doorway.

"This is the foyer," Marcella announced.

The foyer was not a room as much as a covered space between the inner and outer yards. The side facing the outer yard was blank stone, with the doorway in the middle. On the inside, a row of columns overlooked a courtyard garden. The foyer floor and ceiling were limestone slabs. At the far end on the right was a small doorway.

Marcella pointed to it. "That's my office. You only set foot inside when you're told to. Understood?"

"Yes, ma'am."

Marcella marched between the columns into the garden. Eight triangular flowerbeds radiated from a central fountain. Statues ringed the pool, set amid a stunning display of roses. The figures were either huntsmen or warriors, armed with bows and spears. Arian followed Marcella onto a flagstone path between the flowerbeds.

"Those are the guest rooms. You'll be assigned to clean them whenever someone stays overnight." Marcella indicated doors on the left. "And there..." Now she pointed to the most imposing of the doorways, directly facing the foyer. "...is the salon. Doyenne Pellonia used it to entertain visitors. We don't know what plans Doyen Xeranius has."

"Yes, ma'am."

The block containing the salon was the only two-story section of the villa. A veranda ran the length of the upper floor, overlooking the courtyard. Marcella turned right at the fountain. This side of the courtyard had an arched passageway in the middle, and a flight of wooden steps climbing to the veranda. A frieze of running deer, carved in low relief, decorated the wall at head height.

"The upper floor was where Doyenne Pellonia had her private rooms. You'll have no need to go there," Marcella snapped as she stalked passed the foot of the stairs.

"Yes, ma'am."

Arian glanced up before entering the archway. Three doors opened onto the veranda. One must be the study where the murder took place.

They emerged from the short passage into an area of cobblestones. This was obviously the domestic section, servicing the villa. A stone trough in the middle of the yard had a water pump at the nearest end, and a sloping surface along one side for pounding laundry. The building directly ahead was obviously a dairy. Other structures must be storerooms and workshops. A double gateway in the far corner lead back to the outer stable yard, although currently it was shut and barred with a thick wooden pole.

Marcella shoved open the door to the kitchen, where four women were at work. She indicated the eldest of them. "Decima is the cook. You'll take orders directly from her." And, for Decima's benefit, Marcella added, "This is Ana, who'll be working for you. The gods alone know why they couldn't send Nirva or Aelia back. But nobody asked my advice." She treated Arian to a withering look. "I get the sense somebody wanted rid of this one, but we'll see. Sometimes first impressions are wrong. Anyway, she's all yours now." Marcella stomped away.

Once the door closed, one of the women looked up and smiled. "Don't mind her. She's like that with all the new people. You should have heard what she said about me."

"And she was right," another one said, prompting laughter.

Arian relaxed. At least her co-workers seemed friendly. "She might be right about me as well." This earned her a smile from the women.

"Where have you been working, pet? The big mansion in town?" Decima asked. She was easily a couple of decades older than the others.

"Yes."

"Been there long?"

"Not really." It was safest, in case she was asked about other staff working there.

"You'll find things a lot quieter up here."

"Now all the excitement is over," another woman said. "Oh, I'm Illa, by the way. That's Sal and Halie." She pointed them out. "You heard about what happened here?"

"You mean the murder?" An easy guess. "It's awful."

"Isn't it. Did you ever meet Lady Cassilania?" Halie asked.

"I saw her a few times."

"The whole trial was rigged against her, you know. She didn't do it." Everyone nodded in agreement with Halie.

Bran had been right about the servants' eagerness to talk. "That's what I heard too."

"The only person from here who gave evidence in court was Marcella. Not that it did any good. Maybe that's why she's been in such a foul mood ever since. They should have called more of us to speak. We could have set things straight," Illa said.

"Were you all working here when it happened?" Arian asked.

"Yes. Me and Sal were serving wine to the visitors in the salon."

"And I was running errands," said Halie. "I was in the foyer when—"

"Come on now," Decima cut in. "It's time for work, not tittle-tattle." She looked at Arian. "The dairy floor needs washing. It's on the other side of the kitchen yard. A mop and bucket are over there already. Let me know if you need anything else, pet."

"Right." Arian headed out the door, but then leaned back in and said, "But when it's time for the tittle-tattle, please come and get me." She left to a round of laughter.

The mop, bucket, and water were easy enough to find, although by that point a few doubts were creeping in. Arian had seen housemaids washing floors on numerous occasions, but had never studied exactly what they were doing, or how they were doing it. In Breninbury, the floors were bare earth, with loose rushes to soak up the damp. She stood in the middle of the dairy, mop in hand, and looked around. Just how difficult could it be?

What Arian soon discovered, once she had mastered the knack of making the water go where she wanted rather than over her shoes, was that washing the floor was straightforward, but tiring. By the time she finished, the daylight was fading and she was tired, hot, and sweaty—apart from her feet which were cold and wet. Her arms and back ached.

"Hey. You finished in here?" Illa stood at the door, holding an oil lamp.

"Just about." Arian stepped back. "Do you think it's all right?"

Illa tilted her head to one side and held up the lamp. "To be honest, it looks a bit greasy. Did you add enough vinegar?"

Vinegar? "Umm...maybe not. I didn't want Marcella accusing me of being wasteful."

Illa laughed. "Don't worry. You can't win with her." She picked up the bucket. "Come on. I'll help you put the stuff away and show you our bunkhouse. Dinner will be ready soon."

Illa led the way along a narrow path behind the dairy, pointing out a small building on the way. "Decima and Marcella both have their own private room in there. Lucius does as well." She stopped outside another door. "While we're all in here." She pushed it open.

Accommodation for the junior female servants was a twelve-foot square room with two pairs of bunk beds on opposite walls. A thin table with benches ran up the middle. Illa added her oil lamp to the two already there. Even so, they seemed to cast more shadow than light.

"We all get our own beds here at the lodge. Don't have to top and tail." Illa delivered the line as though it could only come as unexpected good news. "That one, that, and that are all free. You can take your pick." She pointed out three of the upper bunks.

How am I going to climb up? There was no sign of a ladder, and Arian's arms felt ready to drop out of their sockets.

"Dinner's here." Halie entered the room carrying a large iron pot. The table creaked when she put it down.

Other women followed her in, one with a basket of hard-baked rolls, each the size of a cabbage. There was, apparently, no option regarding the menu. Arian could only hope it would prove edible. She copied the others, slicing the top off a roll and pulling out the soft inside to form a bowl. The contents of the pot turned out to be a vegetable stew with an odd, though not unpleasant, fishy aftertaste. It would never be Arian's first choice for dinner, but was far from the worst example of Kavillian cuisine she had encountered. The bread roll, after soaking up the juice, was her favourite part.

Chatter bounced up and down the table throughout the meal, mainly concerning an incident involving one of the stable hands and a dung heap.

"Are you married?" Illa leaned across the table, during a lull in conversation.

"No." Arian shook her head.

"Got a lover?"

"Yes. Sort of."

Talk faded around the table, as the others broke off to listen. Someone laughed. "Sort of? Yup, I've been there."

"More than once," another voice added.

"What does he do?" Illa paused. "Or is it she?"

"She." Even after almost four years in Kavilli, saying it to strangers still felt awkward.

"Hey, is that a blush?"

It was. Even the skin dye could not conceal it. More laughter erupted.

Halie was sitting to Arian's right and nudged her with an elbow. "Pay no mind. They're just jealous because nobody wants them."

"Speak for yourself." Sal laughed, while lobbing a squashed up piece of bread roll at Halie.

Thankfully, the table talk veered off into good-natured banter. Arian concentrated on finishing her meal and bracing herself for the climb into bed. Much as she wanted to leave the lodge and get back to Kavilli as soon as possible, she was not up to doing anything that night. Digging up information about the murder could wait.

Halie showed her the latrine in an outbuilding, shared by the servants. The running water under the seats was not enough to fully prevent the smell of ammonia. Afterwards, Arian hauled herself onto one of the upper bunks.

Sleep would not come. She lay awake a long time, staring into the darkness. Competing snores came from different corners of the room. Haystalks stuck out of the thin mattress, scratching the exposed skin on her neck and ankles. Her whole body ached, hands, arms, legs, back. Before, when she was in Breninbury, the work would not have been so taxing, but the years of living like a Kavillian noblewoman had made her soft. How was she going to last through the next few days?

She wanted to get back to her villa with its friendly wolf statue, her own comfy bed, the small private bathhouse, and servants to clean and cook for her. She wanted her choice of wine and cinnamon cakes. Conditions in the servants' bunkhouse were basic. Yet, thinking about it, they were still far cleaner and more comfortable than anything to be found where she grew up, even as a member of the royal household.

The walls of the bunkhouse were plastered with lime cement, rather than horse dung and straw. In winter, the wood-burning, iron stove had a flue to the outside, rather than let smoke seep out through the ceiling. Smoke could not get out that way anyhow, since the roof was made of pottery tiles, not leaky grass sod. The floor was granite flagstones. There was running water to hand. A latrine that did not need to be dug out each night. Clean smelling lamp oil. Foodstuff from all over the empire. And a room full of people who did not care whether her lover was a man or a woman.

How could she ever go back?

The gate between the service section of the lodge and the stable yard was unbarred. Arian pushed it open and stepped through. The chickens were lying in wait. They came charging from all directions. Being the centre of attention for the ravenous horde was faintly unnerving. However, apart from a few inadvertent collisions with her ankles, they came to a halt in an impatient mob around her feet, scrambling over one another, clucking, squawking, and flapping.

One white hen tried experimentally pecking Arian's shoelaces. She shunted it aside with her toe and reached into the bucket. The contents were mostly kitchen scraps, the vegetable peelings and burnt bits nobody had wanted at breakfast.

Feeding poultry was one task Arian felt quite confident in her ability to perform. As a child she had often been charged with tending to the flock of ducks, geese, and hens. Arian cast the scraps in an arc, aiming for as wide a dispersal as possible. Thankfully, her arms were feeling better after a night's rest. She could only pray today's work would be less strenuous.

The hens scrambled over each other in a desperate battle, clucking continuously. A lucky bantam ran away with an unbroken length of apple peel fluttering from its beak like a war banner, chased by two others.

Soft laugher came from behind Arian. She checked over her shoulder. One of the stable hands was close by and had stopped brushing a horse to watch the show. He was a young man, in his mid-twenties or so, with a lean, rangy build, and a good-natured expression.

Carefully, so as not to step on any birds, Arian shuffled closer. "Good morning. I'm Ana. I arrived here yesterday."

The man gave a nod. "I heard they'd sent someone, after Marcella got snitty about being short-staffed. I'm Hal."

"Nice to meet you." She tossed out another handful of scraps.

"Likewise."

Arian had spent breakfast thinking up various creative ways to get people talking. She need not have bothered. Hal did the job for her.

"Did you hear about the murder we had here a month back?"

Is there anyone in Kavilli who hasn't? "Were you here when it happened?"

"Yup. I was the driver on Lady Cassilania's carriage. I brought her and two of the guests up here." He paused, scowling. "It's awful the way she got stitched up for the murder. She didn't do it, you know."

"That's what the others told me." Arian scattered more food for the chickens. "Who do you think it was?"

"That old cow Lilliana. We all know it was her. She and the doyenne always hated each other. It goes back to them being sisters, once upon a time."

As if sisterhood was something you could change at will. "So come on, tell me what really happened."

"Phww." Hal blew out his cheeks. "Well, I didn't see much. Like I said, I drove Lady Cassilania's carriage up from the city with a pair of guests. Got here midafternoon. The doyenne had something fancy planned for them. You could tell from the way they were shitting themselves as they went in. Jak had already brought up a couple of others, and they were doing no better."

"Any idea what was going on?"

"Nah. Politics stuff. The old doyenne was always having fun with the other families in the Senate. Anyway, it was crap weather that day, so I was getting the horses under cover, when another carriage showed up. That was Lilliana and her friend."

"The one who's just become principal magistrate?" Arian tossed more scraps to the chickens.

"Yup. That bitch. They weren't supposed to be here. Marcella got in a right old state. Lilliana swanned through like she owned the place, and Marcella had to chase after her."

"What about the friend, the new magistrate?"

"She tagged along at the end."

Arian emptied the final few scraps. "I guess that was the last you saw."

"Are you kidding?" Hal grinned. "We weren't going to miss watching Marcella flap around, squawking like one of your chickens. After they'd all gone inside, me and Jak snuck up the steps to the foyer and peeked in."

"So what happened next?"

"To be honest, not a lot. Lilliana barged into the salon, with Marcella on her heels. The magistrate dawdled around the garden, sniffing the roses. Cocky bitch. They weren't her roses."

"She didn't go into Marcella's office to drop off her cloak, or anything like that?"

Hal frowned. "No. Why do you ask?"

"No reason." Arian shrugged. "I'd just heard she's really nosy and likes poking into things that don't concern her."

He shook his head. "Nah. Apart from anything else, she'd left her cloak in the carriage. After she'd finished with the roses she went into the salon as well. Then Marcella came back and told me and Jak to clear off." Hal sighed. "So I carried on seeing to the horses. Everything was quiet, must have been for well over an hour. Then that prat who's in charge of the Senate came out, swearing like a drunk sailor and threatening all sorts if me and Jak didn't drive him back to town. But we had our orders, so we told him to go speak to the doyenne. You could see he was scared shitless of her, but he went off in the end. Next thing, Lord Xeranius came racing out, and he says he needs the fastest hor—"

"You aren't paid to gossip. Get back to work. Both of you." Marcella's strident voice. The housekeeper was standing in the gateway behind them, hands on hips.

"Yes, ma'am." Arian made haste to return to the kitchen, but Marcella grabbed her arm as she sidled past.

"Decima asked you to clean the floor of the dairy last night." Was that a question or a statement?

"Yes, ma'am. She did."

"I've just looked in there. It's filthy. Were you gossiping then as well, rather than working?"

"No, ma'am, I di—"

"Go wash it again. And do a proper job this time."

"Yes, ma'am." Arian scuttled back to the kitchen yard.

How much vinegar was the right amount? Was there any way she could ask someone, without wrecking her charade of being a housemaid? With hindsight, she should have done more research before leaving Kavilli. Laelia could have given a few worthwhile tips.

On the positive side, she had made progress gathering information, even if it was not what she had hoped for. Vessia could not have taken the brooch from Cassie's cloak.

❖

The muscles in Arian's back and arms were screaming a complaint. Her knees were on fire and her fingers rubbed raw. The bottom half of her dress was soaked. The material clung to her legs, cold and wet, turning movement into a battle. Several times already she had taken a tumble. The only blessing being, since she was kneeling, she did not have far to fall.

Marcella had clearly decided floors were her speciality. After finishing mopping the dairy, Arian was now scrubbing the one in the kitchen. Once more, she dunked the brush in the bucket. The vinegar stung where her skin was chafed, but at least the concentration was now right.

Illa was peeling vegetables. She smiled down at Arian, sympathetically. "How are you doing?"

Arian grimaced in reply.

"Have you heard the news?"

"What news?" Arian continued scrubbing the floor.

"Doyen Xeranius is coming here tomorrow. It'll be the first time since he took over."

"Tomorrow?" *Damn.* What chance she could stay out of sight? Xeranius would surely recognise her, even with the dye. Or had Bran forewarned him?

"Yes. Maybe we'll find out his plans for the lodge. I don't suppose he'll want to live here, like Doyenne Pellonia did."

"It's a sodding joke." Halie slammed a ball of dough onto the counter and thumped it with both fists. "Lady Cassilania should have been doyenne. Everybody knows it. She's the only one who can hold a candle to her mother."

"They can't vote her in as doyenne when she's in jail, and about to be executed," Illa said.

"Do you think I don't bloody-well know that?" Halie punched the dough more forcefully than before, venting her anger on today's dinner. "It's not right the bastards are going to burn her."

This time, Arian's grimace had nothing to do with the pain in her arms and legs.

Decima gave Halie a strained look, but then spoke to Sal, the youngest of her assistants. "I need help turning the cheese in the store. Put down what you're doing and come with me."

Nothing more was said until the pair had left the kitchen.

Illa broke the silence. "Come on, Halie. You shouldn't say things like that about Lady Cassilania with Decima around. You know how it sets her off."

"I just said she ought to be doyenne. It was you who brought up the execution."

"Is Decima upset really about Cas…" Arian caught herself. "Lady Cassilania?"

"We all are," Illa said. "But she takes it more to heart. Decima was her wet nurse, back when Lady Cassilania was a baby. She's always had a soft spot for her. Well, you would, wouldn't you? The poor thing couldn't stop sobbing for days after the trial."

Arian moved on to the next patch of floor. If she and Bran failed to save Cassie, she now knew where she could find a sympathetic shoulder to cry on.

"Everyone's upset and angry about how the trial went. And Marcella being a complete pain in the arse ever since doesn't help." Halie continued violently kneading the dough.

Arian dropped the brush in the bucket and sat back on her heels to give her arms a rest. "You mean she used to be cute, sweet, and lovable?"

"No."

"She was born crabby," Illa said. "But she's getting worse. Maybe she blames herself, because she spoke at the trial, but that's no reason to take it out on us."

Halie picked up the dough and slammed it down on the countertop, making the whole table shake. "Even so, it's not her fault. It's whatever prat picked the witnesses. It should have been me at the trial. I'd have told them it wasn't Lady Cassilania who murdered her mother."

"What could you have said?"

"Lots." Halie stopped assaulting the dough. She leaned forward, resting her elbows on the countertop. "On the day of the murder, I was helping Marcella."

"You were with her the whole time?"

"Mostly. She sent me to the stores for a mop to wipe muddy footprints. Another time she wanted hot milk. Lord Xeranius…"

Halie pouted. "Doyen Xeranius, as he is now. He sent me to the kitchen with a message about more wine for the salon. But that was it. The rest of the time I was with her, except she was in her office, and I was outside in the foyer."

"Did you see something?"

"It's what I didn't see. I didn't see Lady Cassilania go up the stairs."

"Except for at the end, when she found the body?" Arian suggested.

"To be honest. I didn't see her go up then. Loudmouth Tribonus was out in the stable yard, shouting himself red in the face. I was watching him instead. But it doesn't matter, because the doyenne was already dead by then, and had been for a while. Well, that's what we found out later." Halie twisted off a knob of dough, then slapped it back on the main lump. "But I heard they tried to make out she'd snuck up to the study after leaving the loopy old woman crying in the guest room. But she didn't. Lady Cassilania came out and went straight back to join the others. I saw her. And that was the only time she left the salon."

"Any of us who were there can confirm that bit." Illa said. "I told you I was serving wine to the guests, didn't I?"

"Yes. You mentioned it yesterday." Arian hesitated. Actively interrogating them would be a mistake, but this was the perfect opportunity. Both were eager to talk, and surely a genuine housemaid would want to hear all the gruesome details. "Do you know anything else?"

"You won't believe it." Halie leaned forward again.

I probably would.

"Two of the men came into the courtyard to have an argument. You'll never guess what it was about." Halie's voice dropped to a stage whisper.

"What?"

"One of them murdered his wife, forged her will, and got the other to cover for him. And that one had already done the same thing, only it was his grandfather he bumped off to get his money. They were both threatening to drop the other in the shit."

"Wow." Arian tried to look suitably surprised. "You heard them? Didn't they see you?"

"I was hiding behind a pillar, but I had a clear view of the courtyard. It was while I was listening to them I saw Lady Cassilania leave the old biddy in the guest bedroom. She went straight back to the salon. She never went upstairs."

"How about those two men? They'd already murdered their relatives. Could they have killed the doyenne as well?" Arian asked.

"No." Halie shook her head. "After they finished threatening each other they went back to the salon."

"And the old woman? What about her?"

"Juliana." Illa provided the name. "She's doyenne of the Nerinae family. The gods alone know why they picked her."

"Did she go upstairs to see Doyenne Pellonia?" Arian asked.

"No." Halie looked scornful. "She was still sobbing in the guest room when Lord Xeranius came looking for her. I don't know what upset her. He sent me off with the message about wine. When I came out of the kitchen he was with her at the water trough, helping her wash her face."

"So who did go up the stairs?"

"That's just it. Nobody. I was there. I'd have seen them." Halie picked up the dough once more and thumped it onto the counter.

"Someone had to. Someone murdered Doyenne Pellonia." How to make sense of it?

"What Halie means, is that none of the visitors went up the stairs except for queen bitch Lilliana," Illa said. "She's the only person who could have done it."

All of which proved…what? "You said Marcella sent you on a couple of errands. Couldn't someone have snuck up while you were away?" Arian asked Halie.

She shook her head. "Marcella came back from the salon after the fuss about Lilliana turning up. That's when she saw the muddy footprints and sent me to get the mop to clean it up. But that was when everyone was still in the salon." Halie shrugged. "I took the mop to the workshop after I finished. By then the doyenne and

Lilliana had gone up to the study, but I was back before the old bitch came down again."

"How about when Marcella sent you for the hot milk?"

"I was away for longer that time, but that was after everyone had gone back to the salon, including the one who'd been crying in the guest room."

Illa nodded. "And nobody left the salon again until Primus Tribonus went off to swear at Hal and Jak."

"And the thing about asking for more wine?"

"Lord Xeranius came out of the salon and asked me if I knew where what's-her-name was. I told him she was in the guest room. Marcella shot out of her office as soon as she heard his voice. He's always been her favourite. He said about the wine, so she sent me off with the message while they talked. There's no way Doyenne Waterworks could have snuck up the stairs with them both standing in the foyer. And by the time I left the kitchen, he'd already dragged her out of the room and had her washing her face at the pump."

Nothing added up. "You were in the foyer when Lilliana and Vessia arrived."

"Yes."

"When Marcella chased after Lilliana, you stayed behind."

"Yes."

"And Vessia didn't go near Marcella's office?"

"No. Why do you want—" Halie's expression changed abruptly. She snatched up the lump of dough.

Arian had a sudden awareness of something moving behind her, then pain erupted in her ear and the world jolted sideways. She ended up sprawled on the wet floor.

"I've warned you about gossiping when you should be working." Marcella loomed over her. "This is your last chance. Get on with your work." She glared at the other two women. "And the same goes for you." She turned and stomped out.

Halie slapped the dough down again. "Yup. She's definitely got the arseache over something."

"Sorry," Illa said. "I should have spotted her coming."

Arian got back to her knees. Her ear throbbed in waves, running around the side of her face. "That's all right. I think I'd already blown my chance of becoming her favourite person."

"We all have. I don't know what's up with her, but she's getting worse. I mean, she was never the friendly, chatty sort, but you always felt she was on your side, but now…" Illa frowned. "Something's got under her skin."

Arian picked up the scrubbing brush, about to dunk it back in the water, but stopped. The skin on her hands was lighter. The vinegar was removing the dye. Before long, maybe before the day was out, somebody was sure to notice. She was running out of time to question the staff.

Another floor, this time in the foyer. Fortunately, it only required sweeping rather than washing. Arian used the end of the broom to dig a wad of dead leaves from the corner at the back wall. They joined others in a neat heap as she continued methodically working her way around the edge. All the while, her thoughts churned.

Who else did she need to talk to? From what she had discovered so far, it appeared impossible for anyone to commit the murder. All the servants were convinced Lilliana was guilty. Was there any chance they could be right? Somewhere, somehow, a clue was missing. But what, and how to unearth it?

As she approached the housekeeper's office, the door opened. Marcella stepped out, then stopped, glaring at Arian and the pile of leaves. She was clearly looking for something to criticise but had to settle for a disapproving "Humph" before marching away. The beat of her footsteps faded.

Arian hesitated. Was it worth checking the office? Just how hard would it have been to take the brooch from Cassie's cloak? Could the murderer have done it without Marcella noticing? It was definitely worth finding out. Ears peeled for the sounds of Marcella's return, Arian turned the handle and opened the door.

The room was smaller than expected. A desk took up a quarter of the floor space. Above it, a window gave a view into the stable yard so the housekeeper could see who was arriving at the lodge. Bookshelves filled with ledgers lined the walls apart from at the back, where a double row of hooks fanned out on either side of a log-burning stove. In summer, the fire was unlit, but presumably that was where the cloaks had hung to dry.

Anyone sitting at the desk would have their back to the door, but given the size of the room, sneaking by would be impossible, unless Marcella was asleep. Even then, the murderer would be taking a chance, and Marcella was surely not the sort of woman to doze on the job.

A growl made Arian jump. In the dimly lit corner, a bundle of fur raised its head. Why had nobody warned her Marcella kept a dog? It was a small terrier, of the yapping sort. Arian quickly closed the door, muffling the irate "rah-rah, rah-rah-rah," and carried on sweeping.

❖

The latrine stunk of ammonia and rotten eggs. Men's aim was notoriously poor, something that was as true in the Kavillian empire as it had been back in Breninbury. Arian set down her mop and bucket just inside the doorway. Already, her eyes were starting to water.

No. Just no.

This went far beyond what she had agreed with Bran. She sent the bucketful of vinegar solution cascading over the floor and stepped back into the fresh air.

In daylight, the fading dye on her hands was unmistakable. She could not stay at the lodge another night, especially with Xeranius visiting tomorrow. The sensible option was to grab her bag and leave immediately. Or was it worth making one last attempt to dig for answers? Because answers were in desperately short supply.

Nothing made sense. Two witnesses asserted Vessia had not gone into the housekeeper's office, which meant she could not have taken the brooch from Cassie's cloak. Between Marcella's testimony at the trial, and what Halie added, it was impossible to see how anyone else could have done it either, especially with the dog there. And even after taking the brooch, nobody could have climbed the stairs without being seen.

Which added up to...something.

Arian pinched the bridge of her nose. Maybe if she saw the scene of the crime, she would be able to think of a fresh angle, a new insight to make everything fall into place.

The noon bell rang out as a drizzle of rain began falling, driven by gusts of wind, Lunch was not taken in the bunkhouse. Servants had a simple meal of bread, cheese and dried fruit at their workplace, and with the rain, nobody would be sitting outside to eat. This might not be the perfect opportunity to investigate Pellonia's study, but it was the best she was going to get in the time available.

Arian hid the bucket and mop behind a stack of barrels and crept to the end of the passage. The area around the water trough was empty. All the doors opening onto the service yard were closed. She tiptoed across the cobblestones and through the arch to the garden courtyard.

The creak of the wooden stairs and the patter of rain were the only sounds as Arian reached the veranda. Then voices echoed in the passageway, getting louder. Arian eased open the nearest door and slipped inside.

Light from a casement window revealed a large desk in the middle of the room. Other furniture consisted of a set of chairs, bookcases, a chest of drawers, and two large cupboards. She was in luck. This had to be the study, the scene of the murder.

Evidence of Vessia's search was all around. Locked drawers and cupboard doors had been forced open, splintering the wood. The wall beneath the window was a gaping hole that had once been a secret compartment. Pellonia's strongbox was still there, bolted to the wall behind. Arian could not help smiling at the layer of ash inside, imagining Vessia's face when she opened the lid.

A bittersweet smile. That ash might once have bought Cassie's freedom.

Arian took a seat at the desk and tried to imagine herself in Pellonia's shoes—the conflict with her sister, the frightened visitors downstairs, the victory in her grasp, the decades of intrigue and blackmail, power plays and extortion. It did not help.

The door was directly in front of the desk. No one could have entered without Pellonia seeing. Climbing through the window or down the chimney was out of the question. Quite apart from the difficulty, both would create far too much noise to go unnoticed.

Yet someone had come there with murder in mind, and Pellonia had not raised the alarm. She had let the killer stand behind her, without looking back. She had not seen the knife poised beside her head. And this was a woman for whom the concept of unqualified trust existed only as a cute fantasy for the simpleminded.

Arian leaned back in the chair. She was missing something. Something important. Could there be another way into the room? A secret passage?

The walls were lumpy white plaster, divided into panels by wooden struts. The timber looked like branches cut from trees and used without any further input from a carpenter. It was a rough and ready style, repeated throughout the lodge.

Arian rapped her knuckles along the wall behind the desk. The second to last panel sounded different, higher pitched, with the hint of an echo. Was she imagining it? A closer look at the struts on both sides revealed gaps, barely big enough to squeeze a fingernail in. Yet the panel would not move when she pushed. Perhaps there was a catch or release mechan—

"What do you think you're doing?"

Arian slowly turned around. Marcella stood in the doorway.

"I um…" What could she say? "I heard so much about the murder, I just had to see wh—" Playing the idiot was the best idea that came to mind.

"Are you insane?"

Quite possibly.

Marcella advanced into the room. "That's it. You've had your chance. Get your stuff and go."

"Where?"

"I don't care."

"Can I get a ride into town?"

"You're joking." Marcella was now close enough to grab Arian's shoulder and drag her from the study.

The rain started coming down in earnest as Arian set off on the ten-mile walk back to Kavilli, carrying her small bag of belongings. Fortunately, it was downhill all the way, and if she was right about the secret passage, the hike was worth it. Plus, all things considered, it was still preferable to scrubbing the latrine floor.

CASSIE

"Your lunch is here." Orthias's tone implied he wished she would choke on it. He was by far the least friendly of the warders.

The woman bringing the basket was familiar, although not an ordinary housemaid. Cassie recognised her as Rufina, one of Bran's favourite agents. She was, presumably, playing the role in order to pass on a message, but the timing was unfortunate. Another warder on duty would have been preferable.

At the other side of the room, Orthias leaned against the wall, arms crossed, showing no sign of leaving them alone. His combative manner was an attempt at intimidation, rather than due to recognising Rufina. He was the same with genuine housemaids. The other two warders would not have hung around.

"I hope you've brought something tasty." Cassie took a seat at the table, positioning her chair so Rufina would have her back to Orthias while laying out the contents of the basket.

"The cook has made a special effort for you, my lady." Rufina then dropped her voice to a whisper, while sliding a plate across the table to mask the sound. "Master Branius has followed up on a couple of leads from his notes." A degree of lip reading was required.

"Did he have much trouble finding the ingredients?" Cassie spoke at a normal level.

Orthias gave a snort of contempt and finally went, although leaving the door open behind him. He was possibly still loitering outside, but Rufina could safely raise her voice a little.

"The trial of Lord Galvinius was short on evidence, but Magistra Vessia found him guilty regardless, and sentenced him to permanent exile. Doyenne Lilliana was unhappy with the result, but she was out-bribed."

"Really." How interesting.

Cassie had known Galvinius was Lilliana's second cousin, but not that Vessia was the judge. His trial for sedition had taken place five years ago, in one of the outlying provinces—obviously Basalonia. News reaching Kavilli had created a minor stir at the time, and then been forgotten. The general assumption was Lilliana herself had arranged for the verdict, as part of an internal family dispute. Apparently, this was not the case.

"Has Bran found out who did bribe Vessia?"

"That's what he's been hunting down. The clues point to Primus Tribonus, although he wasn't leader of the Senate back then."

"Thank you." It was definitely information she could work with. Vessia had taken a huge risk, and Tribonus was playing well above his league. "There must be something major behind it."

Rufina nodded. "That's what Master Branius thinks. He's still digging. But it's not easy now the original papers are gone."

"Please, thank him for me."

"Yes, my lady. Will that be all?"

"How is Arian? Has Bran kept her out of trouble?"

"He's done his best. She's up at the lodge at the moment, in disguise."

"She's what!" Cassie's voice was louder than she intended.

Sounds of movement came from outside the cell.

Rufina glanced toward the door and back. Her voice returned to a hushed whisper. "He thought she would be safer there, rather than leaving her to poke around on her own at the Konithae mansion. Which is what she was going to do otherwise. It was the only way he could think of to get her out of harm's way for a while."

"But what's she doing, and why the disguise?"

"Master Branius asked her to question the servants and find out what they knew." Rufina gave a small shrug. "Who knows, she might even discover something of use."

Did Bran have a valid point? Just what sort of disguise? How long was Arian gone for? Who else knew? There were too many questions she could not ask. It needed more time and privacy than could be worked into a meal delivery, especially since Orthias picked that moment to return.

"Tell the cook the broth is not up to his usual standard. Maybe he can add more seasoning to dinner." Cassie pulled at the neck of her gown. "And this needs washing. Could the maid who comes with my evening meal also bring a change of clothes?"

"Yes, my lady. I'll pass on the request." Rufina bobbed a curtsy before going.

Alone again in her cell, Cassie tried to muster enthusiasm for the food, but her stomach had turned to lead. Exactly what was going on with Arian? Answers would have to wait until Rufina returned that evening with dinner. Fortunately, Orthias was not due on duty then, and neither of the other warders would be so crass as to insist on standing watch while she changed clothes.

Cassie was sitting by the window, attempting to read, though the daylight was fading fast. Dinner was late. She lit a lamp using the tinderbox, but rather than continue with the story, her eyes drifted to the city skyline. The rain had tailed off and ragged gaps appeared in the clouds.

The key sounded in the lock. "The maid's here with your dinner."

She glanced around as Marcus ushered in a housemaid carrying two baskets. The woman was not Rufina or anyone else Cassie recognised in the lamplight. Was this another of Bran's agents, or was something else going on? Regardless, hopefully answers would be forthcoming.

"You can leave the food on the desk. I'll eat it later. But I believe you've brought clean clothes for me." She slid her book back into its leather cover.

"Yes, my lady. And I was told I had to collect your laundry to be washed." The voice was a different matter. The flutter in

Cassie's stomach had nothing to do with the baby growing inside her.

"That will be good." She nodded but kept her eyes averted, waiting until she heard the door close before adding. "I prefer you blond." She put the book down and turned around. "I heard you were at the lodge in disguise, but I had no details. What were you doing there? Were you..." *Safe.* Just how angry did she need to be with Bran?

"I was pretending to be a housemaid."

"Did things go all right? Were you recognised?"

"No. And it was mixed." Arian took a halting step towards the bed. "I need to sit down. I've just walked all the way from the lodge."

"You walked? Why?"

"Marcella kicked me out." Arian collapsed on the bed with a groan.

"She did? What did you do?"

"I spent too much time talking, and I didn't get the floors clean enough. Bran thinks it's funny I lasted less than a day working as a housemaid."

"You've spoken to him since you got back?"

"For about ten seconds. I got to the mansion just as your dinner was ready to go." Arian swivelled into a sitting position on the side of the bed. "I thought I might as well benefit from the disguise before I washed it off."

"I wish..." *Things were different.* Which was too banal to be worth saying. But Arian was safe, and if Marcella had dismissed her because of dirty floors it was obvious nobody had seen through the disguise. Cassie sat beside her on the bed. "I'm pleased you're here."

Arian smiled. "Do you think I'd miss the chance to see you take your clothes off?"

"Not fair."

"I'd offer to do the same. But it would be hard to explain if the warder comes back."

"True." Or was it worth the risk, to lie naked in Arian's arms one last time? She settled for a slow, passionate kiss, before forcing her thoughts down another, safer, route. "Did you learn anything at the lodge?"

"Yes. All the servants are very upset about the verdict."

"I'm not thrilled myself. Anything else?"

"I think there's a secret entrance to the study. It's the only—"

"It's not a secret."

"You know about it?"

"Yes. It's how Bran got back in, even though Vessia had posted a guard outside the door. The other end of the passage comes out in a cow barn below the lodge. Mother used it when she wanted to talk to folk who couldn't visit her openly."

"Could the murderer have got in that way?"

"No. It's normally locked from inside the study. Except Bran had the foresight to release the bolt mechanism while everyone was milling aimlessly around Mother's body." She peered at Arian in the lamp light. "Is that a bruise on the side of your face?"

"Yes. Don't ask."

"You've been hurt." Maybe Bran did have something to answer for, after all.

"It's nothing. Honestly." Arian took Cassie's hand and squeezed it. "All right. Apart from the not-so-secret passage, two independent witnesses told me Vessia couldn't have taken your brooch. She never went in the housekeeper's office. Nor did anyone else. And Marcella has a yapping dog in there."

"Ah." The arithmetic did not look good for Marcella. Who else could have taken the brooch? "Anything else?"

"Yes. One of the housemaids, named Halie, was assigned to help Marcella. She was in the foyer virtually the whole time. She says nobody used the stairs, between Lilliana coming down and you going up."

"I didn't see her in the foyer."

"She was hiding behind a column."

"Hiding? Why?"

"She was listening to Bellorion and Ellonius having an argument."

"Did she hear anything interesting?"

"Some would say so." Arian gave a wry smile. "One of them murdered his wife."

"Yes, Bellorion. I mentioned it to you before."

"And the other murdered his grandfather."

"That's a new one." But unfortunately, not very helpful.

"Wasn't your mother bothered about inviting murderers into her home?"

"As long as you take sensible precautions, they're the easiest people to deal with. It's the virtuous, honest ones who give the most trouble. They're the ones who'll charge straight ahead, doing the right thing and not care whether they personally end up better or worse off. Honest people are so hard to control. People like you."

"I'm not that virtuous, or brave."

She was wrong, but why argue? Before meeting Arian, integrity and a refusal to compromise had seemed like weaknesses that could only betray anyone afflicted with them. Now, at least in Arian's case, the qualities seemed endearing, formidable, and nerve-racking in equal parts. "Anyway, as soon as someone shows they're willing to bend the rules to suit themselves you know you can make them do whatever you want if you push hard enough in the right spot."

"Does that apply to you as well?"

"Of course."

Arian frowned but did not pursue the issue.

Cassie continued. "But going back to this housemaid, she said she was watching the stairs the whole time?"

"Not entirely. She was sent on a few errands, but only when everyone was accounted for. Except..." Arian wrinkled her nose in thought. "My guess is she wouldn't have been concentrating the whole time. After all, she was listening to two men talking about murdering their relatives. Who's going to be paying attention to a staircase with that going on?" Arian shrugged. "For what it's worth, Halie was adamant you went straight back to the salon after you'd finished talking to Juliana."

"She probably kept a close eye on Bellorion and Ellonius as well, after they finished their chat, just to see if they'd murder each other. Did she say anything about what Juliana did after I left her?"

"She stayed sobbing in the guest bedroom until Xeranius dragged her out and took her to wash her face. That was one of the times when Halie was away on an errand, but only after Marcella had come out of her office to talk to Xeranius. Juliana couldn't have dashed up the stairs and back without being seen."

"So what does all this add up to?"

Arian ran a hand through her dark brown hair. The colour was not looking any less strange on her. "I was thinking about it all the way back from the lodge, and there's only one solution I can come up with. Marcella murdered your mother."

Cassie sighed. It was the obvious conclusion.

Arian continued. "She's the only one who could have taken the brooch from your cloak. With her yapping dog in the office, nobody else could sneak in unheard. There's no other possibility. When things calmed down and everyone was back in the salon, Marcella sent Halie to the kitchen to fetch a drink of warm milk. Obviously, Halie had to wait for the milk to heat up. This gave Marcella plenty of time to visit the study."

"Mother trusted her." As much as she had trusted anyone.

"Which is another point towards her. How many people would your mother have been willing to let stand that close behind her back?"

"A few." But not many. Certainly not Lilliana or Vessia.

"Also, everyone kept going on about how much Marcella has changed since the murder. Something's upset her. It could be a guilty conscience. She was like the bitch from hell with me."

"Was she the one who gave you that bruise?"

"Yes."

"And she chucked you out of the lodge and made you walk back to Kavilli?"

"Yes."

Things were not looking good for Marcella. "Bran needs to talk to her. Discuss it with him when you get back to the mansion. He can arrange for her to come down to Kavilli."

"If we get a confession from her, they'll have to reverse the verdict."

Cassie shook her head. "It won't be that simple. Shunting me out of the way is just too big a win for our rivals. They'd try to bury the story."

"The truth would come out in the end."

"The end might be a long way off. I'm not interested in a posthumous pardon. But…"

"But?"

"I'm working on a plan. It's still vague, but I'm hoping to get my sentence commuted to exile. If I can do that, we'll have as long as we need."

"Then a confession would help."

"It won't do any harm."

There was more to say, but time was not on their side. Soon, Marcus would want to know what was going on. Cassie stood and began to loosen the ties on her dress. "I guess I better swap over my clothes. Assuming you really have brought fresh ones."

"Bran had them ready. He said they might not be your nicest, but the maid who selected them went for those with a fuller waist."

Which was going to be needed. The baby was showing.

Arian levered herself off the bed and came close. "I'll help you change."

"Are you sure that's not just for the chance to get your hands on me?"

"Maybe."

Arian's arms slipped around her waist, pulling her close. Their lips met in a kiss. The touch was at the same time so familiar, and yet so surprising. How would she ever reconcile all the contradictions Arian inspired in her?

Finally, she pulled back and stared into Arian's mesmerising green eyes. "Have you ever seriously wondered whether I really did kill my mother?"

"No. As I said before, it wouldn't make a difference to me."

Maybe not now, but it would in the end.

Cassie peeled Arian's arms away. "Sit down. You're not speeding things up at all."

Arian plonked herself on the side of the bed again, with the demeanour for a petulant schoolgirl. "Do you want me to close my eyes as well?"

"No. Peek all you want."

❖

Working together, Marcus and Orthias tilted the footlocker up on its edge, so they could check the underside for concealed objects. Needless to say, they found nothing. The resounding thump, as they dropped it back down, was enough to raise a row of tiny dust fountains from between the floorboards.

Cassie watched from her out-of-the-way position in a corner, trying not to let her amusement show. The iron-bound, solid oak footlocker probably weighed as much as she did, which raised the question of how they thought she might have been able to hide anything under it in the first place. Even without being pregnant, there was no way she would be able to lift it on her own.

As the one-month anniversary of her imprisonment drew near, the warders were clearly confused. They knew she was up to something, and they were right. But would it ever occur to them the something might be a case of doing nothing, just to worry them? This was the third time her room had been searched in the space of five days. Each time, the scope of the search was expanded. Even her regular examinations by the midwives were getting noticeably more intimate.

With the fruitless search over, Orthias stomped out, scowling as though he had been personally insulted.

Marcus managed a strained grimace, masquerading as a smile. "That's it. You can go back to what you were doing." As though the room search might have interrupted her in the middle of an important task.

"Thank you."

In fact, she had only just woken up. The dawn search was undoubtedly intended to catch her off guard. The warders were getting increasingly suspicious. Was it time to move forward, or should she let them stew a few days more?

Arian's visit yesterday evening, even with the brown hair, had been an unexpected blessing, and they were a huge step forward in identifying the murderer. Even if Marcella had not struck the blow, she was in league with the person who did. Best of all, there was no risk of Arian playing at being a spy in the Konithae mansion, unless Bran's interview with Marcella took a completely unexpected turn.

Cassie stared vacantly out the window, mulling things over. While searching her cell, Marcus had looked so confused, so concerned, so sure he was missing something. But then, he was handicapped by not having the first idea about what he ought to look for. The biggest irony was that the items she needed lay in plain sight. Cassie nodded, decision made. It was time to use them.

She took her seat at the table and opened her weapon of choice, the writing case. The letter was short, little more than a note. She folded the paper in a knot, sealed it with wax, and wrote on the outside, *Doyenne Lilliana Tacita con Avitae dom Konithae*, then pulled the bell cord.

Orthias appeared. "What do you want?"

"I'd like to speak with Prefect Marcus."

"Why him?"

"He's the senior warder." Which was true in a strictly factual sense, although not her reason for choosing him.

Orthias grunted and left, to be replaced by Marcus. "You wanted to see me?"

"Yes. I need you to do something for me. I promise you'll be well rewarded."

"I'm your guard, not your servant."

"I know but…" The acting needed to be right. A touch of hesitancy, a touch of pleading, with just an edge of self-importance. Cassie held out the letter. "You have to see this message gets to Doyenne Lilliana."

The name clearly caught Marcus by surprise. He stared at the folded paper in his hand, as if waiting for it to burst into flames. "I don't…"

"It must go to her, and no one else. Here—" Cassie slipped a silver bracelet off her wrist. "Take this. You'll receive more. I swear. But you must tell nobody else about this. Not my family. Not others in the prefecture. No one."

"What's it about?" After the confusion at Lilliana's name, Marcus was pulling his wits together.

"I can't say. But please, promise you'll give it to her, for your sake as much as mine." Cassie firmed up her tone, not quite to the level of threat, but one to make him think twice. "Doyenne Lilliana is not someone to cross. You..." A pause to add sincerity. "You don't want her as an enemy."

Marcus drew a breath, as if about to speak, but settled for a sharp nod. He left the cell taking both the note and the bracelet.

Of course, the letter would never reach Lilliana. There was no doubt about where Marcus's loyalties lay. He would already be on his way to Vessia, probably at a run. When she opened the letter— of which again there was no doubt—she would find a message written in code, although not one complex enough to cause her excessive difficulty. Within a day or two Vessia would be able to read:

I got your message the day after the trial but haven't heard from you since. I trust you aren't thinking of forgetting our deal. You know she is a liability, and I know you want to see your cousin again. I can arrange for you to get the evidence you need. We both stand to gain by working together.

Cassie smiled. The game had begun in earnest. And good riddance to the ugly bracelet. She had never liked it.

ARIAN

A rian held out both arms in front of her, then examined her legs and feet. She checked her face and hair in the polished silver mirror one last time. All traces of the dye were gone. The chafing on her hands was obvious, and would be for a few days more, but was nothing she could not explain away. The story she had invented about visiting a thermal spa in a nearby town provided a ready excuse. The bruise on her face could pass off as an accident, such as slipping in a pool.

She selected a clean dress from her wardrobe and slipped it over her head. The light blue satin caressed her skin, flowing around her. A silver link belt secured it at her waist, while not hindering her freedom of movement. The pleats swished around her ankles as she moved.

The coarse, itchy, homespun clothes she had worn as a housemaid, along with a small bottle of dye, rags, and cleansing powder were tied up in a bundle on the floor. Bran had suggested she keep them, along with a few other items, for when she needed to don a disguise again. Arian dumped them at the back of the wardrobe and closed the door.

She had overslept that morning. Feran would have already left for school. She could check up on Eilwen, assuming she was in the villa and not off with a friend. Or she could make a few social visits of her own. Maybe, by now, people would have found a topic of conversation other than asking how she felt about Cassie's conviction. How did they think she felt? How would anyone feel in her situation?

Sunlight streamed through the open window. Arian selected a thin lace shawl. The day was too warm for anything more. After the miserable rainy spell, summer had returned, even though its peak had passed, and the days were getting shorter. She hesitated over two pins in her jewellery box. Both had a modest design, one with three amber beads, the other with twisted scrollwork. Identical copies of either could be bought in a dozen shops around the city. If only Cassie had worn a similar commonplace item, the prosecution case against her would have been much weaker. But of course not. Because Cassie, and everything about her, was exclusive.

The bedroom door creaked open. Arian turned around, surprised. She had not heard a knock.

Ulfgar stood in the entrance. "Arian. I…I did not know you were back."

So what was he doing in her room? Eilwen had mentioned him sneaking in when she was away. But surely a priest would not steal. "I returned late last night, after dark."

"I thought you intended to stay longer at the spa town."

"I did." Arian held up her red, blotchy hands. Not that it was any of his business. "Unfortunately, the mineral water didn't agree with my skin."

"Right. I…" Ulfgar began to retreat, but then stopped. "Is there any fresh news from Earl Kendric?"

"No."

"You're still determined to stay here, in Kavilli?"

"Yes. And I've nothing more to say on the subject." Not until Feran was safely at the academy.

"I warn you, I'm running out of patience."

"That's your problem."

Ulfgar glared at her in undisguised anger. With each month, he had grown more belligerent in his demands. "I need to sacrifice another bull." His tone made it a challenge, daring her to call him out.

Finally, the picture slid into focus. Why had it taken her so long to see it? *As soon as someone shows they're willing to bend the rules to suit themselves you know you can make them do whatever you want if you push hard enough in the right spot.* Cassie's words from yesterday. Up until now, Ulfgar's status as a priest had prevented her from recognising the obvious truth.

If Ulfgar was truly outraged by her taking a female lover, he would have tried to make her stop, not use it as ammunition for blackmail. And, whatever his real reason for wanting to return home, he was prepared to put it on hold in exchange for money.

Arian shook her head slowly, as if in sorrow. "I'm not sure. The first bull didn't help much."

"You refuse?"

"Yes."

"You don't leave me any choice. I've told you what will happen if you insist on staying in this cesspit of corruption and immoral lusts."

"Yes. You have, repeatedly."

"Yet you persist in your vice."

"As do you."

"I will not..." Ulfgar's voice died, as he registered her words. "You...you." He pulled himself upright. "What do you mean?"

"I mean it's regrettable, when honest people fall for the lure of earthly riches and debase themselves." Regardless of what was going on with Ulfgar, money lay at its heart.

"Are you accusing me?"

"Why? Have you done something I could accuse you of?"

Ulfgar's face said it all, but still he tried to bluster his way out. "I've warned you."

"I shall consider myself duly warned. Now, is there anything else you wish to discuss?"

Ulfgar turned and left without another word.

❖

Arian walked unnoticed through the city streets, wearing a magical necklace of invisibility around her neck, otherwise known as a slave collar. When combined with cheap clothing, it rendered even her yellow hair mundane. She just needed to remember to step out of everyone's way, except for those also wearing collars, who she could jostle aside in the normal fashion.

The directions in Bran's note brought her to an ordinary looking bakery in the affluent part of the city. Counters outside were stacked with flat round loaves. The owner stood at the front, loudly promoting her wares. Her eyes flicked in Arian's direction as she slipped by, but the baker made no move to stop or question her. No doubt, she had been warned Arian would be coming. The sales pitch continued without as much as a pause for breath.

A cobbled yard at the rear of the shop had tables, a donkey-powered millwheel, and a row of ovens. Two journeymen were measuring flour into a vat while a younger apprentice stoked the fire, and a small girl guided the donkey. One of the journeymen looked up when Arian arrived and silently pointed to a door at the far end of the yard. It led to a storeroom, piled high with sacks of grain. Arian squeezed though a narrow walkway between them, until reaching yet another door. Here, she paused, reached up to her neck, and pulled open the hinged halves of the collar.

The fastening rivet was a fake. The difference removing the iron band made to her neck and shoulders was surprising. She twisted her head left and right, easing the cricks. A slave collar was a burden that could not be measured on a weighing scale—but was it any worse than in Breninbury, where slaves captured from enemy tribes were denoted by minimal clothing, downcast eyes, and even branding?

The sound of sliding bolts followed her knock, and a servant opened the door. "Please, follow me."

Their route cut through a maze of yards, staircases, and alleyways. Despite Arian's frequent visits to the Passurae mansion, none of the buildings looked familiar. Only the occasional silver fox emblem confirmed she was actually there, presumably in the service quarters.

Finally, her guide stopped outside a door. "Master Branius is expecting you."

The room she entered was small, lit only by a high, barred window. Bran sat at a table in the middle. He looked up as the door opened and gave a not very welcoming smile. "Have you recovered from working at the lodge yet?"

Arian ignored his emphasis on the word "working." "Yes, thank you." A second chair was pushed against the wall. Arian positioned it a suitable distance from Bran and sat. "When's Marcella due to arrive?"

"She was supposed to get here a while ago."

"I wanted to be here from—"

"Don't get upset. You would have been. I was going to let her stew for a bit in a locked room before we spoke."

"I assume she hasn't shown up."

"Correct."

"Any idea where she might be?"

"No. And I won't mind if you don't want to hang around waiting."

"I'll stay."

"Your choice." His tone made it clear he thought her presence unnecessary, if not an outright handicap.

"I spoke to the people at the lodge. Heard what they knew about who was where and when. If Marcella starts spinning lies, I'll be able to catch her out."

"Are you sure that's why you want to be here?"

"Of course."

"It's not so you can take revenge on her for making you work? A chance to put her in her place?"

"No. I'm just furious with her for helping to frame Cassie."

Judging by Bran's expression he didn't believe her. "No hard feelings on your own account?

"She was unpleasant. But the other housemaids were pissed off with her as well."

"They've lasted longer than a day."

"Only because they haven't been caught snooping around the murder scene, looking for evidence." Arian drew a deep breath, trying to maintain her composure. "Let's be honest with each other.

You accuse me of looking down on you because you were a serf. How about admitting you look down on me because you think I got it easy and had everything handed to me as a gift?"

"You want to argue you didn't? I was a serf. That's a half step up from being a slave. I worked on the farm, doing what I was told, when I was told, else I'd have been flogged as a warning to the others. And we serfs were supposed to be grateful, because in return for slogging our guts out, dawn to dusk, we had the king's warband to protect us." His face flushed with anger. "We both know how that worked out."

"I'm sorry for everything that happened to your family, but it wasn't my fault. There's nothing I could have done."

"Nothing? Yep. That's exactly what you and all the other nobles would have done if I'd escaped from the enemy warband and returned. Would any of you have said, 'Oh, sorry we didn't keep up our side of the bargain. Here's all the food we took from you and your family back. Now go off and do whatever you want.'" Bran scowled at her. "Like fuck you would. Some noble would have claimed me and put me to work on his farm."

"It wasn't..." What could she say?

"I've been lucky. Lucky the enemy had more prisoners than they needed so they sold me on. Lucky Lady Cassilania bought me and wasn't bothered with what I was born as, only with what I could do. Maybe you think I'm a traitor to our people. But do you know why I give my allegiance to the empire? It's because here I get to choose who I am and what I do."

"I didn't choose to be a princess any more than you chose to be a serf."

"It must have been really tough for you." His words oozed sarcasm.

"It was, in some ways."

"You think so?"

"I know so. I lived it."

"You know nothing. There isn't a serf in Lycanthia who wouldn't have swapped places with you in a heartbeat."

The beat of a heart. Arian clamped her jaw shut, fighting for self control.

Bran continued. "Come on, tell me about how hard you had things."

"All right then." Arian turned on him. "Let's talk about our life back there. Did you have a bedfellow?"

"Yes. And she's probably a slave somewhere, if she's still alive. She got captured in the same raid as me."

"Did she make you happy?"

"What's that got to do with anything?"

"When the two of you lay together, muttering stupid, silly things, making love. When you watched her face as she slept beside you. Were you happy?"

Bran shrugged. "Happy enough."

"My children are a result of me getting blind drunk at festivals, so I was on the point of passing out and taking my chance with whichever of the stag dancers picked me." Arian's hands were gripping the table so hard her knuckles were white. She forced them to relax. "I never knew what it was to lie with the lover of my choice, someone I actually wanted in my bed. Someone I loved."

"Are you going to pretend it's the same thing? You couldn't manage a day working like a commoner."

"You've got a wife now, and a son, so I hear. Imagine you had to choose, you could either take them with you, go back home, and become a serf again. Or say goodbye and never see them again. Which would you pick? What's more important to you?"

"You want to make up fairy tale games of what if?"

"Quite right. It is a fairy tale. Because you'll never be stuck in a situation like that. It's never going to happen. You're safe. You've got the lover of your choice. And it's just tough shit for anyone who isn't as fortunate."

Bran opened his mouth to speak but fell silent.

"I didn't sit on my backside all day back in Breninbury. Believe it or not, even the king's sister had to work. But my only real worth lay in having a son to be my brother's heir. You might have been treated like a workhorse. I was a brood mare. I did my duty by him and the tribe." Arian swallowed. "And now? If the only way to save Cassie's life was to sell myself into slavery, I'd do it. In a heartbeat. But that's just another fairy-tale game of what-ifs. I may lose her and there's…" She could not continue.

Tension hung heavy in the room. At last, Bran said, "I still think you're a stuck-up wuss."

"And I think you're a loutish pain in the arse, but we could call a truce?"

"Truce." He pouted, but his anger had faded. "For now."

The following drawn-out silence was broken by distant voices. Arian sniffed and dislodged a tear with her fingertip. "What's happened to Marcella?"

"That's a very good question."

"She can't have got lost."

"No. I'll see if there's any news." Bran went to the door. After a brief conversation with someone outside he returned to his chair. "You won't go back to Lycanthia when your son is older?"

"No." The stark realisation came in a moment of certainty. "No matter what happens, I can't go back to that life. I probably won't be able to anyway."

"Why?"

"Ulfgar, the priest. He's threatening to send a report back about me."

"Saying what?"

"Guess."

Bran looked thoughtful. "Is there a reason for the threats?"

"He wants us to leave Kavilli immediately. He's been on about it for months, but he's getting more and more desperate. There's something going on with him."

"You don't know what it is?"

"I'm worried he's allied with rebels and wants to place Feran in their hands."

"I didn't mean the question that way. I know why he wants to flee."

"Why?"

"He owes a lot of money to men you don't want to mess around with."

"Who does he owe money to?"

"All the bookmakers at the racetrack. Doyenne Pellonia had me check who was running up debts. She was after people whose vote for principal magistrate she could buy. Obviously, your priest doesn't have a vote, but..." Bran shook his head. "He's been a very silly boy. Digging himself in deeper and deeper. Gamblers are like that. They never learn from experience, always sure the next big bet is the one where they'll win everything back. That's his problem. Now he wants to run far away from nasty men who're threatening to break his legs." Bran laughed. "Tell me, have you noticed things going missing? Things that are easy to pick up and sell?"

"You think he's been stealing from me?"

"I'd be amazed if he hasn't."

"Priest aren't supposed..." Arian sighed. Eilwen had been right.

"To steal? They aren't supposed to gamble on horses either. But he has. I'd guess he's stolen enough for a few down payments on his debt. Though more likely he blew it on his next gamble. Either way, he's too far in to dig himself out. Running away is his only option."

Arian slumped in her chair.

"What are you thinking?" Bran asked.

"Cassie said honest people are hardest to handle, because they'll do whatever's right even if they lose out by it. But once someone starts putting themselves above the rules, you can push them into doing whatever you want."

"I won't argue with that."

"I assumed Ulfgar was virtuous because he was a servant of the gods. Which was silly, given how he'd already taken money from me. But if I know he's dishonest, I just need to work out what matters to him."

"I think not getting his legs broken comes quite high on his list."

Arian frowned. "I was worried he's in league with rebels who want Feran dead so they can make his cousin king."

"Is the cousin going along with this?"

"He's only four. I doubt he has much of an opinion. Except he won't be happy at being kidnapped and held hostage." Arian glanced at Bran, meeting his eyes. "Sometimes royalty have fewer options than you'd imagine."

"What are you doing about it?"

"I've arranged for Feran to go to the military academy." Getting Lilliana's support was one success she had achieved over the previous month. "It's something he's been nagging me about, ever since his friends went. I thought he'd be safe, surrounded by the Kavillian army."

"Does Ulfgar know what you're planning?"

"No. I haven't told anybody. I want Feran gone before Ulfgar has a chance to react. I discussed the possibility with his bodyguards, to get their opinions, but they don't know I've gone ahead with it. They thought it was a good idea for him, and they'd be able to find other work without a problem."

"As long as they're together, they'll be happy."

"Are you sure?"

"Of course. They're lovers. Didn't you know?"

"What?"

"You're not the only one making the most of the freedom Kavilli can offer. Although they've been more discreet about it than you." He shrugged. "Discreet or not, I doubt they want to go home."

"How do you know?"

"Like I said, it's my job to spy on everyone."

A knock sounded at the door.

"What is it?" Bran called.

A servant came in and whispered to Bran.

"Right. Thanks for that."

"Did he have news about Marcella?" Arian asked after the man left.

"Not directly. There's no sign of her in Kavilli. A rider is going up to the lodge, to check she left, but…" Bran shook his head.

"You think she's run away?"

"That's where my money goes. And it amounts to an answer of sorts, though I'm not sure where it leaves us."

"If she isn't coming, I suppose I'd better go back home."

"Right. I'll see what a full search shows up. Don't worry, we'll find her."

Arian stood up. As she reached the door Bran said, "Take care, wuss."

"You too, lout."

❖

Arian sat in the courtyard, basking in the early-morning sun. It was not yet hot enough to seek shade. What could she read into the wolf's backward stare today? Doubts over the way taken felt closest to her current mood. Not that she had the slightest doubt about where she wanted to go, but was she on the right path?

Marcella had conspired to murder Doyenne Pellonia. There was no doubt. Equally, there was no proof. It simply could not have been anyone else. Marcella absconding confirmed the case against her, yet it would not be enough. Bran had to find the former housekeeper and get a confession. However, two days had passed and Marcella was still missing.

How much longer would finding her take, and how much time did they have? Cassie said the baby was not due for another three months, but she was looking big. Perhaps she was having twins. Perhaps the baby would come early. Perhaps Cassie would suffer a miscarriage, which would end the baby's life, and thus hers, within days.

Arian closed her eyes. She had to believe they would get both Marcella and the confession in time. Surely then, regardless of what Cassie's enemies might want, the guilty verdict would be overturned. Arian chewed her lower lip. Or might Lilliana launch a scheme to outplay them?

Waiting for news was agonising, but there was nothing she could do to speed up the search. The situation with Ulfgar was simpler, though still not straightforward. Bran's information made clear the extent to which Ulfgar was bluffing. He was desperate to evade his creditors, which meant his threats were empty. He dared do nothing which might prevent her returning to Breninbury, because that meant he too was stuck in Kavilli. The final irony being, had he come to her at the start and admitted the truth, she could have released him from his duties as tutor and sent him home. However, he had chosen to threaten her and turned himself into her enemy.

Ulfgar was unaware Feran was going to the academy. Once this happened, Ulfgar would be free to go wherever he wanted. Unfortunately, he had shown himself to be dishonest, a liar, a fool, over-fond of money, and he now held a grudge against her. Dare she let him return to spread rumours? There was no reason to think he would even restrict his stories to the truth.

For herself it made little difference. She had no intention of going back. Some things about Breninbury she would miss, but the life it offered was not one she wanted. However, the future was unpredictable and keeping her options open was wise. Beyond this, Feran did not want to start his reign fighting scandalous gossip about his mother.

The future king was currently sitting nearby, playing with toy soldiers he had named after his absent friends. Arian smiled at him indulgently.

"My lady, there's a messenger for you." Leasilla entered the courtyard.

"Who from?"

"She said the fuel merchant."

She? "Send her in." Arian tried not to sound overly eager, but this had to be news about Marcella.

The woman who entered the courtyard was vaguely familiar. Arian remembered seeing her around the Passurae mansion.

"I've got the receipt for your next delivery, my lady. The merchant asks if you can make a part payment today." The woman held out a folded note.

Arian opened it.

We've found Marcella, but it's not quite as expected. I'm sending this message with Rufina. She has more information.
Bran

"Ah, yes. Come with me. I've got coin in my room." *As long as Ulfgar hasn't stolen it.*

They entered Arian's bedroom and shut the door. "You're Rufina?"

"Yes, my lady." On a closer look, Rufina was younger than a first impression suggested.

"What did Marcella have to say for herself?"

"She ain't saying anything. She's dead."

"What?"

"Master Branius had us search the road from Kavilli to the lodge. I don't know if he was expecting her to be dead, or just hoping we'd find someone who'd seen her. Kal was the one who spotted blood on the road. He followed the trail and found her body in a ditch. She'd had her throat slashed and her belongings were gone. And there was no sign of the donkey cart she'd been driving."

"It was robbery?"

Rufina gave an ambivalent shrug. "That's what it was made to look like."

"Are there many such attacks on the road?" The one she had walked down alone just a few days earlier.

"Not like this. Highway gangs go after rich pickings— merchant shipments along trade routes. The cheap thieves who target lone women usually hang out around the city streets after dark."

The conclusion was obvious. "It's too much of a coincidence. Marcella must have had an accomplice who decided to silence her."

"That's what Master Branius thinks as well."

"I take it the prefects have been told."

"Yes. Not that they're going to get as worked up over the death of a housekeeper as they were over a doyenne."

"Right." Arian ran a hand through her hair. "Is there anything else to report?"

"Master Branius said to tell you the laundry is due again in six days time, if you want to be the one to take it to the prison."

"Thanks. I will." How could she pass up the chance to see Cassie?

"You'll need to contact me. He's going to be out of town for a while."

"Where's he going?"

"I don't know, my lady."

"Is it to do with finding the murderer?" Who was now guilty of two deaths.

"I don't think so. Doyen Xeranius has a mission for him. Master Branius leaves this afternoon. While he's gone, you can leave messages for me at the bakery."

"Right." Arian paused. "Don't the agents for other families know about the secret back entrance to the mansion?"

"Oh, of course they do, my lady. Just like we know all the secret ways into their houses."

"Then what's the point?"

"It'd take too much effort to keep a watch on all of them, all the time. We only bother when there's something serious going down. If you come to the house through the bakery? Well, I can't guarantee nobody will be watching, but it's not as likely to be noticed as it would if you went in through the front door." Rufina gave a reassuring smile. "Will that be all, my lady?"

"Yes. Thank you."

Rufina ducked a curtsy and left.

Arian moved to the window and stood, staring down at the courtyard. She had not liked Marcella, and the woman had been in league with the murderer, but had she deserved to die like that? And where did it leave their attempt to prove Cassie's innocence? What options were still open to them?

A knock at the door.

"What is it?"

Leasilla entered holding a small bound scroll. "Another message for you, my lady."

Arian opened it.

Darling. Have you still not recovered from the ill effects of the spa water? I feel so guilty. I wish I'd never spoken to you about the place. Please say you forgive me. I simply must, must, must see you, just to reassure myself you're all right. I'm having a small party at my place tomorrow night. Please say you'll come. I've missed you so very much.

With love
Your one and only Vessia

Arian groaned. It was the third such letter she had received since returning from the lodge. The excuse about blotchy skin would not work any longer. Too many people had seen her. The most cursory checking up on Vessia's part would expose the truth.

Maybe she could invent a new illness? After all, the thought of seeing Vessia made her feel sick. Arian pouted at the scroll in her hands. Or was there the faintest chance she might pick up useful information? Because, at the moment, she was completely out of ideas.

No matter how nauseating the idea was, she needed to keep in contact with Vessia. In fact, it might be Cassie's only hope.

❖

For anyone arriving at one of Vessia's gatherings, the steps followed a predictable routine. Vessia would greet each person enthusiastically, as if their entrance was the single most eagerly anticipated event of the evening. For a while, the new arrivals could bask in Vessia's enthralled attention before she left them with "someone you simply have to meet." Her focus would then switch to a new subject, until the next person arrived.

Once you understood what was going on, minor fluctuations became clear. Usually there were one or two people, normally members of senatorial families, who received more of Vessia's time than others. Beyond this, there was a distinction between those who were dumped off haphazardly, freeing Vessia to move on to more important guests, and those where she deliberately set up introductions, where one guest was hoping to profit in some way. This was done not so much for any direct benefit to Vessia, but in the hope of the favour being reciprocated.

Entering the apartment, Arian clenched her teeth. On the night of the murder, the guest most in demand had been herself. Why had she not spotted what was happening, before giving up the details about the brooch? Regardless of whether what she said made any difference to the outcome of the trial, it was pathetic of her to be so gullible.

True to form, Vessia descended on her the moment she walked through the door. "Arian. I'm so pleased you were able to come." Vessia slipped an arm around her waist and nuzzled a kiss on her neck.

Arian fought the urge to shy away. "What's the celebration for?"

"I'm moving out of the Konithae mansion. I've bought a villa of my own nearby." She drew back slightly. "My husband will be coming from Basalonia to join me. I know these things bother you, but please, darling, don't be upset." As if his arrival could, in any way, be compared to Cassie's marriage. "We're going to get divorced." Vessia shrugged. "I haven't told him yet, but you know how these things go."

Did she?

"I don't suppose you've heard from Lady Cassilania recently?" Vessia's voice held a sharper edge. She was after something.

Arian settled on a bland smile. Whatever it was, Vessia would not learn it from her. "How would I hear anything from the prison? And why would I want to?" Insincere questions, but not outright lies.

"Oh, I know. It's silly." Vessia gave a forced giggle. "The time you visited her, she didn't ask you to take a letter for her?"

"No."

"Or mention plans to contact anyone?" What was Vessia after?

"Do you have anyone in mind?"

"Oh no, darling. It's just you know how devious she can be. I merely wondered if you knew anything. Forget I spoke. It's just me being silly. You wouldn't…" Vessia's voice faded into an even more forced giggle. She urged Arian across the room. "Anyway, darling, there's someone here I want you to meet."

Did this mean a guest wanted a favour from her? If so, it was probably a trade deal with her homeland. Vessia had pulled the same trick before, ignoring Arian's protests about how little influence she had. The men in her tribe were the ones who made the decisions, and trying to pretend otherwise was a fraud. She ought to stand her ground and refuse to go along with it. On the other hand, apart from not wanting to appear rude, talking to anyone other than Vessia would be an improvement.

They stopped in front of a large chair. "Darling, this is Doyenne Juliana Balbina pars Drusae dom Nerinae. I've told her all about you and she's just dying for a chat."

Doyenne Juliana huddled down as though trying to make herself appear even smaller than she actually was. She gave an insipid smile. "It's nice to meet you."

Vessia gave Arian's waist one final squeeze. "You two have fun." Then she headed off to accost a pair of middle-aged men who had just arrived.

Arian's share of Vessia's attention had been more fleeting than normal, even with the strange questions about Cassie. She looked across to where Vessia was hanging onto one man's arm and giving her sunniest smile. Of course, now the election was over, and Cassie no longer a threat, what benefit did Vessia gain from continuing with their relationship? Maybe her husband was not the only one Vessia was preparing to ditch. With luck, she would do it before the end of the evening. Arian had intended to plead a stomach upset as an excuse not to stay overnight, but perhaps it would not be necessary.

Meanwhile, Juliana was smiling up at her with an odd expression that could only be classed as hopeful anxiety. Obviously, the arranged meeting was her reward for either her vote in the election, or for her testimony at the trial. Arian was tempted to turn and walk away. Except this was a chance to question a new eyewitness. Was it conceivable Juliana might have anything useful to say?

Arian pulled over a cushioned stool, covered in sheepskin and signalled to a nearby servant for wine. Juliana was already holding one of the decorated glasses, although she was showing no sign of drinking.

"It's nice to meet you too. I saw you at the trial, though we didn't get to speak—Lady Cassilania's trial." Arian added, as though there might be confusion over which one.

"Oh."

"You were actually present when the murder happened?"

"Yes."

"Wasn't it appalling of her to kill her own mother."

"Yes."

The servant handed Arian wine from a tray. The pale blue glass was painted with a gold-and-red griffin, the Konithae family emblem. The design was familiar, after all the meals she had taken at the mansion. Lilliana must have dozens of the glasses, each one identical, a way of showing off her wealth to guests. Vessia had always traded heavily on second-hand prestige from her patron. What was she going to do now?

Arian took a sip of wine. "Lady Cassilania and I, we used to be...well, you know."

Juliana nodded. Obviously, she did know.

"I never thought Cassilania would do something like that. Did you?"

"No."

"It must have been terrible for you."

"Yes."

Juliana clearly needed encouragement to talk. Arian gave her best show of morbid curiosity. "What actually happened?"

"I...I..." Juliana shrunk down still further in the chair.

"I heard Doyenne Pellonia lured a group of you up to her lodge. I know it's wrong to say bad things about the dead, but even when I was with Cassilania, I never liked her mother. Did you get on well with her?"

"No." Juliana shuddered visibly.

"Cassilania was just as bad at times."

"She could be nasty." At last Juliana volunteered more than a simple yes or no.

Arian gave an encouraging smile. "I know."

"She tried to bully me."

"I'm not surprised." Arian raised the glass to her lips, then lowered it without drinking, as if struck by a thought. "Was that in the guest room? I remember what you said about it at the trial."

"Yes. I wanted to leave, but they wouldn't let me." Juliana clasped her wine glass with both hands. "She was trying to force me to vote against Vessia. She threatened me."

"That must have been so upsetting."

"It was. I got rather emotional."

"Anyone would in your place."

"I was so pleased when she finally left me alone. But then that other woman, the housekeeper, came and got me. She wasn't very nice either."

Which meant everyone was in complete agreement about the woman. "Marcella was her name. I've heard she's just been found—"

Arian broke off as the implication of what Juliana just said scattered her thoughts. Had she misheard or misunderstood? Because otherwise it meant she had to rethink everything she thought she knew.

Meanwhile, Juliana was waiting for her to finish the sentence. Arian covered by glancing over her shoulder, as if fearing eavesdroppers, then leaned forward and lowered her voice to a whisper. "She's just been found dead as well. Murdered."

"No."

"The prefects think it was a robbery, though they aren't saying much at the moment. She was on the way into town. Everything was stolen. Even the donkey cart."

"That's awful."

"Isn't it."

"I didn't like her but, even so." Juliana took a mouthful of her wine.

"You said she was unpleasant when she came to get you from the guest room."

"Most unsympathetic."

"Was Xeranius with her?"

"No." Juliana shook her head. "He was waiting for us outside in the courtyard. When he saw me, he insisted I wash my face before we went back to the salon."

But how much difference did it make? With Halie taking the message to the kitchen and Marcella in the guest room, it meant Xeranius had been alone in the courtyard. Even if the dog did not bark at him, would he have had time to rush to the office, find Cassie's cloak, go upstairs, kill Pellonia, and be back waiting when Marcella dragged Juliana outside?

"Did the housekeeper say much to you?"

"She told me to hurry up. So rude. A servant, ordering me around."

"I hope you made her wait."

"Not on purpose. But I needed to compose myself."

"Of course. It would've served her right if you'd made her stand there for five minutes."

"I wouldn't have done that. She made me nervous, glaring at me."

Arian sympathised. Marcella had possessed a vicious glare.

Juliana continued. "I only took a few seconds."

Which, even allowing for Juliana wildly exaggerating the speed with which she had pulled herself together, did not leave enough time for Xeranius to commit the murder. The new trail led nowhere. Arian was about to take another sip of wine, when a young man walked by, clipping her elbow. The glass was knocked from her hand and shattered on the tiled floor. Heads turned.

Vessia appeared at her side. "Are you alright, darling?"

"I'm fine. I'm sorry about the glass. I know it belongs in a set." And it had to be expensive.

"Don't worry. They get broken all the time. The craftsman at the glassworks has a copy of the design to make replacements." Vessia smiled and patted Arian's shoulder. "But how has your little chat gone?"

"I...we haven't got to that part yet." Juliana looked apologetic.

"I'll leave you to it. Don't worry about the glass. I'll have someone clean it up and get you a new one." Vessia breezed away.

Juliana cleared her throat. "There was a matter I wanted to talk to you about."

No surprise there. "Yes?" Arian tried to look politely interested.

"Your people have ore mines, don't they?"

"Yes." It was the only reason the empire had any interest in the land.

"And there's gold?"

"A little. It's mainly iron and tin."

"It just that my family…"

Are all avid goldsmiths.

Juliana nervously took another gulp of wine. "As doyenne, it's my responsibility to ensure my family doesn't get overlooked. I do what I can, but I'm not the best at negotiating, and we don't always get a fair deal, and I…" She looked awkward, verging on tears.

"Your family must have faith in you. They picked you as doyenne."

"The role of family leader is hereditary for the Nerinae. My father was doyen before me, and I'm his oldest surviving child. It should have been my brother, but he died in a battle, just before he was due to leave the army. It was so sad. My daughter…" Juliana's mouth worked as she searched for words. "She doesn't want to be doyenne, any more than I did, but she doesn't have a choice."

It explained a lot.

The Lycanthi also relied on birth order to select their kings, going through the female line. Her brother had been king because he was their uncle's eldest nephew, the son of his sister. Feran would be king because he was her brother's eldest nephew. But her brother had been a total disaster in the role. Bran would have been an infinitely better choice as king. In truth, any of the chickens she fed as a child would have been a better choice.

How would Feran fare? Supposing he did not want the throne. Supposing he lacked the skills and temperament. Perhaps her people should take something from the empire and open up the selection process. Cassie should be doyenne of the Passurae, not because she was her mother's daughter, but because she was the best person for the job. Sharp, hard, utterly unique, and far more dangerous than she appeared—just like her damned brooch.

A housemaid arrived with a pan and brush. Arian shifted the stool back to give her room to work. Shards of glass lay in a pool of wine. The largest fragment displayed the painted Konithae griffin, still intact.

Half an idea hopped into Arian's head, cutting up the timeline of the murder and then sewing it back together. She stared at the griffin, pulling at the threads in her memory and weaving it into a tapestry, finally coming together to make a complete picture. It all made sense.

You filthy treacherous...

Arian stood up, swaying slightly from anger, rather than alcohol. She looked down at Juliana. "Please give my apologies to Vessia. Tell her I was feeling unwell. But..." Was Juliana the nicest person in the room, or merely the most incompetent? Either way, she could do with a lucky break. "I'll see what I can do about gold imports from Lycanthia."

"Thank you so much. I'll pass on your message to Vessia. I hope you feel better soon."

Arian hurried from the room. She needed to think, and she needed to talk to Cassie.

CASSIE

W hat's happened to Orthias? He isn't sick, I hope."

"Humph." The new warder was not in the mood to talk. He finished the morning inspection of the cell and left, locking the door behind him.

Cassie allowed herself a smile. Everything was running to plan.

Orthias's belligerence had been the sure sign of someone who wanted to feel powerful, more than he wanted to perform his job well. No doubt he believed he deserved better than he received, both in terms of promotion and pay. He would be the warder most inclined to accept bribes and lie to his superiors. Even if there were no issues with his work, he was unlikely to have many friends among his colleagues. Now it had come back to bite him.

Over the previous few days, she had paid both the other warders to carry letters to Lilliana, knowing they would go straight to Vessia instead. But not Orthias. His departure surely meant Vessia was, at the very least, considering the possibility he had taken the money and passed on a letter as requested. All of which in turn meant Cassie could be confident of a visit from her sometime that day.

In fact, Vessia arrived just before lunchtime, clearly angry and ill at ease.

Cassie looked up from the book she was reading and gave her most patronising smile. "To what do I owe this honour?"

Vessia waited for the warder to close the door, then sat in the chair at the opposite side of the table. "I've received a request from Doyen Xeranius, asking for your sentence be commuted to beheading. I have to decide whether to grant it."

"I'm grateful to you both for your kind consideration of the matter."

"Don't be. Because at the moment I'm tending towards refusing."

Ah. Threats. How original. "Any reason?"

"You know why. I'm not here to play games."

That's what you think. Cassie nodded slowly. "Out of interest, can I ask which of the three warders passed my note to you."

"They all did."

Vessia spoke tersely with a falling cadence, while her eyes focused briefly above Cassie's head. Did she always do that when she lied? Cassie made a mental note of something to watch for.

"That's a shame. I hoped one might…" Cassie sighed. "Never mind."

"What deal have you got with Doyenne Lilliana?"

"I don't have one."

"I'm not stupid."

"Of course not. I wouldn't dream of suggesting it." Cassie let her smile say otherwise.

Vessia leaned back in her chair. The forefinger of her right hand tapped out a beat on the tabletop. "What is the deal?"

"There isn't one."

"I don't believe you."

"If you're going to doubt every word I say what's the point of talking to me?" Cassie made no attempt to hide her smile. Whoever would have thought telling the truth could be so much fun? She shook her head, as if in disbelief. "Oh, come on, use your common sense. What possible deal could I have going with Lilliana?"

Vessia pushed away from the table and lurched to her feet. She took two steps towards the door, before turning back to face Cassie. Judging by her expression, she had come up with at least three ideas by way of an answer. *I wonder what they all are.*

The great thing about bluffing people who had a guilty conscience was that you could let them do the hard work for you. She just had to volunteer nothing and leave Vessia to fill in the blanks. The more answers Vessia invented, the cleverer she would think she was being.

"Admittedly, you're not Lilliana's favourite person at the moment." Cassie put enough confidence into her voice to imply she was speaking from knowledge, rather than conjecture. "But I'm sure she understands why you hung onto your report into the Roldanian fiasco. Anyone would have done the same thing in your place. You could have taken better care of the key to your strongbox, but we all make mistakes." Cassie let her smile broaden. "What's done is done."

Vessia returned to her chair. She glared across the tabletop. "What do you want from me?"

"Nothing. You can't change the verdict." Cassie stressed "you."

Vessia pounced. "So that's it. You think you can get me dismissed from office so the flunky you installed as my deputy can take over."

"What makes you say that?"

"It's obvious."

"Really? You think so?" Cassie laughed. "Anyway, even if you were dismissed, your deputy could only retry cases if it was proved you'd taken bribes to convict innocent people. You haven't done that, have you? I mean, with Lord Galvinius there was all the evidence about…" She waved her hand vaguely. "Whatever it was."

While taking bribes was an everyday occurrence, getting caught at it was a different matter. Vessia drew a breath, as if to speak, but then, without another word, stood and marched from the cell.

The door did not close immediately. A housemaid came in, with the basket containing lunch. Clearly, she had been waiting outside for the principal magistrate to leave.

"Good. I'm ready to eat." Cassie paused. "Once you get back to the mansion, could you pass on a message asking Doyen Xeranius to visit me whenever he gets a chance."

❖

Xeran strolled into the cell with the casual air of a man at a friend's party, although the narrowing of his eyes spoke of heightened alertness.

"Thank you for coming so quickly." The housemaid had left less than an hour before. As doyen, Xeran did not need Vessia's permission to visit a family member.

"I was heading to the Senate. You were on the way." He smiled. "What's up?"

"I need a favour."

"I imagine you could do with several. What are you hoping for?"

"I've been working on Vessia. I've got her rattled."

"Congratulations." Xeran laughed as he took a seat at the table. "They should have known it would take more than locking you in a cell to take you out of the game. How did you do it? What naughty tricks have you been playing?"

"I've convinced her I'm working with Lilliana to get her dismissed from office."

"How did you manage that?"

"By denying it. Vessia has such a suspicious mind."

"But how did you put the idea in her head to start with?"

"I pretended to bribe the warders to carry a letter to Lilliana."

"Pretended?"

"I gave them letters and a payment. But I knew they'd pass the messages to Vessia instead."

"I assume there's no truth about you being in league with Lilliana."

"None at all."

Xeran's elbows were on the table. He rested his chin in a cupped hand, looking confused. "That doesn't surprise me. What does surprise me is Vessia buying the story. What benefit could there be in it for Lilliana?"

"Vessia knows she's on shaky ground with her. After all the money Lilliana poured into the election campaign, they were at the point of conceding. All due to Vessia's carelessness. And there's more. Bran read the contents of Vessia's strongbox before passing it to Mother. In particular, there was evidence of a bribe Vessia took to convict Lilliana's cousin Galvinius of sedition."

"A bribe from Lilliana?"

"From someone else. Lilliana was not pleased about it."

"Ah, right. I see."

"Unfortunately, the evidence is lost. But we know where Vessia has buried the bodies, so to speak."

"I've sent Bran off on an assignment. Do you want me to recall him?"

"No. We don't have enough time to do the digging. Well, I don't have enough time." Cassie patted her bulging abdomen. "The baby will be born before we turn up the hard proof we need to get Vessia dismissed. It might not even be possible. We don't have a lot to go on. But she doesn't know that."

Xeran scratched his head. "I think I'm following you."

"The thing is, if we prove Vessia took money to convict an innocent person, it would be grounds to get her dismissed from office and her deputy take over."

"Luckily, our man got enough votes for second place." Xeran's expression brightened. "He could order retrials."

"Yes. Then Lilliana could get her cousin back from exile, who would be of more use to her than a liability like Vessia."

"I take it you'd want him to retry your case as well."

"Of course. The thing is, I don't want the verdict overturned posthumously."

"I can see that." Xeran laughed. "But you've got me confused. What do you want me to do?"

"I'd like you to visit Vessia. Tell her you don't trust me. Tell her you think I'm working a scheme to get the verdict overturned, and you're not at all happy about it."

Xeran raised his eyebrows. "I'm not?"

"No. Because if I was declared innocent I could demand a fresh election for doyen, on the basis I'd been unfairly prevented from running before. Don't worry, I'm not going to do it. You're safe. Not least because challenging the family vote has to happen within twelve months, and there's no way we'll get Vessia removed in time."

Xeran looked uncomfortable. "Time's not an issue. If you get declared innocent, I'll stand down as doyen, and we can have a fair vote."

"You don't have to."

"I don't want it said I only became doyen because you were falsely imprisoned."

"Thanks. But we can wait to talk about it. For now, when you see Vessia you can say you've been keeping a close eye on the housemaids bringing my meals, after you found out I was using them to pass on secret messages."

"Wouldn't I simply have stopped the kitchen providing your meals?"

"No. Because intercepting my messages was the best way to find out what I was up to. You could easily afford to out-bribe me. Except I stopped doing it. When you heard Vessia had been here, you came to see me to find out what was going on, but I wouldn't tell you." Cassie smiled. "You know I'm up to something, and you'd like me out of the way before I can pull any tricks. Who knows what I might do in three months."

"You want her to poison you?"

Cassie laughed. "No. I know how to spot most poisons, and with my meals coming directly from the family kitchens it would be awkward to explain." She shook her head. "There's one quick and simple way Vessia can ruin whatever scheme I have going. She can commute my sentence to exile. I could be gone from Kavilli within days. Somewhere a long way away, where she can control who talks to me, and who I talk to."

"That won't be much fun for you."

"Better than the alternative I'm looking at now. And I'd hope you and Bran could do the digging to eventually get her out of office."

Xeran looked thoughtful, rubbing his chin. "It could work. Anywhere in particular you fancy going?"

"Ideally somewhere warm and sunny. But anywhere will do."

"All right. I'll see what I can manage. Is that everything?"

"Yes. And thanks again."

Xeran stopped at the door and looked back. "No matter how things turn out, I truly am in awe." His smile broadened. "I pray I never find myself on the opposite side of an argument to you."

"The feeling is mutual."

Alone in the cell, Cassie returned to the view from her window. She had made her play. Now it was all up to Xeran.

❖

The cell door opened and Arian was ushered in, her skin and hair again dyed dark brown. The colour was not growing on Cassie, but the visit was good timing. Finally, there was progress to report. Plus, if all went well, she could be sent to a place of exile on an hour's notice. Who knew how long before they met face to face again?

Cassie waited until Marcus left, closing and locking the door. "It's good to see you." She left her seat by the window.

Arian put the baskets she was carrying on the desk and stepped into the welcoming embrace. Cassie rested her forehead on Arian's shoulder, with her arms holding Arian's body tight. A deep sense of peace welled up inside her. She could happily spend eternity like this. However, Arian pulled away.

"I know who murdered your mother."

"It's not Marcella?"

"No. I'm sure of it. In fact, I don't think she was involved at all."

"So what's changed? Who do you suspect?" Cassie sat on the side of the bed.

Rather than join her, Arian leaned against the wall by the window. "It was something I heard a few nights ago at a party at Vessia's."

"All right." Cassie kept her face calm while fighting back the surge of jealousy.

"Don't look like that. I didn't stay the night."

Damn. She's getting better at reading me.

Arian gave a wry grimace, and added, "I couldn't have. Just the thought of her touching me makes me feel sick."

Cassie tried not to smile too broadly. "What did Vessia say?"

"Not her. Doyenne Juliana was there. She was the one I talked to."

"And she had something interesting to say?" Astonishing was too weak a description.

"Yes. It wasn't Xeranius who got her from the guest room. He sent Marcella to do it."

"Which means…" A surge of nausea kicked at Cassie's stomach. *No. Please not him.* Or was Arian aiming at a different target? "If the housemaid was away on a errand, and he told Marcella to fetch Juliana, there was nobody in the foyer. Xeran could have dashed over, got my brooch, and then…"

Arian shook her head. "No. Even if the dog didn't bark, he wouldn't have had time to search the office and go upstairs as well. Juliana and Marcella were together in the guest room for a very short time."

There was still little comfort to be had. The pattern of events was shifting, and the end picture was not looking good. Cassie could feel it in her bones. "Then what are you thinking? Who was it, if not Xeran?"

"Oh, it was him all right."

"Talk me though it." Cassie shifted back on the bed, trying to block the sick feeling, spreading from her stomach and up her throat.

"An accident at the party got me thinking. I dropped a wineglass, one of a set of expensive, hand painted glasses. But Vessia said it didn't matter, because the craftsman had a record of the design and would make more." Arian pursed her lips. "I think Xeranius tracked down the craftsman who made your brooch and got him to make a replica."

"Mother was adamant about there being no copies."

"That's because she didn't want them sold on the open market. It was a special gift, just for you. But I can think of half a dozen stories Xeranius could have spun. Your mother had changed her mind and wanted one for a cousin. It had been stolen or lost. You wanted a matching pair and had got your mother to agree. Anything would do."

"It's possible. But supposing you're right and he had an identical brooch. Xeran can't have known how things were going to play out at the lodge."

"He could have had the brooch made months ago, even years. We don't know how many other events he's been to with the replica in his pocket, waiting for the opportunity. The meeting at the lodge was the time everything fell into place for him." Arian folded her arms. "Two questions. Who suggested he leave the salon to find Juliana?"

Cassie closed her eyes, digging through her memory. "He did. I think."

"And who suggested you go to your mother's study to find out why she was taking so long?"

That question was easier. "He did."

"That's what I thought. He waited until Bellorion and Ellonius returned after their argument. Then he left the salon and sent Halie and Marcella off on errands. As soon as he was alone in the courtyard, he dashed up the stairs."

"Would he have had enough time? You said they weren't gone for long."

"He didn't need long. If Halie had gone straight to the kitchen and back, she might have seen him. But with everything going on, it was a safe bet she'd stay to chat. As for Marcella…" Arian crossed the room and plonked herself beside Cassie on the bed. "I've wondered about her. I think she glanced back and caught a glimpse of him running up the stairs. She was loyal to the family, and according to the other servants, she had a soft spot for him."

"But she wouldn't have covered up for Mother's murder." Surely not.

"No. But like everyone else at the lodge, she'd be certain Lilliana was the guilty one. She'd have assumed Vessia took the brooch from your cloak. Marcella wasn't the sort to gossip with

Halie or the stable hands to get their accounts. Regardless, she'd know Xeranius couldn't have taken it. The only time she was away from her office, he was in the salon."

"It would explain why she got flustered when I questioned her."

"Exactly. She'd seen him go upstairs, but was sure he was innocent, so didn't want to mention it at the trial. But then you were found guilty, and she was left wondering whether she ought to have said something. After all, if Lilliana had already murdered your mother, Xeranius would have discovered the body. He could have spoken up and cleared your name. Marcella didn't know what to do, or who to talk to, and that's why she became the bitch from hell."

"Anything else?"

"Yes. Xeranius insisted Juliana wash her face at the pump, but that was so he could clean the blood off his hands."

"And his clothes." The memory of his soaking wet sleeve slipped into place. "He even made a point of showing me."

Arian nodded. "Finally, after you'd found the body, he volunteered to summon the prefects. He sent Marcella to you, so he could remove the real brooch from your cloak before racing away. It wouldn't matter if the dog barked, because Marcella knew he was in her office getting his own cloak."

"You've worked it all out." Admiration for Arian was mixed with self-disgust. Xeran had played her for a fool at every point. It was too much to hope he would still help with outwitting Vessia.

"I've had four days to think about it. I wanted to come sooner, but had to wait until you were due a change of clothes."

The sick feeling solidified in Cassie's stomach. If Arian had come just a few hours earlier, maybe something could have been rescued from her scheme. With a bit of extra work, it might yet have been possible to get her sentence commuted.

Cassie stared at the wall. Was there anything Arian had overlooked? "Marcella could have carried out the murder on her own. Or been working with him." Not that it made the outlook any better. "He wouldn't have needed a replica. She could have handed him the real brooch before going to get Juliana."

"If Marcella acted alone, then who murdered her, and why? It's too much of a coincidence for her to have run into a robber on the very same day Bran was going to question her." Arian paused. "You heard about that?"

"Yes. The maid who brought breakfast told me the day after her body was found."

"And if Marcella was working with Xeranius, I'm sure he'd have killed her a lot earlier, rather than take a chance on her silence. If my guess is right, he didn't even know she'd seen him go upstairs. When Bran summoned her for questioning, she contacted Xeranius to ask what she ought to say. She might have assumed he had a good reason for concealing the truth—some scheme he was working on. But when he realised she'd seen him he arranged to meet her on the road to Kavilli, and murdered her."

"It fits."

"I've had four days to think it through. And I know what to do next."

"What?" Was there a shred of hope?

"If Xeranius had a replica made, I can track down the jeweller and get a sworn testimony. Furthermore..." Arian put an arm around her and gave her a hug. "Did you look closely at the brooch?"

"It was coated in blood and sticking out of Mother's ear." Not one of her favourite memories.

"That's a no."

Cassie nodded.

"You didn't examine it later?"

"The prosecutor waved it around at the trial. It looked like mine."

"The point is, a replica won't be absolutely identical, no matter how good the jeweller is. I've held your brooch. It's got smooth patches on the back from seven years of rubbing against your cloak, and a scratch on the fox's ear. The point is worn from being pushed through your cloaks. A new brooch won't have any sign of wear. It'll prove the weapon used to kill your mother wasn't yours."

Tears threatened to fill Cassie's eyes. She leaned on Arian's shoulder. Her enthusiasm was adorable but misplaced. "You'll need more than that to get the verdict overturned."

"One step at a time. Do you have any idea which jeweller made the original?"

"Mother's favourite jeweller had a shop on Goldsmith Lane. He had an odd sounding name like…" She closed her eyes. "Alentisco. He may be dead by now. It was years ago. I can't be certain she used him for the brooch anyway."

"Do you—"

The key sounded in the lock.

"Quick." Cassie swivelled around and lay out flat.

Arian shifted off the bed and knelt at the side, placing a hand on Cassie's forehead.

"Aren't you done yet?" The new warder glared at them.

"She's feeling faint," Arian said. "It's the baby, it's—"

"If she's got problems, ask for the midwife. Now you hurry up and get on with what you came for, or I'm kicking you out regardless."

"Yes, sir."

The door closed again.

Arian dropped a quick kiss on her lips. "We better get moving."

Cassie hooked an arm around Arian's shoulders before she could move away and held her tight. They had so little time left.

Eventually, Arian pulled back and looked into her eyes. "Are you all right?"

No. Of course not. I've screwed up. Cassie tried to control her expression, but knew the grief was spilling through.

"I love you." Words she had never said before. "I love you with all my heart. You're the most important thing in my life. The only important thing in my life, and I was stupid not to realise it a long time ago. I'm sorry."

Arian closed her eyes and rested their foreheads together. "You don't have to apologise." Then she lifted her head and smiled. "I think pregnancy has made you overemotional."

There was no point saying more. Cassie let herself be helped off the bed.

After Arian went, she wandered to the window. The skyline of Kavilli was unchanged. How much longer did she have to look at it? An unaccustomed feeling of guilt washed over her. Arian looked so enthusiastic, so hopeful. She was dreaming they had a future together. Cassie closed her eyes. It was only going to result in more pain, and she had already hurt Arian far too much.

"I'm so sorry, Arian. I love you and don't want to leave you. But there's no other way this can end."

❖

Marcus stopped just inside the door. "There are changes to the conditions of your imprisonment."

This was not going to be good news. Cassie braced herself for the worst.

Marcus continued. "It has come to our notice you've been abusing the privileges granted you. All visits by your family employees will cease. From now on, you'll be eating prison rations. All other amenities will be provided solely by the prefecture."

"Anything else?"

"The request for commuting your sentence to beheading has been denied." To give him his due, Marcus looked genuinely apologetic.

Cassie nodded slowly. "Thank you for letting me know."

So Xeran did not want her alive and in a position to challenge him, and Vessia had been more than happy to oblige.

Arian

Goldsmith Lane had as many perfumeries as goldsmiths, which made it one of the more pleasant streets in Kavilli to walk along. Arian strolled from shop to shop, trying to ignore the sellers who pestered her every time she stopped to look. Half the establishments had the owner's name displayed prominently on a board outside. This generally denoted jewellers who saw themselves as artisans rather than craftsmen. Their merchandise came with higher prices, while not necessarily being any better than the others.

Pellonia could have afforded the most expensive items on offer. But equally, she was a shrewd woman who knew her own mind. She would have chosen objects she felt affinity for, and not cared about the cost, either high or low.

Goldsmith Lane ended at a junction with the main boulevard through Kavilli. The noise level increased, while the scents carried on the air became markedly worse. Arian paused, thinking. None of the written names had looked anything like Alentisco. Did he no longer have his own shop? Did he view himself as a simple craftsman? Was Cassie's memory faulty? Alentisco might even be a nickname, reserved for friends and favoured customers. She was going to have to ask. Arian retraced her steps and stopped at the first jeweller's shop.

The owner, a woman with an over-elaborate hairstyle, bustled up. "How are you, madam, on this bright sunny morning?"

"Very well, thank you."

"What can I help you with today? Rings? Necklaces? Amulets? Someone with beauty such as yours deserves the very best." Which was flattery she undoubtedly bestowed on every potential customer. "Please, sit down. Let me show you the finest workmanship in all Kavilli."

Arian waited to get a word in. "I'm actually looking for a particular shop a friend recommended. It's owned by Alentisco. Do you know of him?"

The shopkeeper held out her hands in a dramatic gesture. "No. But why would you want to go to this man. I promise, nothing he has will be half as good as what I can show you. Please, come inside. Let me—"

"Thank you, but no." Arian backed away and carried on walking. Was it worth asking elsewhere, or would it be more of the same?

On her return down the street, Arian walked more slowly, shifting her attention from the names written on boards to the shops behind. The risk of grab and run theft meant few items were on display, although most shops had some cheaper items nailed to a board that was guarded by well-muscled men carrying quarterstaffs.

The fifth shop she passed had a larger than average display, including a pendant in the shape of a stork on a silver chain. Beside it were a butterfly and a cat in similar style. Arian came to a halt. What was it about them that put her in mind of Cassie's brooch? The use of colour, the proportions, the sleek lines? There was definitely a shared feeling to the work.

Of course, as soon as she was standing still, the shopkeeper homed in. "Good morning, madam. What can I help you with?"

"That pendant is quite unusual."

"I see you have a discerning eye. Come inside, please. I have many other wonderful pieces for you to view."

"It's just the pendant and the two items next to it that interest me. Did you make them?"

The shopkeeper's expression changed to one of regret. "No. It's a sad story."

"In what way?"

"Why don't you come inside, where it's cool?" Even though the peak of summer had passed, the midday sun was scorching.

Arian let herself be steered to a chair close by an open doorway at the rear of the shop. Through it was a busy workshop. In truth, the shade was welcome, although occasional gusts of warm air from a furnace were less so.

"You said it was a sad story. What happened?" she asked, before the shopkeeper could resume his sales pitch.

"Poor Leni. He was a neighbour of mine for many years."

"Leni? That would be Alentisco?"

"Yes. A dear man."

"What happened to him?"

The shopkeeper raised both hands in an exaggerated shrug. "Who knows? His body was found, floating in the river. Maybe he was drunk and fell in."

And maybe he was pushed and held under. "When did this happen?"

"A year ago, or a little longer. His widow needed money and sold all his merchandise. We gave her a fair price for it, of course. The Goldsmiths' guild takes care of its members and their families." His smile returned. "But enough of sad things. Let me—"

"Do you know where his wife is now?"

"She went back to her family. Both of them came from the eastern provinces."

"The cat and the butterfly were made in Alentisco's shop as well? Did he craft them?"

The shopkeeper's smile stretched tighter. "It was made by a man who worked for him. But why don't you—"

"Do you know which one? Where is he now?"

"Why all this fuss?" Signs of impatience were showing. "Do you want to buy the stork? I can offer a very good price."

"Perhaps. But first I want answers. Do you know who made them?"

The smile was getting more forced. "One of his master craftsmen. A man named Rikko."

"Do you know where Rikko is now?"

"Yes. He works for me."

How convenient. Arian leaned forward and lifted up her coin purse. "How much would you charge for me to have a private conversation with Rikko?"

The shopkeeper stared at her. He probably viewed her as a time-wasting eccentric. Were it not for sight of her purse, he most likely would have summoned the guard to throw her out. Eventually, he said, "It's free of charge." He stuck his head through the doorway. "Rikko. There's a lady here who wants to talk to you."

A hunched, balding man appeared. He was dark-skinned, even by Kavillian standards. His hands and clothes were stained with black powder and grease. "Yes?"

"You're Rikko?"

He nodded.

The shopkeeper left them and returned to his position by the street entrance.

"I have questions about an item you made."

Rikko nodded again.

"It was a brooch in the shape of a silver fox. It was used as a cloak pin. Do you know the one I mean? The pin could be pulled out and locked into place."

"Yes, my lady. I remember it. It was a special job, years ago. I was given a drawing." He spoke with a heavy accent. "Master Alentisco had me make the fox, because the drawing looked like pictures from my homeland in the far south."

"Did you keep the drawing?"

"Yes. It reminded me of my childhood. And it was good luck that I did so." Rikko gave a toothless smile.

"Good luck?"

"Else I could not have made another one."

"You made a replica?"

Rikko nodded. "The lady lost the first. It was a gift from her mother, who would be angry if she found out. So the lady sent her brother to have a copy made, in secret."

"When was this?"

"I finished the job, it must have been..." He frowned. "A month before Master Alentisco died."

Xeranius covering his tracks. "What did her brother look like? Did he give a name?"

"He was Lord Jadioleus. He was about forty, maybe older, maybe younger. This tall." Rikko waved his hand two inches above his head.

Arian had only met Cassie's brother, Jadioleus, once. As a high ranking army officer, he was normally stationed with his legion. Jadioleus was three years younger than Cassie, which made him only thirty-three, although estimating age always held a touch of guesswork. He was also a few inches taller than Rikko indicated, but this was hardly conclusive. Probably the most glaring discrepancy was that Jadioleus would have given his title as Legate, not Lord.

"He was an army officer?"

"Oh no. No." Rikko shook his head. "He wasn't wearing a uniform."

Which did not prove anything. Although what would be the point of Jadioleus hiding his identity behind civilian dress and title, but then giving his real name?

Arian leaned back in her chair. Where did this get her? She had a witness proving Cassie's brooch was not unique. Possibly, Rikko could identify Xeranius if they met face to face. And then Rikko would have an accident and be found floating in the river before a lawyer got to certify his testimony.

If Bran were around, possibly they could keep Rikko safe. But Xeranius had sent Bran away from Kavilli on assignment. Arian could only hope the mission was genuine, and Bran was not in danger. He was better able to look after himself than most, but not immune to treachery. Nobody was.

Arian smiled at Rikko. "Thank you. That's all."

"Yes, my lady."

"But, Rikko?"

He had been part way through the door but stopped. "Yes, my lady?"

"Be careful who you speak to about this."

He nodded "Yes, my lady." But, from his expression, he too had added her to his list of time-wasting eccentrics.

The shopkeeper had been keeping an eye on them and, seeing Rikko leave, now came back. "Is there anything else, madam?"

"How much do you want for the stork, and the other two pieces beside it, the butterfly and the cat?" It was unsafe for Rikko to have such clues on display outside his place of work.

"Eight gold imperials."

Arian made a minimal attempt at haggling, and ending up paying no more than double what they were worth. She could have done better, but her heart was not in it. She left the shop with the three items in her purse.

She knew for certain who had murdered Doyenne Pellonia, and now had crumbs of proof to back up her claim. Unfortunately, it did not add up to anything like enough evidence to demand a retrial. She did not need Cassie to tell her as much. Getting either Vessia or Lilliana to back down would require a serious bargaining chip on the table, and she did not have one. Arian bit back a groan. If only the document implicating them in the grain fraud was still readable. If only…

Arian came to an abrupt standstill in the middle of the street, struck by an idea. Maybe not her best, but it might work. She needed to talk to Rufina.

❖

"I'll tell Doyenne Lilliana she has a visitor. Please wait here." The housemaid gave a curtsy and closed the door.

"Thank you."

Arian's heart pounded in her chest and her hands were sticky. Her stomach was threatening to empty its contents on the floor. She closed her eyes and concentrated on breathing, slow and steady. This meeting was too important to let nerves get in the way. She had to relax.

Had Cassie felt like this, sitting in court, with her life on the line? She had looked so calm and self-controlled. But of course, Cassie had years of practice and training to hone her public persona. Arian had this one chance to master the technique, and she dared not fail. Slowly, her pulse rate eased.

The housemaid had shown her into a small reception room, containing a few high-backed chairs. A potted plant with long waxy leaves stood on a round table. The walls depicted scenes from mythology, winged nymphs chasing a golden stag into the sea. Above the paintings, a row of small arched windows were too high to allow a view of the world outside. Thick glass tinged the sun's rays green, as they fell in bands across the white tiled floor.

Arian selected a chair where she would have her back to the light and put her small leather bag down at one side. Verbal duelling with Cassie's mother had been a game for fools, and not one Arian had ever chosen to play. Now she must take on Pellonia's older sister.

The door opened and Lilliana breezed in. "Lady Arian. This is a pleasant surprise. I understand you wish to speak with me."

"Thank you for seeing me."

Lilliana took a seat facing her. "Would you like food? A drink?"

"Only if you do."

"No." Lilliana waved away the housemaid who had accompanied her. "That will be all." Once they were alone, she asked, "What can I do for you?"

Take your time. Don't fidget. Don't lick your lips. Remember to breathe. "What would you say if I told you I have evidence Cassilania did not murder her mother?"

Lilliana looked politely interested. "Is that something you're likely to say?"

"I have proof. Or, more accurately, Principal Magistrate Vessia has proof."

"You're surely not accusing her of withholding evidence?"

"Oh, no." Arian allowed herself a small gesture of disavowal. *Don't overact the part.* She returned her folded hands to her lap. "I merely think she hasn't properly examined what she has."

"Really?" The hint of a combative edge entered Lilliana's voice. "Please, explain."

"I've found the jeweller who made the brooch Doyenne Pellonia gave to Cassilania."

Lilliana sat motionless, saying nothing. Her expression appeared, if anything, amused, except for the ice in her eyes.

"Just over a year ago, a man visited the jeweller to ask for a copy to be made."

"Did this man give a reason?"

"He said Cassilania had lost the original and wanted a replacement made in secret, so her mother wouldn't find out."

"Did he give his name?"

"He claimed he was Jadioleus. Cassilania's brother."

"Claimed? You think he was someone else?

"I'm actually quite sure he was Xeranius. Doyen Xeranius as he is now—a change in status that was only possible because both Cassilania and her mother were out of contention."

A flicker of Lilliana's eyebrow denoted either surprise or curiosity. "That's a very bold claim."

"We can be certain the man wasn't Legate Jadioleus, since he was stationed with his legion, over eight hundred miles away at the time. We could also summon the jeweller to meet Xeranius to see if he can identify his customer. But I fear such an encounter would have a detrimental effect on the jeweller's health." Arian's smile did not have to appear genuine, as long as it was not sickly.

"Can I assume you think Xeranius murdered Doyenne Pellonia?"

"Yes."

Lilliana nodded slowly, clearly thinking things through. Even though this was Lilliana at her most dangerous, Arian let her take her time. Rushing would be a mistake.

At last, Lilliana said, "So you're claiming Cassilania is innocent on the basis of a story told by a common craftsman who you don't wish to produce. And, even if he did come forward, it would only be to say the replacement brooch was ordered by one of her relatives at Cassilania's own request. Have I understood the situation correctly?"

"Not entirely. The jeweller's testimony is merely to give the background. If you remember, as I said at the start, Principal Magistrate Vessia has the evidence in her possession."

"Yes. That was quite intriguing. I was hoping you'd say more on the matter." Lilliana's smile held no warmth.

"The murder weapon was supposedly a brooch Cassilania had owned for seven years. During this time she'd used it on a regular basis."

"Ah yes. Supposedly. I assume you're going to claim Doyenne Pellonia was actually murdered with this duplicate you purport to have found evidence for?" There was no doubting the challenge in Lilliana's voice.

"Of course. And this is where the indisputable proof arises. If you examine the murder weapon, retrieved from the scene, you'll see there's no sign of wear on it. No scratches, or smooth spots where it's rubbed against a woollen cloak. You merely need to look at it to tell whether it's a cloak pin Cassilania has been using for years, or a newer copy, kept hidden by Xeranius until he found the chance to frame her."

"I see." Lilliana nodded slowly. "Would you be desperately upset if it was discovered the brooch had gone missing? I'm afraid this can happen to evidence once a trial is over."

"I'm sure, with enough diligence, it can be found."

"I fear you may be disappointed." Lilliana's manner eased perceptibly.

She thinks the brooch is all I have. While it was good to be one step ahead, the conversation was like dancing with a cobra. "There is more."

"Go on."

"It might be considered circumstantial, but if you tie together accounts from all the servants at the lodge, not just the one selected for the trial, you can see how Xeranius manoeuvred people into position for his plan. You can also find witnesses to the fact Cassilania didn't go upstairs to see her mother, prior to her finding the body."

"You aren't worried about the health of the lodge staff?"

"I think if they all were to suffer tragic misfortunes at the same time it would be…" Arian paused, as if searching for a word. "…awkward to explain."

"Anything else?"

"Regarding proof of Cassilania's innocence? No."

"What are you hoping will happen now?"

"I'm hoping the verdict will be overturned and the real murderer arrested."

Lilliana tilted her head to one side. "And how do you rate your chances of this happening?"

"With your help, I think my chances are very good."

Lilliana smiled. "Why would I help you?"

"I'd like to think it would be because it's the right thing to do. Pellonia was your sister, and I can't believe you'll be able to sleep at night if you know the man who murdered her is walking around free. Not only free but enjoying his new status as doyen of his family."

"Oh, Arian." Lilliana's manner relaxed still further. "You can be most delightfully innocent at times."

"Is that your way of saying you don't want to help?"

"Quite apart from it not being in my best interest, I couldn't do it if I wanted to. The verdict and sentence are purely a matter for the prefecture. I've no control over the administration of justice."

It was time to heat up the contest. Arian leaned forward. "Speaking bluntly, we both know that's not true. You have Principal Magistrate Vessia on a very short leash."

Lilliana's eyes narrowed in response to the change in tone. Her sympathetic smile held venom. "I know this must be distressing for you b—"

"How about if I change things so that helping Cassilania becomes in your best interest?"

Silence hung in the room. Lilliana's eyes on her were sharper than before. "Do you think you're able to do that?"

"Yes." *Stay calm, stay calm, stay calm.*

Lilliana gestured with one hand. "Then be my guest."

"I know the reason you wanted to talk to your sister in private at the lodge."

"Which is?"

"You were going to withdraw Vessia from the election."

"I was?" Lilliana's face had become a blank mask.

"Yes. And I have the evidence here." Arian reached into the bag she had placed by her chair and pulled out the folded document. "This is the notice to that effect, signed and sealed by both you and Vessia. You left it with Pellonia in her study when you went back to the salon." Arian crossed the room and handed it over before returning to her seat. "You may keep it."

"You're giving this to me?" Lilliana had moved to the defensive, apparent in her tone rather than the words.

Now you know there's more coming. "Yes."

"Why?"

"Partly because I don't need it. And partly so you'll know you can believe me when I tell you about what else I have."

For the barest instant, Lilliana's face dropped, before the mask snapped back into place. "Go on."

"When you left her study, Pellonia had two documents on her desk. You must have hoped she locked them in her strongbox, and they were turned to ash, along with everything else in there. But, in fact, both documents were still out when Xeranius murdered her. One of those documents you're now holding. I'm sure you know what the other was. It starts, *Having concluded my investigation into the matter of the supply of wheat to the Roldan Pass garrison, it is my firm conclusion, supported by the evidence listed below,* and then goes on to give the evidence and name the guilty party. At the bottom it is signed and sealed Magistra Vessia Gallina ado Prefectae. I'm sure, if you ask her, she can tell you what the rest of the report says. I doubt she'll have forgotten."

"You don't have that document with you as well?"

"Do you really think I'd be foolish enough to bring it here? It's somewhere very safe."

Lilliana settled back in her chair, staring at the floor midway between them, her expression frozen. Arian waited, listening to faint sounds from outside, the chirp of birds, the rustle of leaves in the wind, and the distant shouts of children at play.

Eventually Lilliana raised her eyes. "What are you hoping for from me?"

"I've already told you. I want Cassilania's verdict overturned and the sentence revoked. Do that, and you have my word I'll give you Vessia's report."

"That's not possible."

"Make it possible."

"I can't." For the first time a trace of raw emotion fired Lilliana's voice—anger, impatience, maybe even alarm.

"That's unfortunate for you."

"I…" Lilliana sucked in a deep breath. She let it out in a sigh. "The best I can offer is the sentence commuted to exile, but I'll need the approval of three senior members of the prefecture for it."

"I think you can count on Vessia."

"She's just one."

"No others you have dangling on a string?" Arian let sarcasm slip into her voice.

"It's not as easy as you seem to think."

"Then how about I give you a second one."

"Who?"

"Doyen Bellorion murdered his wife."

"That's unproven, and even if you've dug up evidence, he's not a member of the prefecture."

"No. But apart from killing her, he had to forge her will, since she'd destroyed the real one. If you look carefully at it in the Senate archives, it's an obvious fake. He coerced Scribe Ellonius into certifying it as genuine."

"Do you have proof of that?"

"I know how to get it. Bellorion was able to pressure him into certifying the will because he has evidence Ellonius murdered his own grandfather. I'm sure if you threaten Bellorion about his wife's forged will, he can be persuaded to hand over his evidence against Ellonius, who is, I believe, Chief Scribe of the law courts. Is that senior enough for a second prefecture approval?"

Lilliana nodded slowly. "You're not as innocent as you seem."

Who could be, in Kavilli? "I've been taking lessons from your niece."

"But not, I think, in all things. You give your word to hand over the report?"

"I do."

Lilliana gave a half smile. "Do you know how many people there are in Kavilli, whose word is worth as much as a sparrow's fart?"

"Probably more than you think."

"And probably fewer than you think. I wouldn't place any trust in my niece's word. But with you…" She pursed her lips. "If I get the necessary approval for commuting the sentence to exile, what terms do you want?"

"Talk to Cassilania. If she's happy, then I am too."

"Then we have a deal."

CASSIE

A chill draft squeezed through gaps in the wooden slats. The weather was slipping towards autumn, with cold nights that took longer to dispel after sunrise, although, as yet, leaves on the trees showed no trace of yellow. Until the day warmed up, Cassie was forced to close the shutters on the unglazed windows. The feeble light was sufficient to walk around the room, but not enough to read or write, and sitting alone in the gloom with only her thoughts had long since become tedious.

"A visitor for you." Marcus opened the door.

Which had to be a welcome diversion, regardless of who it was, with the possible exception of the executioner, come to measure her up for a set of padded robes, ready to be soaked in oil. Though, if it came to it, she would be willing to engage even him in conversation. More than the plunging quality of her meals, the complete absence of news from the outside world was fraying her nerves.

Lilliana entered the cell. Cassie got to her feet, but apart from this, neither moved until the door was shut and locked.

"This is an unexpected pleasure. I hadn't thought to see you here."

"How could I stay away?" Lilliana matched the ironic tone, before becoming more serious. "How are you and the baby doing?"

"As well as can be hoped, in the circumstances." Cassie returned to her seat. "I take it there's a reason for your visit, beyond enquiring about my health."

"You haven't received word from your lover? I'm assuming you've rekindled your romance."

What had Arian been doing? "You must excuse my ignorance. I've missed so many social engagements over the last month, I'm rather out of touch with gossip around town. If you're referring to Lady Arian, she visited me briefly, at the start of my incarceration, but I've not seen her since. Has she done something I should know about?"

"You might say that. She talked me into using my influence to get your sentence commuted to exile."

She's done what?

Cassie concentrated on remaining calm. Hopefully, the dim light concealed any blatant display of surprise. Before getting excited, she ought to make sure she was not dreaming, or worse still, the victim of a malicious trick. Although what reason could Lilliana have to lie?

Cassie left her chair and opened the shutters, letting in a stream of sunlight. The cool air on her face was reassuring, as was her failure at willing herself to levitate and float out the window, a feat she routinely managed in dreams.

Without turning around, she said, "That's unbelievably kind of you."

"Kindness had nothing to do with it." Which was easy to believe. Nobody had ever accused Lilliana of acting out of compassion.

"Whatever Arian said must have been very persuasive."

"You don't know?"

"No. As I said, I've not been in contact with her."

"You don't want to guess?"

"Is there any point?" She had to be careful. Lilliana would be, correctly, assuming she was lying about them being in contact, but would also assume she was aware of whatever trick Arian had pulled. Revealing the extent of her ignorance would be a mistake. The only way to get information was to let Lilliana think she already knew it.

Cassie continued looking out the window. "I'm sure you haven't come here to play twenty questions with me."

"Quite. I'm here to tell you the terms we've agreed."

"Are you sure you're not here to discuss those terms?" If everything was finalised, an underling could have delivered the message. Lilliana would only come in person if she had to approve the deal.

"There's nothing to discuss. Permanent exile in secure accommodation."

"Three years exile. No longer."

"You're joking. Three years for murdering your doyenne, your own mother?"

"Except you know I didn't." Surely Arian had revealed what really happened.

"Fifteen years."

Lilliana had gone from permanent exile to fifteen years far too easily. Arian must have a major hold over her, which meant there was more room to negotiate. "Fifteen? For a crime you know I didn't commit? Come on. Be reasonable."

"Ten years. That's my final offer."

Except it was not. Cassie could hear it in her voice. She turned around. "Seven, at a location of my choosing."

Lilliana had not moved from her position by the door. "Where would you suggest?"

Now there's a question and half. And one Cassie had previously given much thought to, back in the days before Xeran's betrayal. "The Isle of Thalos. I hear it has a comfortable villa that's currently unoccupied." As well as pleasant year-round weather.

Lilliana was silent for the space of a dozen heartbeats. "Agreed."

Cassie returned to her chair. A feeling of light-headedness battled with the urge to giggle.

Lilliana continued. "Will you write to Lady Arian, confirming we've reached mutually acceptable terms?"

So that was the bargain Arian had hammered out. "Of course. Do you want me to do it now?"

"If you don't mind."

Cassie pulled a sheet of paper from the shelf under the table and opened the inkwell.

"Do you have plans for Xeranius?" Lilliana asked, while she wrote.

Obviously Arian had named the true murderer. "Nothing as yet. But he'll be dealt with."

"If you, or your agents, require assistance, I may be able to help."

"Did you agree to this also with Arian?" Surely not. Although if Arian was to help assassinate anyone, without a doubt Xeran would top her list.

"No. It's because Pella was my sister."

Cassie finished writing. "That's not something I expected to hear you say."

Of course, if anyone murdered Jadio she would not rest until she had made them pay. But their sibling bond was quite different. The only emotion Mother and Lilliana had ever shown for each other was bitter rivalry. And yet, Lilliana seemed unexpectedly troubled.

"Pella was just two years younger than me. As children we were..." Lilliana sighed. "We were close, except everything turned into a competition. I don't know if it was my doing or hers. It was a game we played. At least it was a game for me. When she married your father, I thought she'd divorce him in a few years and return to the family. But then she agreed to adoption and renounced us."

That was easy to explain. "Because if she'd stayed in the Konithae she'd never have been doyenne. You'd always have taken precedence over her."

"But she didn't need to turn everything into a battle."

"You didn't need to prove yourself. She felt she did."

Sunlight glinted in Lilliana's eyes, looking suspiciously like unshed tears. "She already had. The Konithae were a powerful family before I was born. The Passurae had been in decline for decades. She turned your fortunes around, built the Passurae into one of the empire's foremost families. I started at the top. She fought her way there. If our positions had been reversed, I doubt I could have done half as well as she did."

"You're selling yourself short." Cassie handed over the note.

"That's a matter for speculation. I'm going to miss sparring with her. Xeranius would never be an adequate substitute. I hope your family pick someone better to replace him." Lilliana put the note in her purse. "Once you arrive at Thalos, you need to write to Lady Arian, confirming your safe arrival, so she can hand over a certain report as she has promised."

The Roldanian affair. Everything suddenly made sense. Clearly, Lilliana had not seen the state the document was in and was taking Arian at her word. How ironic. It was quite possible Arian was the only person in the entire city who could have got away with the bluff. With anyone else, Lilliana would have demanded far more assurances.

How would Lilliana react when she discovered the truth? Cassie was quite sure Arian had not told a single lie, but would Lilliana see it that way? Would she accept she had been outplayed, or would she want to settle the score? Or maybe she would accept alternate payment?

"Before you leave, I'd like to make a suggestion," Cassie said.

"What?"

"Have you ever wondered whose money paid for the conviction of your cousin, Galvinius?"

"Possibly."

"If ever you're tempted to do something rash, contact me. We might have the basis for a deal."

"I assure you, I never do anything rash. But I'll keep your offer in mind." Lilliana nodded slowly. "You'll be leaving before first light tomorrow. I want you gone before anyone has a chance to work out if they want to argue. I'll send word ahead to Thalos to expect you."

"I'd like to select my own staff." Preferably ones without a sideline in assassination.

"I'm sure that can be arranged." Lilliana knocked on the door. "I'll see you in seven years."

"Count on it."

❖

The sky was still dark, dawn an hour away. The carriage standing in the moonlit stable yard had boarded up windows. Looking up at the prefecture building, Cassie fancied she could pick out lamplight at the window of what had been her cell. To the north, the constellation of Draconis was rising, the imperial dragon, guardian of the empire. Surely it was a good omen.

Armed guards escorted her to the carriage. The seats were without cushions, or much else by way of comfort, though the interior did have a few added features, such as iron rings fixed to the walls. Thankfully, the guards did not feel the need to manacle her, but after the door closed came the unmistakable sound of bolts sliding into place, locking her in. The vehicle shook as the driver took his seat atop the cab.

On the drive through Kavilli, Cassie closed her eyes, picturing the scenes outside in her mind's eye. The familiar streets rolling by. The open plaza in front of the Senate building. The wide boulevard leading to the city gates. The temple of Yelathi, with the huge dome she had gazed at from her cell window. The markets, taverns, statues, shops, and squares. The dangerous back alleys and palatial mansions. Kavilli was noisy, crowded, perilous, dirty, and home. She was going to miss it.

The carriage stopped just outside the city gates. The bolts were drawn back and the door opened. Someone held up a flaming torch that snapped in the wind, sending dancing streams of sparks amid acrid smoke. By its light, two women entered the carriage and took their seats. Cassie recognised both faces from the lodge, before the door closed, leaving them in darkness.

"Good morning, my lady." They spoke in unison.

"You're coming with me to Thalos?"

"Yes, my lady. Word came to the lodge yesterday evening, asking if we'd be willing to go with you. Of course we said yes." Judging by her voice, it was the older one, speaking for the pair. "I'm Decima, and this is Halie. I've been working as cook at the lodge, but I'm happy to turn my hand to whatever needs doing. Halie is an all-purpose housemaid."

"Thank you." People she could rely on. The rest of her staff could be sorted out later.

The carriage set off again to the grind and rumble of iron-bound wheels on flagstones. After a while, the quality of the echoes changed. They were now passing between fields and hedgerows, no longer surrounded by stone buildings. Paved road had changed to gravel and mud. The first daylight squeezed in through cracks around the door and window boards, enough to see the two women opposite. Cassie shifted on the hard seat. She would not return to Kavilli for seven years. But she would be back.

The journey to the Isle of Thalos would take at least six days. First, they would travel due south, along well used roads on the way to the coast. The voyage to the island was another half-day sailing. With the baby's birth still two months off, there was no problem getting settled in time.

Unlike being in prison, she would not be cut off from events. No one had mentioned a ban on her receiving letters, or even visitors. Mother claimed living at the lodge was a way to hold the world at arm's length and gain a better perspective. Maybe she would be able to turn her exile into an advantage. But even if she could not master Mother's trick, all things considered, her prospects were infinitely improved on how they had stood at the same time yesterday morning.

The baby stirred, kicking forcefully at Cassie's stomach and sending a stab of pain through her pelvis. She groaned and curled forward. In an instant, Decima switched sides in the carriage and put an arm around her shoulders.

"It's all right, my lady. I worked as a midwife for a few years. I'll take care of you."

Arian

Arian was shown into the same room as before, although this time two glasses and a full wine decanter were standing on the table next to the potted plant, and Lilliana was already there, waiting.

"Can I offer you a drink?" she asked once Arian had taken her seat.

"Thank you."

"I hear you've received news from Thalos."

"Yes. Cassilania has arrived safely at the island."

"There's no word yet of the baby?"

"No. But it's not due for a while." Arian accepted a glass of wine from the housemaid, then waited until she left before continuing. "I'm pleased you were able to resolve things to everyone's satisfaction."

"Maybe not quite everyone."

"Well, it's true Vessia no longer wishes to see me, but I'm trying to live with the disappointment."

"The principal magistrate may soon have more serious matters to concern herself with. As might Doyen Xeranius. I hear his spymaster has been recalled to Kavilli."

"Yes, I know." If Xeranius was hoping Bran would protect him, he was going to be disappointed.

Lilliana settled back and steepled her fingers. "But to business. I've fulfilled my part of the bargain. I take it you're ready to fulfil yours."

"Of course." Arian opened the leather bag and pulled out the document. "Here's the report as promised."

Lilliana left her seat. She unfolded the paper, then stood in silence, staring at the blood-soaked parchment.

Arian sat, sipping her wine, waiting for a reaction.

Surprise on Lilliana's face shifted to annoyance, and then, unexpectedly, she exhaled in something sounding close to laughter. She met Arian's eyes. "I see my niece has taught you well. When you next contact Cassilania tell her I now understand the background to her offer. And yes, I would be interested in taking her up on the deal."

❖

"Come in," Arian called out in response to the knock.

"You wanted to talk to me?" Ulfgar remained in the doorway.

"Yes. And close the door."

Ulfgar stomped halfway across the room, but then froze, seeing Bran sitting to one side. "What's he doing here?"

"I've asked him to help me."

"You consort with traitors." His arrogance was disgusting.

"Only honest ones."

"Honest…"

"You know what I mean. People who come straight out and tell you what they stand for and why. They might not be loyal to the things you feel they should be, but you know where you are with them." Arian weighted her words carefully. "On the other hand, you have dishonest traitors. The ones who'll declare undying allegiance, when they'll happily sell everything out in a flash if it's to their advantage."

Ulfgar pointed at Bran. "You mean the way he's sold out our people to—"

"No, no, no. I'm not talking about Bran. I'm talking about you."

"What do you mean?"

"You claim to be loyal to the king. My son. Feran."

"Dare you question it?"

"Yes. I do."

"I'm entrusted with the sacred duty of defending our people and our laws." Ulfgar glared at her. "Laws you trample underfoot in the pursuit of your own degenerate lusts."

"That's as may be. But we're not talking about me and my shortcomings. We're talking about you."

"I've done nothing."

"Really?" Arian turned her head. "Bran. How much does he owe, and who to?"

Bran unfolded a sheet of paper. "Lucky Jacko, five gold imperials and sixty silver marks. Tarrius the Ram, eight gold imperials and twenty-three silver marks. Nethius of Demia, twenty-three gold imperials, twelve silver marks, and four copper half-bits." Bran frowned. "He's the biggest one, though I'm not sure how the half-bits fit in. You'd think he'd write them off. Loria—"

"What do you mean?" Ulfgar was trying to sound defiant, but his face had bleached pale.

"Bran means you owe a large amount of money to various people." Arian signalled to Bran. "What's the grand total?"

"Sixty-six gold imperials, twenty-three silver marks, plus the four copper half-bits." Bran smiled and rolled up the paper.

"You've been digging into my affairs. Setting spies on me." Ulfgar retreated into a show of anger.

"Bran didn't get those figures by consulting an oracle."

"It's muckraking."

"It's all your muck."

Ulfgar turned to the door. "I'm going."

"If I were you, I'd have a look out the window first."

"Why. What's there?"

"Two big men, looking not at all happy, standing in the courtyard."

"What?" Ulfgar hurried to the window. "Who are they?"

Bran answered him. "They work for Nethius of Demia. They're responsible for sorting out his debt collection problems."

"What are they doing here?"

"I told them they could wait down there for you." Bran smiled.

"I've promised to pay him. He knows I…" Ulfgar clutched Arian's sleeve. "You have to help me."

"I do?"

"They'll…"

"Don't worry. They might break a few bones, but that'll be all. They won't kill you. Dead men don't pay debts." Arian yanked her sleeve free. "They're not like the rebels in Lycanthia who'd murder Feran without a moment's hesitation if he fell into their hands."

Ulfgar still stared through the window. Arian pushed his shoulder so he was forced to face her. "You claim to be honest, but you've been stealing and lying. Pilfering things from me to buy yourself more time, while you dug yourself even deeper into debt."

"I'll pay you back."

"With what? And even if you could, what of your claims of loyalty to your king? You'd risk Feran's life, just because you couldn't control your gambling. You wanted to run away from people you'd promised to pay and didn't care if it meant Feran was killed. You've broken every trust anyone has ever placed in you. To your king, your fellow priests, your people, even yourself. Some of it I could overlook, but not putting your bad habits before my son's life. That I'll never forgive."

"What are you going to do?"

"Bran can escort you down to the courtyard. I don't want them coming up here and getting blood all over the furniture."

"You're bluffing."

"You think so? You've gambled and lost every time. But if you want to try your luck…" Arian pointed to the door. "Go ahead."

"You wouldn't have called me here just to taunt me." Ulfgar pulled himself up straight. "What is it you want? I can give my sacred oath never to say a word about you and the women you defile your body with. Is that it? Is that what you want? All right. I'll swear any oath you'd like."

Did he really think her so gullible? "It's a sorry thing to say to a priest, but I wouldn't place any trust in your oath. You'd break your word the first time it was to your advantage."

"What then?"

"I'm going to give you a chance to redeem yourself in the sight of the gods. Have you heard of the Holy Isle? It's off the west coast. A hermitage open to the followers of each and every god. You can go there, and spend your life in prayer, surrounded by devout men and women from across the empire. You can share the knowledge of our gods and learn about theirs."

"You think I'd agree to this?"

"Or you can talk to the men in the courtyard. Either way, you're not staying a member of this household a day longer. Do you think you can walk back to Lycanthia on broken legs?"

"Supposing they follow me, even to this island you spoke of?"

Arian picked up a heavy purse and shook it so it jangled. "In here are sixty-six gold imperials, and twenty-four silver marks. I rounded up the copper half-bits. If you agree to leave immediately, once you're gone, I'll take care of your debt."

"I don't know. I..."

"Be quick. You don't have long to make your mind up."

"I..."

"You could think of it as a chance to redeem yourself in the sight of the gods. And you'll be out of temptation's way. I'm informed there are no racing tracks on the Holy Isle."

"All right. I'll go."

"Do I have your word on it?"

"Yes."

"Good. I thought you'd accept my offer. Bran's arranged an escort to get you safely to the island."

"They won't be needed."

"Why? You weren't thinking of breaking your word again and running off as soon as you were outside Kavilli, were you?"

"No. Of course not." Ulfgar's expression said differently.

"Goodbye, Ulfgar. It's my earnest hope we never set eyes on each other again."

Ulfgar scowled and left the room without another word. His footsteps faded.

Bran closed the door behind him. "Well done."

"Compared to Lilliana, he was child's play. The escorts are waiting in his room?"

"With his things packed and ready to go. He'll be on his way without delay." Bran grinned. "Do you think he's planning on absconding as soon as he's left alone on the island?"

"I'm sure he is. So it'll come as a nasty surprise when he learns the boat trip is one-way only." The hermits took their pledge to forsake all worldly temptations very seriously.

"He's not the only one heading for a nasty surprise. Xeranius has offered me a huge amount of money to keep him safe." Bran looked disgusted. "He thinks he can buy my loyalty."

"What are you planning?"

"You don't want to know."

Which was probably true. "Tell me once Ulfgar has gone, and I'll give Feran the good news."

The military academy took new cohorts of boys on a quarterly basis. Just over a month remained before the next group was due to depart. She had that much time to spend with Feran at home. Already, the thought of separation was miserable. But Feran would be free to decide for himself, picking his own path in life. Both her children would.

Bran nodded toward the window. "Shall I pay off the men down there? Let them know they've done their bit?"

"Yes. Do that." Arian peered down at the two heavyset men. Both were working hard to give off an aura of menace. To be honest, they were overplaying the part. Fortunately, Ulfgar was a poor judge of acting. "Where did you find them?"

"They work at the blacksmith's next to the bakery."

Cassie

Sunlight burnished the southern horizon, turning the sea to gleaming silver. The breeze was heavy with salt. A seagull floated into view, rising on air currents coming up and over the cliff. Others wheeled against the clear blue sky. Their raucous screams competed with the incessant crash of surf from below. Cassie sat outside the villa with a blanket wrapped around her shoulders, watching the dance of the seabirds.

The Isle of Thalos was a limestone crag, jutting from the water, two miles long, and a half mile across at its widest point. On the southern side, the land sloped down to the ocean and a beach of soft white sand. On the northern edge it cut off in a sheer, hundred-foot-high cliff. Once the baby was born and she had recovered, Cassie would be able to walk the whole way around it in a couple of hours.

Spindly trees and coarse bushes covered most of the island, with denser patches of ferns and moss in sheltered corners. Curly-horned sheep grazed the hillsides, in the company of a colony of rabbits. Seals visited isolated coves, hauling themselves onto the sand. The largest land predators were stoats, feeding on both rabbits and seabird eggs. The villa and associated outbuilding were the only signs of habitation, apart from sheep pens and the jetty on the beach.

The villa was decent, with bright, well-sized rooms, set around two linked courtyards. Currently, less than half the space was in use. The remainder was in need of repairs, though nothing too major. The interior decor was showing its age, as was the furniture. However, the basic structure was sound and well positioned. With a modest outlay, the accommodation could be brought to a comfortable standard. With a chunk more money, it could even become luxurious.

Cassie was on the raised terrace, with a view of the mainland coast, fifteen miles to the north. Every ten days or so, a small sailboat came over with provisions from the closest town, Salabolli. Currently, the latest delivery was approaching. The boat drew steadily nearer, bobbing over the waves, until it rounded the end of the island and slipped from sight, heading for the jetty.

Several people had been standing on the deck, more than just the ship's crew. Hopefully, they were the staff she had requested. The villa was currently short-handed. Apart from her, Decima, and Halie, the only people on the island were those essential for the upkeep of the villa and flock, a caretaker and his wife, plus an elderly shepherd. Even with Cassie in residence, the villa would not require a large workforce, but a few more employees would allow life to run more smoothly. It should even be possible to start repairing the villa.

The boat would also bring news from the outside world. Living conditions on Thalos were a vast improvement on the prison cell, but the feeling of isolation had intensified. Over on the mainland, just fifteen miles away, the empire would be forging ahead—battles, parties, arguments in the Senate, trade deals, elections, and love affairs. Things were happening. *Dammit all.* Even if she could not take part, she wanted to know about it. *Seven years.* How was she going to cope?

Cassie drifted into a light doze, waiting for people off the boat to climb the path from the beach. The sound of voices and footsteps roused her from a tangle of semi-dreams. Then a shadow fell across her. Cassie opened her eyes. Or was she still asleep and dreaming? Arian stood beside the chair.

"Sorry if I woke you."

"You can wake me anytime." Cassie had slipped down in her chair. She pulled herself up. "It's good to see you."

"I couldn't stay away." Arian crouched beside the chair. "How are you feeling?"

"Better for having you here. I hoped you'd visit but didn't—" The words stuck in her throat. Cassie twisted awkwardly in the chair, wrapped her arms around Arian's shoulders and buried her face in Arian's neck. Tears tried to squeeze between her eyelids. The latter stages of pregnancy always made her so emotional.

Arian pulled back so their lips could meet in a soft, slow kiss. Now there was no warder to worry about. No need to rush, as long as Arian did not intend to return with the boat.

"How long can you stay here?"

"As long as you'll have me. Bran twisted some arms to get permission for me to join you."

"What about your children?"

"Feran has gone to the military academy. That's why I wasn't here sooner. I waited until he was admitted. Eilwen's here with me. I left her on the beach, looking for seashells. She wasn't thrilled at leaving Kavilli but was prepared to go along with it when I told her you were here and there's a proper bathhouse." Arian bit her lip. "There is a bathhouse, isn't there?"

"Just a small one."

"Hot water?"

"Yes."

"That's a relief. We'd have been facing a mutiny otherwise."

Cassie was about to speak when a cramp twisted her insides. She clutched Arian's hand. "I need to stand and walk around for a bit."

"Are you all right?"

"I will be." She heaved herself to her feet and stood swaying, until the dizziness passed.

"Are you sure?" Arian slipped a supportive arm around Cassie's waist.

"Yes, but we should find Decima. She's got experience as a midwife."

"I see."

"It might be a false alarm."

"Do you think so?"

"I'm not sure. But either way, it can't be much longer." Cassie rested her head on Arian's shoulder. "I'm pleased you'll be with me for the birth."

Arian rubbed her back. "Me too."

❖

Repairs to the villa were nearly complete. Cassie wandered from room to room, examining the results. The holes in the plaster and water stains were gone, as were the cracked roof tiles. All the doors now opened and closed without sticking, and the windows had glass. The hypocaust had been cleared out, ready for next winter, evicting several families of rabbits. In future, log burning stoves would not be needed to keep the main building warm.

The wall paintings were still faded and had irregular blank spots filled with new plaster. The mosaic floors were in a similar state. Full repairs to both would require the skills of professional artists, and undoubtedly cost more than Xeranius was willing to pay from family funds. Her own personal finances were subject to a raft of petty restrictions for the duration of her exile. Yet, all in all, Cassie was happy with the way things were looking.

The roundabout route brought her back to the bedroom, where baby Ana was taking an afternoon nap in her cot. Cassie stroked her pinkie against Ana's palm, entranced yet again by how the tiny fingers instinctively clasped around her. Each miniature nail was perfect. Her daughter. Would she grow tired of the sight? Or would Ana have turned into a boisterous toddler first?

Ana made a tutting sound and yawned, round-mouthed, all without waking. Cassie carefully slipped her pinkie free and wandered out through the open doorway to the terrace. She shaded her eyes from the bright sun. The weather was warming.

Arian sat nearby. "Have you finished prowling?"

Cassie dropped onto the bench beside her. "Prowling?"

"Like a caged cat."

"I was inspecting the state of the work."

"Has it changed much in the past hour?"

"I was admiring it."

Arian pointed to Eilwen, who was sitting in the shade a short way off, with a book open on her lap. "I'm wondering if you should talk to her."

"Why?"

"She's a little too absorbed in what she's reading."

"Isn't that a good thing?"

"It's about poisons."

"That's what I was reading at her age."

"I know. She told me. That's why she'll listen to a warning from you. I don't want her experimenting."

Cassie laughed. "I never poisoned anyone, and I doubt she will."

"Doubt isn't good enough."

Halie arrived on the terrace. "Excuse me, my ladies. I don't know if you noticed, but the boat from Salabolli is coming into dock."

"I was indoors." Cassie looked to Arian. "Did you see it?"

"No. But I haven't been paying attention. I didn't think it was due for a few more days."

"It's not." Cassie stood, uncertain.

Arian smiled at her, indulgently. "If you want to go down and see what's up, I'll stay here and keep my ear tuned for Ana."

"Thanks."

Despite her enthusiasm for the book, Eilwen had obviously been listening in. She bounced to her feet. "I'm coming too."

The sandy path zigzagged down the hillside, between fresh growth of heather and other shrubs. Everywhere, wildflowers were bursting into bloom. Spring was on the way, turning the island into a garden. Eilwen pointed out the oleander and belladonna.

They reached the beach just as the passengers began to disembark. The first person off the jetty was Bran.

Cassie stood at the top of the beach, waiting for him to reach her. "This is a surprise. I assume you've brought news."

"Yes. It's about Doyen Xeranius."

She had suspected as much. "Come up to the villa. You must meet Ana. And you can tell me about Xeran on the way." Cassie turned back up the path. Bran fell in beside her, while Eilwen tagged along on the other side. "Is it serious news?"

"Yes. He's suffered a mishap."

"Fatal?"

"I'm afraid so."

"What happened?"

"He drank too much wine before going to bed. Enough to make him clumsy. He must have knocked an oil lamp over, because his blankets caught fire. People heard him screaming but…" Bran shook his head, as if in sorrow. "It was too late. There was nothing anyone could do."

"I assume the prefects looked into it."

"Yes. Doyenne Lilliana even sent her own personal physician to examine the remains. Everyone agrees, it was just a tragic, awful accident."

Cassie nodded. Unpleasant, but all things considered, quite fitting. "Has the family elected a new doyen yet?"

"Yes. That's something else I had to tell you about. The voting was very quick. There was only one candidate put forward." Bran came to a halt and gave a formal bow. "Congratulations, Doyenne."

"Me?"

"Yes." Bran continued walking. "There was nothing in your terms of exile to say they couldn't pick you."

"I'm still a convicted murderer."

"Except nobody in the family believes you're guilty."

"Is there any consensus on who the murderer really was?"

"Different people have different ideas." Bran shrugged. "Some of them are even correct."

"It was Xeranius of course," Eilwen said.

"Why do you pick him?" Cassie asked.

"You mean, apart from listening to you and Mama talking?" Eilwen rolled her eyes. "It's obvious. He was the person who gained the most. You shouldn't have bothered looking at anyone else until you'd completely eliminated him from suspicion."

"And there you have it." Bran laughed.

"You should let me work for you as a spy. I'd be really good at it." Eilwen skipped along sideways, looking up at him.

"I think your mother might have objections."

"Why? She let Feran do what he wanted."

Bran held up his hands. "I'm staying out of that discussion."

Before Eilwen could argue further, Cassie returned to the previous topic. "Wasn't anyone concerned about me being absent from Kavilli?"

"Your mother was never in town. It didn't cause her problems."

"I'm a lot further away."

"Some issues will need sorting. You'll have to nominate a senator to speak for you in the Senate. We'll need to speed up the flow of information to the island. That's part of what I'm here to discuss. The boat will have to come much more often, maybe daily. And I'll station relay riders between there and Kavilli."

"That sounds good." In fact, it sounded much, much better than good.

"I'll need an administrative office in Salabolli. I might even make it my main base and get a house in town for Tessa and the baby."

"Or they could come and live on the island. There's room for them here, and Tessa would make an excellent chief of staff." Plus Bran's son would be a playmate for Ana.

"Thank you. I think she'd like that."

The path levelled out as they reached the top of the island. The white walls of the villa were only a dozen yards away, stark against the brilliant blue sky. Arian was still sitting on the terrace. She got up to greet them.

"Mama, Mama, you'll never guess what." Eilwen ran to her. "The Passurae have picked Cassie as their new doyenne."

ARIAN

A rian put down the letter. The sun was sinking towards the sea. Its rays created a dazzling golden path across the waves, while the first hints of pink smudged the sky. Seabirds swept past in waves, coming back to their nests on the cliffs. To the east, the full moon was a translucent silver orb set on washed blue sky, rising above the mainland haze.

"How's Feran enjoying the academy?" Cassie asked.

"He's loving it. All his friends are missing their mothers, but he's having a great time." Arian picked up the letter again but did not open it. She stared at her name written on the outside in Feran's bold, purposeful handwriting. "I don't know whether to be happy for him or to feel snubbed. You think he'd be a bit homesick without me."

"I'm sure he is. But some boys simply drop straight into the life. Jadio was like that. I know I missed him more than he missed me or Mother. I should have guessed he'd become a career soldier. My oldest son is the same. I won't be surprised if he stays on in the army after he completes his twelve-year stint. The younger two are a different story though."

"Feran is king of the Lycanthi. He can't stay in the army." Much as she wanted him to make his own choices in life, that would be a step too far—or would it?

"Don't worry. If the army does one thing, it instils a sense of duty."

"Shame I can't send Eilwen."

Cassie laughed. "I think even the army might struggle with her."

"She's badgering Bran to let her work for him as a spy."

"She's got a good eye and a nose for things out of place, but she thinks it's a game. That's dangerous but understandable when you're young. In a few more years she'll have a better appreciation of the risks involved." Cassie looked thoughtful. "I can't see her going back to your homeland though. Feran will do all right as a warrior king, just not the sort of warrior your people are used to. But Eilwen isn't going to be happy, trundling along the rut they'd want her to stick in."

"I know." And it was impossible to blame her.

"Anything else? I saw you got another letter."

"It's from Earl Kendric. Everything's going well. My nephew, Perrith, is happy to be back with his family. Trouble is calming down. Merchants from all over are moving in and trade is increasing. There's the beginnings of a town in the valley below Breninbury, including the first public bathhouse." Before long, Lycanthia would be just like every other province of the empire. Did it matter?

It's not as if I'm ever going back.

Arian stopped admiring the sunset. Cassie sat a few feet away, cradling Ana in her arms. Cassie's expression, as she looked down at her sleeping baby daughter, could only be described as soppy and sentimental. It was a side of Cassie few people would ever see. Watching her, Arian suspected her own expression was not so very different.

The wolf statue from the courtyard in Kavilli had come to life and wanted her to do something, but she could not make sense of its whining. She left the courtyard, and immediately found herself in a forest. No one would tell her where she was, and she had to pass on the wolf's message. And then she was trapped again between stone walls that stretched ahead forever.

Arian's eyes snapped open. Moonlight cascaded into the room, casting harsh shadows over the bed. Cassie lay curled beside her. Carefully, so as not to wake her, Arian lifted Cassie's arm from around her waist. She slid out of bed, pulled a robe around her shoulders, and left the bedroom.

The beauty of the full moon over the sea was enough to stop her dead. Arian leaned back against the wall, drinking in the scene. She stood alone on the edge of the world. No one else was with her to share the wonder.

The statue's backward stare. It did not have to be just one thing or the other. Regret, relief, doubt, or even hope. It could be everything at the same time. Still, Kendric's letter nagged at her. The world was changing, and she could not deny her own part in it. Many would find fault with her decisions. In truth, she was more of a traitor than Bran. His actions affected only himself. Hers changed their people's future. She could only pray it was for the best. Feran's blood might be Lycanthian, but the heart it pumped through would be Kavillian. Meanwhile her people would be seduced by bathhouses and sewers, sweet red wine and cinnamon cakes.

Arian sighed and ran a hand through her hair. But even if she could, did she have the right to deny her fellow tribesfolk the same choices she had taken advantage of? Was it not the height of arrogance to think the freedom to choose might be right for herself and her children, but lesser folk needed their paths decided for them? If her people did not want to eat the cakes or drink the wine, nobody would force them to. They were free to ignore the sewers and the bathhouse if they chose.

The wolf had been looking back, but it was still moving forward. Despite her doubts, she was happier than she had ever been before. She would not change a thing. Life without Cassie was not one worth living.

Arian allowed herself a while longer, soaking in the splendour of the moonlit sea, until the nighttime chill penetrated her robe.

As she slipped back into bed, Cassie mumbled something incoherent.

"What did you say?" Arian asked, unsure of whether Cassie was awake enough to answer.

"I love you." The words were more breath than sound.

"I love you too."

Arian planted a kiss on Cassie's naked shoulder then snuggled up behind her, spooning their bodies together. For now, this was all she needed, all she wanted. Tomorrow she would deal with when it came.

About the Author

Jane Fletcher is a GCLS award-winning writer and has also been short-listed for the Gaylactic Spectrum and Lambda Literary Awards. She is a recipient of the Alice B. Reader Appreciation Awards Medal.

Her work includes two ongoing sets of fantasy/romance novels: the Celaeno Series—*The Walls of Westernfort, Rangers at Roadsend, The Temple at Landfall, Dynasty of Rogues*, and *Shadow of the Knife*; and the Lyremouth Chronicles—*The Exile and The Sorcerer, The Traitor and The Chalice, The Empress and The Acolyte*, and *The High Priest and the Idol*. She has also written five stand-alone novels: *Wolfsbane Winter, The Shewstone, Isle of Broken Years, Silver Ravens*, and *A Fox in Shadow*.

Her love of fantasy began at the age of seven when she encountered Greek mythology. This was compounded by a childhood spent clambering over every example of ancient masonry she could find (medieval castles, megalithic monuments, Roman villas). Her resolute ambition was to become an archaeologist when she grew up, so it was something of a surprise when she became a software engineer instead.

Born in Greenwich, London, she now lives with her wife in southwest England, where she is surrounded by enough historic sites to keep her happy.

Website: http://www.janefletcher.co.uk/

Books Available from Bold Strokes Books

A Wolf in Stone by Jane Fletcher. Though Cassilania is an experienced player in the dirty, dangerous game of imperial Kavillian politics, even she is caught out when a murderer raises the stakes. (978-1-63679-640-6)

New Horizons by Shia Woods. When Quinn Collins meets Alex Anders, Horizon Theater's enigmatic managing director, a passionate connection ignites, but amidst the complex backdrop of theater politics, their budding romance faces a formidable challenge. (978-1-63679-683-3)

One Last Summer by Kristin Keppler. Emerson Fields didn't think anything could keep her from her dream of interning at Bardot Design Studio in Paris, until an unexpected choice at a North Carolina beach has her questioning what it is she really wants. (978-1-63679-638-3)

StreamLine by Lauren Melissa Ellzey. When Lune crosses paths with the legendary girl gamer Nocht, she may have found the key that will boost her to the upper echelon of streamers and unravel all Lune thought she knew about gaming, friendship, and love. (978-1-63679-655-0)

The Devil You Know by Ali Vali. As threats come at the Casey family from both the feds and enemies set to destroy them, Cain Casey does whatever is necessary with Emma at her side to bury every single one. (978-1-63679-471-6)

The Meaning of Liberty by Sage Donnell. When TJ and Bailey get caught in the political crossfire of the ultraconservative Crusade of the Redeemer Church, escape is the only plan. On the run and fighting for their lives is not the time to be falling for each other. (978-1-63679-624-6)

Undercurrent by Patricia Evans. Can Tala and Wilder catch a serial killer in Salem before another body washes up on the shore? (978-1-636790669-7)

And Then There Was One by Michele Castleman. Plagued by strange memories and drowning in the guilt she tried to leave behind, Lyla Smith escapes her small Ohio town to work as a nanny and becomes trapped with an unknown killer. (978-1-63679-688-8)

Digging for Destiny by Jenna Jarvis. The war between nations forces Litz to make a choice. Her country, career, and family, or the chance of making a better world with the woman she can't forget. (978-1-63679-575-1)

Hot Hires by Nan Campbell, Alaina Erdell, Jesse J. Thoma. In these three romance novellas, when business turns to pleasure, romance ignites. (978-1-63679-651-2)

McCall by Patricia Evans. Sam and Sara found love on the water, but can they build a future amid the ghosts of the past that surround them on dry land? (978-1-63679-769-4)

One and Done by Fredrick Smith. One day can lead to a night of passion…and possibly a chance at love. (978-1-63679-564-5)

Promises to Protect by Jo Hemmingwood. Park ranger Maxine Ward's commitment to protect Tree City is put to the test when social worker Skylar Austen takes a special interest in the commune and in Max. (978-1-63679-626-0)

Sacred Ground by Missouri Vaun. Jordan Price, a conflicted demon hunter, falls for Grace Jameson who has no idea she's been bitten by a vampire. (978-1-63679-485-3)

The Land of Death and Devil's Club by Bailey Bridgewater. Special Liaison to the FBI Louisa Linebach may have defied all odds by identifying the bodies of three missing men in the Kenai Peninsula, but she won't be satisfied until the man she's sure is responsible for their murders is behind bars. (978-1-63679-659-8)

When You Smile by Melissa Brayden. Taryn Ross never thought the babysitter she once crushed on would show up as a grad student at the same university she attends. (978-1-63679-671-0)

A Heart Divided by Angie Williams. Emma is the most beautiful woman Jackson has ever seen, but being a veteran of the Confederate army that killed her husband isn't the only thing keeping them apart. (978-1-63679-537-9)

Adrift by Sam Ledel. Two women whose lives are anchored by guilt and obligation find romance amidst the tumultuous Prohibition movement in 1920s California. (978-1-63679-577-5)

Cabin Fever by Tagan Shepard. The longer Morgan and Shelby are stranded together, the more their feelings grow, but is it real, or just cabin fever? (978-1-63679-632-1)

Clean Kill by Anne Laughlin. When someone starts killing people she knows in the recovery world, former detective Nicky Sullivan must race to stop the killer and keep herself from being arrested for the crimes. (978-1-63679-634-5)

Only a Bridesmaid by Haley Donnell. A fake bridesmaid, a socially anxious bride, and an unexpected love—what could go wrong? (978-1-63679-642-0)

Primal Hunt by L.L. Raand. Anya, a young wolf warrior, finds herself paired with Rafe, one of the most powerful Vampires in the Americas, in an erotic union of blood and sex. (978-1-63679-561-4)

Puzzles Can Be Deadly by David S. Pederson. Skip loves a good puzzle. Little does he know that a simple phone call will lead him and his boyfriend Henry to the deadliest puzzle he's ever encountered. (978-1-63679-615-4)

Snake Charming by Genevieve McCluer. Playgirl vampire Freddie is on the run and a chance encounter with lamia Phoebe makes them both realize that they may have found the love they'd given up on. (978-1-63679-628-4)

Spirits and Sirens by Kelly and Tana Fireside. When rumored ghost whisperer Elena Murphy and very skeptical assistant fire chief Allison Jones have to work together to solve a 70-year-old mystery, sparks fly—will it be enough to melt the ice between them and let love ignite? (978-1-63679-607-9)

A Case for Discretion by Ashley Moore. Will Gwen, a prominent Atlanta attorney, choose Etta, the law student she's clandestinely dating, or is her political future too important to sacrifice? (978-1-63679-617-8)

Aubrey McFadden Is Never Getting Married by Georgia Beers. Aubrey McFadden is never getting married, but she does have five weddings to attend, and she'll be avoiding Monica Wallace, the woman who ruined her happily ever after, at every single one. (978-1-63679-613-0)

Flowers for Dead Girls by Abigail Collins. Isla might be just the right kind of girl to bring Astra out of her shell—and maybe more. The only problem? She's dead. (978-1-63679-584-3)

Good Bones by Aurora Rey. Designer and contractor Logan Barrow can give Kathleen Kenney the house of her dreams, but can she convince the cynical romance writer to take a chance on love? (978-1-63679-589-8)

Leather, Lace, and Locs by Anne Shade. Three friends, each on their own path in life, with one obstacle…finding room in their busy lives for a love that will give them their happily ever afters. (978-1-63679-529-4)

Rainbow Overalls by Maggie Fortuna. Arriving in Vermont for her first year of college, an introverted bookworm forms a friendship with an outgoing artist and finds what comes after the classic coming out story: a being out story. (978-1-63679-606-2)

Revisiting Summer Nights by Ashley Bartlett. PJ Addison and Wylie Parsons have been called back to film the most recent Dangerous Summer Nights installment. Only this time they're not in love and it's going to stay that way. (978-1-63679-551-5)

The Broken Lines of Us by Shia Woods. Charlie Dawson returns to the city she left behind and she meets an unexpected stranger on her first night back, discovering that coming home might not be as hard as she thought. (978-1-63679-585-0)

Triad Magic by 'Nathan Burgoine. Face-to-face against forces set in motion hundreds of years ago, Luc, Anders, and Curtis— vampire, demon, and wizard—must draw on the power of blood, soul, and magic to stop a killer. (978-1-63679-505-8)